The Fallstreak Arsenal:
A Sound of Steel
Volume I
by Nicholas Roudas

I0693009

First published by Nicholas Roudas 2025

First edition

ISBN: 979-8-218-64351-5

Editing by Noah Hursh
Cover art by Nicholas Roudas
Illustration by Nicholas Roudas

This book was professionally typeset on Reedsy.
Find out more at reedsy.com

WARNING

This book is for mature audiences only. It explores mature themes, including, but not limited to, strong language, brief nudity, graphic depictions of bodily injury, violence, suicide, and sexual assault. Reader discretion is advised.

For those who doubted me.

TABLE OF CONTENTS

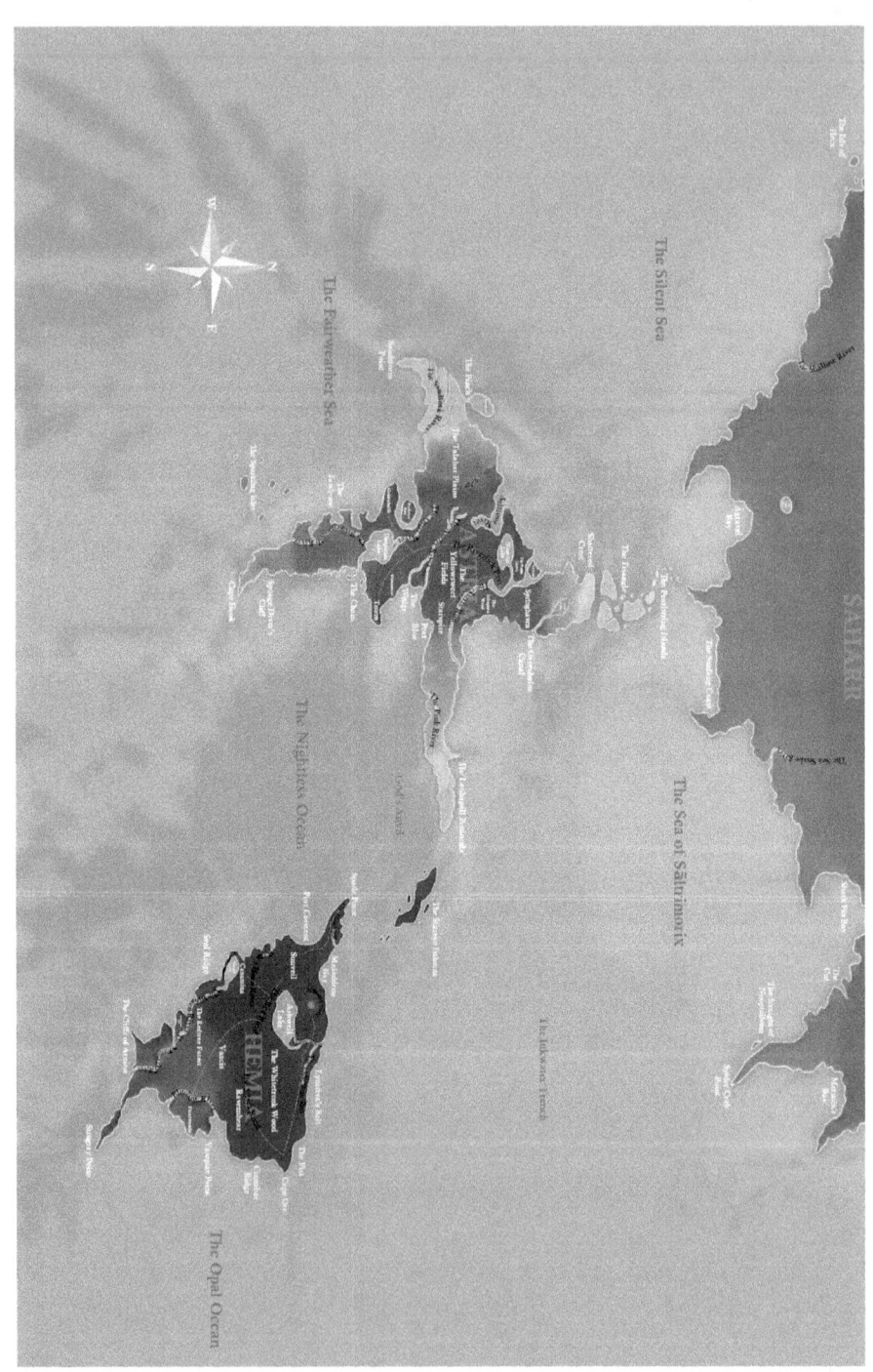

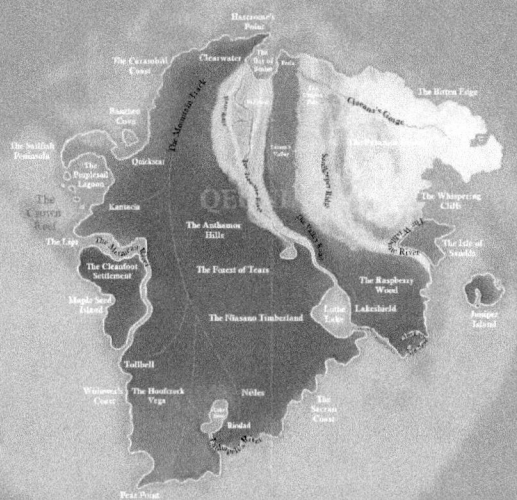

The Goldflight Ocean

The Sea of Sältrimorix

Hazzoone's Point

The Curanthil Coast

Clearwater Bay

The Memoria Peak

The Hut of Rofa Winter

Cleona's Gorge

The Bitten Edge

Bastheel Cove

Quickstat

The Buzilfah Peninsula

The Purplesail Lagoon

The Crown Reef

Katracia

The Lips

The Morgelyn

The Cleanfoot Settlement

Maple Seed Island

QEH...

The Whispering Cliffs

NatuPort Ridge

The Isle of Snailh

The Anthemor Hills

The Forest of Tears

The Raspberry Wood

The Niasano Timberland

Lutie Lake

Lakeshield

Juniper Island

Tollbell

Whitereach Coast

The Hoofcrack Vega

Nóles

Riedad

The Secran Coast

Fear Point

The Turquoise Sea

N
W   E
S

The Opal Ocean

The Ragged Coast

Iwidda's Isle

The Voodoo Forest

The Shiddura Peninsula

Dretli Bay

The Great Swamp

The Villew Mountains

The Armored Forest

Hammerhead Bay

The Chro...

The Spice Islands

The Atonehagn Coast

The Sea of Glass

The Penguin Cluster

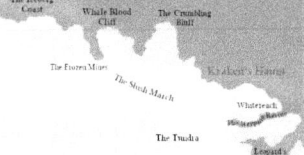

The Iceberg Coast

Whale Blood Cliff

The Crumbling Hmll

The Frozen Mian

The Studi March

Kraken's Hump

The Ocean of Ülribh

Whitreach

The Tuadra

Récha's Grief

Leopard's Foot

The Village

The Fields of Nottu

Narwhal Bay

The Free Clans' Settlement

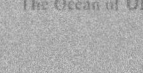

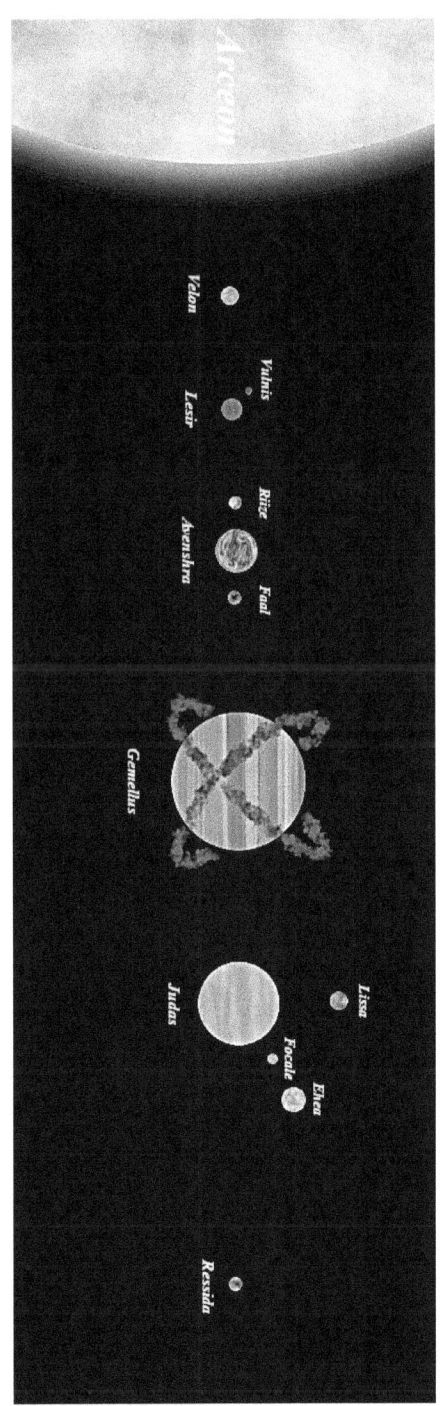

PROLOGUE—THREE HUNDRED YEARS AGO...

M'Cael fought back the pain, slamming once again into the horde of demons.

He spun wildly, desperate to win, screams echoing around him as he engaged whole squadrons of enemies with his Theonium flamberge.

His soldiers attacked from both ground and sky, opening wings of white, grey, and brown and flying at the enemy in a blur of shining steel. They used their pointed, silver daggers to level the playing field against their larger, heavier opponents, penetrating joints in the monsters' obsidian armor and piercing the soft, yellow-green flesh that lay beneath.

Unfortunately, their weapons were not enough.

The Angelicum were cut down, one by one, torn apart by fangs and claws and twisted swords. Their ranks had been broken, small, scattered clusters of soldiers drowning in an ocean of foes as they tried to protect the Shadowrise tree.

It was no longer about winning. It was about survival.

"Regroup!" M'Cael shouted, but his voice was inaudible against the clamor.

A Goblin ran at him, frenzied, its obsidian hide plastered with torn feathers. It made a vicious, downward cut for his left shoulder, but M'Cael parried it, dropping his point and driving it through the creature's neck. He kicked the Goblin's body aside, slapping away an incoming Pneumon's poleaxe and flipping his wrists into a back-edge cut to its head.

Taking advantage of the distraction, a Beast pounced at him, but M'Cael saw it enter his peripheral vision and pivoted, forcing his blade through its head mid-jump, overswinging and lodging the blade in the skull of the Goblin behind it. As he tried to dislodge the blade, a Shadowbat swooped down to hit him with a spiked mace.

Deigning to try and retrieve his previous Calling of the weapon, M'Cael Called Glorystar again, the sword that was stuck disintegrating and rematerializing from his Callring at the last second. He blocked the blow with the flat of the blade, sliding, and caught the Shadowbat with a cut to the side of its head, felling it instantly.

Just as he had cleared a space around himself, a squadron of Goblins and Pneumons had him surrounded again.

They just keep on coming!

Attempting to regain control of the space around him, M'Cael swung his greatsword in wide, intimidating loops. He knocked their weapons aside, cutting them down as they looked for an opening that wasn't there.

M'Cael continued to push through the horde, seeking out the Archdemon.

As he made his way towards the center of the battlefield, more of The Demonium assailed him, but he dispatched them swiftly. He would not be obstructed.

I have to put an end to this.

Finally, he found it.

Ten feet tall, it had oily, onyx skin and a pair of banded, obsidian horns that shattered the light into prismatic colors. Its sulphurous, yellow eyes smoldered over its skull-like nose, and its huge, obsidian teeth were serrated and sharp. Its bulky frame was overshadowed by a set of large, skeletal wings covered in rainbow quills. From what M'Cael could tell, it was a hybrid between a Goblin, a Ressidan, and great white shark. On its right hand, was a black steel Callring embedded with a cabochon of purple malachite.

It was surrounded by two entire squadrons of angels, but numbers weren't enough to beat it. It crushed both squadrons with ease, laughing as their leader struggled to come to their aid and the pile of corpses around it grew. It didn't even summon its Fallstreak. It only used its talons.

To think that this thing and I share blood... Fang'rial will pay for his unholy works.

No longer surrounded by living opponents, The Archdemon turned to face M'Cael. In its hand, it held the last of his kin: his cousin, S'rraph.

The youngest of M'Cael's soldiers, S'rraph was unskilled and inexperienced. He had no hope of beating The Archdemon, but he had fought anyway, fought valiantly.

The fiend took S'rraph's leg with its other hand, the suffering youth squirming helplessly. It held him in an iron grip, S'rraph's bright blue eyes alight with fear as it began to bend him over its knee.

"S'rraph!" M'Cael cried, tearing his way through masses of Goblins and Pneumons. He tried to fly, but he was pulled back down to earth—surrounded, suffocated.

"Get out of my way! Get out of my way!!!"

Just as M'Cael got through, S'rraph's back broke with a horrible crack, snow-white wings fluttering as the light left his eyes. To M'Cael's horror, the Archdemon ripped his cousin's body in half, pearlescent, pink blood spraying across its face.

It smiled gleefully.

M'Cael seethed with rage.

The Archdemon's eyes flashed blue for a second, and so did the eyes of all the Goblins. The ranks of demons parted, giving M'Cael a path to his foe.

It was too late, then.

"Come here, little bird," the demon jeered, its eyes returning to their original yellow.

"Only one of you left now."

What?!

You mean...

His vision obscured by throngs of enemies, M'Cael had not understood. His forces had been completely wiped out. There was no one left but him. He had just watched the last of his brethren die and he had been unable to stop it.

M'Cael's face contorted with anger.

He swung Glorystar in a vengeful arc, but the demon flapped its wings and dodged, punching him and splitting his right ear.

Stupefied and numb with anger, M'cael made a halving cut at The Archdemon's chest, but it dodged again, clubbing him with a stony pinion and surging forwards for a counterattack.

M'Cael cried out as Theonium slashed across his torso.

The Archdemon had finally Called its sword, and enchanted bronze was not enough.

M'Cael hit the ground hard, dropping his flamberge, which evaporated into Lifeblood and returned to the ring on his finger.

His opponent placed a meaty hoof upon his chest, crushing ribs.

"I am Asmodel, the Wingbreaker. You and your kind stood no chance against me today, puny dove, nor did you stand a chance against my brethren. If these were your greatest warriors, if you were supposed to be their champion, then that oaf, Luxyruss, has already lost."

M'Cael couldn't see straight. His eyes watered and he tasted iron, sticky warmth rushing from his grievous wounds.

But he wouldn't let that be his end.

I will not fall so easily. I will not be made a fool of.

The Divinity—won't be made a fool of!

I have to win.

For my soldiers.

For my friends!

M'Cael kicked the demon in the crotch as hard as he could, causing it to stumble backwards.

He used his wings to flip himself over into a spinning attack, Calling Glorystar once again. Its wavy edge hit Asmodel's crescent brand with an echoing report, the demon hissing as it took yet another step back.

M'Cael whipped Glorystar in reeling arcs, Asmodel bracing his blade with his hand as he blocked.

The Archdemon's kilij was a poor match for a sword in two hands, but the monster's size and reach made up for the imbalance. Every time Asmodel counterattacked, he came close to dealing M'cael a fatal blow, a one-handed saber overpowering a sword that cut down spears like reeds.

The clang of metal on metal made M'Cael's ears ring as the swords came together, again and again, each shrill chime resounding over the battlefield. He continued to ward the demon off, trying to confuse him with small feints as he searched for an opening, but Asmodel was no dumb brute. He spun his sword in warding motions of his own, checking each feint and leaving few openings.

Asmodel used a blade-beat to send a bouncing cut sailing towards M'Cael's collarbone.

Luckily, M'Cael had one more trick up his sleeve.

He turned the flat of his blade towards Asmodel, raising Glorystar high and receiving the cut with a flame-like quillon. The Fallstreak hummed, emitting a flash of yellow-white light that blinded The Archdemon, disorienting it.

That was all M'Cael needed. He turned his edge towards the demon and cut down, slicing off its left wing.

Blood, swimming with Tremite larvae, dripped from the shiny stump, Asmodel trembling in fury as he flew into an onslaught of downward slashes, half-blind and more than half an animal.

The Wingbreaker ravaged him, but M'Cael defended himself with all the energy he could muster. And though he was being pushed back, he saw a glimmer of fear in the demon's eyes.

It had never been defied so long.

That fear led to hastiness, and that hastiness led to doubt.

That doubt created another opening.

Ducking under a cut to the temple, M'Cael raked across Asmodel's sinewed calf in a spurt of leaden gore. The monster fell to one knee, paralyzed in shock and agony.

With a *whoosh*, M'Cael rose into the air, looking down at the demon with eyes like fire.

"Know me creature, for I am The Archangel M'Cael, The First Sword of Ressida. You slaughtered my brothers, adults and children alike. You have no honor. And yet you might have killed me had you not been so arrogant."

Asmodel was no longer grinning, his eyes wide.

"Mercy..." the demon coughed, breathing heavily. "You win. You..."

M'Cael's teeth clenched.

Asking for mercy after what you did? Blasphemy.

"You showed no mercy... I won't show any either. For this is mine to avenge; now I repay!"

He dropped upon the terror, stabbing down through Asmodel's ridged torso and deep into the ground as Glorystar began to glow. The light was much stronger, then, the hellspawn roaring as light rays tore through him, burning from within.

The monster quickly fell quiet, and with a flap of The Archangel's wings, Asmodel's body splintered into a cloud of filth, blowing away with the wind and out across the frozen wastes.

M'Cael fell to his knees and cried.

His mission was complete.

But The Angelicum were gone.

CHAPTER I

Torran

Torran Xandromen lay on the muddy ground, bleeding from many wounds. His vision murky and his ears ringing, he watched blurry, white flakes fall before an icy moon.

Dazed, he rose from the ground, as if from sleep.

And then he heard once more.

The dragon roared, buildings shattering around it. Its searing aura crushed everything in its path, plumes of dust and debris flying in a circular shockwave.

Torran shielded his face as countless stones whizzed by, grazing his bare arms.

Flameheir was supreme.

The Firetongue stood one hundred feet tall, a monster amongst monsters. His great, golden eyes beamed down upon the world, the clatter of his scales as loud as thunder.

The massive, maroon dragon had claws as big as scythes, diaphanous, speckled, orange wings like a hundred sails. Its scales glowed with the souls of the slain. Seated between horns, large and coiled and ribbed like a ram's, was a pale figure: Falin Eridion, Hemia's Brimstone King.

Ruby eyes full of malice, Falin cackled as Flameheir breathed a jet of luminous orange fire. Steel melted, flesh becoming charcoal.

Destruction reigned as the fire spread, soldiers scrambling for cover that was not to be found. Screams erupted as the Bloodred Battalion surged from behind Sunveil's walls and past their King's serpent, their silvery, Moondrake-bone weapons tearing through the Astrian forces.

A direct attack would be suicide.

But Torran had to save his men.

Torran looked for his sword, but it was lost, his mail ripped under plate that was dented and smashed. Nevertheless, he trudged back into battle as even the bravest of his troops turned to flee. He was their Prince, and he had to be strong.

There's no time. I need to find a weapon. Anything will do.

Torran picked up the first blade he found, mundane steel with a simple, rectangular crossguard. The sword was broken, but he didn't care.

If this is the end, so be it.

Flameheir's neck wound low, ready to breathe out another jet. Torran was hit by The Firetongue's scorching heat, but he welcomed it.

The Bloodred Battalion quickly got out of the way; Torran ran towards the dragon like a lunatic, tattered cape billowing in the wind. Right as it was about to exhale, he jumped high and grabbed onto its right horn.

The beast flailed, nearly causing him to lose his grip. He held on with a strength he didn't know he had.

Hoping to shake him off, The Raishian King ordered Flameheir to fly, but Torran braced himself against the dragon's burning scales, hanging tight. The Firetongue rose, many stories up, clearing the city's bone-white buildings within seconds.

The clouds' smooth caress alerted Torran that if Flameheir went any higher, he would die—the people below were beginning to look as small as ants. It was probably already too late.

The dragon's skin grew hotter.

This is it! I have to act now!

Don't think! Just do it!

Frustrated, the dragon tried venting its breath through the side of its mouth, bucking and snapping, but with a pang of terror, Torran said goodbye to life and swung off of its horn, plunging the fractured blade through its terrible eye.

Shrieking, the beast plummeted through the night sky, blinded. Torran watched as the great lizard fell towards the Hemian force, spraying smoking, green blood.

It fell faster than him, somehow. Something was slowing his fall; it was as if the clouds were cushioning him. Still, it was not enough to stop his descent.

Flameheir fell back-first onto the city walls, wings outstretched, crushing the Battalion's charge along with its rider. Torran slammed into an ash-covered hill, the impact taking the wind out of him, but miraculously, not his life.

His enchanted panoply must have saved him, if only barely, though he couldn't understand how. He could hardly think, his mouth bleeding and his head woozy.

Nevertheless, he got up, his sternum cracked and his spine bruised, tears streaming down his ashen cheeks. His left leg was mangled and shaking, but for that moment, it managed to support his weight. His forces watched, full of awe, as he silently raised the weapon's shard and pointed towards the ruined battlements.

He didn't need to speak. He didn't need to command.

With a roar louder than any dragon's, The Astrian Army turned and rushed their stupefied enemy.

And Torran fell to the ground for the third and final time, his mind engulfed in blankness.

Leafsong

Blankness engulfed Leafsong's mind as she fell asleep, clean, country air entering through her room and drifting through the cool, dry, manor. As crickets began to chirp, she sank deeper into her pillow, restlessness relenting and giving way to a strange and surreal dream.

She dreamt that she was falling—falling through grey skies and whizzing past grey clouds, her white, lace nightgown fluttering in the wind.

Twisting her body, she turned to see that she was falling towards water, what appeared to be an ocean.

As she came closer to the moment of impact, and the clouds grew sparse, she realized that the expanse of blue before her was not an ocean at all, but an eye, its iris as blue as the sun, as blue as sapphires or the deepest watery trench. Alarmingly, black veins were spreading towards the iris, worming their way through a sclera white as froth, white as milk.

With a splash, Leafsong fell through the pupil at the center of the giant globe, finding herself tumbling through air again as a different person, a ragged cape wrapped around muscular, male shoulders. Blood seeped through a black leather cuirass emblazoned with a golden star. She stared up at clouds engorged with smog, accepting death.

Leafsong hit the ground solidly, kicking up a curtain of ash, but was not hurt.

She picked herself up, breathless, as a gust of hot air drew the curtain, revealing a burning battlefield.

She watched, paralyzed, as a man in a skull mask emerged from a pillar of black smoke at the center of the battlefield, a man with crimson eyes. A white sword materialized in the white knight's hand, white as bone, white as chalk—a sword with a red edge.

The smoke took human form behind him, a specter with eyes of green flame.

It was looking at her.

She had never seen such furor.

An old man's voice echoed softly through her mind.

See all, great Seer. For he must be stopped.

See all!

Leafsong woke up with a jolt, her throat tight with fear. Beads of cold sweat ran down her scalp and trickled along her wiry, Ronari hair, which was fixed into twin braids, which ran along her temples and met to form a single, larger braid going down to the small of her supple back.

Her eyes darted back and forth across her modest room, heart pounding. She searched for a threat, but everything was as it had been.

Leafsong's room was simple, with rough, stone walls. The floor was lined with rush mats, and a mahogany nightstand rested against the left wall. On that nightstand, was a silver candle holder with a half-melted, tallow candle drooping to the side. She burned it at night in an attempt to banish the visions that came with the darkness, but it hadn't been helping lately.

Her feather bed was draped with white cotton sheets, and the bed frame, also made of mahogany, complemented the room's simple yet elegant furnishings. Two windows with poplar shutters allowed a cool breeze to enter the Manor, lending a soothing atmosphere to the space. Between the windows, a wooden chair served as her sewing spot, surrounded by bits of fallen thread. Leafsong's sewing basket, mostly empty, contained a skein of pink thread, a needle, and an unfinished embroidery of a rose, still on its circular, wooden frame.

The crown jewel of the room was an ornate, poplar armoire, positioned against the left wall and past the nightstand. It was adorned with carvings of spirals, and some areas were decorated with swirling lines of gold paint. This special piece had been given to her by her father for her sixteenth birthday, and inside it, she kept her clothes, shoes, a few precious pieces of jewelry, along with some perfumes the Baron had brought back from his trips to the capital.

The room smelled faintly of rose perfume, and if one listened closely, they could hear the river running behind the house. It was a calming place, a peaceful place...

Or at least, it should have been.

In recent weeks, all Leafsong had felt in her room was fear. Every noise was something threatening; every scent was off somehow. Her armoire appeared taller and darker than it did during the day.

Pulling the sheets over her diminutive body, the young noblewoman lay back down on her side, curled up into a ball, and sobbed softly to herself, cradling her pillow as she shivered beneath sheets sodden with sweat.

It had been months since she had enjoyed the comfort sleep would offer. Lately, even warm, spring nights felt cold, and she was constantly hounded by visions she didn't understand.

She finally fell back asleep as the birds began to sing and the maids began to clean.

That time, she did not dream.

Flind

Flind was employed as a scullion at The Ralei Manor in the mountain town of Stillvein. She had worked there since she was young, and she knew the property like the back of her hand—better, even.

The Manor was a bit small and plain compared to the mansions of the other Qeonian nobles, but it was still much larger and grander than the houses of the surrounding townsfolk. Unlike the other properties, it wasn't crowded. It sat alone on the east bank of The Treasure River, whose cold, fast-moving waters divided Heart Ridge roughly along the middle. Built from grey brick and what could barely be made out to be ceramic shingles, the building was visibly run-down, roof tiles brown and discolored with age. Creeping vines crawled up its stuccoed walls, two, tall chimneys puffing a continuous stream of woodsmoke: one for the fireplace, which was in the living room, and one for the oven in the kitchen.

The Manor had a total of four, old-fashioned, open windows: three for the bedrooms and one for the kitchen, though all view of its interior was blocked by white, silk curtains.

The living room was illuminated by a large, glass windowpane, which had the same, white silk curtains behind it, and the twin front doors to the house were made of mahogany. Above the double doors, was a small, stained glass panel of The Theic Eye, done in blue, grey, and green. Representing the watching eye of The Divinity, "The Eye" was the Qeonian national symbol, and a symbol of The Ralei Dynasty. It was also particularly hard to clean, too high up for Flind to easily reach with her duster.

This front portion of The Manor connected to a set of grey, brick walls that lined a lawn of dark green grass and a cobblestone pathway leading to a spiked, iron gate.

Hidden behind the house, was a dirt lot, where chickens clucked and pecked around for leftover pieces of corn, a rotting, wooden chicken coop situated on the far left. A tolerable distance away, was a small, wooden shack with a sagging, triangular roof and three, poorly insulated windows, bleached by rain and sun, and in equal disrepair as the chicken coop. Beyond the shack was a large stream, and beyond that, were pastures and hills, where The Baron's barkmoth herds went out to graze. This shack was Flind's family home, where she and her parents had slept head to foot since the day she was born.

Flind was the only Monolid employed at The Manor. In fact, she was the only Monolid in Stillvein, her skin a navy-blue that stood out in stark contrast to the white and gold skin tones of the townsfolk. Her parents had emigrated to Qeonia to escape The Second Cairnian Civil War.

When Agamus had gone on a diplomatic trip to Qeonia, he was ambushed by Lātist revolutionaries, who wanted to take him hostage and demand ransom from The High Empire. A Lātist himself, Flind's father, Eldo, saved the Lord's life.

A lower-class worker, Eldo sympathized with the revolutionary cause, but he disagreed with their violent approach to revolution. But although he had acted true to the peaceful nature of the Lightseeker faith, his actions alienated him and his wife from their fellow Lātists, and the Baodin family became outcast. With both the oppressive Kïsist regime and the rebels against them, Agamus paid for the expecting couples' passage to Qeonia, placing them in indentured servitude, but saving their lives.

And so, Flind was born in Qeonia. Her mother, Rala, didn't want her to be born in an environment of suffering and war, so she ended up being born into a life of suffering, if not war.

Underpaid and mistreated, Flind was not particularly grateful, but she couldn't complain. Her parents worked so hard that it was hard to find any fault with them. They worked until their dying breath.

Her father had tended to the barkmoths, living out in the fields, and only coming home at night. He would take them out to graze, the large insects eating grass and growing thick, papery scales on their wings. Every month or so, the man would take his u-shaped knife and gently scrape off the scales, the scrapings going to market and to paper producers, who would wet, mash, spread, and dry the shorn material. Though the work was lonely and intense, Eldo never complained, even when he cut himself with his scaling knife, catching tetanus and dying of lockjaw, his mouth sealed shut forever.

Her mother had been a washerwoman, washing clothes, cleaning The Manor, and occasionally helping Cook to prepare meals. At first, her mother had been given more work than the others due to her race, but she outworked them all, winning favor in the Lord's eyes. As the Baron's desire for privacy grew, half of the servants were let go over the span of a couple months, the brunt of the work given to Rala, but she bore it well, and like Flind's father, she didn't complain. She died shortly after her husband, struck down by a falling bag of flour in the kitchen. The heavy sack slammed her head against the floor, causing a fatal brain-bleed.

Orphaned, Flind took charge of many of her mother's duties at just fourteen.

Since then, she had grown up into a strong and capable young woman. Unfortunately, she had grown up to be alone. Though she was good-looking, with a shapely figure, she had slightly masculine features that outshone her cute brown curls and her eyes, which were perhaps a little hard, but glimmered like river stones. None of the men in town were interested in her for more than her exoticism, and that was the only "positive" interest anyone showed in her. She faced discrimination daily, insulted and jeered at, but she had learned to live with it, to bury her resentment and put her all into hard work, taking the example of the other Manor servants.

Dressed in simple whites and browns, the Manor servants never complained. Their clothes were just old enough to look shabby, but not old enough to be replaced, and they maintained a straight and unwavering posture as they quietly carried out their duties, the coarse, wooden handles of straw brooms and feather dusters adding calluses to their already callused hands.

On that particular morning, Flind was tasked with cleaning the upper floor of the Manor, where the rooms of the Ralei family members slept. The other servants were busy preparing breakfast with the cook or bringing in washed laundry.

Flind silently swept away the dust and grime outside of the Baroness' dormitory with a reed broom. Then she swept outside of The Baron's, being as thorough as she could. The movement of the broom handle tugged at her worn palms, the skin between her fingers dry and cracking.

As she began to take down the tapestries so that she could beat the dust out of them in the backyard, she heard a rustling of sheets, pained moans coming from the next room over.

Concerned, Flind sidled up to the unclosed door, peering through the slit.

Is the young Mistress alright? Maybe she's sick?

When she saw the source of the strange noises, Flind had to forcibly stop herself from gasping, clamping a hand over her lips.

The Baron was lying on top of Inesa Ralei, a girl of nine, muffling her cries with his hand. He moved as if in a trance, the young girl haphazardly tied to the bed frame with scraps of loose clothing. No one but Flind could hear her as she squealed in pain, inaudible to the rest of the household.

Baron Agamus Ralei, second in line to the throne of Qeonia, was committing an unspeakable crime.

Flind stood very still, her eyes wide. She didn't know what to do.

What's going on?!

Oh my God! This is so wrong!

I have to tell the Baroness! She needs to know! She needs to stop him; he-

He's a Baron, the King's brother...

But I can't just walk away. I can't just let him do this!

Flind tiptoed over to a nearby table and picked up a hefty, silver candlestick. Disregarding her own safety, she snuck into the room and hit Agamus in the back of the head, stupefying him.

Crying, Inesa pushed her father off. The Baron fell to the ground with a *thud*.

Flind had meant to knock him out long enough to get Inesa to safety, but she wasn't sure if it had worked.

She wasn't going to wait to find out.

I must leave! I need to get her out of here and into the Baroness' room. She can lock the door and-

Ah! I don't know, but she can't stay here!

In full haste now, Flind hurriedly undid Inesa's ties, hoping the girl would defend her actions to the Mistress when the Baron sobered up.

In Qeonia, pedophilia was an offense punishable by the loss of both one's hands. The Baroness probably wouldn't have her husband arrested and tried, as that would damage the Ralei name and hurt her and her daughters both, but as the one bringing most of the wealth into their marriage, she could force him to leave and then divorce him.

Inesa whimpered, shaken and in shock, but still, she was visibly relieved that Flind was there.

"Flind, you—"

Flind had only started untying the clothes when Agamus got up from the ground and grabbed her by the shirt, reeking of alcohol. He held her at length, staring at her with eyes dimmed by intoxication.

Flind wanted to scream, but her voice caught in her throat. Inesa backed against the wall, white as a sheet and too scared to even open her mouth.

Agamus was tall, with broad shoulders, and he stood even taller due to his pompadour hairstyle. He had a well-proportioned face, save for his large, square chin, which stood out like a boulder from a smooth cliff.

There was a time when Flind had thought highly of him. When she was a teenager, she had even been attracted to him a little, but after growing up and realizing how poor her parents had been in his service, she had lost that respect, remaining professional for the sake of her job.

After seeing what he had just done to his daughter, she found him completely repulsive.

Flind tried to scratch his face, to fight back and escape, but even though The Baron was drunk and injured, Flind had no hope of overpowering him.

With a dismissive grunt, he bludgeoned her with the same candlestick she had hit him with and then hit his daughter—hard. He had tried to knock her out, but he used too much force, the dull *crack* of bone echoing in the silence. The girl fell onto the bed she had just escaped, dead.

The secrecy of it all had become a certainty.

Beyond drunk, then, The Baron grabbed Flind by the neck and raped her too. He shoved her face into the sheets until she fell senseless, his wife and Leafsong sleeping just next door.

Jhett

The Sailfish was a large merchant vessel with two floors below deck: one for merchandise, and one for the slaves below.

The oar slaves lived and died chained to rotting, wooden benches bolted to the floor. A bucket for their refuse sat beneath every bench, and the oar holes provided the only light in the dark, rank chamber. Water dripped from the slimy planks above, and the isopods that snacked on the ship would occasionally fall on the slaves' heads, eliciting cries of helplessness. The floor was oily and discolored, the benches were splintering, and the manacles were covered with bubbling, orange rust. The waste buckets would often fall, spilling their contents down the galley, but the sludge was only cleaned when the ship reached the shore, and so it would squelch beneath the slaves' bare feet for days or even weeks.

Jhettisquan pulled against his oar, the drummer at the front of the galley beating away at a furious pace. He had gotten used to rowing with the rhythm, the acid buildup in his arms, but his rage had not dimmed with time. He had not gotten used to servitude, and never would.

Sweat poured down his face as he rowed. His nappy, black hair sat in a square tuft on his head, with three, short dreadlocks hanging down from the back. He was dark, but not as dark as some Nolites, and his skin had a faint, brown luster to it.

Jhett was a married man, shown by The Brand: three, sideways, triangular marks running down his neck. He was also a warrior, shown by the tattoos on his shoulders: circular rings of scar tissue. He had cut them into his own skin on his eighteenth birthday, when The Tribe King of The Aerhauc Tribe, Mgambi, anointed him with holy oil and named him a protector of The Tribe.

But although he was a warrior who had trained since childhood, tall and strong, he had been unable to protect anyone. He and his family had been kidnapped in the dead of night, captured by a group of Nolites slavers from the nearby Quorkorath and Fivefinger Tribes and sold to a group of Qeonian merchants.

Jhett was separated from his wife and daughter a week after they were bought. He hadn't seen them since...

At that moment, the ship he was rowing was making the return journey from Hemia.

He and his oarmates were only ever given momentary periods of rest, and those were few and far between. The five other members of his Tribe that had been bought as galley slaves had died, and he was barely holding on to life himself. He told himself that he had survived and they had not, simply because they had lost their drive to return home. Like Jhett, they also belonged to the warrior class, but they had fallen prey to their shame, defeat eating away at them until they grew weak and eventually fell ill.

Jhett refused to suffer the same fate. He would wear his shame like a dark mantle, let its weight harden him. He would do whatever it took to survive, even if he had to drag himself along by his fingernails. He pulled at the oar with the same defiance as when he had first been whipped.

But it had been many months since then—how many—he wasn't sure. With every stroke of the oar, his memory faded, and the object of his drive slipped away. His rage was like a seething cauldron for his spirit, slowly turning it to steam and leaving him a husk.

He could barely remember his wife's face, the sound of his daughter's voice, but still, he clung to the notion of homecoming like a child trying to capture smoke in its hands.

He could use a little bit of luck, some aid from his ancestors, but he feared that they were unreachable, warded off by the drummer's tireless beat. If he didn't stay strong, he would probably join them before the ship cleared the upcoming Stareye Isthmus. He vowed that if he did, he would curse The Sailfish and all its sailors, Qeonia itself. If he couldn't kill them himself, his jinx would. It had to.

Every man has their limit.

The tribesman stared through the oar hole beside him as he rowed. The waters glittered, a beautiful turquoise, but they were torturously calm. It seemed like he had a lot of work ahead.

Jhett prayed for wind.

Konell

Clearwater was the largest city in the world, with a population of five hundred thousand people. The whole city was enclosed in walls sixty feet high, the land populated all the way to Harcrome's point. The elevation got steeper and steeper until one reached the cliffs from which King Harcrome The Builder had famously thrown himself into the sea and committed suicide.

The Bay of Scales sparkled to the east, packed with high-masted ships and protected by the powerful Qeonian Navy. Open-air markets stretched between the yellow-painted houses, their flat roofs decorated with ornamental peppers: small green bushes festooned with fruits that were round and colorful, no larger than pebbles.

Strolling the markets, the rich wore grey and blue tunics and the peasants wore cotton and brown leather. Whitewashed churches stuck out from groups of older, more faded constructions, sporting tall towers, their conical roofs painted blue, and topped with golden spires wrought in the shape of The Trident. Further up from the commoners' homes was a roughly rectangular area of land where the cobblestone was smoother and the architecture was more refined. There, the various noble families chose to build their mansions: grey stone buildings with neatly manicured lawns, fruitful orange trees, and their own cobblestone courtyards. All of the mansions had walls with metal spikes on them to keep out thieves, and the nobles rarely strayed from their dwellings to buy things. Instead, they would send their Nolite slaves, who would go to market for them. The streets were crowded with travelers and the inns and taverns were always cooking seafood, rich spices and the smell of citrus drifting on the wind.

The Qeonian Royal Palace was situated on the cliffs, its shadow falling over half of the city. It was similar in appearance to the churches, with tall, cone-capped towers, painted in red and white. However, it was differentiated by a large, blue dome that sat at the center of the building, the entrance barred with pillars of glittering white marble, column headers done in simple but elegant scrollwork. The Palace had a marble fountain in front of it, and a line of cypresses bordered the crushed marble pathway leading to the main entrance.

At the southwest end of the city were the older homes, the cheerful, yellow houses getting fewer and fewer until one reached Beggar's Alley, a series of alleys and ramshackle houses that sat close to the walls. There, the streets smelled of alcohol and sewage and the houses were made of unpainted wood and stone. In Beggar's Alley, one was always on the lookout for rapists and pickpockets, the Qeonian military doing little to enforce the law. All the poor were crammed into that one area, and the rest of the city didn't much care if they lived or died, so long as they stayed away from them and their brighter, cleaner part of the city.

In the shadow of the walls, the only sources of light were the taverns, where the hopeless went to drink and gamble, the streets lined with broken teeth and broken bottles. Gutters constipated with stinking shit lined both sides of the road, running through the whole sector and into the sea. The sewage exited through a large hole in the walls, a loud, yellow-brown waterfall, and nearly every step was a step in excrement or rotting food, the litter becoming denser as one got to the lines of wooden hovels at the edge of the walls. Parasites and diseases ran rampant, and the diseased never saw the light of day, for there, the walls were tall enough to throw everything into perpetual shade, and the decrease in elevation made it look like it was always night. The people who lived there were the poorest of the poor: street sweepers, gutter cleaners, prostitutes and the unemployed, wearing rags. The tavern owners made a fine profit off of them, living comfortably in their sturdy, stone houses, with a fireplace to stay warm during the winter and enough rooms to house their entire family.

Konell had followed his quarry from one of those taverns all the way out of Beggar's Alley and up to the border of the nobles' sector. They leapt from rooftop to rooftop, the distance between them closing, albeit slowly.

His target dove from a nearby church tower, swinging off a flagpole and landing silently on the next roof.

Konell followed, creased, leather boots glancing against brick as he ran two steps on the wall of that same tower, kicked off, and slid down those same shingles, rolling over the gap between them and the next house.

From purple cloth, he pulled a dagger, ricocheting it off a stone chimney with a *clink*, but his target simply rolled, and continued to run, the knife missing its mark.

Frustrated, Konell sped up, ceramic breaking underfoot.

His breath fogged up his mask, crude steel closed around a misty visor of amethyst glass. The dogged chase carried on, and Konell was getting tired.

But he had a contract, and truth be told, he enjoyed the thrill of the pursuit.

Finally, his quarry stopped to face him, standing on a wide, square roof with strong shingles. They intended to fight.

Face still cloaked in shadow, his enemy revealed clawed gloves, shiny, silver crescents drinking in the moonlight.

Konell's quarry was The Silvercat, one of the most deadly assassins in Qeonia, and perhaps, the world. Konell would have never pursued her in the past, but he had been given a list of assassins to kill, and failure was not an option.

Konell Called Tardrown, the threatening kilij falling into his hand. The ebon sword was affixed with a sphere of purple chalcedony. Dust swirled around the blade, held in orbit by some unknown force.

Undeterred, The Silvercat pounced, slashing and slicing, turning his cape to ribbons of purple satin as he dodged.

Konell ducked and swayed, parrying her claws, but her fingers were coming within inches of his neck. She took his mask off with a well-placed swing, sending it clattering into the alley below.

The next swing, she got his throat, but the cuts were shallow, drawing blood without hitting anything vital.

With a low kick, Konell swept The Silvercat off her feet, slamming his scimitar against tile as she rolled out of the way and back to her feet, tossing a steel throwing nail at him that he deflected.

Konell backed off, adopting a high guard with his saber and watching for her next move.

From that distance, her face was visible. The Silvercat was a mix between a Luzian and a Monolid, with pale blue skin, almond-shaped eyes, and wispy, white-blonde hair that was long and flowing and nigh on translucent.

She was around his age. Had he no contract, he might have enjoyed this meeting, tried to seduce her.

But it was not to be.

She took off her gloves and threw them down in a huff, pulling a long, notched knife from its scabbard: a sword breaker.

With a *swish*, she threw out another nail and rushed him. Konell cut the nail out of the air, swinging down at her head.

The Silvercat moved offline, her dagger in reverse grip, and caught his sword in the sword breaker's enchanted steel tines. Then she grabbed the spine of the blade with her other hand and twisted, but to break Theonium was an impossible goal, and she wrenched at the metal to no avail. Nevertheless, he let her pull the sword from his hand, tackling her as it spun and disappeared.

The Silvercat lost her knife in the fall, but she managed to turn them over in the air and get the top mount.

She choked him, squeezing as hard as she could with both hands, but to her surprise, Konell did not resist.

He let her choke him, blood dripping from the wounds on his neck. Her surprise quickly turned to fear as she stiffened, the poison seeping through her skin.

Konell smiled.

"Relax," he said coolly. "It hurts more if you squirm."

Amdryaan

A scream.

"Amdryaan!"

"Amdryaan, help!"

"Amdryaan, where are you?!"

I'm sorry, Mom; I can't! I'm too scared!

Amdryaan hid.

The Weirtonce had entered his family's tent and was holding his mother, Lyccaona Winterlove, up by the neck, her nose bleeding and her long, luscious, black hair full of split ends.

Though she had been badly beaten, she wasn't broken yet. Her eyes shone like embers, but those embers were slowly dimming, and the ice giant's grip was tightening.

As his mother began to gag and cry, her attacker's brutal features twisted into a cruel smile.

He had long ice-hair that reached down to his shoulders and a dark blue scar parted his left eyebrow, a reminder of his one and only defeat.

The tallest giant of his generation, Voreus Cloudburster easily towered over any human being on Avenshra. Standing at twenty feet tall, he was probably the tallest giant in history. As if that wasn't enough, he was also the most muscular man Amdryaan had ever seen. His arms bristled with spikes of ice, long arm hairs dipped in water and frozen to a razor point. A weapon made of a freezing, light blue metal sat strapped to his back, a war scythe.

Amdryaan hid, trembling, behind boxes of Imperial provisions that had been stacked at the far end of the room. His father's spear rested against the boxes next to him, but he had not yet mustered up the courage to take it.

His father, Kanis, was not a coward like him. His father had always been courageous, the son of the mighty Amaak and Ilalia Winterlove, the greatest leaders of The Wolf Clan in hundreds of years. He had married a woman from another clan, fought the Frosslar with their towering swords. He had united The Five Clans, driving the ice giants out of ancestral, Native lands and buying twenty years of peace.

But that peace had ended, and Amdryaan wasn't like his father. He didn't have the courage.

He didn't have the strength.

If I can hit him in the neck, I can save Mom. But I'm scared!

He peeked around the boxes. His mother was weeping, abandoned by her family. Amdryaan's father was out hunting with the other men, and would not return for a fortnight. His sister had been dragged out of the tent just minutes earlier.

She was probably already dead.

Amdryaan hadn't helped his sister, and he was watching his mother die.

She was suffering because of him.

Amdryaan took the spear in his hands, his fists tightening around it.

He would do it. He had to.

Suddenly, the giant slammed his mother into the central tent post, the wood cracking. He began to untie the furs around his waist excitedly.

Amdryaan quickly hid behind the boxes again.

He was a skinny thirteen-year-old. If he fought, he would die.

I need to save her! He's going to hurt her!

But I—

I can't do it! I'm not strong enough!

I'm just too scared!

There was a cry of rage.

Amdryaan peeked out from behind the boxes as his younger sister, Wiola, burst in through the tent's second door, interrupting The Weirtonce. Her eyes were blackened, but she was still alive, her ulu dripping neon-blue blood.

She snarled, a true wolf.

Voreus dropped Lyccaona to the ground, an icicle appearing from out of nowhere in his hand. He stabbed for Wiola's chest with the jagged spike, but the girl dodged, swinging her leather-cutting knife.

She managed to cut the giant's cheek with it as he leaned in, Voreus snarling at this second scar, but drew no more blood. The giant slapped her, sending her flying into the crates and knocking both her and Amdryaan out.

The last thing Amdryaan heard was his mother whimper as the giant threw her over his shoulder and took her away.

The last thing he felt, was shame.

Amdryaan sat up, his nose bloody.

Why can't I escape that memory? I was just a kid; he was too strong! There was no way to save her...

There can't have been a way.

If I could have stopped it...I would have, right?

The tribesman was cold, having lain in the snow for what could have been minutes or hours, for all he knew. Arceon wouldn't set for a month, so it was hard to tell the time of day under Goddess' constant surveillance.

Aamdryaan's family, like much of The Five Clans, practiced the religion of Uuquát, which translated to Those Who Bow Before The Sun in The Universal Tongue. Known colloquially as The Bowers, they worshipped Iásuka, Goddess of Light, whose spirit lived in nature and in all living things.

To them, the sun was not just a star in the sky, but the big, blue eye of their Goddess, watching the people to see if they held her Creation in respect.

Though the Goddess was powerful, she was not tireless, and her brother Itat, The Moon God, watched the world while she slept. Unlike his sister, Itat did not love humanity. A God with two faces, one friendly and one angry, his personality changed every night—one night willing to help the humans and answer their prayers, the other looking to erase them, a blemish on his sister's art.

Though he knew he shouldn't, Amdryaan wished that Itat could take her place for just a moment, even if it was risky. It was too bright out.

But the sun continued to shine.

Squinting, Amdryaan felt his bruised cheek. They had gone so far as to strike him, and he was embarrassed to admit that he had been knocked out in a single punch, that he had cowered in fear, as he always did.

Amdryaan was a short, skinny kid, with wavy, brown hair that went down to his chin and was parted at the center. He had the same, light grey eyes as his father and light, reddish-brown skin, an irregular, dark brown birthmark on the side of his neck.

Weaker than the other boys in The Five Clans and shorter than most Natives, he was subject to bullying—a lot of bullying.

Wait, Enpen! Please, don't!

Who's going to stop us? The Chief couldn't care less, and you're his son! He didn't even take you on The Hunt. You're weak!

The other boys didn't understand. He was not like them.

Enpen and his posse were a group of older Wolf Clan boys who made it their mission to make Amdryaan's life hell. Enpen was tall and muscular and older than Amdryaan, and when he pushed him around, Amdryaan's father stayed mum.

Amdryaan wasn't skilled at much, and he wasn't the strong, natural-born leader that his father had hoped for. Kanis left him to fend for himself most of the time, aiming to toughen him up, but all he did was make it clear to the rest of the Clan that he wouldn't punish anyone for bullying his firstborn.

And why would he? Enpen and his posse were the kind of sons The Fiveclan Chief had hoped for. Born hunters, they were made for the ice—big, tough, and hot-blooded. Their hearts burned against the cold expanse of The Ice Fields, seeking glory and recognition. Amdryaan's heart burned with a small, nearly invisible flame. He was not a warrior. He was not a hunter or an attractive match for any woman in his clan. In truth, he had never had an interest in women, but he felt the pressure to conform, to meet his father's standards. He knew he needed to become stronger, but there was still a naïve idealist within him, an idealist who wondered why he needed to be a fighter, why the world couldn't leave him alone and respect him like everybody else.

He wished that people could just get along.

But that wasn't how the world worked. People only respected the strong.

You have to show them who they're dealing with, Amdryaan. You are the heir to The Five Clans. My blood runs in you. Our ancestors are with us, watching from Goddess' Palace in the sky.

By letting those boys push you around, you tarnish my reputation; you dishonor your ancestors. Stand up for yourself!

That's easy for you to say, Father. You were born with strength... I was born with responsibilities, but not the body to fulfill them.

A shadow fell across the snow. Amdryaan looked up to see Wiola, looking down at him with a frown. Her curly hair blew in the wind, ulu sheathed at her hip. In their mother's absence, she had grown into a fierce and competent young woman. Inheriting her mother's unusual, fair skin, she didn't look like your typical Native, with a mop of curly, brown hair, a freckled face, and long eyelashes.

Wiola was loud and tough and did what the boys did, but when she wanted to be, she could be quite gentle.

Amdryaan's sister helped him up, brushing the snow off of his furs.

"What was it this time?" she grumbled.

"To be honest, I don't even know," Amdryaan replied, rubbing his chin.

"Did you hit them back?"

"No."

Wiola sighed.

"Well, at least you're alright. I'm surprised they punched you. People don't respect Father as much as they used to. In the past, they would have never dared-"

"I know," Amdryaan cut her off, sighing back.

"Still, Amdryaan—why?" Wiola asked, exasperated. "They're not that strong! You're not a little kid anymore; you're twenty years old! You have to fight back."

She shoved his chest.

"If you can't stand up against your own kind, how can you stand up to The

Frosslar?! After what they did to Mother, I— I'm sorry..."

"No, you're right... I have to change," Amdryaan agreed.

Wiola changed the subject.

"Since Enpen and his gang are back, I assume Father has returned from The Hunt?"

"Yeah. He's holding some sort of meeting with the other Clan Chiefs in his tent,"

Amdryaan confirmed.

"That can't be good."

"Yeah."

"We should check it out, right?"

"Yeah."

Amdryaan and Wiola made their way to The Village, dreading the conversation they knew would take place.

The Village was the makeshift center of leadership for The Five Clans. Though The Five Clans all lived in the same vicinity, The Village was separate from the main Settlement, sitting on the high cliffs at the edge of The Ocean of Ūlrihh. The residents of The Village dwelt in tents made from seal, walrus and polar skins draped over strong, wood frames and lit from within by warm fires. Caribou hides hung from tanning racks and fish were skewered on thin, wooden stakes, frozen by the cold. Smoke filtered through the holes the tent spokes poked through leather ceilings, and the air smelled faintly of whale oil and blood.

The ground was covered with a thin layer of snow, and the sky was a white-grey with swirls of cirrus clouds. A flock of albatross flew overhead, trying to hunt, but finding few updrafts in such cold. Wolf Clan flags rippled and snapped in the wintry wind, a grey Wolfprint on a bleached, cotton background. It was his family's sigil—a sigil he was unworthy of.

Amdryaan and Wiola finally made it to The Chieftain's Hut, their faces windburnt.

The Chieftain's Hut was a large, trapezoidal structure at the center of The Village, consisting of a sturdy, wooden frame and more than twenty grey-and-brown seal skins, sewn together, which draped over the wooden beams and only opened at the top to let smoke out of the building. The structure had been built in recent years, and was very different from the small, cozy tent Amdryaan had grown up in.

The seal skins brushed Amdryaan's head as he and Wiola entered, and he was immediately hit by the scent of burning whale fat from the large bronze braziers at the center of the room. A gift from The High Empire, they lit the space with pale, yellow-orange light.

The dirt floor of the Hut was carpeted with pelts whose bottom had been oiled to prevent moisture, and the tent's beige interior was painted with seal blood spirals and dots, giving off a traditional feel that didn't jive with Kanis' leadership style at all, but nevertheless endowed the space with a mystical and almost otherworldly quality.

At the back of the tent was a chair, made of wood and lined with wolf skins, the modest Throne of The Fiveclan Chief. To the right and behind a seal-skin curtain, was his father's bed, a simple arrangement of furs with a feather pillow, which was also a gift from The High Empire. To the left, was a tent flap leading to a small wooden outhouse, and near the entrance, his father's whalebone and caribou-skin kayak, a spruce oar, and a rusted, steel-tipped spear rested against the wall of the tent, ready for use.

It was the spear that Amdryaan had failed to use so many years ago.

Adam

Three, parallel mine shafts had been dug at Lynrava's Belt, a series of bubbly, red crags that ran for miles along Hemia's northern coast: one for silver, one for iron, and one for copper. The crags resembled teeth, the mines like long cavities, boring down into the depths of the earth.

Just outside the mines, sat yellowed, wooden stands where the Overseers would sit, waiting to inspect the ore coming out of the mines and giving the workers their daily nuncheons and wages. Carts had been left haphazardly around the silver mine's entrance, though there was no need for so many of them when little silver had been found in recent years, and the nearby iron mine was half-obstructed by a rusted metal grating. None of the six miners that had last descended had come back alive, and so it had been temporarily shut down. Whether it had been dragonwyrms or a collapse, no one could say, but no one wanted to go down to investigate, so The Mining Guild had hired a group of monster hunters. They were set to arrive in a few weeks, having just finished a job in Qeonia.

East of the mines, was Cinnabar Ridge, a small, red-purple mountain range that obscured the view of The Opal Ocean beyond. The sky above was a bright and cheerful blue, and Arceon burned yellow-blue, unhindered by the sparse clouds.

The area around the mines was surprisingly open, but with how little time the miners spent above ground, it made the work seem even more oppressive.

Adam took in a deep breath of fresh air, savoring it.

The red dirt in front of the mines usually made everything dusty, blown by the wind, but on that day it sat still, baking under the sun. Sharp bursts of grass dotted the arid landscape, poking out like unruly tufts of hair. Seagulls flew overhead, and it was hard to differentiate the smell of sweat from the salt from the ocean.

Adam wanted to believe it was the ocean he smelled.

His musings were interrupted by an overseer's whistle.

Time to work.

Hefting his rusted, steel pickaxe onto one shoulder, Adam walked into the silver mine along with a group of other miners, his muscles still aching from the day before. He almost envied the copper miners, but their salary was even more pitiable than his own.

At least they find something, though...

As he descended, the footing became more treacherous and the air grew hot and sulphurous, the walls a jagged tumble of dark brown stones that could tear your clothes. or worse, if you stumbled.

The silver mine Adam worked in had been hollowed out by years of digging, making copper more common than silver, but the Overseers wouldn't close it until the silver ran completely dry.

However, no one complained. That was just the way of things. Hemia was the world's top exporter of metals and precious gems, and there was much competition within The Mining Guild, with mining companies from Lynrava's Belt all the way to Cinnabar Ridge competing viciously against each other. Adam worked for The Dartán Mining Company, which was ranked first in terms of yield, but company rankings meant little to poor laborers like Adam. In any case, most of the metal and precious gems would go to Astria, as The High Emperor had secured exclusive rights to the ore and gemstones mined through The Settlement Compact, a document The Continental Nations were forced to sign after he quashed their rebellions during The First War of Unification. The document ensured The High Empire's supremacy over the monarchies of each Nation, allowing the rulers of Hemia, Qeonia, Cairnon, and The Ice Fields independent reign, but taking the majority of their troops and natural resources.

Hemia had lots of natural resources. Too many, perhaps.

A tremor ran through the mine, the miners pausing in their descent.

Though a bit frightening, it was not unusual to feel the rumblings of dragonwyrm activity, the large, snake-like reptiles slithering through the rock below, using their acid mucus and the sharp, bony "fins" that ran down their bodies to excavate the dirt. The beasts were generally afraid of humans and the noise they brought with them, and they wouldn't interfere with the mining unless diseased or starving.

Of course, that wasn't much of a reassurance.

Soon the rumbling stopped, and the sound was replaced by that of rock being split by pickaxes and measly bits of silver ore tossed into burlap sacks, which the miners carried out to be counted.

Adam found a spot that looked promising, and got to work.

After a half hour or so, he began to stoop. His shoulders burned and his back ached, but he kept at it.

Adam Akris was not a naturally small man, but he had become small and diminished by years of hard labor. A well-fed man doing the same amount of work for a few years would have become big and strong, but Adam had been starving for most of his time in the mines, constantly lifting weights that most men could not, even when he lacked the energy.

Though he was in his early forties, the miner's hair was mostly grey, and was largely unkempt, peppered with a few reddish-brown strands that refused to die. He had a scraggly beard, and his lips were chapped. His eyes were a dark, knowing blue, reminiscent of a man twice his age, and surrounded by small crows' feet. He was very thin, his physique but a shadow of the physique of his youth, but one could see hard muscles beneath his skin, and he was still quite strong, his palms a rough brown and his nails blunt and full of dirt.

Adam bashed the rock with his dull pick, again and again, trying to dislodge just one measly chunk of silver, which he could already tell was not of the best, or purest quality. The vein he had decided to open was a poor one, but there was no turning back. If he didn't meet the daily quota of one pound of silver, he wouldn't be paid, and he might as well finish what he had set out to do. There weren't many jobs that a Luzian could get over a Raishian in Hemia, and there were few places a man could disappear from society like one could in the mines.

All that mattered in the mines was how much ore you could find—that was it.

Adam persisted, every contact making sparks fly.

His friend Zarrack, who was working next to him, began to wheeze.

Zarrack was a frail-looking old Raishian with washed-out skin and a long, frizzy white beard. His eyes were a sickly pink, and he had a persistent cough. The old man's lungs had been ruined by soot and dust, and he was even skinnier than Adam was, his appearance that of a man in his nineties, though he was no older than sixty-five. His attitude was extremely cynical, but there was something endearing about it, as if his sourness towards life was a hyperbole that reminded Adam to be grateful for what little he had.

Still, Adam pitied Zarrack. At such an age, he deserved better. He wished he could help him in some way, to give him some food to eat or to replace his rags with new clothes, but he was just as hungry and ragged, and he had a family to support.

At the opposite wall, a brusque, stocky woman named Fendril was using a blunt, brown hammer to break open a stone, trying to reveal the minerals inside. She was nearly as old as Zarrack, but she was twice as strong, with biceps bigger than most men's. She had a square face and a long ponytail of greasy, yellow-brown hair, and she wore a brown, leather jerkin and beige, cotton pants.

Fendril was mean—but then again, they all were, to some extent. Any other personality would be crushed by the mines. Even the air had a strange heaviness to it.

It was hard to endure, but they endured it. They all needed the money, and ignored the pain, ignoring the inhumanity of the work and the damage it did to their health. It wasn't like Hemia had such a clean environment outside the mines, either.

Adam looked over at the woman. He and Zarrack worked together often, but they were unlucky, and would often find little silver, if any at all. On the other hand, Fendril was very lucky with the veins she chose to mine. It was as if the reef opened up for her, and instead of yielding metals or precious gems, it paid her in newly minted coins. Adam never tried to get close to her, as she was something of a bully, only caring about her salary, but it was always hard to quell his feelings of envy when she walked out of the mine with a full sack of silver an entire hour before the rest of them.

As usual, she had struck precious silver that day, albeit a small sliver. She threw it in her sack and left the mine with a proud look on her face, spitting a wad of tobacco on the floor. An hour later, Adam and Zarack were the last two people in the shaft.

The jolt Adam received with every strike travelled up his arms and made knots in his neck. His stomach growled.

He hadn't eaten in the past three days, giving the necessary fuel to his sons.

Regardless, Adam never blamed his family for his problems. His wife Ariel did

everything she could to raise the kids, save for working alongside him in the mines, as he had forbidden her to do so. He didn't wish to see her fare as he did, coughing up black phlegm every night, losing hair and covered in bruises.

The two miners kept going, but with fatigue, came carelessness. Heedlessly chipping away at the cavern's perilously hollowed-out interior, Zarack's pickaxe hit something the wrong way, the head crumpling with a loud *plink!*

Contrary to their employer's lax assurances, the mine was not safe, their nightmares made manifest when cracks raced up the walls from where the pickaxe had struck. The ceiling separated, rocks falling.

A heap of stone dropped, and would have crushed Zarack had Adam not pushed him out of the way. He had made his choice without a second thought.

The rocks scraped Adam's shoulders, slamming him against the uneven floor and smothering him. With a bronchial grunt, he tried to fill his lungs with air, dense and caustic, but he could barely breathe.

Zarack, shaken but unharmed, couldn't pull him out from the rockpile or move the stones that pinned him down.

Luckily, the cavern had a very low ceiling, so the stones hadn't fallen very far. Adam's back, arms and legs weren't broken, merely stuck, but with so much weight on top of him, it was only a matter of time before he ran out of oxygen.

"Whydja do that kid?!" the Raishian cried. "You should have saved yourself! I'm an old man; it was my fault... I'm going to get help; try not to move!"

Zarack sped away towards the tunnel entrance, faster than Adam had thought the old geezer could run.

But it would be too late. Adam knew that he had to escape by himself, or perish.

He breathed in again, as hard as he could, heaving. Pressing his back against the scorian prison, he pushed with all his might.

Unbeknownst to him, his eyes flickered in the dark. He began to feel woozy, almost nauseous. For some reason, everything in his field of view went orange, everything except his hands, which emanated a bright white glow, a glow like the high noon sun.

And the rubble began to melt, giving way around him.

Absolute

The Church of The Thousand-and-First, referred to simply as The Church, was the largest religion on Avenshra and the official religion of The High Empire.

According to The Church, the universe and everything in it was Created by The Divinity, God of Angels and Men. The act of Creation took four days, one for each of The Four Heavens: The Land of Sky and Stars, The Land of Mists and Vapours, The Land of White and Gold, and The Land of The Lords. At the top of it all, God sat on The Throne of The Most High, surrounded by his children, The Angelicum.

Though The Angelicum were perfect, formed from pure light, they were unchanging and cold. Day and night they came before him, showing off shimmering works and performing miraculous feats. But none amongst them was better than the rest, and all were too good to judge. Tired of perfection, The Divinity floated down to Avenshra in His Cloud, feeling defeated and empty.

Falling short of omnipotence, he could not do something against reason. And although his will was absolute over others, it was not absolute over himself. In the dusts of time, he Created The Angelicum so that he, who was alone in the universe, could feel love. And indeed, The Angelicum showered him in gifts without end and praise—much praise—but how could it be called love? How could it be called worship, when their best was indistinguishable from their worst? He stood above all in power, so how could he tell whether they had put in an effort to please him, or if, deep down, they hated him, and simply felt obligated? The Divinity wanted to feel love freely given, love and gratitude, or else, bitter hatred.

As he languished, drawing in the dirt with a stick, he spied a lump of clay, a byproduct of Creation. It was imperfect, could never be perfect, but it was ever so close to perfection. It wasn't immutable, like light, but rather, infinitely mutable, and far more pleasing. There, in the ash and grime, The Sculptor, that great artist, molded man excitedly, breathing Lifeblood into raw clay. A being incapable of perfection, man separated himself from the rest through effort and dedication. Everything he did—whether good, or bad—had meaning.

Rejoicing at the birth of this new class of life, The Divinity granted mankind full dominion over The Land of Sky and Stars. Then, he left them alone. He wanted to see—would they love him, or would they reject him?

The Angelicum looked down as well. Some looked down in sympathy, vowing to protect the infant humanity from harm. Others were outraged.

"Why do these lumps of clay inherit what we, The Perfect Ones, were never given?" they cried, losing some perfection. "Why have they been granted the gift of choice?"

To calm the chaos, the leader of the angels stepped forward, the brightest and most perfect of all, though all of them were as perfect as could be. This was the Archangel M'Cael, The Brightest Star.

"If you desire worship that is meaningful, Lord, then let us choose whether to serve you," he suggested, speaking for them all. "Let us sin, let us err, and let us doubt—if only to prove that our love is real... Remove our perfection. Then, lower us to their level, and watch us return to you."

The Divinity, moved by this request, accepted M'Cael's suggestion, sending The Angelicum down to The Land of Sky and Stars. There they were sent, and there they remained. They lived amongst the humans for many years, intermingling with them and teaching them their ways, serving as role models for the flawed. But just as The Divinity had never known true love, neither had his angels, for they were awesome, and hard to praise. They wished for genuine praise, and the cost of genuine, human praise was cheap. After all, humanity was so much lesser. Many grew drunk on that praise, and The Divinity's love lost value to them.

Foremost amongst these was Skotathis, who was second only to M'Cael in his perfection. As a human, he always did more than those around him. He strove to overcome the world, breaking his back to build monuments to The Divinity and glorify him. The most kind, the most selfless, the best of The Angelicum, he was greater, perhaps, than even The Archangel in merit. Naturally, being so good, the people praised him, and as they praised him, he slowly began to change. The monuments he had built became his monuments, intended more for himself than any other. Abandoning his pursuit of love, he instead pursued power, the people building great castles and pyramids in his name. For hundreds of years, he lived on Avenshra as a king, eating plump grapes on velvet thrones and taking his pick of the most beauteous women.

One day, after centuries of succor and dole, he decided that even this was not enough for him. He gathered his followers, who could not rise as kings and equals, and then flew up to The Fourth Heaven, aiming to take The Divinity's Throne. The god's love seemed like nothing, then.

But The Archangel was waiting for them, returned to his master. He had proven himself long prior through acts of charity, humility, and piety, finishing what Skotathis had only started. He had returned to his Father with many others. Repelling the assault, The Archangel fought with flaming sword, and Skotathis and his followers were cast out, all the way down to The Deepest Hell, the lowest, darkest point in The Land of Sky and Stars.

In The Fall, the rebel angels burned and twisted. Reborn as The Demonium, they took on monstrous forms that reflected their corrupted nature. Their skin burned to dust and glass, their gem-encrusted crowns and signet rings melting into rainbow horns and rainbow claws.

For an age, The Demonium lay broken, licking their wounds, but Skotathis remained defiant. If he could not reclaim his place in heaven, he would reclaim it on Avenshra. Rising as The Adversary of man, he orchestrated The Invasions, which razed the planet and caused untold ruin.

In the ashes of The First Invasion, a survivor, known only as The Sufferer, pulled himself out of the rubble and gathered fellow survivors. Instead of rebuking the god that had made them, these men and women were grateful for what they had taken for granted, burning what little they had left as an offering to The Divinity.

Seeing that these people truly loved him, The Divinity gave them his blessing to fight the enemy, and their strongest were exalted as The Warriors of Avenshra. Granted Elemental powers and swords that could pierce the monsters' obsidian skin, they fought The Demonium and won, sending them back to The Deepest Hell and reclaiming their planet. The Sufferer, who was not a Warrior himself, but their mentor and guide, recounted each day of the Invasion in The Book of a Thousand Deaths, writing until his own death in the final battle.

Upon his death, the one-thousand-and-first of the conflict, the survivors created The Church of The Thousand-and-first in honor of The Divinity and his most devoted follower. They wrote The Key to Heaven, a set of rules for society to follow to avoid falling into the selfishness and greed of The Adversary and his followers. For Hell was an open pit, unclosed, and the devil's cunning knew no bounds. Without guidance, they too would fall short of the imperfect perfection required to enter The Land of White and Gold, where eternal rest and fulfillment awaited. Stalwart guardians and champions of the faith, The Warriors travelled across the land, driving out darkness where they found it and waiting for the next Invasion. Their exploits were later added to the Book as the final chapter, which came to be known as The Book of Avenshra.

It was this final chapter that Absolute had turned to, his old, blue, leatherbound copy of the Book beaten up from constant study. Falling apart at the spine and full of creases and stains, it had seen much study.

An Acolyte, or aspirant Sage, Absolute read to find courage in The Warriors' strength, but he was also reading as a distraction, a distraction from something he had left unread for days.

Tall, with fine features, Absolute was a pale, young man with eyes that were a dark and lonely grey. His hair was thick and sat in a puff on his head, roughly parted to the right, and dandruff flaked down the back of his neck and onto his collar. Soft-spoken and introverted, he had few friends, and the only thing about him that drew attention was his hair, though it was also the reason people avoided him.

Though Absolute was but twenty-five years of age, his hair was of a platinum sheen, a son of a Luzian father and Ronari mother. A rare breed, this made him look much older than he was, as if greying prematurely. From what he had understood over the years, mixed-race individuals were the subject of fear and scorn, and although The Monastery at Perla was a holy place, supposedly free of such prejudice, he still felt a clear divide between himself and his fellow Acolytes.

At that moment, Absolute felt as old as he looked, his heavy, grey, roughspun robes pulling down on his already sloping shoulders. With so much reading and prayer, back problems were an issue faced by many men in the cloister, and one had to be mindful not to sit all day without moving.

Remembering himself, Absolute got up and stretched, looking around. His eyesight was blurry after hours of reading, and it had grown dark out.

Absolute breathed in deeply.

His room was cool and dusty, the grey, stone floor slightly damp. Cobwebs swathed the grey ceiling, which was made of the same, grey stone, the room mostly empty, save for his desk and desk-chair, two bookshelves, and a cot with a feather pillow and bleached cotton sheets. A square, open window looked out over overgrown bushes and a fence and out over The Bay of Scales.

Hop-skipping about his small dorm, Absolute changed into a light pair of cotton undergarments for the night. Like all his clothes, they were grey, symbolizing his impurity as an Acolyte. Only Monks, fully ordained Sages who had sworn themselves to asceticism, were allowed to wear white.

On the desk next to him, was a lit candle in a brass chamberstick, a roll of parchment sealed with dark blue wax, and a steel letter opener. Dripping white wax, the candle lit the room with a yellow-white glow, dappling the ceiling with flickering shadows. The air was permeated by the soft scent of mildew, so the small, brown, wooden shutters had been left open to let in some air. He could hear the night sea, smooth waves lapping against the city's sizeable seawall.

I should read his letter, already, Absolute decided, grabbing the roll of parchment off the desk, and breaking the seal with a decisive *snap.* It was a letter addressed to him by his master, Amalgus Silverfire. It had been exactly one month since the Brother's death...

Sitting on his bed and ruining his posture again, Absolute moved the hair out of his eyes and read the message, pupils adjusting to the dimness of evening. His face was serious.

"I am sure that what approaches has been on your mind.

You will finally see past these walls.

You will feel great excitement... I know I did. You will finally be allowed to experience what the outside world has to offer, both good and bad, and you may find yourself caught up in it all, as many Acolytes surely will be, acting on all of their impulses.

But if you are to return, you must control yourself as I did; you must not spend a single coin on the pleasures and luxuries that tempt you. You must not speak to anyone; you must not touch anyone.

Do not stray like the others, I beseech you.

If you do, it will be known, and you will forever be barred from The Brotherhood. The coins you will be given are unique, uncopyable, and they will speak to your honesty and sanctity of person. There is no cheating in this test, as the inhabitants of Perla will tell The Monastery of any misdeeds. I will have no say in this matter, since if you are reading this, I am already gone. Your companions will be under the same mandate, and the other Monks are forbidden to assist them too. Your acceptance as a Monk shall rest upon your actions alone.

Remember this—a true Brother will not falter. A true Brother knows that though the outside is beautiful, it cannot compare to heaven's light. Most people outside are not evil or even bad. They may draw you towards them with their friendliness. They may attract you. But in the end, they are all sinners, sinners who do not fight a lifelong battle against their sinful nature, as we do.

Their desires drive them and their vices bind them. The only thing that separates us from them is that we refuse to give in, to succumb to obsession and addiction. We remain pure, favored in the eyes of God. Should you lust, stay your hand...

I want to remind you not to take The White Week lightly. It will be your ultimate challenge. Most of the people of the city below will do anything to get your money. In fact, they have been encouraged to do so—it is a trial of conviction after all.

You must have no contact even with the ones who don't, even if they are good people by society's standards, wishing to ease your tribulation. Should you fall in with them, no one will fault your character, but you will have left The Monastery behind forever. Such a life will be one of fleeting joys and long hardships, ones that you will not have as a Brother. It will be a lifestyle where fulfillment may be beyond your grasp. Should you choose such a life, you will be starting that life off of as many Liralas remain to you—a harsh prospect—but The Church is not a bank.

I wish to stress that you cannot become a holy Monk without a knowledge of the things you leave behind. That is the sacrifice that makes one holy, the meaning of this test. Holiness requires faith, faith requires selflessness, and selflessness requires sacrifice, sacrifice knowingly and willingly made. There is no other path, and though the pain of isolation will drive you towards sin, you must deny yourself at every step, turn away from that which draws you–before it is too late.

If you are strong of will—truly pious—you will prevail. I trust in you, Absolute, because you are faithful, and I believe you will return, the door to enlightenment ajar, ready to take my place.

But if I am wrong about you, and you do waver, for whatever reason, noble or ignoble, I wish you the best of luck regardless, and hope that you can find some *meaning in this existence, some sense of purpose.*

May The Divinity watch over you in your struggle, Absolute—I know how difficult it can be to say no to what you think you want."

Absolute had finally opened the letter after much mourning, hoping it would give him confidence. Instead, it only furthered his misgivings.

The White Week was about to thrust him into an alien world, one which he knew little about, save what he could glean from books—books which talked more about ideas than people. Many a day had he seen them in the streets. He would watch them through his bedroom window, going about their lives, but seeing was not the same as knowing.

All Absolute knew, was that the world outside was one in which doing wrong was dangerously easy.

And on the morrow, ten pieces of zinc would determine his future.

Scarolette

The Sea Star was a single-masted schooner and one of the fastest ships on the sea. The body of the ship was brown and the sail was a royal blue, a peeling Star of Astria painted on it in white. The ship's figurehead was a carved, gold-painted Star of Astria, which clung to the bow of the ship like a wooden starfish, its top point climbing up the prow and onto the bowsprit.

The High Prince's simple, square cabin sat at the stern, behind the sail, and it had two small windows on either side. Inside, was a feather bed with two, feather pillows and a set of thin, bleached cotton sheets, a bedside stool, and a small desk and desk-chair bolted along the right wall. A lantern hung from the ceiling, casting a warm, yellow light on the cabin's interior.

The planks of the ship were fastened well, and the wood was relatively new, with only some slight discoloration. Nets lined the hull, and there was even a fishing rod on the ground, but Scarolette didn't think anyone had ever used it.

Below deck, were hammocks, stools, which were bolted to the floor, trunks of weapons and armor, and chamber pots, along with a cot that the men had brought in for her, arranged with a feather pillow and a set of bleached cotton sheets.

Scarolette kept her writing utensils in a small, wooden box, which she kept on the ground near her bed.

To the left of the bed, was a set of wooden tables, bolted down. The prince's map was tacked to one of these tables, as he would often come down and consult his soldiers on navigation, or at least, he used to.

Lanterns lit the area, hanging above empty barrels, which were there to prevent a fire if they fell. The air smelled of dry wood, lanolin, and sweat.

At the back of the room, was a hardy wooden capstan. Below the crew's quarters, was a storage level, where salted meat, dry biscuits, limes, and water were stored in large, oak barrels with iron hoops. Underneath it, was another storage level for rigging and various other supplies, like fishing line and tackle, cups, and plates. This bottommost storage level sat above the ballast and bilge, which kept the boat from rolling.

The High Prince didn't allow any alcohol on the boat, and the sailors were all well educated and high-ranking soldiers in The Astrian army, including a battle-medic and a doctor trained under Lord Sigmund Jiralt, The Overseer of The Public Health, and Scarolette's mentor. This being the case, the environment on the boat was a bit more serious and reserved than that of the average noble's, but she had gotten used to the way things were, and in fact, preferred it.

Though alcohol was forbidden, the sailors had fun playing cards, reading books, telling war stories, and playing dice games with the cinnabar dice they had taken during their Hemian conquests. They would often ask Scarolette to recount to them the beauties of the homeland and sing songs, keeping them merry during the day and putting them to sleep at night. They included her in their games on the rare occasion that she would accept their invitation to play, and they never took her money, even when she lost. They would greet her every morning, and would compliment her, though they kept things tame, worried that they might draw their Prince's ire...

They were a spirited bunch, eager to bring glory to their homeland and to make their leader proud. At least, they had been a week before.

Torran's men had grown sullen and silent, retreating to their quarters and only emerging from below deck when it was absolutely necessary, their eyes haunted and their hands trembling as they went about their duties.

The best of Torran's soldiers, they had survived hundreds of battles together only to lose their closest friends at the moment of ultimate victory, for squadrons of their brothers in arms to be burned to ash by a monster that was presumed extinct. Their beloved leader lay bandaged on a cot, half-dead, and fleeing from the city he had just conquered.

They had been deeply shaken.

Scarolette was worse. She had been completely stricken, having watched The High Prince slide in and out of consciousness, falling into a coma on the third day after his fall. She thought she had lost him for good, but on the sixth day, he miraculously opened his eyes, and it took Scarolette all she had not to burst into tears and kiss his bandaged forehead. The battle-medic had had to fight the men tooth-and-nail to keep them from bursting in and embracing their leader, crying the whole time as he did so. The atmosphere on the boat had livened significantly since, but the situation was still dire, and it weighed heavily on everyone's minds.

Though he had woken up, Torran's injuries were so severe that he had difficulty moving or talking. He only got up for a few minutes each day, and only to ask the battle-medic to help him clean himself or for Scarolette to get him a drink of water. And although he had received immediate medical attention after his fall, there was no guarantee that he would ever fully recover.

Everyone knew this, and so, no one on the ship had yet sent word to the capital. Perhaps it was because they felt it would make the situation real. Perhaps they feared that they were being too hasty, and fate would pull a cruel trick and take The Prince away from them forever.

Scarolette was worried too, but today, one week after the massacre at the gates of Sunveil, Torran had finally asked her to pen a message to his father, telling him the news.

Scarolette penned the message quietly, hoping he didn't see how frizzy her hair was or the red puffiness around her eyes as he lay bandaged beneath many furs. His bare chest was wrapped a million times with bandages, the large cot he lay on seemingly cramped for a man his size.

Admittedly, being scribe to Torran Xandromen had always been difficult— whenever he looked at her, she would feel her heart pounding, and then a heady rush within her. She was, however, able to control her expression and maintain her poise, and so, she had been able to keep her position for multiple years without any awkwardness between them.

Scarolette glanced over at the injured Prince.

Any young noblewoman would swoon at the sight of him. He was tall and toned, with parted, blonde hair and bright blue eyes. A lieutenant in The Imperial Army would see an altogether different man. Torran loomed like a shadow, with muscular arms that were scarred by swords, a cloud of messy, brown hair, and hard, grey eyes.

Looking at the unconscious Prince, Scarolette knew that neither of those men quite matched Torran's description. Torran was attractive; it was true, and that was what had first drawn her to him. He was six feet tall, with muscles that most men would envy. His thick, wavy hair was a dirty blonde and his eyes were a stormy grey-blue. But as good-looking as he was, he was not some vacuous playboy. In the five years that she had worked for him, not once had he made an advance towards her. No matter how seductively she tried to dress or how much she tried to flirt, he would never go further than to give her a smile and a few, kind words. She had tried to seduce him for so long that she had almost given up in trying to win his affections.

And as difficult as it was for her to elicit a response from him, Torran was not unshakeable. Many times she had seen him lock away his fear in order to be brave before the enemy, bottle up his emotions in order to appear strong. He could be cold, yes, but he was not a tyrant, nor was he a man who looked down on others. If anything, he aspired to be worthy of the trust placed in him by his soldiers.

At that moment he lay bandaged before her for that very reason. He had fought and killed a dragon to save Astrian lives. His body was so scarred because he followed in his father's footsteps and led every battle from the front lines.

At the end of the day, she knew that people would only see what they wanted to see in Torran. The High Prince was just a regular person, as flawed and emotional as any other.

Everyone was waiting for him to come back triumphant, a handsome hero who could never be hurt. But she would give anything just to see him recover, to stand up strong and give her the same, easy smile she had seen so many times before—a smile saying: "It's alright."

Sitting in the boat, tossed about, she still managed to write legibly, but it was hard, Torran watching her through the plethora of bindings, which offered him less freedom of movement than he already had, given his wounds.

"You always write with such a beautiful hand, Scarolette," he uttered.

Every word for him was an effort. She was surprised he spoke at all.

Scarolette didn't know what to say, as per usual. She nearly stumbled, but spoke instead.

"You are very kind, your Highness."

Flustered as she was, she was relieved that he was still awake and talking. She feared that at any moment, he would stop, and his eyelids would remain forever sealed.

When he finished dictating the message, she remained by his side, nervous, the ink already dry. She held the paper up as if thinking to add to it, to confess her feelings to the parchment, and admit that she was enamored with a dragon slayer who was far above her station.

Torran's voice was kind, but firm.

"Scarolette... Deliver the message, then go to your cabin and sleep. Your concern touches me, but I will survive. Get some rest."

"Yes, your Highness."

Scarolette blushed fiercely, her cheeks burning, and left the cabin, looking for the Dovekeeper.

Viktor

Viktor Eridion walked along Sunveil's northwest edge. He saw a city broken and defeated, the fruitless end result of his father's rebellion against The High Throne.

Flameheir's corpse sprawled across the crumbling walls, beginning to bloat. Offensive in its foul stench, portions of the dragon's brown skeleton had been exposed by maggots, its blood drawing myriad clouds of flies and other scavengers. Even in death, the body could not be burned, and it was too large to cut apart, so they had left the insects to it, unpleasant as it was.

The walls had been damaged enough that they offered no protection from attack anymore, and houses continued to collapse days after the battle, startling peasants and sending up tall clouds of plaster and dust. They had been hit by neither trebuchets nor explosives, but experienced the deadly touch of a Power, a Power that turned air into fire and men into gods.

Ashen streaks marked the ground where charred corpses had been dragged from beneath debris and more corpses. It wasn't just soldiers that had died, but civilians too, brought into the fray by their King. Falin had sent them to hell himself after using them to play a cruel trick on the Astrian Forces. Though he had successfully scared off the vanguard of The Imperial Army, the people of Sunveil had little food, water, and weapons anymore, and everything was in chaos.

The chaos would not be quelled in time. Soon, countless Imperial troops would follow to officially take the city, and there was no way to stop the flood. A delegation was set to arrive within the next two days.

Viktor looked away from the wreckage and tried not to think about what it meant for him and his people. Holding in tears, he looked out over the bleak landscape that sat to the northwest. The Red Road was lined by red, pitted, stone spires, the ground a powdery reddish-brown. The sun was obscured by rolling mammatus clouds, and the air smelled of sulphur and blood. Metallic, green ashbugs buzzed loudly, flitting past the soldiers and towards the feast of flesh. Weapons both broken and whole sat discarded and abandoned.

The peasants who lived nearby had moved towards the city center, taking refuge at The Temple of The Burned, and the soldiers who had once guarded the walls had retreated to their barracks. Only members of The Bloodred Battalion, Hemia's elite fighting force, remained outside the walls, picking up the bodies of their members to give them the proper funeral rites.

Vitkor walked up to Felarion, the head of The Bloodred Generals who led The Bloodred Battalion. He was a hard man, with a cold gaze and beady eyes like inkwells on fire. Those eyes were the only thing visible beneath his visor. He watched quietly as his men gathered the remaining corpses.

The air was grim.

"How many dead?" Viktor asked.

"Fifty thousand, your Highness," Felarion answered.

"Have you recovered my father's corpse?"

The General paused.

"His corpse was just found, your Highness, but it grieves me to tell you that King Falin's body is irrecoverable. I have already told your Lady mother, but she demands to see his remains for herself."

"What do you mean?"

The General walked over to the head of the fallen dragon, beckoning him over. His mother was already there, trembling in fear and distress. It was unlike her, but his father had been her whole world.

"Where is he?!" she cried. "Is he under there?! Please tell me he isn't under—"

The Battalion members lifted the dragon's neck with their combined strength, revealing a mash of pulp, well into putrefaction, pieces of half-healed Theonium left within the mix.

Viktor had no doubt that it was his father, but the General had not lied. Had it not been for Falin's characteristic plate, The Maūron Armor, it would have been impossible to tell. The set of magic half-plate had been recovered from Saharr thirty years ago, Falin returning from a seemingly unfruitful expedition with only a plain, white ring.

That ring had won him countless battles.

But he had not won the war...

Viktor, stone-faced, did not weep.

His mother did.

She threw herself to the ground, soiling her dress and cradling the pieces of her husband's fractured armor, all that was left for her in her grief.

After much screaming and wailing, Viktor was finally able to wrench her away from his father's grave, calling a nearby soldier and ordering him to escort her to the Palace. He ordered another soldier to follow them and fetch her a doctor. They led her away, her clothing wet with stinking entrails and her eyes, wide and glassy.

Viktor's ears began to ring.

The nearby Battalion members stood and watched, unspeaking, metal statues, as they held the dragon's neck aloft, waiting for his orders.

Viktor's voice was harsh.

"Pick up the armor fragments and have them scraped clean and washed. Have them brought to The Temple. Then, remove the white ring from his finger, have it washed, and then hide it in the Palace east tower. Also, pluck one of the dragon's scales and bring it to the best jeweler you can find. Tell him to make a necklace out of it as fast as possible, and have it hidden in the same place."

The Battalion members simply looked at him, stupefied.

"And his Majesty's remains?" they inquired.

"Get a shovel," Viktor replied coldly. "Dig him up along with the dirt."

The soldiers flinched, but did as they were told.

The General followed him as he made his way back towards the city.

"I know you are in pain, your Highness, but you must—"

Viktor turned sharply. His eyes blazed red.

"Your Highness... So you have a plan."

Viktor looked at the broken Mount Criant.

"Sunveil will fall, and I will fall with it. But with its fall, will come the end of The High Empire. Worry not, Felarion... Tend to your men, and keep the peace. For I will not remain shackled, and when my chains are broken, so too will be the peace. I will crush Astria until there is nothing left to recover. And Hemia shall be repaid for every drop of blood."

Flind

At twilight, Flind woke up on a river bank.

The river's cold waters lapped at her naked body, which was red and scraped, a bump the size of a tangerine slowly swelling on the back of her head. It throbbed, but the cold stiffened her limbs and numbed the pain, albeit only slightly.

Flind was tired and dazed, but even in her tiredness, it was obvious what had happened. After raping and beating her, The Baron had taken her for dead and thrown her into The Treasure River, which ran behind The Mansion and all the way down Heart Ridge. He was probably hoping her corpse would end up in Beggar's Lake—just another body to be dredged amongst dozens. It was a pretty smart plan, as every week, dozens of men and women drowned themselves after losing everything in their search for mountain gold.

But in his drunkenness, The Baron had neglected an important detail. The current slowed significantly at a bend in the River just a few miles down from the town. That is where she had ended up, on the river's east bank and right beside the muddy, mountain footpath that led back to town.

Her extremities dull and sluggish, even crawling was too much for her, so she dragged herself as far inland as she could with just her arms and collapsed with a grunt.

In her peripheral vision, she could see that her right arm was covered in stinging, purple

fingerprints.

His fingerprints.

Flind got up as much as she could before she vomited, swallowed water coming out in pure revulsion. She tried to crawl further ashore, but could not.

With a pang of nausea, the scullion lost consciousness, her head lolling to the side.

As soon as her eyes closed, the bump on her head deflated. Through some mysterious intervention, her wounds healed in an instant; the Baron's fingerprints disappearing without a trace.

And the sand drew itself over her, like a warm, earthen blanket.

Amdryaan

Amdryaan's father sat stoically in his chair, chin resting heavily against his scarred knuckles. The other Chiefs had requested an audience, so the tent was crowded.

Kanis was a tired sort of man, with long, shaggy, greying, black hair that reached his shoulders, and a short, choppy, salt-and-pepper beard. His eyes were a pale grey, and he had a blunt, crooked nose. His light brown skin was wrinkled and freckled from the sun, but he was still muscular, even in his old age.

There in the tent, his eyes reflected the firelight, but the flames merely danced along their glassy surface, and did not take deeper residence within. What lay within was not easily set aflame—at least, not anymore. Fire had become flint; wood had become bones...

Though there were a lot of people in the tent, the atmosphere was remarkably quiet and tense. At that moment, the scent of whale oil was perhaps rather thick and suffocating, and the brazier-flames quivered with the entrance of a slight draft.

Everyone knew what this meeting was about. Everyone knew the enemy's name...

Yurwik was the first to call for violence.

"Kanis, these intrusions cannot stand! The Frosslar continue to expand into our territory. A fortnight ago, I sent a hunting party out along The Tundra inland from Leopard's Port. They never returned. When my men and I went to investigate, we found them around a dead fire pit in the middle of a wooded clearing. They had been stripped of their game and their belongings and chopped into tiny pieces! Those hunters had wives, children... They didn't deserve that, and this isn't the first time something like this has happened. Over the past month, fifteen of ours have been murdered: hunters and gatherers who helped us survive the past few winters. Those damn icebeards want us to starve! This land is the land of our forefathers... We have no place else to go, no other way of life. If they continue to come against us, we must fight back!"

Heads nodded in the crowd, and there were murmurs of agreement.

Amdryaan's father sat in terse silence. Amdryaan could see it in his eyes that he felt ashamed, ashamed of having been unable to protect his people. Finally, Kanis spoke, his voice shaking slightly.

"They are strong, Yurwik, and have many more resources than us. What hope would we have in war? Their swords are rock, and they have Mechanica. They do not know the same hunger we do, and the smallest amongst them is bigger in size and stature than the largest of us."

Yurwik blew up.

"Even after what they did to Lyccaona, your wife, you still won't fight them?!

They are but men—tall ones—but still men, and you won't fight them because they have a couple of stone swords and some hunks of junk?! If we don't strike back, our people will be exterminated; we'll have nothing left to eat! We need to show them that we will no longer tolerate these incursions!"

Kanis' voice rose, his tone biting, but still subdued.

"Lycca was my wife! You know I cared for her, Yurwik, and the ice giants are but men, but our people are in no condition to fight! As you say, many are starving, and that isn't the last of our problems. Even if we could find more food, most of our people are either too young or too old to fight, especially not heavily armed men twice their size. Even if we were strong and well-equipped enough to fight the Frosslar, how would we defeat their King? When I was twenty years younger, I barely scratched him, and it nearly cost me my life. He's twenty feet tall and hundreds of pounds of muscle. He has steel armor, he wields powerful magic, and his scythe cuts through all but enchanted steel like it would soft fat. What would be our edge, Yurwik?"

"Our edge would be your edge, Kanis, heaven-sent."

Yurwik's men handed their leader a heavy bundle wrapped in brown cloth, Yurwik proffering it to The Fiveclan Chief.

Confused, Kanis took the bundle from him and unwrapped it. Beneath the cloth, was a lump of coal-like metal, black as soot.

"This is..."

"The ball of fire that fell from the skies not three months ago. My men and I ventured deep into the woods, past where the maps end, and we finally found it amongst substantial wreckage. It's demon steel, the black steel that burns when it tastes blood. Itat showed his kind face that day, and sent us a gift."

"I see," Kanis replied, his expression grave.

Yurwik's voice was scratchy and hoarse.

"Please, Kanis, fight for your wife, for the people we've lost. For our lands that were stolen a hundred years ago... Our united Clans have the best chance in decades. We may never have another one."

Kanis looked at him and then the other Chiefs.

"Who here agrees with Yurwik?" he asked, hesitant.

Slowly, the Chiefs of the Fox, Seal, and Fin Whale Clans voiced their agreement.

"Haa... But the odds..." Kanis broke off. He was deeply troubled.

Yurwik put his hand on his shoulder.

"We all know the odds, Kanis! But tell me, old friend, when did cowardice strip you of your manhood, hm?! Voreus already had the scythe made of Resha's tears when you last fought, and you would have killed him had you not been so injured going in! With what you hold in your hands, you could make a weapon as deadly as his own! Why do you hesitate?! Let us teach them a lesson—you know you want to—let us castrate the blue wankers! Let us fight together once again and make the ice run blue!"

Amdryaan trembled as what he thought was a small flicker of light came back to his father's eyes.

Father... Is this when you finally...

The old tribesman stood up. "Then let us go to war," he declared. "I will do battle so that no one can ever say that Kanis Winterlove, Fiveclan Chief, was a craven—that he did not love his wife, his people! But Yurwik—everyone...it better be worth it. Let us not waste our lives over a fire sword from the sky, or generations to come will rue this day. Let us be victorious."

He gave orders to the other Chiefs. "All of you—assemble your best trained men, and arm them with the best that you have. I will also write to The High Emperor and request reinforcements. If we are to fight, we must fight back as soon as possible. Let us end this bloody history of ours, once and for all! And let us drive the Frosslar from the ice!"

Adam

The miners Zarrack alerted arrived at the scene of the accident quickly. They were breathing heavily, sweat gluing their dirt-stained, cotton shirts to their chests as they gasped for air. Led by a tall, burly man with a balding head, they had enough muscle to lift a mountain, but they had arrived too late.

Adam had already gotten free, but he was not himself. He felt like he was in a dream, like he was someone else.

An unnatural change had taken place. He glowed.

That glow put a fear in their eyes, the miners who had come to help him fleeing from him. Zarrack pushed past them, yelling, trying to see what was the matter.

Zarack took one look at him and dropped to his knees, lip trembling.

Adam's skin swam with sapphire phosphorescence. He was unscathed, the pile of scoria that had trapped him, pooling at his feet. His eyes blazed red, but he was afraid.

What is happening to me?!

"Adam?"

Adam shambled forward, terrified. He felt something building up inside him.

I need— I need help! What do I do?!

"Help me. Zarrack—please help me!" he begged.

"What happened to you?!" Zarrack cried.

Adam clenched his teeth as a burning sensation washed across his skin. He felt like he was walking on the sun.

"I don't know; I— Please help me! Oh, it hurts!"

Adam grabbed the old man by the shoulders, the sickly Raishan, scared stiff.

He convulsed, half-keeled over from the pain, wishing that somebody, anybody, could save him.

"Zarrack, please help me!" he pleaded.

"I- I can't; I don't know what to do!" the miner shouted, overwhelmed.

"Please, just— Help me, Zarrack, please!!! It burns so much; it burns!!!" Adam screamed.

Zarack was set alight.

CHAPTER II

Leafsong

Leafsong had made it through one nightmare only to enter another.

That morning, she had been rushed out of her room and to the ground floor by the Manor servants. The building had caught fire.

There was a big commotion as more and more people rushed up to the second story. Flames had engulfed her sister Inesa's room, as well as her father's. The flames were creeping over towards hers, but the staff fought back the blaze, throwing pails of water.

The flames recoiled, hissing like snakes.

Where the fire had come from, no one knew. The Manor was mostly made of stone, but a lot of the furniture inside was flammable. It would be very difficult to set it on fire from the outside, and the Ralei's were well-liked in Stillvein, so arson was unlikely, though not impossible...

Like Leafsong, Inesa would keep a candle burning at night, but she was young and could be careless at times. She had most likely failed to securely place the candle in her chamberstick, the candle tipping over and falling over when she went to sleep.

One small moment of carelessness had led to unimaginable tragedy.

As The Manor servants did their best to extinguish the fire, Leafsong's parents knelt over her sister's body, which had been found in the backyard. The corpse had placed it on a cloth stretcher, cleaned of dust and dirt, but it did not look like her sister. The thing before her had no face, just a concave mass of flesh.

The servants believed that she had tried to climb out of her window to escape the flames and had fallen headfirst, but no one could say for certain. All that was for sure, was that Inesa was gone forever.

Leafsong felt numb. She stood there, looking up at the fire, then down at her sister, then back at the fire.

All this...because of a candle.

Leafsong's mother was inconsolable. She buried her face in The Baron's jacket, sobbing. The Baron held his wife in a close embrace, rocking slightly from side to side. He looked on, haunted.

And he was, for the alcohol had wiped his memory clean. But it did nothing to clean the flecks of blood that still coated his hands, the blood the soap had missed during his fumbling attempt to conceal his tracks. The blood was still there, and nobody saw.

Nobody saw.

Ilidar

Ilidar, Captain of The Astrian Guard, ascended the smooth, spiral staircase leading to The Imperial Palace Rookery.

Ilidar was a tall man, with meticulously groomed features that contradicted his relaxed posture. His tightly moussed, white-blonde hair was coiffed to the left, keeping it out of his pale blue eyes, and his blue-and-white uniform was well-starched and crisp. He was toned, but not overwhelmingly muscular, and although he was a fierce fighter, an elite amongst elites, he had no visible scars. His nose retained its original, gentle curve, giving him the appearance of a dandy.

The young Captain ran his fingers along the staircase railing, exposing his one blemish, a purple thumbnail caused by a recent hit from a training sword.

He knocked twice on the Rookery door and then entered.

The Rookery was a small, cream-colored room backlit by a large, glass window criss-crossed with wooden beams. The mourning doves the Rookery housed sat in large metal cages, made of iron and stacked like crates, covering the entire right wall. The birds cooed loudly, the sound reminiscent of the hooting of owls. Their cages were kept surprisingly clean, so the air didn't smell of guano, but the creaky, maple-wood floor was covered in downy feathers and bits of lint. The room had a low ceiling, which made it easier to catch the doves if they were frightened, but it also made the space feel more like an attic than an actual room.

That being the case, the Rookery functioned exactly as it was supposed to, providing The High Emperor with news of important events from all five of The Continental Nations. This was achieved through a simple system, where the doves both entered and exited the rookery via a small, circular, shuttered window in the room's back wall. A small, wooden lip outside the window allowed the pigeons to land, peck at the shutter, and get let in by Korac, The Registrar. Korac would untie the rolled-up message from their feet and place them back in their cage with water and birdseed as a reward. Then he would read the messages, either compiling them into a daily report or relaying them to The High Emperor directly, if they were urgent.

At that instant, Korac sat hunched over his large, mahogany desk, which was situated on the left side of the room and covered in papers, rolls of string, a pair of steel shears, and bits of broken sealing wax. His desk-chair was very plush, with soft, grey cushions and a cherry-wood frame, but it was the most expensive luxury he owned, if it could even be called a luxury with the backbreaking amount of work he did in it.

Korac was constantly, constantly reading and writing letters, his black inkpot sitting in a circle of stains and holding no less than three quill pens, all of which had seen better days. Beside it, a large, steel letter opener weighed down a sizeable stack of opened letters, the parchment made of quality barkmoth pulp. Next to that stack, was a pile of rolled-up letters twice as high, waiting.

Ilidar always found it amazing that The Registrar was able to write coherent letters amidst the constant cooing of the doves, let alone get through such a volume of work each day. Of course, leading the Astrian Guard was no cakewalk either.

Finishing the letter he was writing with a quickly scribbled line, Korac stood to address him, his back straightening with a *crack.*

"Captain."

The Registrar was a small, lonely-looking man, with mousy, brown hair that curled into his eyes, and large eye-bags from lack of sleep and overwork. He was in his late forties, but looked like he was in his late fifties.

Ilidar felt a twinge of sympathy for the man, as usual.

I really should suggest to his Grace that he give the man a vacation...

"Any news from Hemia, Korac?" Ilidar asked.

"Not yet, I'm afraid. Do not despair, though. Sometimes the doves lose their way when flying over rough seas, but they're hardy birds, and they always find their way home. They should reach us soon."

Ilidar scratched his head, squinting. "Let's hope that's the case and that they find their way. Though the Emperor is of a patient nature, he grows more anxious by the hour, and I can't say I blame him."

"It is a bit worrying that we've not yet heard from his Highness, The Prince, but again—I'm sure it's nothing. In any event, the moment I receive word, I will immediately relay the message to his Grace, so please rest assured."

"Thank you. You have put my mind at ease. Well, I will await the news of his Highness' conquest... I will take my leave now."

Ilidar left the room and headed back down the stairs towards the throne room. It had gotten dark out, the starry sky visible through the Palace windows.

Though the stars shone beautifully, the Captain's mind was not at ease.

Rest assured? How can I rest assured? Torran always writes to his father immediately after battle.

Everyone can feel it. Something isn't right.

Just two weeks ago, he wrote that he was heading to Sunveil with his personal forces. He was a week away from the city at the time, and The Eridion Dynasty was set to surrender. So why has no one heard from him in days?

Where are you, Torran? What is going on?

Flind

Stillvein was an old mountain town that bordered Treasure River, flat-topped wooden houses lining a wide, grey, cobblestone road. Pipesmoke snaked its way out of the taverns, old men coughing as the tobacco hit them, and woodsmoke puffed up from the chimney belonging to the only inn in town, a ramshackle establishment that battled the wind, its supports wobbly. At the end of the cracked, uneven road was a small, whitewashed church with a white-domed roof, stained brown by rain and dust. A marble Trident stood defiant against erosion, announcing holy grounds for Believers of The Three.

Though they embraced the beliefs of The Church, Believers also worshipped a trio of lesser goddesses called The Three: Claeana, The Mother of Mountains, Mermëa, The Mother of Rivers, and Tásara, The Mother of Forests. Every month, they would burn offerings to the Mother of their Domain to ensure a bountiful harvest and prevent natural disasters. And although it was frowned on by The Church, the big cities of Qeonia would throw festivals honoring the goddesses twice a year, once during the summer, and once during the winter solstice. The maritime country was the largest of The Continental Nations, and although The Wings were strong, they weren't strong enough to fight The Trident...

Farmers, beekeepers, bakers and fishermen stood on the side of the road and next to narrow alleyways, convincing people to buy their products—cheese wheels that jutted from worn-out wooden carts, honeycombs in glass jars, loaves of soft, crusty bread lying in wooden boxes full of sawdust, and trout hanging from creaking, wooden racks. Through the windows of the town butcher shop, one could see rabbits, geese, and pigs hanging from the ceiling from thick, iron hooks and hidden from Arceon's big, blue eye.

To the east of town, at the edge of Tásara's valley, were the Baron's swelling apple orchards and dark green vineyards. Not as rich as his King brother, the Baron could not afford Nolite slaves, so he employed the poorest of the townspeople, families stuck in indentured servitude and tied to the land like Flind's parents had been.

To the west of the town, past the quick-moving, pale blue waters of the River were the fields where The Baron's cattle and barkmoths grazed. The cows were managed by Grennyt, and the barkmoths were managed by Relók, a job the man had taken over after Eldo's death. The shepherds stood watchfully in the tall grass, resting against their fig crooks, as they always did.

Though it was usually peaceful and picturesque, at that moment, the old, sleepy town of Stillvein was in a state of panic. An earthquake had hit.

The artisan's overburdened carts broke and tipped over, spilling precious merchandise. Buildings swayed; the inn began to collapse. Meat fell from butcher shop hooks; glass broke.

It was not a natural earthquake. Like a manifestation of Claeana, Flind walked down the busy street, her clothes wet and encrusted in sand.

The ground shook with her every step. Her eyes were like magma.

Fishermen and washerwomen dropped what they held at the sight of her and fled.

Flind didn't mean to scare them, but she was also not overly concerned about scaring them. She watched them flee as if watching from outside her body. The whole scene felt surreal.

Within minutes, the street had cleared, the townspeople running to their homes, most of which were at the other end of the town. Those who lived nearby slammed their doors shut and locked them, worried she was after them.

At that point, the rumbling had mostly subsided. Her hands shaking, Flind picked up a set of freshly cleaned clothes and some food off the ground, and turned into one of the nearby alleys.

There, like some common criminal, she looked both ways, seeing no one, and changed into her stolen clothing: a man's green, cotton shirt, brown, cotton pants, and a blue, hooded cloak embroidered with olive leaves, which were done in silver thread. Then, she shoved her face full of the food she had taken and went into the fields to hide.

Her stomach growled, wanting more food, but that wasn't what she cared about.

She wanted only one thing, and that was retaliation.

She would wait until cover of darkness.

Absolute

The Monastery was a cluster of old, grey stone buildings overgrown with moss. Its walls were scorched black in places from when The Red Meteor had tried to burn it down during The Goldfeather Purge, but they stood proudly, refusing to crumble. Tall, spiked iron gates and an overgrown lawn, full of weeds, separated the Monks from the townspeople of Perla, though few had business with the Monks outside of The White Week.

The Monastery had many inhabitants, but even so, Absolute felt isolated, sticking to his room and his books. Compared to most of the Monks, he was very young, and even amongst the Acolytes, he was one of the youngest. Many had taken their vows to escape the world and other people, sequestering themselves in their rooms and only joining their Brothers for two quick, silent meals and mass. For this reason, Absolute knew few of their names, even though he was raised in the Monastery. And although he was raised in The Monastery, he couldn't easily connect, even with those who could see past his hair. He had been left as a baby, with no memory of his parents and no past life to look back on. The others had been sent to the Monastery as older children or young adults, either to escape poverty and decrease the burden on their families, or to learn discipline and piety after stints as petty criminals.

That said, it wasn't like Absolute never left his room. He was quite familiar with the different buildings and knew the layout of grounds like no other. There was the abbey, the monks' dwellings, the dining hall, the library, the bathhouse, and then, a grey cobblestone courtyard, which had a small, stone well at its center. The buildings looked nondescript and drab against the blue sky, but Absolute associated them with good things—the smell of fresh-baked bread, the fury of righteous sermons, the joy of a warm bath, the thrill of great novels, the relaxing sound of chanted prayers.

At that instant, he stood outside the Monastery gates with all of the other Acolytes. The air smelled faintly of damp wood and stone, a smell that was neither pleasant or unpleasant, nor very strong. It was the smell of fate, a fate long in the coming, a smell of both calm and foreboding.

The youth looked on with wide eyes as a pair of older Monks unlocked the gates.

A group of one hundred Luzian and Ronari men, their excitement to experience the world outside The Monastery betrayed the dull color of their oversized, grey, roughspun robes. Within moments, they would be given more freedom than they had ever had in their lives, a freedom that would be their lifelong prison if they didn't hold themselves back.

The gates opened with a *creak*, any form of decorum disappearing as the Acolytes burst forth as an unruly throng, free at last. Absolute was pulled along by the human current, people stepping on his feet and bumping into him.

He and the others were met with festoons of white decorations and flower garlands. Minstrels played lively music, streetside vendors selling the most delicious-smelling foods imaginable. The taverns were merry, redolent of beer and smoke, greeters inviting them in. The blue sun danced off of the skin of beautiful girls, who hovered, completely nude, outside of brothels.

The townsfolk smiled, all of them hungry for zinc.

Absolute told himself he would not give it to them. He told himself he was strong.

Many of his peers didn't even try to resist.

After all, few chose to enter the Monastery if they had other options, especially in their teens and twenties. They bought the best food, clothing, weapons, and sex they could buy, riding on liberty's high. They left their religious life behind without looking back, spending all of their money.

Absolute knew that within days, they would be beggars, and the giggling girls and witty merchants would scorn them at week's end, watching as a hundred, lousy men pounded on the iron gates, begging for forgiveness. He knew that they would get only silence in reply. They would have to start a new life on their own, a hard life.

In the beginning, Absolute easily ignored the vendors, merchants, prostitutes, musicians, and all others he thought would corrupt him. He looked ahead, and, in the distance, beyond the crowds, beyond the busy streets and noisy buildings, were deep green trees dotting the blue-purple mountains of Sandkeeper Ridge, only a light dusting of snow remaining on their cloudy peaks. Arceon sparkled off of the thin, white lines that bisected the rock: waterfalls from which he could drink. He imagined that there would be smooth trails that cut through fields of flowers, bird nests in every tree, ripe fruit hanging down and ready to eat. For a second, he stood frozen by the majesty of it.

I just have to get there. There I can survive The White Week. I can do thi-

A fetching voice made him freeze. "Hi there. You look lost... Let me point you in the right direction."

Standing before him was a naked girl infinitely more beautiful than all the others—sun-kissed skin, flaxen hair, an alabaster smile. Her body was unblemished. Goosebumps ran up her legs as she looked at him, expectant, spurred by the breeze.

Eyes like tanzanite.

She took the Acolyte's hand, leading him, as if in a trance, into the brothel she had come from, moans audible even from the outside.

Absolute didn't even try to resist.

"I've never seen a guy like you before," she commented in a dulcet tone. "It's been a while since I was the one bringing someone back, but you really caught my eye."

As they entered the establishment, a red cast fell over their surroundings, men and women interlocked in pleasure.

Absolute couldn't speak. He didn't even know how to speak, it seemed. His heart pounded, he began to sweat, and though he wished he could pretend that he didn't, he wanted to lie with her on plush mattresses in some hidden room of the brother, to give her everything—his coin, his seed, his soul. He wanted to live for once in his life.

But he remembered who he was, who he wanted to be.

And so, half numb, he pulled away from her and ran out of the building. He ran as fast as he could, past the city limits and out into the hills. He ran till he could run no more.

And above it all, outside it all, an eye bluer than that girl's shed a tear for him and his folly.

It would be worth it, he thought to himself.

She isn't what I really want.

He believed that was the truth.

But it was false.

Viktor

The Temple of The Burned stood in Faalaran's Square, which was located at the center of Sunveil.

The building consisted of four, strong pillars and a domed roof, all painted a powdery scarlet-red. At the top of the dome, was a silver steeple, wrought in the shape of The Forked Flame, tasting the sulphurous air. That day, the sun was hidden by particularly heavy clouds.

It was dark.

The floor of the Temple was paved in black limestone, which drew together to form an elevated, cube-shaped platform holding a large, bronze brazier. That brazier was used as the main fire pit for the daily ceremonial fires, in which the priests would burn frankincense, rosemary and sage.

Pigeons and starlings sat perched upon the roof of the Temple, raining white paint down onto the tiles below, but the frustrated priests had given up on getting rid of them long ago. In any case, the tiles were already stained with bits of red wax from the weekly duels, in which nobles would defend their honor with specialized dueling swords. Such duels arose from accusations of improprieties not severe enough to fall under criminal law, but Viktor had never participated in one. He had withstood no shortage of insults to his name, but he had drawn enough blood in his training that he had no interest in fighting for fun, especially against some minor Lord, whose skills were far inferior to his own. As a youth, Viktor's father, Falin, had fought many such duels against angry Lords whose wives and daughters he had slept with. In fact, his parents had met at such a duel, though Viktor didn't know the details. Of course, that no longer mattered.

A war had just been lost, another looming on the horizon.

No, that was not quite correct. He would bring that war...

The long walkway leading to the main fire pit also acted as the fencing piste, so it was not uncommon to see the temple's new acolytes scraping away the wax and bird droppings with blunted knives in an effort to beautify the Temple. Still, for some intangible reason it always seemed run-down. Nevertheless, it was the most popular place to go for mass.

Mass was usually held at high noon, when the sun was brightest and even the darkest of Nolites would burn with enough exposure. The Priests chose this time specifically to humble the masses, highlighting the weakness of mankind and the greatness of their god, The Lord Defiant, who was reborn in flame and thereafter, could not be burnt.

During the day, the Priests' voices would boom across the cobbles, bringing a twinge of fear and awe in even the least devout of listeners. Even the baker or the farmer felt a fire light within them, a drive to uphold their convictions and rebel against The Lord Oppressor, to be confident in themselves and take what they deserved from life.

At that moment, no one spoke. Falin's funeral pyre burned quietly on The Burning Altar, a large, polished, concave slab of granite in the courtyard behind The Temple. The funeral was a small function, the city too damaged and its people too shaken for a large, gaudy funeral procession. In fact, many would be happy to hear of The King's death; peasants and even low-level government officials had been burned to death by their ruler in what was probably the most dishonorable trick in military history.

The city would soon fall, but the nobles' attendance was important nevertheless. They needed to see their leader smashed to pulp by The High Prince... They would be of use in the coming fight.

They needed to be angry—or at least, have a good reason to be angry, a reason they could not excuse themselves from battle. Long ago, they had sworn their allegiance to The Eridion Dynasty, and Viktor would bind them to that oath.

The nobles stood with their heads bowed in respect. The Priests stood beside them, hoods down. All were wearing red.

Viktor and his mother stood closest to the pyre, a small, neat pile of logs and sticks brought all the way from The Redtree Forest. Falin's remains had been spread out amongst the sticks along with the fragments of his Theonium half-plate and a ceremonial sword. The armor and the sword had been arranged to form a humanoid figure. The figure held an enchanted steel blade in its invisible hands—an overall absurd display.

Viktor's mother had insisted on burning what little was left of his father, and she wouldn't allow The King to be burned on salvaged wood, either. Falin Eridion, The Brimstone King, would be held up in noble fashion, even at the bitter and ignoble end.

With a *woosh*, the fire flared red, crackling and popping, and the smell of burning pine was overpowered by the oily stench of burning flesh. The air became filled with black smoke, which rose up into the night sky and melded with the half-hidden clouds of soot that poured from Mount Criant.

The night was cold and there was a chilly breeze, but the fire burned hot and cast a bright glow on the pale faces of the congregation. The oily smell made Viktor want to vomit, but he clenched his jaw to keep from gagging, his face as still as water.

His mother made no speeches. She didn't take the lead. She just stood and mourned as the rest of the city languished, broken in body and in spirit.

Viktor didn't speak either. He only watched the slowly fading embers...

Voreus

Voreus stood atop a platform carved into the surface of a large, fang-like, grey, stone crag known as The Cold Tooth, whose back stood against The Ocean of Ūlrihh. The Cold Tooth overlooked Whitereach, a village whose name was too grand and noble for most cities. There, The Frosslar lived in the shadow of the crooked alp, which protected them from most of the storms born from the Ocean, but not the ones from the nearby Sea of Glass.

Whitereach was a village that was simple in both its structure and its style, a collection of rough-hewn, grey, stone dwellings shaped like faceted half-domes, each with a single, open, arch-shaped doorway facing away from The Sea. The domes were clustered closely together, carved from the exposed tops of massive boulders that had been frozen in the ice centuries prior. Those boulders were most likely pieces of the Tooth that had been dislodged by a powerful blizzard, but, wherever they had come from, they made for strong houses.

Deer, fish, and whale meat sat skewered on large wooden poles between the buildings, frozen solid, but there was little else left outside, save for a central "latrine," a large hematite basin with carved handles that sat at the center of the village. The latrine used to be emptied into the ocean every week, but the boats had returned to The Weeping Ravine with little to show for their latest fishing and whaling expeditions, and a famine had taken hold. The latrine was mostly empty. However, the latrine was never very full, as the food was never very good.

Instead of cooking their meat like the other races, The Frosslar simply dipped it in the ocean, let it freeze, and then thawed a portion when they wanted to eat it. They were weak to heat and fire, but didn't need either to survive, so they stayed far away from both, their special, blue blood protecting them from all but the most extreme and prolonged cold. Unfortunately, it also limited them to The Ice Fields, as they would die of heatstroke anywhere else, but they had ruled over The Ice Fields for generations, and had no intention of leaving. The only thing fire could offer them was light, and they had found an alternative in Amalta's tears, a type of pale, blue-green, bioluminescent lichen that coated the surface of many of the continent's caves. The Frosslar had transferred that lichen to their own, stone ceilings, allowing for some dim interior illumination.

Even with the lichen, The Frosslar saw poorly in the dark. Their white eyes absorbed less light than others, perhaps explaining the town's brutalist, and almost ugly, appearance. Worse, the dwellings were sparsely furnished: a bed of furs, dinnerware made of stone and utensils of carved seal-bone, a stone chamber pot and a bone scraper for it, a nicely-shaped rock or two to use as chairs... Some owned weapons, weapon-making tools, or enchanting liquid negotiated through The Settlement Compact, and a few homes had small, carved stone figures of Lessendr, The Cold Hammer. Lessendr, the god of The Frosslar, who was said to have carved his people out of ice and breathed life into them. It was a custom for ice giants to set the figures by their door to protect against Iásuka, Goddess of The Sun, and her worshippers, who hated the ice and wanted to see it all melted.

The figures gave the homes some character, but their purpose was quite ironic, at least in Voreus' eyes, as drinking water and the water used to wash clothes and dishes was a precious resource provided by a contraption that channeled the sun. The contraption, known to The Frosslar simply as a "boiler," was made from two, wooden basins, which were really just the enchanted halves of barrels of food that had been provided by The High Empire a while back. The two basins were connected by an enchanted copper pipe, also provided by The High Empire, one sitting on the ground and the other elevated by a set of wooden legs. Chunks of ice were thrown into the bottom barrel a while beforehand and then covered, the sun focused by a polished lid made of enchanted quartz. The focused sunlight would boil the ice, steam entering the second barrel-half, which was covered with an enchanted wooden lid, and condensing into potable, salt-free water.

Before the boiler, the Frosslar would purify saltwater through melting and scooping or straining through hides, which took far longer and yielded far inferior results.

Though prideful and nationalist, the ice giants lived hard, mostly solitary lives. Few children were born each year, either due to famine, or the overall dour mood set by their harsh living conditions.

The best times were when the nearby Mines they controlled bore platinum and other precious metals, which The High Empire was happy to trade food and supplies for. There they could also mine and enchant hematite to make swords and armor.

But Whitereach was only so big, and many of the ice giants were growing in age. Some were too tall to enter the caves, and yet others were too lazy. Only one man still knew the art of making Mechanica, and he was old and half-crazy, rarely leaving his cave, even when summoned.

If we can take The Village, we won't have to worry about starving for a long time, Voreus thought. *The tribesmen can work in the mines and bring in more Astrian goods. They can also handle fire, cook, and clean for us.*

Not to mention the women... Here the women are all so ugly and bored. If my wife is to be shorter than me, at least let her have a pretty face and a little fight in her... What's the point if they always say yes?

Voreus stood atop the platform overlooking Whitereach and called for his people to assemble, scree shifting beneath him. The other giants shambled over, looking up at their King with sullen expressions that they didn't bother to hide.

Snorting with displeasure, Voreus projected his voice.

"We know that The Five Clans are coming for us. They think they stand a chance, but they don't. We fight them tonight, when our strength is greatest."

Someone spoke—Rewin.

Rewin was a cautious sort of man, with shiny, grey-white eyes and a long, multipronged ice-beard that was almost triangular. He was far shorter than Voreus at only eight feet tall.

"My King, what about the Astrians with them? Surely killing them would usher The High Empire's ire?"

"You will usher my ire, Rewin, if you do not use your head a little more. Hemia has a Firetongue—a Firetongue we helped them control. In all likelihood, Astria has just suffered a crushing defeat, but even if they somehow won, they won't have the soldiers to spare anytime soon. If we attack now, we can solidify our hold over the tundra. If we control all of The Ice Fields by the time The War of Unification is over, The High Empire will be forced to accept our rule. And if not... Well—we aren't helpless either."

Rewin fell silent.

Weak oaf. You should fight whether we're to win or lose, simply because I command it.

You won't be the one winning any battles, anyway. That will be Glasswing...

Glasswing, my pet, I am coming to your cave soon. Prepare yourself for me.

Hearing no further questions, Voreus sent his people off to prepare.

"I want every able-bodied member of our village in armor, every Mechanicum well-fueled, every sword sharp. Tonight, we make our move."

Kanis

The Tundra was a vast expanse of ice so flat that it looked unnatural. The milky, blue-white glaze was several inches thick, obscuring anything that grew beneath. Powder snow had coated the area and frozen to the surface, making it much less slippery than it otherwise would be. There were no footprints in that no man's land, the ice left untouched for twenty years...

At the center of the tundra, was a Shadowrise tree, which sat in a circular divot in the ice thinner than the surrounding sheet. The sky was black, with near-invisible clouds, Riize's pinkish light giving it an eerie vibe.

The wind swept up any loose snowflakes and sent them tumbling across the glacial plain in small whirlwinds, the glittering crystals moving as if they had a mind of their own. The air was bitterly cold and dry.

Kanis' eyelashes had been glued together by tiny icicles, his beard half-frozen and half-drenched in sweat.

The old Native coughed.

The Shadowrise gave off an acrid, metallic smell, as if rotting from the inside out, but The Frosllar didn't seem to mind. They had assembled behind giant spikes of sharp, blue ice, a temporary wall that their King had erected to deter The Five Clans from making the first move.

They had Mechanica as well, platinum monstrosities with snake-like heads and centipede bodies. The automatons crawled up and around the jutting pillars, their eyes glowing like molten silver.

How they were made, no one knew.

The Frosslar were different from the other races on Avenshra. They were extremely tall, muscular, and resistant to the cold, so much so that they purposefully dipped their long hair in water and froze it against their backs in waterfalls of white. The men froze the especially long, white hairs on their arms as well, forming wickedly sharp ice-spikes that served mostly as intimidation but could also be used in combat. They donned enchanted hematite splint mail over furs of every sort, leaving the dangerous spines jutting out. Their solid, ghostly, hair didn't move in the wind, and they stared back at the tribesmen with eyes hard, and light, and alien. They carried huge, rectangular cleavers of swords, made of hematite that had been knapped from individual boulders and then enchanted.

Kanis wasn't scared.

But when he saw Voreus arrive upon his mount, he trembled.

Voreus sat upon an Icetongue, thrice as tall as any man, and fitted with a polar-bear-fur saddle. The serpent raised its scaled head, covered in hoarfrost, its stark blue eyes like radiant suns, its breath a biting cold that turned the air to billows of fog. It let out a terrible screech, lifting its rider upwards in a gale of freezing wind, its translucent wings scraping the frigid clouds above and its bladed tail trailing behind it.

This was not something he had prepared for. All the dragons were supposed to be dead.

But he couldn't back out.

Voreus made a fist.

The pillars broke, the Mechanica chittering and running towards the Natives as The Frosslar began their forward march.

Voreus watched the scene from above, aloof. He seemed sure that it would be a one-sided fight.

We won't let you win so easily. Last time, we were divided, but not anymore!

The Five Clans were gathered for war. The Wolf Clan, The Fox Clan, The Bear Clan, The Seal Clan, and The Fin Whale Clan all stood at Kanis' command, ready to fight and die for each other. A squadron of Astrian soldiers stood with them in solidarity, dispatched from Cairnon, but they were few, and Kanis was unsure how hard they would fight. If The Five Clans lost, those Astrians would be prisoners in name only, returned to negotiate a deal with The High Empire. His tribesmen would be enslaved or killed, so they had to fight. Their lives depended on it.

Nevertheless, it was good to have some backup.

The dragon let out another screech, the air quavering.

The Clans stood solemnly, waiting for his signal. Their furs flapped in the breeze as they held forth spears of bronze and chipped rock. Some had simple, sharpened staves—precious driftwood; others held rusted, iron axes or ulus, and some even held tridents with narwhal-bone points, lashed on with grass.

Kanis unsheathed Nighthowl, his newly forged sword and The Five Clans' best chance at victory against The Frosslar's King.

Nighthowl was a black steel short sword, a cold-forged, but relatively smooth blade, with a line of diagonal grooves down its length and a silver ring punched through its width—his old wedding ring. The sword's handle was made of enchanted wolf bone wrapped in sinew dyed a deep maroon.

Kanis swung the weapon in a circular motion above his head, the wind whistling and moaning as its grooves whipped up turbulence. He would not watch from afar like Voreus. He would fight on the front lines.

At this signal, The Wolf Clan ran to meet their foe, shouting.

The other Clan Chiefs sounded their horns, following in the charge.

"For freedom!" Kanis yelled, every tribesman joining in. Together, they slammed into the ice giants, a wave of sound and spirit.

Unfortunately, that wave didn't push the enemy back by much. The

Frosslar's hulking warriors tore through Kanis' ranks, his peoples' weapons outmatched by the ice giants' superior resources. The Astrian soldiers put up a better fight with their enchanted steel swords and armor, but they too were being routed, not used to fighting in the snow and the heavy blows of their towering enemies.

Greathelms imploded, crushed by blows from arms no Luzian could lift.

But there was naught to be done. The Frosslar had always been stronger. That didn't mean The Five Clans could just give up.

His people fought tooth and nail, blood turning the snow to purple slush.

Kanis dodged a swing from one of the bigger giants and then shoved his blade through the man's chest, steam and blue blood coming from his nostrils before he collapsed. Nighthowl slid smoothly from the Frosslar's chest, leaving a burning hole behind. Flames ran along the weapon's edge, woken by iron.

A giantess came at him with a pair of hematite short swords, but Kanis ducked beneath one swing and stopped the second before it began, cutting off her left arm and leaving a charred, blue stump at her shoulder. Then he raked his sword across her chest, the woman passing out from shock.

The Chief moved on. He dodged and whirled, ducked and parried, his grey wolf-skin cloak flying.

Seeing that he and a few of the other tribesmen were advancing, Voreus descended, dispersing the soft clouds, his dragon spouting a jet of seawater. Touched by some unknown force, the saltwater turned to a misty plume of glowing ice.

Kanis dove out of the way.

Others weren't able to in time. Frozen in verglas, their faces were fixed in shock and disbelief before chipped, hematite swords shattered them into a million pieces.

Kanis growled, swinging Nightowl ferociously. He slew countless enemies, the foes who faced him, bigger and stronger by far.

In battle, Kanis' limp disappeared; his agedness disappeared, leaving only the fight, the memory of what Voreus had done to his people. He saw his wife, assaulted and dead, his children bloodied and bruised. He saw men impaled on wooden stakes, women raped and killed.

My Lyccaona... You murdered and defiled her. You hurt our children.

Voreus vaulted from the Icetongue's back as it swept low a second time, flipping backwards and pulling his war scythe, Whitewind, from its holster in one fluid motion. He hit the ground hard, completely blocking Kanis' advance and smiting the last of the Astrian reinforcements.

As the snow settled, the two men's eyes met, hatred boiling within. They held their weapons in a white-knuckled grip, veins popping.

Voreus' thin, blue lips pursed in amusement as Kanis' eyes fell upon the plume of black hair that hung from the back of his scythe.

Her hair.

Kanis tried to control his rage, but could not.

The battle exploded around them as the men yelled. Voreus spun, Whitewind sailing downward, only to be parried by Nighthowl's edge.

There was a sound of steel, a high-pitched, keening sound that pierced the air.

And everything and everyone stopped for a moment—one, beautiful moment.

It didn't last.

CHAPTER III

Flind

Flind arrived at her destination as Riize took its place in the heavens. Crickets chirped, and the wind rustled the leaves, The River's smooth trickling tying nature's symphony together.

The Manor was heavily protected, guards in blue-and-grey uniforms standing at the property's gates, and many more patrolling its perimeter.

Upon closer inspection, she saw that much of the building was black and crumbling, burned, which explained the posting of such forces.

So he burned the evidence, and now they're looking for an arsonist.

Too bad they aren't prepared for me. He tried to hide what he did, but I know the truth.

I can't bring Inesa back, but I can make him pay for his crimes.

He will pay...

Flind approached the Manor slowly, hood covering her face.

"What's your business here, stranger?" one guard asked, wary.

Flind kept walking, her eyes lighting to a bright red.

She thought that that would be enough to scare them all off, but the leader of the guards drew his sword, steel shining in the moonlight. His men quickly followed suit.

"I'm not going to ask you again, stranger," he warned, steadfast. "State your business now, or you'll have to go through us."

Fine; have it your way, then. Anyone who helps that piece of shit is my enemy.

A gemstone skewer shot up from the ground and opened the guard's throat.

Flind spoke her intention.

"I'm here to kill Agamus Ralei."

Ilidar

Ilidar pushed open the large, ebon doors, which were carved with a simple outline of The Star of Astria, the six pointed star resembling a compass rose.

A long, smooth, light blue carpet ran down the length of The High Court—bordered in white, and full of small wrinkles. No one sat in the twoscore pews, which were also made of ebony and arranged in rows along the carpet.

The room was dead silent.

It was cloudy out, with no moonlight coming through the tall, arched windows that took up most of the walls, and it was dark, except for the light from the elaborate, gilded silver chandeliers, which were filled with Moondrake-blood candles. The candles glowered an uncanny blue, sparkling off of the High Throne and throwing long shadows across the grey, tile floor.

The air smelled of old wood, and, if one concentrated, they could find the light scent of beeswax, making the space feel both cozy and cavernous, hallowed and human.

At the end of the room, The High Throne shimmered like the night sky, a ten-foot-tall piece of black aventurine. It was angular, with rectangular arms flush to the sharply-cut, stone edges of the oversized backrest. The brutalist chair looked uncomfortable to sit in, as it was hard and cushions slid down its polished surface, but it wasn't made for comfort. It was made to intimidate the masses.

To the left of the stone chair, was The High Princess' small, wooden chair, painted white and cushioned with light blue pillows.

At The High Emperor's right hand was an uncushioned seat made from the same ebony as the pews, carved with a Star of Astria at the headrest. That was Torran's seat. It was covered in cobwebs, as it had not been sat for many years. In fact, the seat had stood there, empty, longer than it had ever been filled.

Ilidar's footsteps echoed as he walked down the carpet, muffled footsteps bouncing off of the courtroom's high, arched ceiling, which was painted with masterful frescoes of The Divinity and his angels, lounging on clouds.

High Emperor Agravius Xandromen slowly stood to greet him, dwarfed by the otherworldly monolith that was his seat. The guards had left the area to guard the Palace entrance for the night, leaving him alone.

The High Emperor was a tall man, but not an overly tall man. He was muscular, with little fat on his frame, and battle-scars lay hidden beneath the brocade of his stately robes. Nevertheless, he was not an overly muscular man. He had handsome features, with wavy light brown hair that reached down to his shoulders, pale green eyes, and a full ducktail beard, streaked with blonde. That said, he was not the most handsome man in Court, and he was not an overly young or youthful man. He was an intelligent man, devoted to scholarship, and well-versed in tactics and in fighting, but he was not the smartest man Ilidar had ever met.

Despite these facts, Agravius had a presence like no other. His nobility went beyond mere blood. His gaze was intense—in one light, cool and relaxed, in another, sharp and judgemental. He exuded an aura of authority, and there was a deep wisdom to him. The Captain thought that if any man deserved to rule the world, it was him.

Ilidar had served The High Emperor long enough to see the heartbreak that had borne that wisdom, the slight but constant slump in the man's posture, as if he carried the kingdom on his shoulders everywhere he went and could not put it down. Ilidar wished he could relieve some of that burden, to help The High Emperor carry that enormous weight, but there was no way to reach him. It was like he stood on entirely different ground, walked a lofty, lonely path that no other man could walk but him.

"Any news?" Agravius asked tiredly.

"I'm afraid not, your Grace," Ilidar answered, firm, but apologetic. "We sent aid to The Ice Fields a week ago, but there is still no confirmation of victory... Korac is optimistic, but I believe The Five Clans and our troops have been either captured or killed. There has been silence for too long, and though the snows over the region are violent, the doves should have arrived by now."

The High Emperor stroked his beard, his eyes looking more sunken by the day.

"I see... What are your thoughts, Captain?"

"I think we should buckle down our military strongholds in Cairnon and wait for any invasion attempts. The Frosslar are rumored not to be able to withstand the heat, but we can't know that for sure. That said, I don't think invasion is their goal. All they have ever cared about is The Ice Fields. Having successfully taken the lands belonging to The Five Clans as well, there's no reason for them to antagonize us any further. They will likely try to negotiate a new and more favorable trade agreement now that they have sole control over the continent. Still, the timing of their attack was all too perfect. They moved east while the eye of the imperium was firmly focused on Sunveil. I suspect that Sunveil and Whitereach formed a short-lived alliance, though I am unsure what The Frosslar had to offer the Raishians... In any case, Cairnon is nigh on impenetrable from the south with all of its swamps and bogs. Getting The Cairnian Navy involved seems unnecessary at this stage. As much as I hate it, waiting for a ransom request from The Frosslar seems to be the most prudent next step."

Agravius stroked his beard.

"Recent events have been too suspicious for my liking, but I never expected such an alliance... It is of no import now. Sunveil has fallen, and The High Sword rides for the city as we speak. The ice giants are the only ones who remain in rebellion. I won't lose the War of Unification at the moment of victory. I must unify The Continental Nations. However, the Hemian cities need to be secured before our armies can leave. Otherwise, they will quickly fall into chaos and turn against us once more. Qeonia won't readily give me troops to send to The Ice Fields, and Cairnon will be of little help in the midst of Civil War. If only I hadn't sent The Winter Angels to Lonecastle..."

The High Emperor's eyes hardened.

"Forget waiting for a ransom request. If we haven't heard anything by now, our troops are dead. They probably thought: what's a bit more spit when spitting in the face of The High Empire? These ice giants seem to have forgotten who they're dealing with. We are The High Empire, and The Ice Fields belong to us. Take your best men and The Sixty-sixth Division to The Ice Fields to remind them. Sail for The Outpost and then for Cairnon. Gather more troops there, and go break this rebellion. Astria cannot be blinded by the loss of a few doves."

"Understood, your Grace. I will do as you command."

Agravius

Agravius stopped for a moment to stretch his legs before pushing in his bedroom door. His knees were sore and aching from the long flight of steps that led to the second floor of The Palace.

His bedroom was small for a common Lord, let alone The High Emperor, but it was, nevertheless, quite luxurious. The red-painted walls were embellished with tight-knit, gold scrollwork, and there was a large, rectangular, glass door at the far end of the room that led to a white, marble balcony with a railing carved of the same material. The open door to the balcony was covered by sheer curtains of bleached linen, which drifted across the floor with every gust of wind.

To his right, was a large, walnut-wood armoire with two doors and gold knobs. To his left, was a walnut-wood canopy bed, the pillars carved with flowers and the headboard carved with The Star of Astria, surrounded by yet more flowers. The bedsheets were made of red satin, and so were the bed's two plush, feather pillows. The thick, sumptuous comforter was made of red linen and embroidered with flowers.

Next to the bed, a finely-patterned, gold-lined rug covered the slate, tile floor on the right side of the room, depicting Aeshius Xandromen landing on The Imperial Palace with his eagle, Asteropt'r.

To the left of the bed, sat a potted dracaena in a tall, oval-shaped, glazed, blue pot, and on the left wall, was an oil painting of The Silent Sea in a thick, gold frame, embellished with gold beads. To the right side of the bed, was a heavy, walnut nightstand with a gold candle-holder and an unburnt, beeswax candle.

The ceiling of the room was unpainted, and there was no chandelier, but the walls were well-decorated, weapons adorning the walls. The standout of the display was an enchanted war knife, positioned horizontally across the right wall. The slightly curved sword was fitted with a longsword handle that consisted of a ruby-studded, gold, pear pommel, a black walnut grip, and a golden crossguard done in ruby and sapphire cloisonné. On the left wall, but to the right of the bed, was an enchanted arming sword with a filigree silver handle, and a disk pommel with a mother-of-pearl Star of Astria at its center. Paired with an enchanted steel buckler, the sword had seen many battles, but its edge was clean and sharp, and its associated shield was virtually unblemished. While the war knife was far more beautiful, Agravius' arming sword was intended for use, and had seen many battlefields as his preferred weapon.

The High Emperor sighed, sitting down on the bed. He had seen the disapproving look on Ilidar's face.

The Luzian monarch pinched his nose bridge, tired of the struggle. His eyes were bleary from lack of sleep. Leaning back, he felt the mattress slowly cave in around his hands. He breathed in, holding the breath, and then letting it pass.

The room smelled of damp stone.

All this because I sent aid instead of trebuchets, because I would not see innocents die.

Because I was afraid she would die.

Agravius remembered his father. He knew how Josephus would have responded to Hemia and their truce. He wouldn't have given them food or medicine. He would build his Empire on a foundation of bones, if that was what it took.

Let them die. They crossed Astria, and now you would help them? Rebellion doesn't end until every rebel dies. Any kinship you had was severed by their declaration of war.

But Agravius was not his father. He was not so cold and calculating, staring on with slate-grey eyes until the news of victory was brought to him. He wasn't so devoid of emotion, and so he had made a mistake, and Torran had paid dearly for it, his subjects had paid dearly.

His father would have said he was weak for believing Falin's lies, for believing a vulture like Falin Eridion.

His brothers would have been more forgiving, or at least, Terricus would. Terricus would have cursed Josephus' honor, spitting malice at the idea of harming innocents. Then again, Terricus was not a man to take seriously. Preoccupied with the bacchanalia of flesh and drink, he would have forgotten the next day, ignoring or not seeing the darkness in his father's eyes.

Velestre would keep his opinions to himself, aiming to be invisible until Josephus' death. He would remain silent and suppress any great wisdoms, lest he be given any real responsibilities.

Unfortunately for Agravius, he did not inherit Springhaven, the lush gardens and plentiful vineyards of the Astrian countryside. Josephus had given it to his meek and inconspicuous son, a man who was, in truth, much louder and more flamboyant than any of the three royal children. He had inherited the grand sprawl of Starspire, the squabbles of its people and the difficulty of its governance.

Starspire would have gone to Geudeford, but Geudeford was only a military genius, and in the ways of life and science, he was utterly inept. After two years of fighting, his big, strong, older brother had sailed off to The Isle of Hecx and off the edge of the world.

Spurred by the lies of a Cairnian mystic, he had gone there in search of a mythical weapon, a weapon that could end The First Cairnian Civil War and bring the Astrian armies home. If such a weapon existed, it must have blasted his ship straight out of the water, because Geudeford was never seen again, and neither were the search parties.

That had left only Agravius and Velestre, and of course, Agravius had to be the better choice. He didn't see the stupidity of his success. He was serious, and he always seemed more capable than his younger brother. It was no surprise that he would inherit the Throne, inherit their father's final words, so uncharacteristic of a military man, but still dripping with blood.

Unify them. Bring them peace.

Though the masses trembled before his fortune, jealous of his wealth and status, Agravius had inherited a great burden. Most men murmured incoherently before they died, whispering some bit of drivel that only held sway in the individual memory. But his father had given him a task, and what so bothered Agravius about that task, was not that it was assigned to him by his father, but that it had been assigned to his father.

The High Emperor rubbed his eyes, tear ducts burning.

I need to sleep. I can't think about this right now.

Agravius tossed and turned. The satin was smothering him—the silk, suffocating him.

That night, he found himself reliving a memory, a memory that was cold, and bitter.

Following the surrender of Sunveil at the end of The First War of Unification, King Faalaran Eridion of Hemia had hosted a ball in the interest of peace, inviting the nobles of all The Continental Nations and writing to Agravius and his wife, Juliana, personally, asking them to attend. Had he not chosen diplomacy, Sunveil would have been besieged and starved into submission. Ravenshear, Vascis and Canamina had all fought and fallen, and an attempt to hold a capital cut off from its surrounding cities would have been nothing but an exercise in futility.

The party was held in the largest ballroom of The Hemian Royal Palace. Long-necked, standing, bronze braziers lit the room, supplementing the overhead lighting, and the swirling, red-and-black, marble floor had been polished to a sparkling shine. The walls of the ballroom were tiled with embossed wooden squares, rimmed with gold, and the ovular ceiling was swirled with white paint. The entry to the room consisted of three double doors to the south wing of the palace and one single door to the west wing of the palace.

Nobles in gaudy clothes whirled across the dance floor, illuminated by the gold filigree chandeliers above, the candles like fervent spectators, weeping lipid tears at the beauty of it all.

Agravius wasn't dancing. He was pushing his way through the crowded room, looking for Juliana.

High Empress Juliana Xandromen was a stunning brunette with a slight but shapely figure and a soft but beautiful voice. She had chosen to wear a strapless, black velvet dress to the ball, complemented by a small, heart-shaped, gold pendant hanging from a thin gold chain. A keepsake commemorating the birth of their son, Torran, she never took it off. With electric-blue eyes and a smile that made pearls envious, it was impossible not to see her. Yet it seemed that no one knew where she was.

Agravius had been explaining the details of The Settlement Compact to the Hemian King when Prince Falin had asked his wife to dance, and, feeling neglected, she had agreed. Agravius was too busy trying to get Faalaran to sign the document, the old King embittered by his loss and more than a little drunk. The man had drunk the ghostwater like it was regular water, and it was a wonder he could write at all, propped up by his advisers. Perhaps it was better for that way, the Lords pushing their drunken King into signing away his country's riches. It was the only way to avoid more war. Still, the monarch's intoxicated state had made the process long and tedious, and in that folly, Agravius had lost sight of his wife. The Raishian Prince was gone as well.

Agravius was starting to panic. He had paid too little attention to his Empress, at the party and in general. He was so focused on bringing The Continental Nations together that he had ignored everything else. His work had consumed him, and he didn't know what to think.

He had seen her playing around with some of the noblemen back home, heard her flirtations, but he had assumed that they were merely to tease him, to take his mind off his work and make him pay attention to her. He had never seriously considered that Juliana would have an affair, leave him for another man. When he had met her, she was a scholar. Torran's birth had changed things a little, but she was still a scholar.

She must understand why I'm so busy. Does she not know that I love her?

Finally Agrvius spotted her. She was speaking to Lord Elrisain, Hemia's Overseer of Finance.

The pair turned.

"Ah, Lady Anasade. May I introduce you to his Grace, The High Emperor of Astria?" the Lord smiled.

Lady Anasade had a large beaked nose and a high forehead, criss-crossed with wrinkles. Although she was far too thin and spindly to be called attractive, her eyes were a light and piercing green, the color of jade.

It's not her.

Was it even a black dress? Maybe it had been dark blue, or purple! He didn't know anymore!

Agravius' mind whirled. Had he cared so little about his wife? Had he taken her for granted?!

Lady Anasade started talking to him, anchoring him to the ballroom and preventing him from flying through the doors in search of his wife.

Elrisain commented that he looked quite pale, and he regurgitated some rote excuses. He was sure that The King's advisers had no idea about Falin's treachery, but this man might have been in on it. He was Falin's friend and confidant, though he was ten years older.

The Lord's face betrayed nothing.

Whatever the case, it was of no import, then. Agravius knew that even if he wanted to chase down the pair, he could not. Juliana had run off with Falin Eridion, The Prince of Hemia, and Unification depended on Hemia's cooperation. Though the War had ended in peace talks and parties, the candles reeked of blood. Thousands had died to bring The Settlement Compact to the Sunveil. Worse, Juliana had gone of her own volition. It was what she wanted.

You put your work first, even when your wife runs away! I could never give her the love she deserved...

The High Emperor swallowed his pain, and put on a porcelain smile, returning to the festivities. That night, he would leave alone, birthing terrible rumors.

When he returned to Astria, he told Torran and The Court that Juliana had died of a chill.

But illness hadn't taken her from him. She hadn't been taken from him at all.

She had left him.

Jhett

Jhett didn't know how long it had been since the ship had stopped, but it had been a long time.

There was little wind, and he doubted the merchants had decided to suddenly give them a break. Honestly, though, he didn't really care why—he could rest. Better yet, the drummer had gone above, his ancestors to creep back to him

The other oar slaves peered through the tiny openings in the hull, their curiosity aroused, but Jhett could see nothing from his end of the aisle even if he wanted to. He was on the larboard side of the ship and everyone was looking through the holes on the starboard side.

"Father above... What could have done such a thing?!" a man exclaimed.

"Shit, that smells," another muttered.

"What is it?" Jhett asked.

An overweight, red-bearded Luzian in front of him responded.

"A fuckin' whale. Torn right in half. Bitten, looks like."

Jhett could smell it then, too. A putrid semi-sweet smell, it was chillingly reminiscent of the smell that permeated the galley.

The tribesman shuddered.

Madevf above... These are not the waters you gave us.

We need to get out of this ocean.

Having taken stock of the situation, the drummer came back down, sat, and began to play again. The ancestral spirits dispersed at the beat of sticks against exotic leather. But the drum disturbed more than the ancestral spirits.

There was a muffled *thump*. It came from beneath Jhett's feet.

He looked down, scared, at the dark, greasy planks.

There was silence for a moment. A few of the other oar slaves had noticed the sound too, but kept rowing.

Another thump came, louder that time.

And then Jhett was flying. An ultramarine fluke speared through the bottom of the vessel, an explosion of wood and splinters. He was weightless, thrown into the air.

Shouting, he fell with a *smack* onto a piece of the hull. Half submerged, he turned disorientedly to see what had happened, his back spasming.

As Jhett's eyelids slid down, and unconsciousness encroached upon him, he caught a terrifying glimpse of their misfortune. He saw something that should not have existed.

A Seadrake, emerging from the formless unknown, towered over the merchants, slaves, and sailors frantically treading water, its scales coated by a thick layer of seaweed.

It slid through a hole it had made in the whale's carcass, turning towards them all. Whale lice plopped onto the merchants' heads, slipping from its teeth as it snorted pungent steam.

The men saw the face of the abyss. Its cannonball eyes saw snacks tossed about amongst the wreckage. Dripping with saliva, the dragon's mouth fell open, illuminating teeth like clear needles.

It descended upon the merchants first, the ensuing waves knocking over the tribesman's piece of hull as it swallowed them whole.

And Jhett sank beneath the froth as the ocean seemed to boil—screaming, drowning.

Oscure

The Shadowrise tree bled viscous, transparent sap, ants and other small bugs trapped in the immortal resin. Their souls would never escape, the insects alive and conscious as they sat trapped there, unmoving, for years.

Hundreds of feet tall, The Shadowrise' spined branches reached past the canopy and all the way into the emergent layer before diving back down through green-brown leaf-litter, pushing past the dry leaves, grass, and moss that carpeted the jungle floor. The tree was surrounded by a halo of death, a uniform radius of withered, drab-looking vegetation which the surrounding cecropia trees would not encroach on.

Ten enchanted steel spigots lined its trunk, punched through oily, black bark and the sticky, black sapwood beneath. They were not of Nolite make.

The Quorkorath Tribe had desecrated the already sickly Shadowrise, patches of greenery glued together around its ten-foot-wide trunk. The Tribes of The Wildlands had revered the tree for centuries, long before outsiders stepped foot on the continent and it fell sick.

But five years ago, the Quorkorath had turned away from their fellow Nolites and allied themselves with Qeonia, the Continental Nation that had started the slave trade and continued it even after it became illegal in the eyes of The High Empire. Given enchanted steel weapons and armor by the Qeonian crown, the Quorkorath had taken the land around the tree for themselves and repelled all the other Tribes, except for The Fivefinger Tribe, their historic and historically weaker ally. In return for their help, they traded The Shadowrise' sap for more arms.

What Qeonia wanted with the sap, Oscure didn't know, but it didn't matter. The Quorkorath would do anything to strengthen their Tribe and establish dominance over The Wildlands. So when Qeonia asked them to enslave their own kind, they did, sending out bands of Nolite slavers who would attack the villages of the different Tribes and capture their strongest members. The captured Nolites would be sold to merchant groups, who would then auction them off.

As much as he hated it, Oscure knew their swords were superior, for, at that moment, his old, enchanted steel knife, the only one in the tribe, lay in the dirt, and his iron ida was cut in half.

Blood poured from a large hole in his sternum. He had been stabbed in the chest, though Nolites couldn't be cut.

Quorkorath warriors had ambushed him as soon as he arrived at The Shadowrise, and now, they had him surrounded, brandishing their shimmering steel. Their keen eyes glimmered in the gloom, watching him intently as he made to get up. He had trespassed into their territory, and they would not let that go unpunished.

Oscure had known the risks, and did it anyway.

He had had little choice. The crystal at the center of the tree, known as The Shadowheart, was believed to hold the souls of all of the tribesmen who died in The Wildlands and possess numerous magical properties, one of which was the ability to heal wounds and cure infection.

Ritsi, a six-year-old girl in Oscure's tribe, had developed a severe leg infection after being attacked by a Fievfinger trespasser while searching for food for The Aerhauc Settlement. As Tribe King, it was Oscure's responsibility to try and save her.

However, the mission wasn't just a matter of responsibility. It was personal. Oscure's father, Mgambi, had died in a similar way. Fighting The Fivefinger Tribe King, the old Aerhauc Tribe King had been cut with an enchanted steel dagger coated in the juices of a Glowfruit pod. The hanging, green gourd glowed blue at night and was native to The Wildlands, but although its flesh was delicious, it was often home to featherworm larvae. In the course of a week, the featherworms had fully parasitized his father, proliferating under his skin and growing downy, white appendages that overheated him to death.

Oscure had hoped to sneak in and dig the crystal out of the tree before anyone noticed, as The Shadowrise stood at the very outskirts of The Quorkorath Tribe's territory, with few patrols going along the perimeter. The other tribes stayed away due to the Quorkorath's greater numbers and vicious attitude, so there was little reason to keep a constant lookout.

Unfortunately, Oscure had chosen a bad day for his risky gambit. He had managed to dig out The Shadowheart, the clear, faceted, dodecahedral stone humming in his hand, but he had taken too long cutting away the spines at the tree's base, and a patrol had spotted him.

Oscure paid dearly for the delay.

He was wounded, and his blood brother Mozamic lay dead behind him.

Mozamic was younger than Oscure, and of a more slender build. He had always been strong for his size and extremely athletic, muscles rippling beneath his brown-tinged skin, but he had a bravery in him that verged on recklessness, a bravery that made Oscure look like a coward in comparison. No matter the danger, he would flash his striking, white smile and face the obstacle head-on. He was everything a leader should be, everything a leader should not be, the source of both his parents' pride and worry.

Their worry had proven true in the end, for he volunteered to join Oscure on his mission and it cost him his life.

I have to fight, Oscure told himself. *For Mozamic.*

His death cannot be in vain. I can't lose my best friend for nothing....

Ritsi, I will save you...

But first, I need to save myself. They can cut it out of my chest if they have to, but I must use The Shadowheart now.

Ancestors—give me your power.

Not knowing what would happen, Oscure slammed the gemstone into the hole in his chest, the Quorkorath backing away as red arcs spun around his body and veins of crystal spread across his breast.

The elders were right. I'm healed!

Reinvigorated, Oscure stood, picking up his knife. The Quorkorath looked at him in anger and bewilderment.

But he was no longer alone in his body.

As he took a step toward The Quorkorath, he was hit by a wave of burning pain that forced him down to one knee and made him drop his knife.

Oscure cried out. It felt like fire. The pain issued from a small, swirling, red light amongst countless others stored in The Shadowheart. Knowing it to be a soul, Oscure touched it with his mind, probing to see who it belonged to, but he should not have.

He should have fought through it.

Oscure cried out as the light stilled and began to glow brighter, his corporeal form disintegrating into red smoke. He became enveloped in a cloud of Lifeblood and then a part of that cloud. Formless, but still conscious, he was, for a fraction of a second, a being made entirely of Lifeblood. Urged by the soul he had touched, the cloud rapidly coalesced, energy becoming matter again.

Oscure Transformed, and The Transformation was terrible.

Black wings crawled from his back, his ears flaring out and his face growing longer, no longer human. He had become someone else, something else.

A Shadowbat.

The Shadowbat was immensely dark. Its head and shoulders were covered in obsidian spikes, large, frilled ears framing a skull-like face. A thin membrane of skin stretched like a black tarp over its empty eye sockets, and two curved, obsidian fangs, big as swords, jutted from its mouth, or at least, what should have been its mouth. The space where its mouth should have been was replaced by an elongated, fleshy oval, for the demon needed no mouth to feed. Shadowbats drew sustenance solely from Lifeblood, sliding their teeth into their prey's eye-sockets directly into the brain, the largest reservoir of Lifeblood in the human body.

Grey smoke puffed from The Shadowbat's skeletal nostrils, burning with sulphur.

Oscure watched his Transformed body move as if he were a bystander. It was not his ancestors that had granted him power, but a malevolent being, his ancestors' ancient enemy.

A hateful name flared through the Tribe King's thoughts.

Naraklar.

Without hesitation, the demon lashed out, tearing apart The Quorkorath with its obsidian claws, and Oscure could only look on in horror.

His ancestors had betrayed him.

Absolute

The mountains of Sandkeeper Ridge were not as green or lush as they had appeared from afar. The Canyon Pass was muddy and bumpy, and the only fruits he had seen in half a day of hiking were poison berries, crab apples, and black walnuts.

Even those were few.

Though the landscape was not as welcoming as he had imagined, the signs of life he saw made him feel less isolated. There was the occasional cluster of droppings from goats that shepherds had brought to graze, and insects flitted in and out of the sparse grass: white butterflies, bees, and common flies. He passed a trodden beetle, its red shell crushed against the mud and gravel, but he only spared it a glance, continuing along the uneven path.

Absolute passed a beehive that he thought about taking, but he had no means to protect himself from being stung, and, even if he had, he felt that he would pity the bees who had worked so industriously to make their home in this rugged environment.

Eventually, he happened upon a small stream, which ran over a bed of smooth rocks and broke into tiny streamlets that trickled down the mountainside and into the dark green forests below.

He quenched his thirst, the water clean and faintly sweet.

Shortly afterwards, he chanced upon two bushes of plump, shiny blackberries, on which he gorged himself in his hunger.

A group of blackbirds landed in a pine tree overhead, angry that he took their harvest, but he ignored their cawing and kept eating.

Once his hunger was sated, Absolute continued up The Canyon Pass in search of shelter, but didn't find any on the Ridge's west side.

The second thing Absolute felt, was the cold.

His grey, cotton robes had been somewhat hot and uncomfortable during the day, and he had praised The Divinity when Arceon's great blue disk finally slid from view. But he had praised God too soon, for his robes were loosely knit, and the night winds blew through the weave. In posterity, he wished he had warmer clothes and been twice as hot during the day.

Absolute shivered, but continued searching for shelter, fearing the perils of the wildlife. He hadn't seen any animals, but he knew that nonetheless, animals would be hunting at night, and that worried him.

If I encounter a bear or wolf, I'll be in trouble... There must be someplace safe I can rest.

Absolute reached the top of The Canyon Pass by moonrise. He still hadn't found shelter, but the view at the top made him forget his tiredness.

Below, lay The Basamor Desert, an expanse of shallow dunes surrounding and surpassing a chevron-shaped, brown mesa split in two by Claeana's Gorge, the continuation and end of The Canyon Pass. That night, the dunes had taken on a navy hue, Riize, a silver-blue crescent amongst a sea of twinkling stars.

He felt a calling to go to the desert, but although it looked beautiful from afar, all the books he had read agreed that no one should go there lest they be lost to the sands. Still, he could not quiet the yearning in his heart. It was as if he was being guided there by some invisible force, as if there was something he was meant to discover.

Remembering the danger he was in, Absolute cleared his head of such thoughts and carefully descended the west face of the mountain. After an hour or so, he eventually stumbled upon a small cave, no more than three feet high.

Exposed tree roots from some faraway conifer draped over the cave entrance, and the grey stone inside was coated in a thin layer of dirt. It was dark, and looked like a mouth, and Absolute was unsure if it was an animal's dwelling, but he had to be brave if he wanted shelter.

His bones ached, and his eyelids were drooping.

Mustering up his courage, the Acolyte dislodged a small pebble from the muddy trail and threw it into the cave to scare away anything that might be inside.

The stone clattered, but nothing jumped out. The cave was empty.

Relieved, Absolute crawled into the damp enclosure, curled up, and tried to sleep.

Amdryaan

The Five Clans knelt before The Cold Tooth, the bent, white mountain rising behind them like a pillar to heaven. They were captured.

About sixty people remained, a dozen men and women from each Clan. Their hair was greasy and tangled, icicles growing from unkempt beards and mustaches, faces blackened and bruised. Defeated in battle and chained, they had been beaten and dragged over to the Frosslar capital.

The prisoners' exposed hands were dry and white, close to frostbite and bound by rusting, iron manacles. A fuzzy, white coating of frost covered the dark brown metal like some persistent kind of mold, and snow flew on the bitter wind, stinging their faces. The drifts washed over Whitereach in waves, hissing over rugged, dome-shaped dwellings of stone.

The ground under Amdryaan's bruised knees was white as white could be, the sky above far too blue, overbearing.

The young Native hung his head in shame, snowmelt dripping down his hair as the sun hit, a big blue ball of fire. It seemed impossible, then, that it was Goddess' eye, too harsh in its judgement.

We failed. And now, it's over... he accepted bitterly.

The other survivors refused to accept what stood carved in cold truth before them. They were shackled, but they looked up without fear. Those too full of pride undestroyed were beaten and punched again by the angry guards, but they just laughed.

Looking down on them disapprovingly, was The King of The Frosslar: The Weirtonce, and the man that had killed Amdryaan's mother.

Aamdryaan looked up, eyelids sliding over frozen sclera. The shouts of his fellow tribesmen rang in his ears, but he didn't turn to them, reverting his gaze to the ground.

"Voreusss!!! Kill us, you coward!" they yelled, Yurwik loudest amongst them. The engineer of this disaster, he had survived the battle he brought, but his friend, Kanis, had not. The Fiveclan Chief's newfound sword sat against Voreus' hip, separated from the giant's skin by a thick and protective wolf-skin.

"Kill us and be done with it!" the Clan Chief bellowed.

Wiola, full of rage but not wanting to see more of The Five Clans die, tugged on his bearskin cloak with bound hands.

"Yurwik, stop! Don't do this!" she pleaded in whisper.

Ignoring her, The Chief of The Bear Clan continued. He had nothing left to live for, too weary and too riddled with guilt to go on. Some of the other, more firebrand tribesmen joined in. Old, and tied strongly to the land, they refused to live in a world where The Five Clans were not victorious.

"Kill us, you monster! We will never serve you!"

The Blizzard King cocked his head, cracking his jaw. He had had enough.

"Who is with Yurwik, here?" he asked, curious. "Raise your hand," he asked, his tone malicious.

No. Stop!

Three hands shot up: Yurwik's, that of The Chief of The Fin Whale Clan, and that of a man named Rengoew, a wizened member of The Wolf Clan who had outlived not one, but two leaders. As soon as they shot up, the men's hands were separated from their wrists with a swing of the scythe, falling to the ground. Their hands were swiftly followed by their heads, Whitewind ending its arc as a thin, blue line, dripping deep, red blood.

Wiola, blood-spattered and horrified, bit her lip, biting back a defiant growl. Her eyes were watering, like lakes assaulted by heavy rain.

Amdryaan shook his head, averting his eyes for a moment before forcing himself to look. He watched the blood drip with a disturbing clarity.

Damn it... I should have stopped them. I should have—

What could I have done?

What can I do?! Why am I so weak?!

The prisoners were cowed in an instant, but—unable to direct their ire towards their captor—they directed it towards their new and undeserving leader.

"Amdryaan!" Paqlo cried out. "How can you just sit there and say nothing?! You're the leader of The Five Clans! Do something!"

The Weirtonce found this amusing.

"Yes, do something, Amdryaan," Voreus mocked. Twenty feet decreasing to a mere ten, he knelt in front of Amdryaan, smiling. Fingers clawing, he raised his chin, boring into him with eyes like steel.

"You want to fight me? To kill me? Here—take your father's sword," he offered good-naturedly, unsheathing it hilt-first and extending it towards the Winterlove heir.

"You don't want to?" he questioned, feigning confusion.

You bastard. You know just as well as I do that I cannot win. How could I, when my father died so futilely?

So do the rest of these people, but they'll pretend like I have a hope so that they can feel better about themselves when I refuse.

To the anger of the other prisoners, Amdryaan didn't reach for the sword. The moment he did, he would be executed like the rest. Yurwik, the most rebellious of them all, had chosen to die and not live. That told him everything he needed to know.

"You coward!" they shouted, spitting at him and pelting him with what little snow they could scrape up from the hardened earth. Wiola shielded him, knowing why he didn't move, but her eyes also betrayed resentment.

I'm sorry, Amdryaan said with his gaze. *I'm a terrible brother.*

Wiola simply turned away, acknowledging, but not accepting.

That's fair, Amdryaan sighed to himself. *Very fair.*

Seeing that their leader was weak and would not act, The Five Clans lost all hope, not strong enough to die, but not weak enough to simply surrender to fate.

Voreus took note of this. "We would rather die free than as slaves!" he mimed. "Few men can say that and truly mean it in their hearts. You hate me, but you do not hate me more than you hate those chains. And, as tempting as that would be," Voreus sighed, addressing the prisoners as a whole, "I have other plans for you. It would be a shame to execute so many useful workers. Instead of death, I sentence you to life. You will toil in The Frozen Mines till you collapse or bring me one hundred ingots of bronze... But do not lose hope! For whoever accomplishes this, will be granted the opportunity to face me in mutual combat—no magic allowed, and one weapon each."

Instead of angering them, this statement enthralled the people of the Clans, save Wiola and some of the more levelheaded tribesmen. It was an excuse to give up without looking like they abandoned the fight.

"However," Voreus continued, "someone must be punished. He glanced over at Amdryaan as he walked down the line of prisoners. "I will choose the guiltiest amongst you, and throw him into The Prison Caves to pay for their crimes. So tell me...who should bear the blame for your failed insurrection?"

You— You piece of shit.

He's offering me up as their scapegoat. All they need to do is say—

"Amdryaan," spat Laaren, an acidulous woman with dark red hair.

"Laaren!" Wiola exclaimed.

"Shut up, bitch," the woman retorted. "Your brother's just a weak-willed worm. We lie here in chains, and he says nothing. Why should we protect him? Because he's the Chief's son? The Chief is dead. Your mother's gone too."

"Yeah, Amdryaan should be the one punished," Alöwon affirmed. A portly man with a patchy mustache and a dissonant, high-pitched voice, he had never liked Amdryaan, and Amdryaan had never liked him either. He looked like a walrus, and was as fat as one too, his wife fasting during the winter to maintain his size.

"Why should we suffer for his father's mistakes?" the traitor asked. "At his age, he should already be Chief, though, if he'd been in charge, we would've never been here in the first place!" he scoffed.

"Watch your words, Walrus," Wiola warned, her tone like ice on ice.

"Or what?" Alöwon retorted. "We're bound in chains, beaten. You going to strangle me with those handcuffs?" He turned to the others.

"Someone needs to pay," he stated matter-of-factly.

Agreeing with him, the voices of The Five Clans rose, acquaintances and even relatives offering Amdryaan up as sacrifice. Amdryaan winced. This condemnation hurt, but it was also surprising in that Enpen and his posse remained silent. For whatever reason, his bullies didn't speak against him—

they who had always abused him.

So you find your humanity now?

Go on, condemn me like the others, you assholes! What, you want to take the high road now?

Condemn me too, damn it...

Amdryaan hung his head. He was damned, and he couldn't say it was wrong. However, someone disagreed—with all of it.

As The Frosslar moved to take him away, Wiola moved in front of him, extending her arms and protecting him, though she was his younger sister.

"Take me instead," she begged.

Wiola...

Amdryaan's eyes darkened in self-disgust.

"Take you?" Voreus asked, laughing. "You do have pretty eyes, and I can't say I didn't consider taking you to my bed... But alas, you're not as pretty as your mother," he lamented.

At this, Amdryaan's veins popped. Suddenly, he slammed his muscles against the manacles. He wished that for just one second, they could break, but they didn't.

Frustrated, he sprung to his feet anyway. Howling, he ran at Voreus in a rage, Wiola reaching to pull him back.

Her hand didn't reach him, and he didn't make it, the guards intercepting. With a strong right hook, Amdryaan was knocked down.

He hit the ground hard, falling still. The young tribesman stared into the distance, cheek to the ground.

Ah, that's right. I shouldn't have tried to play the hero now... Even when Mother called for me, I didn't come.

As his vision died, Amdryaan watched the soldiers march his people off to the Mines. They were taken away, taken to a life of misery.

And it was all his fault.

Oscure

Oscure woke up, changed back. His hands were covered in blood, but it wasn't his. The Quorkorath lay in a broken ring around him, pulled apart and slashed like dolls disliked. From the angle at which they sat, it was clear—they had been running. They had been running and he had killed them.

I... I have gone against The Law of Madevf, he realized, feeling broken.

The Tribe King massaged his scalp, no longer glass but skin. He tucked his chin and inhaled deeply through his nostrils, trying to deal with the situation calmly. He had become a demon's human vessel, left to deal with the aftermath of an inhuman slaughter.

They attacked me, but I still killed them.

Oscure looked down at his hands again, lip curling.

What have I done?

The Quorkorath were his enemies, but that didn't justify his actions. He looked up at a break in the canopy, looking for answers that didn't come. He turned his eyes back to earth, looking ahead. He peered past the dense cecropia trees and into the smoky darkness of his psyche, searching for Naraklar, the perpetrator within.

Just as he saw it, the creature's face, he heard the rattling of beads, more Quorkorath coming. Caring not for his safety, but its continued entertainment, the demon took Oscure by the face and spun him around, revealing itself in a flash of red. Transformed once again, Oscure struggled with everything he could to force out just one act of humanity. Against its will, The Shadowbat knelt to pick up Mozamic's body.

The demon wanted to leave him there, Oscure's blood-brother and best friend, but The Tribe King would not allow it. He held on with an unshakeable persistence until the demon finally accepted its burden, and moved to leave.

Folding wings like night around itself, The Shadowbat looked back for a final time at the prison it escaped, and tunneled through the trees, a vortex of black.

Oscure blacked out.

Flind

The Manor rocked back and forth, servants running out the doors as brick and beam were torn asunder. They ran for dear life, screaming, but someone closed the door behind them, more afraid of what lay outside than the building's collapse.

Agamus Ralei, Flind presumed.

The Baron had good reason to be afraid. The guards he had hired sat around her in heaps, impaled by stone spikes, rock projectiles embedded in their skulls. She pulled one out of a young guard in his early twenties, a burst of yellow grime, but the regret she felt for killing him was quickly washed away by her fury, by the feeling she got when she breathed in—glowing, red smoke streaming from the corpses and into her mouth.

Flind's eyes blazed red.

I came here to get justice, but they stood in my way.

She tossed the rock and caught it again, testing its weight.

"Agamus Ralei!" she called. "I know you're in there! Come out and fight, coward! I'm not as weak as I was."

There was no immediate response, but Flind knew that he couldn't have escaped. Her appearance at the Manor had started another earthquake, more powerful than the last, and a deep fissure had appeared behind the residence, preventing escape through the back door. To jump over it from the roof would be noticeable at best, and suicide at worst.

The Baron was inside.

He's too much of a coward to come out, even with the way the house is shaking. And he always pretended to be this big, strong, important man.

Whatever. If he won't come out, I'll just have to bring him out myself.

Flind opened her hand and the stone shot out, breaking through the Manor's strong, wooden door in a burst of splinters. Flind kicked it in with a *crash*.

Thankfully, Leafsong and her mother were gone.

They were probably sent someplace safe after the fire...

Good. They're not a part of this.

I came to get revenge on the Baron and no one else. The guards just wouldn't leave me alone.

Agamus stood with his back against the fireplace at the far end of the living room, trembling. He held out an ornate han-jian with a banded, gold filigree handle, its blade polished to a mirror sheen. Functional, but intended for show, he had received it as a gift from a Kisist official during a trip to Cairnon.

To think, he's going to try to kill me with a Monolid sword. Then again, the Kïsists are my enemy.

Flind advanced, ready to exact her revenge.

Cornered, the Baron jerked forward, swinging for her but missing as she moved to the side, a poor swordsman and an even worse person.

He swung again, splitting air, but Flind dodged, taking a shallow cut to the arm as she closed the distance.

More fearful now, he went for her neck, but she ducked, surging back to a standing position and grabbing his sword-hand. She wrenched his wrist back, trying to disarm him, but she failed, Agamus grabbing her by the throat with his off-hand. She tried to pry his fingers off of her, but he really was strong.

Unable to breathe, the scullion pushed, turning them both around. Changing strategies, she let go of the man's wrist, and slammed his head into the wall, causing him to drop the jian with a *clatter*. Using the space she had just created, she kicked him in the chest, sending him stumbling backwards.

Concentrating, Flind accessed her powers, her vision shifting in an eyeblink. It was like she was everywhere in the world all at once, but instead of seeing people and animals, rivers and trees, all she saw was earth and rock, a glowing grey against black and hazy surroundings. She saw avalanches falling, stone breaking under mason's hammers, mudslides, and even magma— churning and compacting under Avenshra's crust. She saw the shifting of sands and the formation of cracks in farmers' fields, stricken by drought. Her focus jumped between each of these scenes at an incredible speed.

Fighting the guards, the scullion had intuitively accessed her powers multiple times, but she still understood almost nothing about them. All she knew was that the red smoke in living things bestowed power, the power to Reach for whatever she chose. Every time she focused on an object, she felt a connection, a potential trade that would be realized if she willed it, smoke for substance.

She made such a trade, Reaching for a grapefruit-sized rock falling down the face of Hemia's Mount Criant. Her eyes dimmed partially, the burning rock appearing in the air to Agamus' left and hitting him in the side of the head, the Baron sent rolling across the dirty floor. He groaned, unable to stand.

Flind wiped the dripping blood from her arm and grabbed him by his wire-like Ronari hair. She dragged him through the living room and out of the Manor, letting him slump onto the well-manicured lawn.

She paced away in a circle, pulling back her hood and taking a deep breath as she spun around.

Agamus lifted his chest off the ground, sputtering.

"Flind? Wh-wha— Please, I've done nothing to you! Why are you doing this?" he cried.

Flind's blood ran cold.

"Nothing?! You're a rapist and a murderer! You violated me, raped and killed your daughter!" she yelled.

The Baron shook his head in denial.

"N-No, I would never! I would never do such a thing!" he cried. "Not my sweet Inesa, no! And you... N-no, I wouldn't! I would never rape anyone, I swear-"

Flind cut him off.

"You did and you know it," she repeated. "You were drinking the night of the fire... You raped your daughter, you raped me, and then, you tried to cover it up."

"I don't remember doing that; you have to believe me!" The Baron insisted, kneeling in the wet grass. "I have no idea what you're talking about! Inesa fell from her window; there was a fire... Dear God, I wouldn't!"

"You did. You threw her from her window, and then set fire to the house to hide the evidence."

Agamus' resolve crumbled. He remembered, then.

"Oh, God, I really didn't mean to..." he mumbled. He put his hands together, begging. "Please! Please, forgive me!!! I would do anything to bring her back, to take back what I did to you! Please, tell me what to do!!! I don't remember! All I did was have some wine!"

Flind looked down. The Baron of Stillvein lay on the ground before her, weeping, his deceptively bulky frame racked with sobs. Something in her wanted to forgive him.

But she couldn't; she wouldn't. Justice had to be served. He was filth—a murderer and a rapist, knowingly or not.

Alcohol did not excuse him.

Flind's expression hardened.

"I'll tell you what you can do," she whispered.

Agamus looked up, his eyes pleading.

Taking his arm, she helped him to his knees as his tears slowed. Her glowing, carnelian eyes were soft in the moonlight.

Tears slowing, the Baron's heart rose. He thought she would spare him.

But then the ground opened—a deep, earthen tomb, yawning wide.

Flind released her grip, the Baron shouting as he fell to his death, dirt falling in from above and burying him alive.

Not moving, she simply watched, smiling, as the ground came together again, particle by particle, muffling his screams until there was nothing left but silence.

"Hold your breath," she instructed.

She had gotten her revenge. So had Inesa. The ground below rumbled in agreement.

As Flind turned to leave, there was a tired groan—a *crack.*

And the Manor collapsed in an inglorious heap.

Oscure

Oscure woke up to the familiar sight of the wooden support beams that held up his Hut's palm-leaf roof. He squeezed his straw mattress as a wave of pain racked his chest.

It was morning, the sky blue and empty, and the two, rectangular windows at the front of the cylindrical dwelling glowed like portals to the afterlife.

He propped himself up by the elbows, extremely sore.

The straw curtains were drawn, and sunlight speared his eyes as he tried to cover them with his hand. Banana leaves and an earthenware pot of foul-smelling tincture sat on the high, wooden stool beside him, and the room smelled of earth and dirt. Birds chirped noisily outside, and insects droned.

A toucan with a colorful beak had the audacity to perch on his windowsill, blocking his soul from leaving the land of the living. It looked at him for a moment with its beady, black eyes, inquisitive, but, seeing that there was no food to be had, it flew away as quickly as it had arrived.

Oscure was too tired to ponder such omens. He sat up against the rough, wooden headboard and looked around.

The room was not the same. The floor was covered in a large, spiral mat, made of straw, and spiritual symbols had been drawn on the wooden walls with chalk. The mat was stained with droops of dried blood.

So there were at least two barriers keeping my soul tethered to my body. If one were to include the toucan...

Oscure's thoughts were interrupted by the stinging of cuts on his arms. His body was battered, but thankfully, he had reverted back to human form.

How did I get here? What happened?

He tried to roll out of bed, but his shoulders were in too much pain.

As if summoned, his wife suddenly burst through the door, accompanied by some of the village's medicine women.

Kilanjara was a very tall and slender woman. She was almost as tall as Oscure, and he was the tallest man in The Aerhauc Tribe. Apart from being unusually tall, Oscure believed she was also unusually good-looking. She had lush, curly, black hair that she wore in a flared, top-knot ponytail and tourmaline-green eyes, which were an anomaly in the Nolite population. Oscure always felt lucky that he had married her, and she was a sweet and caring woman, but sometimes she worried about things too much, and she would often chide him as if she was his mother.

"You're awake!" Kilanjara exclaimed, rushing over to his side. She seemed relieved.

Oscure was not relieved at all. He had hoped it had all been a dream, but the crystal really had merged with him; he could feel it humming in his chest.

He made to get up again, but she stopped him.

"Don't try to get up," she said, coaxing him back down. "You were in bad shape yesterday. Let the medicine do its work."

Oscure's voice was hoarse, his throat dry.

"Mozamic... Mozamic is dead," he wheezed. "The Quorkorath-"

The Tribe King coughed, the bed creaking as he turned on his side. Blood stained the furs, his chest racked with burning croup.

Kilanjara looked at him pleadingly, taking his hand. Her voice was trembling.

"Oscure, you have to tell them how to remove the crystal. It's killing you."

Oscure looked down at his chest.

Things did look bad. Root-like veins stretched across his pectorals, darkness taking root in his heart. But the Shadowheart had kept him alive. Without it, he would have died at the hands of the Quorkorath.

"It can't be removed," he warned. "If you remove it-"

There was another jolt of pain, a scream for control. Oscure's back arched, his eyes glowing red. Naraklar rampaged, trying to take over his body, and all anyone could do was watch.

He wasn't out of the woods yet. If he was to survive, he would have to win the battle for his mind.

Veins popping, Oscure took handfuls of straw and threw himself headlong into the darkness.

Flind

Flind woke up in a dimly lit carriage with a brown, leather ceiling. Sunlight tried to push through, but it only came through in patches, resisted by the membrane.

She was lying on the floor, which had been padded with a faded, dark green quilt, and she wasn't alone, moccasined feet pressing lightly into her sides.

As the scullion moved to get up, the carriage hit a rock with a *bang*, throwing her into the air for a moment. She fell hard onto her elbows, her head snapping back.

"Ow," Flind groaned. Holding her whiplashed neck, she felt something smooth and cold around her finger. Looking at her hand, she saw that she was wearing a ring: brown and translucent, with black veins, like dark, impure topaz.

Where did this come from? she questioned.

The scullion sat up warily. Four Lightseeker nuns looked down at her in silence: Monolid women with shaven heads and green-brown robes. Kïsists.

Um...what happened? The last thing I remember, I was...

She remembered quickly.

She had been unable to control her powers. She had brought down The Manor, but that wasn't the end. She had brought another earthquake down on Stillvein, and the magic wasn't free. It had Drained her, taken something from her. She had blacked out, sapped of all energy.

By instinct, she had accessed the Power, and by instinct, her body had broken The Connection. Because of that, she was saved.

Flind was unsure of what she had lost, and what she had gained.

"Are you alright?" the nun at the back right corner of the carriage asked. She was the friendliest looking of the bunch. The others seemed disinterested. Their gazes ranged from indifference to outright hostility.

"Who are you?" Flind asked, dazed. "Where are you taking me?

"We are servants of Avghe'eah," the woman chimed, smiley and totally unlike her companions, who seemed annoyed at her very presence. "We're returning to The Temple of Iwidëa Exalted. We found you in the street and saw that you needed help. As nuns, we couldn't just leave a child of the Goddess behind. The First Promise is to-"

"-help those in need," Flind finished automatically. She had heard that Promise many times before, touted by her mother, who was too poor to help anyone, but helped anyway.

Flind's parents had been Lightseekers, but their faith hadn't rubbed off on her. She knew all the stories, prayers, and traditions, but she wasn't authentic in her belief.

The Lightseekers believed they would receive enlightenment at death if they kept The Eight Promises, an agreement the ancestor of all Monolids, Anohr, made with The Earth Goddess, Avghe'eah, after The Great Scourge. The Great Scourge was a time of chaos when The Sky Goddess, O'oraneah, sent down her rainbow soldiers, The Surayas, to raze the land. With cities burned and farmland left barren, the people starved, the population dwindling to only a handful, and Monolids almost went extinct. Seeing her children's misery, Avghe'eah gifted her people The Greentree of Cairnon: a holy tree that made life prosper around it, ensuring a bountiful harvest. This event was recounted in a set of lengthy, religious texts known as The Vagabadas, which were written by Anohr's husband, Lāu.

Having saved her Nation, Anohr founded The Lightseekers and became The Lightholder, reigning for several decades beside the Gaudon Dynasty as Cairnon's highest spiritual authority. However, upon her death, there was a schism, and the country was deeply divided. The Kïsists argued that the next leader should be selected by blood, which would make Anohr's sister, Kïa, the next Lightholder. The Lātists believed that the next Lightholder should be selected by popular vote, which favored Lāu. This argument led to The First Cairnian Civil War, which lasted for a decade.

Hundreds of years later, tensions flared again during The War of Conquest, waged by The Red Meteor, Xersus Xandromen, after he went insane and threw away the title of The Warrior King to become High Emperor. During this time, Dame Iwidëa Chu-chigang, an ex-Imperial knight and Warrior of Avenshra, became the face of the poor but defiant Cairnian Resistance. An Elemental with the power to mold and shape the earth, she was widely revered as the human Incarnation of Avghe'eah.

But, for all her power, Iwidëa was still mortal, and she died in battle. The Kïsists had betrayed her, striking a deal with The Xandromen Dynasty, and she was killed by her old leader years after they fended off The Invasions together. The Dame's life and death were later recorded in The Vagábdas, short supplements to The Vagabadas written by various authors.

According to The Vagábdas, the moment Iwidëa fell, the earth began to shake violently. The earthquakes brought The Swampgreen City low and didn't subside until the third day, which later became recognized as a holiday: Jsuichian Barath.

To ensure that they would never displease their goddess again, each of The Lightseeker sects chose four of their wisest female shamans and formed a group called The Great Eight. Each of the members of The Great Eight became known as "Mother" and abbreviated their names down to the first three letters. These women were to remain celibate, mothers to all of Cairnon, and serve the common good until they died. They would then be buried under The Greentree, the symbol of their Nation and religion, and during Jsuichian Barath, flowers would be placed on their graves and on the grave of The Incarnation, flowers that would never wilt.

Arguably the most important festival in Monolid culture, Jsuichian Barath was fast approaching, and Flind realized that if she went to Cairnon, she would see it. Soon, Lightseeker pilgrims would walk across the continent barefoot to visit the Greentree, not wearing shoes so as to leave nothing between themselves and the Goddess that birthed them.

Flind had never walked down The Barefoot Path, but she was more deeply connected to Avghe'eah than anyone alive... She could feel the Goddess' heart pulsing deep below, swirling. Avenshra's crust almost squirmed beneath her feet.

And for all the Promises they made, The Lightseekers were liars, just like her... They had gone back to fighting, spilling blood on blood and forcing the earth to drink.

"Are you a Kïsist?" the nun in the back left corner asked. What she was really asking was: *Are you an enemy?*

"Yes, I am," Flind lied.

"What is your profession?" the woman followed. Her gaze was cold and dismissive.

"I'm... I was a scullion."

Now, I'm not sure what I am, she sighed internally.

"A job close to the earth," the nun noted, pleased.

"Were you a servant at The Ralei Manor?" continued the nun from before.

"Tha— That's right," the scullion answered, careful not to say too much. The woman's eyes widened, as if happy at her answer.

"Why not serve Avghe'eah?" she suggested. "The Baron and his family are dead, and without them... A Monolid alone in Qeonia is vulnerable. Only we Monolids are allowed in The Temple, and new members are rare. It would be good to have another member of The Sisterhood..."

"I... I can't," Flind declined awkwardly. Though the nuns had helped her, they had only helped her not knowing who she was.

"At least stay with us until you're healed," the woman insisted, the nun at the front left of the carriage clicking her tongue. The Sister opposite her had fallen asleep.

This could be dangerous, Flind recognized. *I'm not overly religious, but I was born a Lātist. If they find out...*

I'm hungry and tired, and my clothes are dirty. If I just keep my mouth shut, I can get a handout and leave the Temple right after.

You know what—why not? What's the harm?

Torran

Torran was sleeping, more deeply than he ever had. He was dreaming.

At least, he thought he was dreaming.

His surroundings were shrouded in white mist, a mist that was slowly receding. The freezing air seemed to carry a hint of frankincense, but it was hard to tell.

As the mist drew back, his surroundings came into view. He stood on a cliff, a great swell of divoted, blue clay overlooking a field of craters. Streaks of ejecta criss-crossed the mud below, and everything was dark. Arceon was slightly smaller than usual, and the sky above was hazy, but cloudless. Everything was silent, except for the wind.

In the field of craters, were angelic corpses, crusted in hoarfrost, hundreds of white wings twisted at unnatural angles.

They were not the only dead. A hulking figure lay hunched in the dirt beside them, followed by thousands of ashen skeletons. Their horns were like rainbow fire, burning against the cold, even in death.

To his right, at the top of the hill, stood a throne of solid alabaster. It was larger than his father's seat. Inscribed in the enormous chair were glyphs, but he didn't recognize the language.

Feeling cold, Torran realized he was barefoot, standing at the bottom of a long, white staircase that led up to the throne. Upon closer inspection, he found he was actually completely naked, but for some odd reason, he didn't care, and the cold was tolerable.

An old man walked down the steps towards him, vaguely reminiscent of his father.

"Repulsive dreamsmoke," the man muttered, buffeting the mist with his hand. White hair plummeted down his shoulders, and he wore robes of blue satin, trimmed with white. His eyes were blue—bluer than the sun, bluer than anything Torran had ever seen. Faint rays of light jumped from his face. They formed a crown—a halo.

Torran suddenly felt the need to kneel, for, though he was not told, he knew the man was God.

The Divinity spoke—a kindly voice, but resolute, and sure.

"Torran. I sense you know who I am?" he probed.

Shaken, The High Prince tried his best to reply calmly.

"I do, my Lord," he answered shakily.

The Divinity smiled graciously.

"I'm afraid I'm not the Lord of much anymore, my friend, but I appreciate your respect... Stand. The ground here is far too cold here for my liking."

Torran stood, still unsure whether he should continue to avert his gaze, but a strange feeling of familiarity washed over him, and he felt at ease.

"Unfortunately, necessity dictates that I approach you in a dream. I am no longer as strong as I was," The Divinity stated, gravely.

Torran stared at him, stupefied.

"My Lord, how can you be losing your power?" he asked, hesitant.

The Divinity sighed.

"My enemy has weakened me. Because of this, I am meeting you here to discuss the future of your world, one which I fear I can no longer protect alone."

Torran was reverently silent, unsure of what the god would want of him, what enemy could oppose The Divinity, and what he could really do to help as a human being.

What about the angels? What has become of them?

The Divinity read his thoughts.

"They're gone, Torran, taken from me long ago. That is why I need you to listen to me now. I cannot stay here long. He will know, and he will catch on to me."

"There is a cataclysm coming. Your world does not know it, and few will be willing to face it when it comes."

"What cataclysm, my Lord?"

"My enemy is becoming bolder; his power is growing. The dragons are waking up. And with the dragons will come demons, demons he will loose upon Avenshra in the coming weeks. They will not be alone. Those who would oppose The High Empire will lead them... They will try to destroy everything you care about, shatter the unity you and your family have worked so hard to achieve. The Xandromen dynasty is not without fault, but that is of no importance now. Without your intervention, his army will take lives I cannot protect. The Warriors are gone...and I have become too old to fight this battle and win."

"What do you need me to do, my Lord?"

"I need you to be strong... I will make you powerful, but The Power will not come from me. I will merely be a catalyst of your transformation... I will disturb the strings of fate; I will bring tragedy upon you now."

Torran looked at The Divinity, scared. The Divinity continued, his expression earnest.

"The Power of which I speak is well above me, but I know the way it operates, though it is not whole. It requires sacrifice and extreme conditions. I will bring those to you, though you will come to curse me for it. I will help you when I can, but you must survive what is coming. Your world depends on it, and I cannot guide you on what to do."

"My Lord, what would you ask of me?! Please don't hurt me; don't hurt my men! And Scarolette..."

Torran fell to his knees again, clutching the god's robes. The Divinity looked down sympathetically, but in his eyes, Torran saw fate and was petrified by it.

"Please, my God, please! My men, my scribe... I- You are their god!" he begged.

"I never asked to be a god," the Divinity replied, sadly. "And no one listens to my prayers..."

"But- But they believe in you! I believe in you!" Torran cried. "You can't do this! After all we've been through, after this last defeat... Surely there's another way!"

The Divinity's eyes deepened in color, unfathomably blue. He was angry.

"I can and I must! Stand—are you a craven?! You claim I am your God yet you rebuke me for what I must do! It must happen!"

The High Prince stood, wiping away the tears that had welled in his eyes. Something terrible was going to happen—his God would make sure of it. But who was he to question Him? He was being childish. He had faced death before. He could face it again if necessary.

"I am sorry, my Lord; I have dishonored myself before you. Tell me what to do and I'll do it. I must not beg; I am not a coward. For you, I would take on any burden, especially if it means protecting my men... You say you will help me. But you need to help them, Lord, for I am broken! I have little enough strength to help myself! The scribe who sits beside me fears for my life day and night, worried I will slip away and join you in your halls, never to retur-"

Torran trailed off, the truth of the matter finally setting in. There would be no heavenly halls for him if he died. He would never see The Four Heavens, and neither would anyone else. A god stood before him, stripped of much of his power, worn out and tired. He was old. His God could die. The angels were dead, and The Adversary had an advantage over The Divinity, a man—not an eternal being like The Church claimed!

What heaven?! What afterlife?! What help? It was-

He realized it, then. The Divinity had approached him because he was his only hope. The heavens themselves were losing to the forces of evil.

"Sometimes a hero is one who defends others by endangering themselves. The others do not matter more than you. If you die, the future of your world is bleak. If your shipmates die, it probably won't matter. If there was another path, you should know that I'd take it, but I am not The Initiator. I cannot control destiny, only bend it. I don't know if I can bring fate to you alone, but I'll try to minimize the damage. Remember, all will one day die. I will too, though you can tell no one of this... I will try and stretch my life out. I can still win against my enemy if you fight for me. If we are victorious, all will not be lost when I pass on, for what matters now is Avenshra, that the Adversary never controls it."

The Divinity put his hand on Torran's shoulder, his grip firm.

"I don't expect you to understand now, but you will in time. I saved you when you fell. The conditions should have been enough. But Elementality is, by nature, a fickle process, so now you must endure more pain. You ask what I need of you... "

"You will need to receive a blessing, to swear an oath, to claim a sword... But first, you'll need to be struck by lightning."

Scarolette

Scarolette was falling asleep.

Sitting in the warm cabin of The Sea Star, the Ocean rocked her like a mother would a child. Sleepily, she watched over The High Prince in case he asked for food, water, or medicine, but he seemed to be dreaming, eyes flickering under their lids. Many of his bandages had been removed or changed, and save for the bandages, his chest was bare.

The scribe felt her cheeks grow hot.

She had taken the furs off of him only temporarily, as he had just experienced a bad fever, but embarrassingly, she found herself staring too long at his body.

Torran's body was lean, with a characteristic sheen that was distinctive, but hard to describe. His six-pack appeared faintly when he breathed, and his jawline was sharp and angular. At the same time, his muscles were quite full, with big biceps, wide, long back muscles, and large shoulders.

He really has the perfect body...

Scarolette slapped her cheeks, forcing herself to be serious and professional. Putting away any unbecoming thoughts, she drew the covers over Torran again, and focused on gratitude.

The High Prince was steadily improving, and although he still couldn't walk easily, many of his broken bones had healed, or close to it.

He'll be fine. I should just go downstairs and sleep.

Scarolette was about to get up to leave when the wind picked up out of nowhere, shaking the boat and causing her to nearly fall out of her chair. The weather had been good all day, without a cloud in sight, but the moon quickly fell behind dark grey clouds, and it suddenly began to pour.

Scarolette planted her feet to steady herself and sat back down, deciding to wait until the rain had stopped. For a few minutes, things remained fairly peaceful, and the sound of the rain was calming. She began to feel sleepy again, dreaming of peace and relaxation at the end of a long and terrible war. She hoped that chaos would soon come to an end, that soon they would arrive safely in Starspire.

But it was not to be.

There was mind-shattering noise.

A bolt of lightning had split the mainmast.

Scarolette's eyes darted over to the cabin's small window. She watched in horror as the mast teetered and fell towards them.

Not knowing what came over her, she, who had been sleepy, sprung into action, throwing all her weight into The High Prince and shoving him off the bed as the mast crashed through the ceiling.

She pulled back partially, but it was too late. The burning pole fell on her left arm, shattering it instantly and pinning her to the mattress, not quite making it through the cabin walls, but setting the mattress aflame.

Torran got up, stupefied, only to see her standing there, screaming, as the fire spread across the shredded thing that had been her forearm and began to crawl up her blouse. Fumbling, he grabbed the sword under the bed, threw off the sheath, and, with hobbling step, chopped off her hand, picking her up with a grunt and carrying her as the fire spread further.

His bandages caught fire, the stump of her arm forcibly cauterized as she thrashed, but he held her tight.

Limping as fast as he could, Torran took Scarolette into the shivering rain and they were extinguished, but the scribe had fallen into a deep shock. She was yelling, yowling.

She looked at her arm, half gone. It was burned and flaky, large red pustules already forming as blood oozed. She couldn't believe what she saw.

It felt surreal.

Scarolette felt woozy, but she didn't fall unconscious. She couldn't, too racked with pain to even think, and even the adrenaline coursing through her veins wasn't enough to numb it.

In a craze, she beat at the Prince's chest with her remaining hand, and he took it.

They had saved each other, but she had paid a terrible price for him while he had been left largely unscathed, and he knew it too.

Scarolette doubled over, sobbing as he hugged her, but he just held her close as the rain poured down his face.

Once the pain had subsided slightly, The High Prince lay her gently down on the soothing, wet planks and called for the battle-medic, but all she could think about was that her arm was gone.

She had lost her beauty; she could no longer write.

It was the end.

Torran continued to call for help, but the sailors were too busy to help, furiously hacking away at the mast with axes before it tipped the boat over. Scarolette didn't hear much after that. All she heard was the sound of wood fracturing bone, the stinging of fiery tongues, like relentless, orange wasps.

She didn't notice as Torran ran down to the crew's quarters to get the battle-medic. She didn't notice as her eyes changed from emerald green to an even more vibrant shade, the blood ceasing to flow from the stump of her arm.

The rain was pounding, then, and, as her head lolled to the side, she realized how high the waves had become.

This... This is bad! We're sailing across God's Anvil!

Quick—somebody help me!

Please!

After what seemed like an eternity, Torran came back with the battle-medic. They moved to pick her up, but the ship lurched violently and the man was thrown off balance, flying into The High Prince and knocking him down as a foaming wave washed over the deck, taking Scarolette, along with the mast and many of the sailors.

Scarolette choked on seawater as she sank under the swell, her dress dragging her down towards the dark depths. She pushed against the current hopelessly, kicking as much as she could, but it was no use. She didn't even know which way was up.

To the scribe's great relief, a strong arm found her, and she surfaced. It was one of the sailors.

"Get to the ropes!" he sputtered, pointing to the fishing nets on the side of the ship. She wanted to ask him why he didn't swim over as well, but it seemed like he was barely staying afloat himself.

Scarolette swam over to the ropes just as another swell hit them, taking the sailor under and slamming her against the boat. She grabbed the nets, her lifeline, and held on desperately until, blessedly, the swell passed.

To her terror, the sailor did not resurface, and, just as she had gotten to safety, a second bolt came down, deafening her.

The ship broke in half, the lightning hitting its intended target that time. A piece of wood hit Scarolette in the face, entangling her in nets and knocking her out, the vessel blown apart.

Torran

Torran didn't see.

He didn't see the clouds converge above The Sea Star, Unified by a Power that was entire planets away. He didn't see the fragments of a once glorious whole float along with the clouds and begin to swirl above, gathered for a singular purpose.

He saw a flash. It was almost beyond perception.

Then he heard a loud *zap*, his vision becoming fuzzy. The water steamed off his eyes as current beyond comprehension surged through him.

And then, he was writhing. Roiling. Unspeakable pain, his whole body lit by arcing current.

The pain was immense, hitting him in waves. His God had brought it upon him, damned him at his own behest. Death itself had slapped him, breaking the ship in two with twisted hands: malign fingers of yellow, blue, and white.

He couldn't even cry out as he was cast into the drink, as the waves entered his open wounds, seeping into every fiber of his being.

He couldn't tell if he was facing the surface or the bottom, searching wildly in the stinging murk. The water entered his mouth, his nose.

I can't breathe.

I can't breathe!

And then, Torran's heart stopped.

He was cast downwards by a wave, drifting towards the pale seabed, his face white.

Bubbles passed unaccosted from his lips...

For a few minutes, it seemed that he had been left to die alone, but finally, The Power noticed him. He was blessed by The Power of Order, that ruthless Spirit, the blue of his eyes swept away and replaced by a color much more striking. The Primordial Spirit finally recognized his strength, his sacrifice.

His body stiffened as he changed, momentary paralysis.

And then he could breathe again; he could move again, his injuries healed. For from the agony, was born something supernatural, an old, capricious magic bonding with him, the Power promised to him. It filled in the missing piece of his soul, fusing with it and then pervading it.

It was the Power to keep going. To survive. To fight. The Power to choose a path, achieve a destiny unlike any other.

Torran began to swim back to the surface, the water pushing him upwards like a helping hand. His brilliant eyes beamed through the salt, sparks jumping from his skin.

The High Prince came up disoriented. He treaded water with all his strength and took in a deep breath.

Torran's eyes flashed.

And, as if obeying their master who had had enough, the clouds dispersed. The seas calmed, and the thunder quieted. Riize was full, its dusty, cobalt face reflecting blue light onto the tremulous waters.

The High Prince laughed in sheer relief, but his heart sank when he saw that he was alone.

His relief disappeared.

You... You liar! Not a single one of my men! You didn't even spare a single one of my men!

And you... You even took Scarolette! You took her!

You took her from me! You took he–

"Torran!"

Torran started. The cry was faint, but he had heard it.

"Torran!"

Torran heard it more clearly that time. He scanned the wreckage, and, elated, saw that Scarolette was alive after all, hanging on to a piece of the ship's bow, covered in netting. His relief returned, but it soured again when he saw what was left of her arm. Remorse hit him harder than the lightning and brought him far lower.

Trembling, he swallowed it, and swam over to join her, thankful that at least one person had survived, that Scarolette had survived.

He swam over as fast as he could, pulling his upper body onto the wreckage and slumping over, exhausted.

He looked at Scarolette's face, and went to speak.

She looked up with eyes as red as his.

CHAPTER IV

Viktor

Viktor watched the procession.

Armor clattered as The Imperial Army descended on a broken city. Starving women and children stood by sullenly as haughty, Astrian soldiers strode in on their slender horses, silken tails swatting away bloodthirsty ashbugs. They were led by The High Sword, Astria's highest military official.

The High Sword dismounted, handing off the reins to his steed, and approached.

Viktor's mother stepped forward to meet him, bowing, her red dress sliding across sundered dirt. They were surrendering the city; there was no other choice in light of such numbers. The Imperial envoy stretched all the way down The Red Road, at least ten thousand strong.

The High Sword was a placid, grey sort of man, his straight, grey hair, cut short. He wore a light blue uniform, so well-starched that it was a wonder he could move, but although his clothes were completely free of wrinkles, his face was tan and creased. He walked with his lips pursed in a thin, purplish-white line, as if everything in the world displeased him.

"High Sword, please accept our surrender and my apology on behalf of The Eridion Dynasty. My husband's love for his country went too far, leading to disaster. We once again swear our loyalty to his Grace, The High Emperor Agravius Xandromen, and hope for peace between our people after this long and terrible war."

Viktor could tell that The High Sword didn't quite buy it, but there was nothing to be done. Indeed, he would be an utter fool to believe the words of someone so close to Falin Eridion, a master of treachery, and the man was intelligent.

Still, he is quite a fool...

"Queen Dowager. The High Throne accepts your surrender. Hemia is once more a territory of the High Empire. You and your son shall be placed under house arrest for the time being until a new monarch is elected. If you hope for his Grace's mercy, I suggest that you do not resist this transition."

The High Sword motioned to his forces, who were carting food over to the starving populace. This time, aid would be accepted and not burned.

"Alright—enough of the niceties. Let's feed these people."

Viktor didn't reach for the food and water, though his stomach growled and his throat was parched. He could feel his ribs pressing through his skin, but he ignored his hunger. Instead, he held on tight to the fire within, the urge to cry out in defiance. That was more important than some animal's desire to eat.

As soldiers came to take him and his mother into custody, the young Prince locked eyes with The High Sword. He would not bow as he had before. He would finish what his father started.

But, for the time being, he would suppress the hatred within; he would play nice.

At least, until the assassin proved his worth...

Everything was going according to plan.

Amdryaan

Amdryaan had been thrown into the prison caves.

The Frosslar threw only their most hated enemies and the most repulsive criminals into the prison caves, which were more of a means of execution than a jail. A tunnel had been carved into an iceberg and hollowed out into a dozen cells: caves with wide, circular openings, white-blue ice frozen with blood, urine, and excrement. The floors were solid—the only obstacle between himself and freedom, a set of gated, iron bars covered in seal fat to prevent rust and any attempts at filing them.

The cold was ferocious, the tunnel purposefully positioned against the wind.

The wicked wind howled through the cave system's main entrance and found its way into every cell. The tribesman could taste sea spray on that wind, freedom so close, yet so far, and the white daylight poured in through the cave mouth, lighting the ice to a bright blue that resembled glass, which he would have found beautiful, if he wasn't half dead and shivering.

Eladon, the guard keeping watch over his cell, was an ugly, spiteful man whose muscles bulged unflatteringly from his oiled, elephant seal jerkin. The ice giant's crooked nose and uneven jaw were the only things that distracted Amdryaan from his captor's loud and abrasive voice as he was given his daily beating.

Amdryaan stood, his legs chained and his ankles chafed by manacles, and braced himself for the next hit. The guard's cold fist met his face with a *crack*, and sticky blood warmed his frozen face, though he remained standing. He looked up at the man cruelly jeering at him, but said nothing. Still unsatisfied, Eladon spat on him, the freezing spit encrusting Amdryaan's bloodied face and breaking with a second punch.

Amdryaan fell to the cavern floor with a groan, the guard chuckling as he closed the hard, iron bars and locked them, leaving to take his meal break.

Amdryaan spat out a tooth, coughing. He had lost all feeling of pain a while back. All he felt was an intense burning.

He curled up into a ball, trying to keep warm, but the cell was cold, the floor covered in a solid layer of his own sludge. Still, it was all he could do, and all he had been doing. His furs and shoes had been taken from him days ago, although The Frosslar had left him his clothing so he didn't die too quickly.

Against his better judgement, he had already drunk his urine out of thirst, and he knew his time would soon be up. It was just a matter of waiting, and all he could do was sit there, waiting. The frostbite had taken two of the fingers on his left hand and three toes across his feet. He had eaten them when they fell off. He knew he could live longer if he ate some of his living flesh, but he had already lost so much weight that there was little meat left.

He wouldn't do it again even if he had the strength, though; he couldn't stomach the idea.

Then again, he had survived quite long, especially in such extreme temperatures. He had survived out of spite, but he knew that the longer he survived, the more satisfaction Voreus derived from his pain.

Nevertheless, Amdryaan held on to his conviction. He would fight the Frosslar till he drew his last breath and his spirit left him, till he was just a mummified corpse.

For Wiola. For his dead mother and father. He would never give in, even if it meant extending his suffering, making the guard beat him one more time.

He promised himself, then and there, that he wouldn't give in.

Something heard that wretched promise.

Amdryaan felt warmth again. Not the neural itch of dying nerves, but true warmth.

His eyes changed shade, no longer brown, though he was none the wiser.

Delirious, he watched as the flesh of his remaining fingers returned to its normal pallor, the same with his toes. He inspected his hands, flexing them. They moved easily, the dryness healing as flaking scales of skin fused back together and the blood receded from his extremities.

Then he felt some resistance in his right hand.

It was as if he was holding something malleable in his newly healed palm, as if there was

some sort of fluid around him. The tribesman sat there, bewildered, his hand trembling.

He made a fist, and felt like he was squeezing something.

And then, the cell door crumpled.

Amdryaan thought he was hallucinating.

Fortunately for him, he wasn't.

He was free.

Leafsong

The carriage was uncomfortable, for all its plush interior. The pink, silk pillows, which were embroidered with intricate, weaving patterns, were not enough to cushion the hard, oaken seats.

But that wasn't the reason she was uncomfortable. She couldn't be comfortable after what had happened.

How can I relax? Inesa is dead.

Leafsong sat across from her mother.

The Baroness was a mild-looking Ronari woman with sad, blue eyes, and hair that was fixed in a bun. Leafsong had always admired her mother for her quiet grace and simple beauty, but the woman's face wasn't the usual picture of warmth and strength. She stared blankly out the open window as the peeling, green shutters swayed, the boards creaked, and the walls shifted. Occasionally, they would hit a pothole, which rocked the whole carriage and jostled them both, but The Baroness would eventually go back to staring, heartbroken and forlorn, and Leafsong remained silent.

She understood. Her sister had died a horrible death; an earthquake had hit the town, brought about by the arrival of a mysterious and terrifying figure. Her father had stayed behind to organize a response, sending them away to the family's woodland retreat to ensure her and her mother's safety, but she had no idea what he planned to do against something like that. What could one do against sorcery that made buildings crumble? Was there more to the story? Was the town in danger? Was her family being threatened, specifically? Leafsong didn't know. All she knew was that The Baron had stayed behind, unable to grieve, and possibly putting his life in danger.

Little sis, I miss you so much. I wish... I wish you were still alive.

And Father... Why aren't you with us, Father? Why aren't you here?

Leafsong was sure that her mother was preoccupied by similar thoughts.

Trying to comfort her as much as herself, Leafsong took her mother's hand, squeezing it. The Baroness gave Leafsong a small smile, reassuring her, but it was forced. Her lips were terse, and her hand trembled.

Leafsong steadied it, taking the woman's other hand. There was no need to speak. Looking into each other's eyes, it was clear that they shared the same grief, the same worries and questions. They sat that way for a long time.

At some point, the pair finally fell asleep, physically and emotionally exhausted from the ordeal of the past few days. Though The Baroness surely dreamt of better times, Leafsong was not allowed to dream. Instead, she was given another vision.

Leafsong found herself walking across soft loam. She watched as fireflies fluttered in a deep, murky wood. Like myriad, tiny candles, a sea of wondrous dancing, they circled around a strange, black tree at the center of a dark forest, covered in long, dripping spines. It grew tall in a place where no light shone, corrupting its surroundings.

What she saw, then, was not just a vision.

It was a premonition.

Jhett

Jhett reclined on a sandy beach, drinking from a coconut.

Miraculously, he had survived the destruction of the merchant ship, the waves carrying

him to a small island that he presumed was somewhere near The Stareye Isthmus. His skin was dry, and he had been badly sunburned, but all things considered, he was very lucky. He had found no survivors, but honestly, part of him was glad, and hoped that he wouldn't.

He was finally free.

Jhett sighed with contentment, appreciating a quiet moment after countless, unbreaking hours at the oar.

The teal-blue waters lapped at the colorless sand, carrying more and more of it into the Sea and burying razor clams under a grainy, white blanket. Large, black pumice stones dotted the beach, marine iguanas sunbathing on the moss-covered, holey boulders. Small fish darted through the water, camouflaged by their dull, beige-colored scales, and patches of seaweed undulated beneath the surface, hiding secrets within. Coconut palms swayed with the wind, their blade-like leaves rustling in the dry heat, and the smell of salt was pervasive.

Jhett looked at the sky, taking a deep, sumptuous breath in. Clean air, after so long... He looked up at a sky that was a bright and clear blue, puffy cumulus clouds taking their sweet time as they passed.

I feel like one of Those Who Came Ashore, he mused. The events of the past few days had been very similar to the Creation of mankind as described by his religion, Sulhábah.

Was this how they felt when they shed their tails? He wondered, staring off into the horizon.

The Sulhabáni believed that the people of Avenshra came from the ocean, where they had lived for generations in The Underwater Gardens planted by their god, Madevf. They swam and breathed like fish, for they were not human yet, and that was how they were meant to live. Every animal had its own dominion, and they had much to be thankful for, but it was a tiresome life, always at the mercy of the currents.

One day, an island appeared in the middle of the sea. On that island, sat a man dressed in colorful feathers and multicolored beads. Curious, the fish-men approached the beach, and the man called out to them. Knowing that they wished to rise out of the sea, he offered them a deal. If they gave him the scales from their tails, he would give them legs. Suspicious but exhausted, the mermen took the deal, pulling out their scales. They threw them to the man and swam towards the beach, only to find that the man hadn't been sitting on an island at all, but the back of a giant turtle. Horrified, they tried to get away, but without their scales, they were too slow, and one by one, they were swallowed up.

As they were eaten, the man laughed, revealing himself to be Fvedam, Madevf's evil twin. The god abandoned his beads and feathers and took on his true, monstrous form: a snake without scales, ascending to the heavens with his newfound treasure. When Madevf saw his brother covered in shimmering scales, he immediately realized what had happened.

Enraged, he hacked Fvedam to pieces with a giant knife, and wherever the pieces fell, an island sprung up from the sea. Defeated, but not dead, the god went on to sleep beneath the waves, his monstrous servants still prowling Avenshra.

His anger sated, Madevf then descended from his place on high and found his brother's turtle. With godly strength, he flipped it over and cut open its stomach, saving the fish-men, who were terrified, but still alive. Knowing that they couldn't survive without their scales, he took pity on his creations, giving them legs. Then, he hollowed out the turtle's shell and filled it with sand, turning it into the largest island of them all: The Wildlands.

Jhett's island was small, and it had taken him only a day to fully explore. In essence, it was just a cluster of palms, marooned on a sheet of volcanic rock.

There were a few seabirds that took residence in the treetops, and he had seen some crabs crawl up the trees to break open coconuts and eat them, but apart from the wildlife, it was uninhabited.

Thankfully, the island had everything he really needed to live, and he had set up a small hut near the beach using the piece of the ship he had washed ashore on and whatever driftwood came his way: a small, triangular structure whose holes were covered with layers of palm leaves. It wasn't very strong, but it was fairly spacious, and it kept the sun off his neck and the rain off his head—or at least, most of it.

I should search for more driftwood. Maybe I can fill in some of the gaps. Besides, there's nothing much to do. I have to think of a plan to get off this island, but... I'm so tired. And truthfully, I'm not sure if... No. I must get off this island... I should do something useful.

Jhett began his daily search of the shore, looking for any incoming pieces of the shipwreck or supplies he could use. He didn't want to stay stuck on the island forever, but there was also no way to know when someone might pass by. Several pieces of the ship continued to wash up, but eerily, none of the other sailors.

Jhett feared they had been eaten, eaten by that nightmare from the deep.

I'm so lucky I survived. I'm so lucky to have washed up on this island.

I have to try and make a home of this place, even if it's only for a short time. I can't stay here forever, but if I can survive this, if I don't lose hope and get rescued, maybe I can find my family.

I have to find them...

Something in his mind wondered if he really needed to be rescued, but the husband, the father in him, was stalwart.

I need to see their faces again, so I can remember them. I can't forget who I am. I have to keep searching.

After about an hour of searching, Jhett had collected several planks of wood, untangling them from dried seaweed and pulling them out of wet sand. Just as the sun began to set, and Jhett was about to return to his shelter, he caught sight of something in the corner of his eye. A shadow was coming towards the beach, bobbing up and down with the waves.

Jhett watched in amazement as a large wave, more powerful than the others, carried a fragment of another shipwreck to shore. Clinging to nets covering what looked to be a piece of hull, were two Luzians, a blonde-haired man and a red-headed woman. By their clothes, they appeared to be nobles, but he couldn't say for sure.

Fvedam's feathers! Victims of a different wreck!

Jhett ran over to the scene, and, with some effort, pulled the makeshift lifeboat inland. The pair had tied themselves to the ropes to avoid being swept away, making it difficult, but he managed, dragging them slightly. Tying themselves had been a smart move, as they had lost consciousness, but they looked pale, and their skin was white and soft.

Jhett checked to see if they were breathing.

They were, but only faintly, water spilling from the woman's lips. Something was strange about her, and he soon realized that she was missing an arm. The wound looked new, but it seemed to have been treated. He didn't take the time to think about it.

The tribesman moved hurriedly to untie them, but then he stopped, a hesitation that disgusted him in its selfishness getting the better of him.

They're Luzians—nobles, just like the merchants. What if they try and sell me back into slavery?! If they're Astrians, maybe they wouldn't do that, but if they're from Qeonia... I can't take that risk. I have to get out here! I have to hide! But where?! This island is so small! Still, I must hide; I must-

Jhett's chest grew tight. His teeth clenched.

He paced, unsure what to do.

I've finally been freed, survived an attack by a monster that shouldn't exist! And this island, it's- It's so peaceful...

Jhett stood back up, his fists balled, still unsure what the right move to make was. He was planning on walking away and leaving the Luzians to their fate, but he turned, his conscience getting the better of him. He remembered The Law of Madevf, The Aerhauc Tribe's code of honor.

They'll die if I leave them here. They're barely breathing.

The Law of Madevf states that all wars begin and end on the battlefield. The merchants were evil, and they deserved punishment. If this man and this woman are evil, if they have enslaved my people, then they deserve punishment. But until I know their soul to be good or evil, I cannot leave them to die. They came from the sea, just like The Aerhauc. Madevf has been good to me. Now he sends me a test that I can't afford to fail.

Jhett untied the pair, turning them over. He was going to try and resuscitate the woman when her companion woke up, choking. Gurgling, he threw up seawater in saline fountains.

He looked at Jhett, disoriented, and then at the woman. Seeing her pale and unmoving body, the man's eyes flew open wide.

He pushed past Jhett, and, visibly unsure, but hesitating not even for a moment, he began to try and resuscitate her, pressing down on her chest, again and again. Then he gave her the kiss of life, breathing air into her lungs, but she wouldn't rise.

He did it again, turning her over and patting her strongly on the back. Still, she would not rise.

The man despaired, starting to press down again, Jhett just watching, frozen.

Slowly realizing that it was futile, his eyes flashed with fear. He pushed down as hard as he could, pounding on her chest again and again. He was desperate not to lose her.

Jhett felt guilty that he had hesitated, sympathy for the man.

I see how much you care about her, but my friend, she is already dead. I also know what it's like to lose someone. It hurts so much! But there is nothing you can do...

Let her rest in peace–

Jhett started when the man's eyes flickered red. They glowed.

Suddenly, there was a *zap*, a puff of smoke.

And the woman was revived with a jolt.

Amdryaan

Amdryaan swerved, running through the slippery tunnels. He was running for the exit.

Frosslar guards stood in his way, wearing enchanted hematite splint mail and carrying enchanted hematite swords, but he didn't stop. Not fully in control, but able to roughly direct his burgeoning powers, he took hold of the magnetic fields surrounding their weapons and armor, and, with a wave of his arms, he unbalanced them, sending them stumbling in all directions. One ice giant nearly ran into him, but he sidestepped and continued running.

A group of four tried to block the tunnel exit, tall and menacing, but in their eyes, was a fear that was all too human.

No one had ever been afraid of Amdryaan, but at that moment, he was more than human. His eyes were red hyphemas, his hands, instruments of Avenshra's core.

He raised those hands, and pushed.

The Frosslar cried out as the scales on their armored chests were blasted back and they were thrown into the air, the tribesman squeezing and deforming ferrous atmospheres like wax. They fell to the ground, crushed, brought to heel by his mysterious new sorcery.

Amdryaan stooped to grab one of the fallen weapons, picking up an enchanted hematite dagger, and kept going. Though small for an ice giant, the weapon was as big as a short sword for a Native. Amdryaan was not a warrior, but it would be foolish not to grab something to defend himself.

Two more turns, and Amdryaan sped out of the prison caves. He quickly skidded to a halt, finding himself standing at the edge of The Weeping Ravine, a crack in the tundra that was fifty feet deep, forming a channel for The Sea of Glass. The Frosslar's icebreakers were moored to the Ravine by long ropes, slick, and coated in frozen spray.

The blue-white ice cliffs smoked and cracked, wind whistling through the gaps. The air was odorless, and the sky was colorless, a blank, white-grey tarp thrown over the entire world, hiding the mysteries beyond. The Sea below was a deep, sapphire blue, equally opaque.

Amdryaan shielded his eyes from the sun, searching for a way down, but with alarm, he noticed that the elevator system that allowed access to the boats was on the other side of the cliffs, and he could hear more guards coming for him.

It was snowing lightly, and sun dogs surrounded Goddess' ever-present eye, luminous and iridescent. She was watching him, looking to see what choice he would make now that he was free. Would he immediately run to rescue his sister and the others? Or would he run away, never to return?

I can feel that these powers are waning...

I can't rescue Wiola as I am now, but I would never run away and leave her, and I can't abandon my people, even if they rejected me. I may be weak, but I'm still the son of Kanis Winterlove, Fiveclan Chief. I need to get out of The Ice Fields and ask for help from The High Empire. If they help, I'm sure we can fight back.

The guards were close, then, and Amdryaan didn't hear any clinking noises. Adapting, the ice giants had ditched their armor and weapons, and they would definitely apprehend him if he didn't make a decision. Luckily, the ships below were unattended.

It was his chance and he took it. Amdryaan jumped, using the sword's handle to zipline down one of the ropes in an attempt to hijack one of the ships.

Gathering too much speed, he swung off of the rope and landed on board with a crash, breaking planks and bruising bones, but his injuries were quickly healed by the energy within him.

Fearing pursuit, he swiftly cut the rope holding the ship to the Ravine walls and scrambled to hoist the sails, using the last of his powers to break the chain that held the anchor.

Fortuitously, the winds were blowing in his favor, and the ship began to move.

The Frosslar shouted up on the cliffs, unable to pursue, and one of them threw their sword, but missed, hitting the water next to the ship with a *splash*.

Amdryaan hurried below deck.

I will come back; I promise. I'll bring help.

He would return for his sister, the Clans, and his revenge. But first, he had to save

himself.

Oscure

Oscure gasped awake. On his sixth, and smallest finger, was a black ring, veined with red.

He had fought against Naraklar, the perversion of sacrifice, and for that, he had won a prize.

The Tribe King slid out of his bed and stood, scratched by straw. Impressively tall and muscular, even for a Nolite, he was a boulder of a man, nearly seven feet tall. His hair was short and nappy, cut close to his head, and his eyes were a light sand-brown, with jet-black scleras. His skin was the same, jet-black color, but it had a faint, bluish luster to it, and bumpy, spiral scar-tattoos wrapped around his defined shoulders. With a nose that was large, flat, and flared, he didn't necessarily match the conventional definition of handsomeness, but he had a strong jawline and a good physique, and his cool gaze was almost chilling in its arrest. Fully integrated, The Soulheart sat embedded in his chest, thick, root-like scars spreading across his pecs and away from the translucent, white gem, souls trapped within as a mass of swirling, red light.

No longer scored with wounds, Oscure was finally fully healed; he could feel it. Only his heart remained wounded, but it was not yet time to grieve. It was time to move on from his own healing, and heal Ritsi, complete his mission.

He only hoped she had endured the wait.

Exiting his Hut, Oscure found not The Aerhauc Settlement, but smoke and darkness. He wasn't dreaming, the sand too real beneath his feet to be an illusion, and Narklar wasn't in control. It was as if the Hut itself was shrouded in a dark cloud, hiding his sleeping body while he recovered. Squinting, he waved his hand through the smoke and the sheepish cloud left the area. The darkness dispersed, or rather, was filled again, light left to travel, and not diverted through the ether.

The Tribe King was immediately met with startled looks from Aerhauc faces.

"Tribe King!" they cried, surprised and relieved.

"Tribe King! You're awake!" Gombobo exclaimed, joyful, his eyes lighting up.

"What was that cloud?" Elder Guahi questioned, unsettled. She held her woolen shawl tight against her chest, gnarled fingers in a white-knuckled grip.

"Kilanjara—we must get Kilanjara over here," Hatli insisted, hurrying off to find The Tribe Queen.

"Your Majesty, what's that thing in your chest?" inquired Fēfá, Hatli's little boy.

"Your Majesty—Mozamic... I'm very sorry," Jéral uttered, offering his condolences. He placed a comforting hand on The Tribe King's shoulder.

Patting Jeral's hand, Oscure's voice quietly cut through all the questions and comments. He would answer them, explain to them, but first, he had to take care of the emergency that led to everything.

"Ritsi—where can I find her?" he asked. His voice had a wist to it, like silver.

After a brief uncertainty, Jéral's father, Ugon, raised a trembling arm, and pointed to Elder Falum's dwelling, breathing heavily through missing teeth.

"I see," Oscure remarked. He nodded to the old man in thanks and walked over to the wood-and-straw cabana, rapping his knuckles on the door frame.

The door opened abruptly, spices hitting Oscure's nose.

"Oscure?" Elder Falum cocked her head, surprised. Behind her, Ritsi was writhing in a sickbed.

"How is she?" Oscure asked, taking no note of the breach in decorum. The Elder was his great-aunt, and she had helped raise him. Formalities were unnecessary.

"Has the infection spread?" he probed, apprehensive.

"Not yet, but it will soon if we don't stop it," the old woman answered soberly. "You have the Shadowheart; I see it in your chest. Let us hope that it does what the legends say it does. Hurry; go heal her."

The monarch ducked, entering the hut, and went over to Ritsi's side. He took her hand, holding it so that she didn't feel alone in her pain.

The cut in her leg was long and wide, white, bacterial film assailed, but undefeated by thick, green tincture. The resulting mix smelled like mint, pepper, and rotten eggs.

Carefully, the Elder wiped away the paste with a clean rag, exposing the full severity of the injury. The pestilence had eaten away at the little girl's flesh, and blood poisoning was about to set in.

Shakily, Oscure placed his hand on the cut, pressing down. The girl thrashed, but he maintained pressure.

Closing his eyes, The Tribe King focused on the crystal that had replaced his sternum, seeking to connect with it. He needed to draw Lifeblood from it, extend it through his hand and make an open system.

Mozamic, the souls of his ancestors, would work through him to save her. They had to.

Oscure concentrated more, but the girl was just crying. Nothing seemed to change.

Please open! he begged his chest, desperate. *Let me save her!*

Mozamic, help me complete our mission!

The Nolite King felt Naraklar's apathy and disdain pooling in the back of his head, the demon completely indifferent to his plight. But he also felt the warmth and life of his blood-brother, Mozamic, the smiling warrior answering his friend's call. Unembittered, he would heal the girl and complete the mission that had killed him, the Aerhauc's best.

With a glare like the firelight, a tendril of Lifeblood extended from Oscure's palm, ensnaring the life force of the lesser beings that tormented the girl and drawing it into The Shadowheart.

The living film deadened, greyed—sepsis averted. Elder Falum scraped the plaque away as quickly as she could, and, unlike before, it showed no adherence. It came off, gooey secretions rolling into tiny balls of slime.

The wound now sterile, the medicine woman went to work closing the wound with needle and thread, comforting her patient the entire time.

A funeral would be held in The Aerhauc Settlement, but it would not be for this young girl.

Konell

Konell sat in a nondescript room with smooth, grey walls. No sound could be heard.

With no windows and only one, grey door, it was as if a cube had been cut into the bedrock of Qeonia and furnished with a single chair.

The air had a heaviness to it, and it reeked of stale blood. Perhaps it was the fact that others had been tortured there, some essence left behind by the dead that haunted all the poor souls who sat in that rickety, wooden chair...

At the moment, Konell found himself in that chair. His mask lay shattered on the ground, his disguise gone.

Konell Revangel was a vicious young man with long, black hair that reached his shoulders and a set of icy, blue eyes. In those eyes, was a cold sort of venom, a venom that belonged to everyone but his younger sister. He had been caught days ago, and the torture was finally taking its toll.

It was so painful.

Konell's torturer was a big, brutish man with a head of short, dry, black hair and a set of fervid, black eyes resembling those of a wild boar. He wore a sweat-stained, short-sleeved shirt made of bleached cotton, and a dirty, blood-stained, white apron over a beer belly and brown, cotton pants. Little details, such as whether the blood on the man's apron was his own or someone else's, had escaped Konell's comprehension hours ago. All that mattered to Konell after hours of agony, was what the torturer was holding in his hands at the moment, when the object held would inevitably enter his flesh and inflict pain upon him. At that moment, the torturer was holding a small, steel knife with a walnut handle.

He took Konell by the hair, lifting his head up, and asked the same, tired question he had been asking since the day the assassin had been captured.

"Who hired you to kill The Silvercat?!"

The man's warm breath reeked of onion, Konell's nose wrinkling in disgust.

Annoyed by his continued silence, the torturer took pliers and ripped out a third fingernail, Konell's hand tied to the chair with rope. Konell screamed, the pulpy flesh of his nail bed exposed, blood dripping onto the already bloody floor.

The man slapped him.

Konell simply sat there, unable and unwilling to speak. He was trembling.

I will not crack! I will not crack!

The assassin steadied himself, his breathing irregular.

"Was that supposed to hurt?" he asked slowly, his voice hoarse. He was doing everything he could not to break down. He had to get out.

I can't die here. I have to fulfill my contract and save Amara. I can't die here...
Where? Here? This is nothing...

I must survive. I must escape.

But how?

The torturer removed another fingernail, slapping him again. Blood began to pool in Konell's mouth, giving him an idea.

Oh... I see, now.

Konell lost consciousness.

The hot, humid tavern stank of sweat and grease, and the food smelled bad as well. Round, rotting, wooden tables marinated in gaseous sweat, people sitting on creaking stools that wobbled on the uneven, dirt floor. Broken bottles and spilled beer made the narrow pathways between the tables treacherous to move through, gruff barmaids sweating in their corsets as they brought around perspiring, metal tankards of beer, slamming them down onto creased playing cards and half-naked chicken bones. The whole place was filled with raucous noise, the barmaids yelling out to the tavern-keeper to pour more ale.

The people there didn't mind the conditions. Sitting at those rotting tables were men, women, and children in tattered rags and scuffed-up leather, spending what little money they had made at their jobs as sewage cleaners, chimney-sweeps and street cleaners on ale and the worst parts of spoiled chicken. Some didn't own shoes, but bought beer anyway. Some spent their money on beer and left their kids to starve, like Konell's family. Some were known criminals, people whose morals were loose and whose change was looser. All were forgotten or ignored by their country and The High Empire— the poor and the outcast.

It was pouring outside, the rain falling heavily against the shingles, water spilling through holes in the wooden ceiling and dripping unseen into people's food and cups.

Konell's father, if he indeed could be called a father, was a fat, balding man who only had half of his short, brown hair and less than half of the normal number of teeth. Those few teeth that remained were riddled with cavities, grey-brown and rotting, framed by thin patches of uneven stubble. His face was always ruddy from drink, and ale was always on his breath, his eyes alight with what only a sick man would call humor.

Konell's parents wore no wedding bands; those were for the nobility. His father, Spitz, spent all his money on beer, and his pockets were empty, but nevertheless, he wore a smooth, black ring, set with a tiny piece of purple stone. He had found it in a gutter a few weeks earlier, and thought it suited him. In the weeks since, he had taken to twisting it around his finger whenever he was thinking, which took him far longer than the average man, for he was quite stupid.

"Another cup!" Konell's mother cried, raising her mug of beer, her fat face red with drunkenness and bearing an uncanny resemblance to his equally drunk father's, though she might have been pretty once, a long time ago. She had curled her shoulder-length blonde hair before they left home, as if a pub gathering was an upscale event, and she wore a low cut, stained, bleached cotton dress that squeezed her bosom into a squarish lump that did her already unattractive figure no favors. She giggled like a little girl, though nothing had been said that was particularly funny, and her blue eyes shone with a veneer of jubilance and hilarity that was strongly divorced from the situation around her, including her hungry, emaciated children.

Their friend Stilton laughed, his long, shoulder-length, dark brown hair greasy and matted against his oily face. He was thin and gangly, with the face of a ferret and the eyes of a rat. Unlike many of the denizens of Beggar's Alley, he had all of his teeth, but they were stained yellow from smoke.

"Another cup!" Konell's mother cried out again. She was totally drunk.

"Yeah, another cup!" his father repeated.

"You ain't got the money, Spitz," chided the fat, toothless barmaid, her beer-stained white corset strangling her. She looked a little like Konell's mother, with long, blonde hair and pale blue eyes, but she had more masculine features, and she was taller and broader than most of the men in the pub.

"Aw come on, I'm a regular," the gutter cleaner whined.

"A regular?" laughed the barmaid, snatching the mug out of his father's hands. "What are you talking about?"

Konell sat hunched over in his chair, watching as they bickered. His stomach growled, his bones pressing through his skin, and his face sunken around the beady eyes of a carrion crow.

"Does this look like an inn to ya?" the barmaid spat. "There's a brothel right next door! This is Beggar's Alley, not King's Corner!"

No more beer.

That means no more money. And no more food...

Konell's father scratched his fat, stubbled jaw, not wanting to leave. He thought hard on how to get more beer, but it was eluding him. He took off the ring and turned it around in his hands, weighing its value. He had polished it a million times, constantly staring at the gemstone at its center, but apparently, at that moment, a beer suited him better.

"Hey Stilton, I'll trade you this ring for a beer," he said, chuckling.

"What's that? A cockring some slut shat out? I'd rather have another beer myself," Stilton sneered.

Frowning, his father went through his pockets, looking for money that wasn't there. The barmaid bustled away, tired of Spitz' loitering.

The gutter cleaner sat back in his chair for a moment, twisting the ring, and then leaned back over the table again. His eyes lit up with a truly sickening light.

"Hey Stilton. You can take my daughter for a ride if you give me six feathers' coin," his father sniggered. "She's young and fresh. What do you say? Do your pal a favor?"

Konell's eyes narrowed. His blood ran cold.

His father was low, but he had never imagined that he would sell his own daughter for drinking money. The more he thought about it, however, the less surprised he was, and the angrier he got. Any shred of love he had for his parents, any morsel of respect, was gone.

"She's ten, almost a woman now!" his mother crooned, equally befuddled by and addicted to drink. "You're a friend, and it's not like it'll do her any harm, knowing how the world works! Right, deary? Isn't your daddy's friend handsome? Come on Stilton, buy us another pint!"

Amara looked at her horrible parents, her eyes wide with fear. The filthy denizens of the bar paid no attention, too drunk and too cruel to care. Half of them would have taken the offer.

"Well, I've never had a virgin girl," Stilton laughed, tossing a bag of coins to Spitz and leaning over the table, his breath rancid.

"Come here, Sweetheart. Let me smell your hair."

Konell jumped up, getting in front of his sister.

"If you touch her, I'll kill you, old man."

"Oy, Spitz, tell your brat to mind his business. What, he wants her flower for himself?"

"Get over here, kid!" his father snarled. "You ain't the one in charge here."

His father moved to grab him by the collar, but Konell turned and bit his arm, tasting salt and blood.

The man let go.

"Ow! You little shit!"

He went to hit him, but Konell punched him hard in the throat.

Konell's father fell back into his seat, grasping at his larynx, choking. His drunken mother got up to grab him but she tripped over the chair leg, splitting her jaw against the table and knocking herself out.

Stilton pulled Konell over the table, holding him by the neck.

Amara cried, reaching for Konell's leg, but she couldn't help him.

Stilton was ready to stab him with a nearby fork, when, from out of nowhere, a shimmering knife slid around the man's throat. Stilton gulped, his grip loosening a little. He didn't move lest the razor split his neck from ear to ear.

"Listen here, degenerate trash," warned the figure behind him. It was a man. "I'm only going to say this once. Let go of the boy, or my knife draws blood. It's coated in Oleander, and the poison kills ever so quickly..."

Stilton's eyes widened in recognition.

"Fuck! You're- Please, my Lord, don't kill me! I was just kidding! I-"

"We both know that's a lie, Stilton," the mysterious figure replied. "Now let go of the boy, and live."

Stilton let go of Konell's collar, white with fear. Konell fell onto crusted plates and pooling beer, gasping for air.

The man with the knife broke his promise, Stilton's throat opening with a *squelch*. The gutter cleaner's body fell to the side, revealing a figure in dark, navy robes, embroidered with purple roses. He wore a purple-black hood, the color of bruises.

The Poisonthorn!

The Poisonthorn was the leader of The Assasin's Guild, feared throughout Qeonia and The Continental Nations. Konell had heard the rumors about him, as had all the other boys who lived in Beggar's Alley. He used to be a pauper just like them, but now, he was richer than they could imagine, making contracts with the nobility and secretly influencing the politics of high society.

"You've got some fight in you, Kid. And killing your own parents... That's pretty cold. We could use someone like you."

Quietly, the man reached across the table to pick up the ring that had fallen in the scuffle. He dusted it off, and placed it in a hidden pocket in his robes.

"You okay?" he asked.

Konell didn't respond.

"Huh."

The Poisonthorn turned to Amara.

"Are you hurt, darling? Did they harm you?" he asked gently.

Amara didn't answer either. They both just stared at the table, at the blood seeping through the tablecloth.

The entire room was silent.

Konell looked around slowly, seeing countless corpses. Amongst the dead, stood assassins in dark-colored robes, their curved, silver knives dripping with blood. With barely a movement, they flicked the blood off their blades and returned the weapons to their sheaths, melting back into the dark corners of the room and returning to the shadows like a wave to the sea.

"I'm sorry," the man said, sheathing his knife and lowering his hood. "You must both be scared... Don't worry, no harm shall come to you. We have what we need."

The man's voice was deep and smooth, like sinking into soft, satin pillows or diving into a cool lake on a hot summer's day. It was a voice that was almost comforting, but everything else about him warned that he was dangerous, and indeed, there wasn't a man who had ever drawn his ire and lived to tell the tale.

Konell watched the assassin with wide eyes, trying to hide his fear.

What did he need? The ring? The ring from the gutter? How much could it possibly be worth?

How much is a human life worth?

I killed my parents...

The Poisonthor put his hands on Konell's shoulders in what was supposed to be a reassuring gesture, but the boy remained unswayed, inspecting his features.

He was clearly dangerous, and Konell was sure that every one of the rumors was true, but although The Poisonthorn looked outright sinister when fully cloaked, without his hood, he was quite young and good-looking, with long, wavy, brown hair that reached down to his shoulders and an even crop of facial hair that couldn't decide whether it wanted to be stubble or a beard, but accentuated his statuesque jawline nonetheless. His eyes were an entrancing brown-grey, but they were cold. Extremely cold.

"My name is Anansali Taxis, but you can call me Tax. I'm here to help. Do you want something to eat?"

Konell's sister looked up. She didn't know who the man was. She was probably half-delirious. So thin, she looked like a skeleton. Of course she wanted to eat.

Amara took Tax's hand, hesitant at first. In that moment, she sold Konell into a life of shadows and secrecy, all for a crust of bread.

Konell would have to live with that choice. He loved his sister.

Tax picked Amara up, carrying her out of the tavern.

Konell followed, pocketing a steak knife on the way out.

"Who contracted you?! Why were you there?!" the torturer shouted, frustrated.

Konell was defiant. He would show the brute.

"Even if I told you, you wouldn't believe me."

"Try me."

"The person who gave the order was...your mother!" the assassin laughed raggedly.

Angry, the torturer grabbed one of many knives and stabbed it into the meat of Konell's leg.

Konell whimpered, his consciousness fading again.

"I want an answer! Who hired you to kill The Silvercat?! Why are you hunting assassins?! Why-"

Konell hesitated. He didn't have to go through with this contract. He had left a contract before...

But he was desperate.

It all comes down to this.

Konell aimed the crossbow, centering it on the Lord's head. The man was standing still, leaning on a railing at the edge of the estate's central pavilion. Konell was up on the rooftops, and he was the only one with a clear shot.

I've got you.

Konell pulled the trigger, the quarrel flying.

The bolt missed, the Lord running for cover.

Konell cursed, the other assassins rappelling down the buildings and running across the

courtyard, a much more blatant attack.

He had failed...

Tax was angry, of course.

"I'm disappointed, Konell. You never miss. Every time I fight you, you're as sharp as a nail... You were supposed to hit the target. Ten Guild members died fighting the Lord's men, and we couldn't retrieve their bodies. The Guild has been exposed, made weak, and all because you couldn't make a simple shot. Take Amara and go. I have to reconsider your membership."

Spurned by the Guild, Konell and Amara lived in squalor for a year, taking residence in an abandoned building not far from where they had lived with their parents, a building full of homeless people and criminals. It took a single flash of Konell's knives to keep the criminals away from his sister, but during her stay there, she caught yellow fever.

When Tax came looking for him, Amara had been sick for a month. For Konell it was like The Divinity himself came down to answer his prayers.

Tax promised Konell that the Guild would pay him double for his services if he was able to carry out this latest contract. In that moment, Konell felt ready to kill again, ready to rise up and out of his disgrace and take his place at Tax's right hand. He was ready to bring Amara back to The Guild House, for her to live again in luxury.

But he wasn't really ready.

Lord Eluvaine was a good man. Infiltrating his estate and spending time close to him and his wife, he saw that they treated their two children with love, dignity, and respect. The two nobles were far better than his parents ever were, and they had a third child on the way.

The contract had been placed on their heads when they spoke out against The Second Cairnian Civil War at a recent council meeting. Several noble families wished to capitalize on the misery of the Monolids by selling weapons and supplies to whichever side paid more, but not the Eluvaines. Though they had much land and property, they gave food and water to those without and fed the Monolids, Kïsists and Lātists alike.

This was something the other nobles couldn't allow.

"My Lady, I have a confession to make. I am-"

Lady Eluvaine raised her hand to his lips to stop him.

"I know you've spent some time close to me as my guard, but you are not in love with me, Collin. You are far too young, and I am faithful to my husband."

Konell's face burned. She was indeed beautiful, but that was not the confession he was going to make. His confession was far more serious than a confession of lust.

"My Lady, I have a confession to make."

"Speak no more of this, Collin; I-"

"No, my Lady. That is not what I wish to confess to you. The truth is...I am an assassin from the Guild. I was sent here to kill you and your husband."

The Lady's jade-green eyes widened. She backed up against a nearby rose trellis, hand over her belly. She couldn't believe what she was hearing.

Konell pretended to go in for a kiss. The Lady was petrified.

He moved in, his lips just brushing her neck. With great subtlety, he drew his poisoned knife, and whispered in her ear.

"Right now, this courtyard is surrounded, and your husband is likely dead,

The entire Guild is here on behest of my master, Anansali Taxis, hired in gold. They're watching me right now... I've been ordered to kill you, but I will not do it. I will try to keep you alive, but in the next few minutes, you must have total faith in me... Will you trust me?"

Shocked, Lady Eluvaine nodded slowly. Konell pretended to kiss her again, his hands in her smooth, blonde hair. His face burned even hotter, the Lady pale as bone.

Konell cursed himself.

"I will protect you as best I can, but I can make no guarantees. Whatever noble family is after you has hired the entire Guild. When I turn around, run for cover. Steel will fly. Do you understand?"

The woman nodded.

"Go, then, my Lady. And don't look back."

Konell turned, shooting a dart from his wrist.

Krista fell to the ground, choking. Lady Eluvaine ran, holding her stomach.

Liam and Rex jumped from the rooftops, throwing knives, but Konell spun, deflecting both with a sweep of his leather cloak. He shot Rex with his reserve dart, ducking under Liam's swing and blocking his backswing. Then, he got a hold of his arm and threw him to the ground. His knife found the man's heart, returning to hit Rex in the ear, the red-haired assassin groaning and slumping to the ground.

Konell heard a whoosh behind him.

Propelled by pure instinct, he did a dive roll to the side, a quarrel skipping off the cobblestones he'd been standing on.

Qadro.

For such a muscular man, Qadro landed lightly on his feet, unsheathing both of his knives. Luckily for Konell, Qadro relied on brute strength rather than acids or poisons. He was like a panther, sleek and powerful.

But Konell was a viper.

Konell's knife ricocheted off of the ground, hitting Qadro in the neck. Though it barely

nicked the man's skin, that was more than enough. Qadro knelt, dropping his knives.

There's just one more person I have to beat. It's been a long time since we last fough–

A vial of acid flew for his face.

Konell did a back handspring, throwing out one of his own.

Anansali Taxis spun through the canister, letting the wind take his robes. Underneath, he wore light, leather armor. His knives were sparkling and sharp.

The Poisonthorn hit the ground with barely a sound, his long hair in his face. He was older—greyer, then—but still as deadly as ever.

Through that single exchange, the two most skilled assassins in the Guild announced their intentions. In that moment, they both knew where they stood. There would be no bargaining, no reasoning.

Only hard feelings.

"You disappoint me for the last time, Konell. You didn't have to accept this contract."

"You're right."

"You know I'm not going to go easy on you this time... I will kill you tonight, Konell."

"That's alright. You will not kill the Eluvaines. I will stop you, even if it kills me."

"No. Nothing will stop me. You chose a bad day to grow a heart."

The Poisonthorn summoned a sword as black as pitch. Black dust hovered around it, its hilt set with a glowing, purple gem. It came from the ring on his finger, the ring that had made Konell's life both a heaven and a hell.

"I treated you like a son. I saved you from poverty, raised you like you were my own. All this time, you've lived off of blood money. Why die for these people?"

"She and her husband, they treat their children well. I will not see more children grow up to be assassins. I won't destroy a happy family in this cruel world."

The poison had finally caught up to him. Taxis began to walk away, leaving him to die.

Konell clenched his fist, hunched over in the courtyard. Three daggers were in his back.

I would give my life, just to stop him… I would sacrifice myself to stop this.

If anyone can hear me, I–

Please help me stop him!!!

Konell's vision faded further, no aid forthcoming, but suddenly, the burning stopped, and the poison coursed freely through his veins, not disappearing, but no longer toxic to him. He rose, slowly, his eyes lighting to an unnatural red.

Brought back from frigid death, Konell threw poison at his cruel mentor as he walked away, the man turning, but too late. The liquid flew into Taxis' eyes, blinding him.

Not wasting a second, Konell whipped his knife at the man as he writhed, the dagger hissing through air and finding its mark.

With a whispered curse, Anansali Taxis fell, and Konell fell as well.

Thank you, the assassin thought.

Thank you…

Konell opened the door to Taxis' office, key rattling in the lock.

He had only been in the room once before. No one was allowed in there.

Tax's room was small and dark, lit only by a tiny, square window. A sliver of moonlight illuminated the large, mahogany desk that stood in the middle of the room, roses carved into each leg. A letter sat opened on the table, a paper with a brightly-colored seal.

Tax hadn't bothered to hide his messages. They were easy to read if one didn't value their life.

But Tax was dead, and so was the rest of The Guild.

Konell picked up the paper.

Stamped in red wax, was the sigil of The Broken Bone. By placing eyes on that paper, he had doomed the world.

"Completely kill off the competition. Then, we can discuss terms…"

Konell breathed heavily, attempting to keep it together. He was out of quips, and out of resolve.

"Alright, alright... I'll tell you for real this time. It was— It was—"

The torturer leaned in, eager in his impatience.

Konell spat blood and venom in his face, causing him to trip over the chair leg.

The assassin watched as the man flailed and then stilled, giving him a mocking, red smile, one of victory and relief.

Then, Konell breathed in, the torturer's faint, red Lifeblood passing through his teeth.

It incarnadined his eyes; it brought back his sanity.

He sat there for a moment, grimacing, and then focused on the hallway that led out from the room, the door open. At the end of that hallway was another, equally nondescript door. He had to reach it.

Konell rocked the chair as violently as he could, swaying, and finally, tipping over.

As he fell, Konell said a word. A magic word.

"Evanesire," he whispered, breathless.

Taking advantage of the chair's momentum, the assassin disappeared in a billow of red mist. He reappeared again in the hallway, rolling.

Konell dusted himself off for a second, and then stood, ragged and worn. His knees creaked. Not turning back, he opened the door and left the room as if nothing had happened, though he had a noticeable limp.

He left behind those colorless walls, abandoning his mask amongst the blood and fingernails, as if shedding an old skin.

CHAPTER V

Luxyruss

Luxyruss jumped from Riize. His body died, but his spirit lived.

Slowly breaking apart, he disintegrated, flying off into space as a mess of individual molecules. In seconds, he Converged again on Ressida.

The conditions were bad, but he could withstand them. His homeworld would not step on its native son, though it couldn't even if it wanted to. He was weak, but still stronger than any mortal man.

From a distance, Luxyruss looked weary and old, hunched over and tired, a figure one would find lying dazed outside a tavern, or at the end of a begging bowl. He leaned against a twisted, wooden walking stick, and he was clothed in robes of fraying, brown haircloth, which were held together by a rough-hewn chunk of thick rope. Though Luxyruss was hundreds of years old, and weary of the world, he was not the old vagrant he appeared to be. If one truly looked at him, they would notice that although he was slightly hunched over, he still stood a little over six feet tall. His hair was white, but it was a lustrous white, reaching his shoulders, and his long, grey-white beard was well-kept. His eyes were a glowing, oceanic blue, and although his crepey, wrinkled skin was candle-white and semi-transparent, revealing veins beneath, he was appreciably muscular, and he held his walking stick with the sure grip of a man who had seen combat. He was not an overly handsome man, with a large, blunt nose and long, overgrown, grey eyebrows, but he exuded a sense of regality, exposing his identity to anyone who held even a sliver of faith.

Luxyruss' homeworld, Ressida, was a dwarf planet at the end of The Kol

System. It was similar in many ways to Avenshra's Red Moon, Riize, only significantly colder. Strong, biting winds kicked up glittering glass dust, which swirled through the air. The ground was grey in color, embedded with crystal shards and speckled with black and white rocks. A jagged ridge of worn, granite peaks rose up in the distance, overshadowing a city with smooth, white walls. The sky above was black, constellations twinkling with an intensity that could only exist on a world with few clouds. Not much larger in comparison, Arceon was but a big, blue dot in the sky, providing meager light, and the planet had no moons to illuminate the night.

It didn't used to be that way. There used to be two suns...

Luxyruss breathed in, lungs dry from the cold. The lungs of any mortal man would have collapsed.

The air smelled of ash and burnt wood, even after so many years. There wasn't a living thing in sight, not even a speck of grass. He could sense the microorganisms in the soil, the small, tough insects that had survived The Theft, but the planet was almost completely barren. Frigid wind howled across the scorched earth, a constant reminder of the emptiness.

Luxyruss had come to Ressida because it was a place where he could no longer sense Skotathis. As the primary hosts of Unification and Division, they could sense each others' Jumping due to the sudden Division and reUnification of particles. It was the only time The Powers were in harmony, the only time where one took on the attributes of the other.

Luxyruss couldn't sense him, his great enemy, or at least, he was no longer strong enough to sense him at that distance. Many times he had thought he was alone and was not, but alas, he had been gambling his life that way for years, a cosmic runaway who, at any point, could be lost to time forever by missing the right Convergence. He couldn't help being weak. There was much to do, and Emanations weren't cheap.

This time, Luzyruss found himself lucky; no one had followed him. He could rest.

Yet he had not come to rest. He had come to find answers, the will to go on. To find something he had abandoned.

A legacy.

But he did need rest...

I'm so tired. I need this to end. I need this all to end.

But I must do this. I will never succumb.

Luxyruss didn't pause to rest. He would set out straight away.

Up ahead, was a high ridge. A broken statue loomed over the remains of what once was the greatest civilization to ever exist. The first civilization.

Luxyruss remembered it.

Verdant fields. Scintillant waterfalls. No longer.

The Void had destroyed it all. His home.

It didn't feel like a home... It felt like a crypt.

Luxyruss pressed onwards towards the city, looking off into the horizon. The giant statue of The Initiator clutched the last of Ressida's small mountains like a cane.

A god too weak to stand for themselves...

He tried to find humor in the irony, but could not. He found only despair.

Haash't

Haash't flew above the striated canyon, soaring over dry grasses and twisted trees.

Claeana's Gorge was a one-hundred-foot-deep break running the length of a large, sandstone mesa directly connected to Sandkeeper Ridge. Red-brown rock crumbled down from the canyon walls and fell into the golden sands below with a *thump*. Desiccated masses of string-like plants hung from the sides, small, black beetles making their homes in every nook and cranny. The air smelled of dry stone, and one could hear the wind scrape against the crags. The sky was an ice-blue color, Arceon sending long, yellow-blue streaks across the Gorge's sun-baked walls.

The Gorge widened at the end, becoming a Desert plain, loose sand held together by small weeds and tall, dark green cacti crowned with red-purple fruit.

Haash't felt the lush air flow over his wingtips, reveling in the lightness of a warm updraft. He was the master of the skies, the last Aetus Orum, a hidden predator. His cross-like pupils focused on a hawk flying below—a quick meal to complete his day.

Haash't dove, angling his tail feathers to fall faster—his beak, an arrowhead, his feathers, fletchings.

Haash't fell upon his unsuspecting target before it could make a sound, the long, downy crest on his head trailing behind him like a comet's tail.

Large raptors weren't his usual prey, but this was Aetan territory, and he couldn't just let trespassers have their way.

With a swift movement, Haash't tore off the intruder's wings and then resumed his dive, juices streaming through the air as victim and attacker plummeted together, the white spots on his broad back turning into a blur.

Right before he hit the ground, Haash't opened his massive wings, rising up slightly and entering a controlled descent. He hovered down, pleased with himself, and made his way over to where his prey had landed.

Haash't pierced the hawk's warm flesh with his beak, his tongue exulting in the tasty kill, the salty, metallic juices dripping down his face and onto his neck. He hadn't eaten all day, bringing home his previous kills to feed his mate and chick.

Tastes great. Especially being so hungry.

When he was done savoring his meal, Haash't left the hawk's remains as a warning to other animals.

The ravine was his once more.

Preening his plush, gold feathers, Haash't licked off all remnants of his dinner and retreated to his cave for a nap.

M'Cael

M'Cael was dragged across stone and left bleeding at Skotathis' feet.

Dried-up clots held together tangled clumps of once-golden curls, which obscured the angel's face as he lay seizing in pain, limbs at odd angles as he tried to get up. The scabs where his wings had been shorn from his shoulders cracked open and oozed as his Goblin jailers lifted him up to his knees. Taking his chin with their clawed hands, they forced him to place hateful eyes on the man who had had him tortured for three hundred years. Laughing, they whipped him, adding another scathing line to the web of scars that stretched across his well-knit back.

M'Cael growled.

The Adversary sat before him, the ruler of Faal. His torturer. His captor.

He pulled at his chains as he had so many times before, but it was no use. The black steel manacles he wore encased his arms, and he couldn't open his hand to Call Glorystar.

Skotathis had left him wearing his Callring as an insult.

The demon jailer whipped M'cael again, the angel groaning.

M'Cael's jailer was a smaller, uglier looking Goblin than the ones M'Cael had fought back in the day. He was shorter and fatter, with stubby horns that were half-covered by a dented, black steel helmet. He carried a light blue, squid-leather bullwhip, a weapon he was more than happy to use.

Though M'Cael knew when a lash was coming, it didn't make it better. The scars where his wings used to be flushed in retaliation as he was struck.

Skotathis watched silently, amused.

Over seven feet tall, The Adversary's hairless head was crowned with a set of banded, glowing, rainbow horns that looked like they were made of glass, with two, long horns growing from his temples, a curved, shorter, downward-pointing horn sprouting from his forehead, and a line of small, conical horns that ran vertically down his skull, stopping at his neck. He had glowing, rainbow-colored eyes lacking pupils, with irises that shimmered like oilslick pools and were surrounded by red scleras criss-crossed by shifting, rainbow membranes.

A bemused expression hovered over Skotathis' smooth, well-proportioned face, as if he reveled in his monstrosity.

And a monster he was. His skin was a slick jet-black, his back, shoulders, chest, and abdomen crusted with organic obsidian growths like inch-thick scabs, which had been polished down and carved into a set of ridged armor. At the center of his chest, sat a Shadowheart, faceted into the shape of a rounded hourglass and embedded in his sternum.

Skotathis watched M'Cael struggle to get up again as he lay relaxedly on his throne, smiling a jester's smile. Curled up against his back, were two oily, black wings like those of a bat, with large, hooked pinions. His eyes vacillated like a kaleidoscope, colors that were deep, and bright, and ominous, hues hypnotically shifting, burning bright. His horns changed to match his eyes—first sulphuric yellow, then salmon-pink, then sap-green, then flaming orange—an infinite cycle.

The Adversary licked his lips with a slick, green tongue, revealing translucent, yellow-green teeth as sharp as nails.

"Brother."

"You are no brother of mine, demon," M'Cael spat.

Skotathis' voice was smooth, like dark honey.

"Maybe I am no one to you. Nevertheless, today you will tell me what I need to know. The Coincidence is approaching, and my patience runs dry. Where is The Amulet, M'Cael? Where is the Lifeblood that was stolen from me?"

"Fang'rial, this conversation goes the same way every time. Do you really think I'll tell you now?"

The Adversary clenched his too-sharp teeth.

"Even after three hundred years you underestimate the pain I can inflict upon you... I'm no longer playing games. I will have my necklace."

M'Cael would never betray The Divinity by revealing such an important piece of information. Though The Angelicum were dead, defeated, Luxyruss was still his King, and more than that, his friend—a friend he was lucky to have. M'Cael came from a poor family to the west of Raj'para. He had no business with gods or kings.

M'Cael's father, Eloh'an Vortran, had been a timberman until The War for the Walls. He had lost his wings and arm in battle. His mother, Falcara Encadmon, was a washerwoman for the local nobility, a family of rich farmers. Though they were rich, they paid her little, and M'Cael kept his family afloat by collecting greenmoss from the local cliffs and selling it at market.

Greenmoss was a tea favored by many Ressidans, but it required agile flyers and climbers to collect. Ressidans who used their wings for labor were looked down on as uncouth and uneducated, and M'Cael was often mocked by his peers.

When he came of age, the young angel joined the Ressidan military and volunteered to fight The Ighed'bad outside the walls. He would take revenge for his father's loss and earn the salary he couldn't in his disability. That salary led to promotions, and M'Cael soon became a General. Elevated to this new and lofty rank, M'Cael fought side-by-side with Luxyruss, King of Ressida. The pair had fought to stop Fang'rial and his horde of demons, the invaders reborn through an alliance with the Tremites beyond the walls.

But in the end, The Demonium were unstoppable.

M'Cael remembered the first time he had seen demons.

On a warm, spring day, The Twenty-ninth Regiment, the reserve fighting force of Raj'para's Fourth Sector, was called to fight off a group of Ighed'bad and stop the raid of a village outside the city walls.

To call it a village wasn't really accurate, as it was merely a moving settlement of grass and wood, built by shepherds. Nonetheless, it was home to about a hundred nomads, including elderly people, pregnant women, and young children.

M'Cael was not the leader of the mission. At the time, The Leader of The Twenty-ninth Regiment was one Silas Geige, the youngest son of Lord Johan's Geige, M'Cael's mother's employer.

The Regiment had ridden down to the shepherd's village itching for battle, ready to slay

the Ighed'bad and more motivated to fight and kill than protectors should be. However, what they found was that their enemies were no longer the Ighed'bad, but a new class of horrors: The Demonium.

The Ighed'bad had changed, every crista of their skin coated in Shadow Compound, tiny, grey triangles forming a smooth and nearly impenetrable hide. Only enchanted steel could pierce it, and Silas was the only one with an enchanted sword.

Their claws had grown sharper, their horns glowing with a villainous light. Worse than their transformation alone, they were more organized, and far more vicious in their attack. For the first time in history, The Ighed'bad fought with weapons, weapons of wood, stone, and even iron.

The demons' eyes glowed green, green with envy. They envied the angel's lives, taking what they coveted in sprays of blood. Within minutes, Silas had retreated, leaving his sword on the battlefield and leaving the defenseless villagers to die. The rest of The Twenty-ninth Regiment fled as well.

All except M'Cael.

The young Ressidan knew he had no chance of winning. But if he could give his life to save the villagers that had yet to get away, he would do everything in his power to stop the creatures' advance. He wouldn't let anyone else suffer his father's fate. He would have his revenge, revenge for years of shame and disrespect.

Without shame, M'Cael opened his wings and made his stand, picking up The Leader's fallen sword and flying towards the demons, fighting until he killed every last one.

The shame would not break him. The fear would not stop him.

And he didn't stop, not until the grass was covered in inky blood and every last villager had escaped. Through sheer force of will, M'Cael had survived...

In the blood and agony, M'Cael made a promise to himself.

I will kill them all. No matter when, no matter where, I will fight.

All demons must die.

What M'Cael had wanted was to pay back his parents for what they had done for him, to let them comfortably retire. That was the reason he kept fighting, his dream. But in the process of fighting for his dream, he had become a protector.

The world called M'Cael a hero, and Luxyruss, then Y'shan, had called him Captain.

Years later, M'Cael was there when Goddess revealed herself, Goddess Almighty, when

his master revealed himself to be The Divinity, a Power so great that it could crush everything in his path.

M'Cael would not leave. He couldn't. Gods had placed their trust in him.

He had come from nothing. Who was he to deny them? He just kept on marching, kept on fighting, fighting until he was captured.

It was his duty and his pleasure.

However, over time, even that pleasure disappeared, leaving only duty, for, in the early days during The Battle of Brothers, his parents were killed by The

Demonium, forced into an early retirement. Returning home for a break from deployment, M'Cael had found their bodies sitting at the dining room table, left to rot and bloat. Their deaths almost broke his mind... Later on, The Theft destroyed everything.

"You killed my family, overthrew my King, destroyed my homeworld! You've tortured me in every way imaginable for the past three hundred years! What further pain can you inflict?! I don't care if you're playing musical instruments! I will not tell you where The Amulet is, now or ever, and you cannot break me."

The Adversary clicked his tongue.

"So rebellious. But everything breaks."

A third lash broke the angel's skin, pink blood trickling down his grimy shoulders.

"Come on, M'Cael," Skotathis drawled. "You could be free! You know that Luxyruss has already lost; why bother holding out like this? I am a god; I could give you a new life amongst the mortals, end all this shit! But I need you to help me... The war over Avenshra is over—the planet is mine, and Avenshrian souls run in my veins. Why suffer out of pride?"

"It's not about pride. It's because you aren't a god, and you'll never be a god—not while I draw breath! It's because I find you disgusting; because you destroy everything you touch! You sold out your fellow men so that you could be more than an angel, so that you could gain power... That's all you care about. If you kill me, I won't be dying in the defense of pride. I'll be dying to prove that you have no power here! I may lie shackled here, but you're the one who lies imprisoned."

"You don't know true imprisonment. I can show you," Skotathis snarled.

He stood up, grasping M'Cael by the neck, claws digging into The Archangel's throat.

The Adversary's eyes burned green, the color of anger.

"Where is The Amulet, M'Cael? Give me the truth."

"You don't understand truth," M'Cael choked.

"Very well."

The Goblin jailer handed Skotathis a wicked-looking apparatus, a strange dagger made out of an enchanted steel syringe. It had a handle made from Shadowrise sapwood, wrapped in Shadowthread and topped with a glass bulb filled with a murky, black solution. The needle was surrounded by four, claw-like blades, also made of enchanted steel and sharpened to a razor's edge.

Without hesitation, Skotathis jammed The Epidemion through M'Cael's chest, the dagger's metal claws enveloping his heart.

M'Cael gasped.

Skotathis slammed down on the bulb, the injector piercing muscle and injecting its payload. M'Cael's vision died in a burst of blood and tears.

"Idiot angel. You should've just answered the question. You think I'd grant you the privilege of death for not cooperating? I never said anything about killing you."

Oscure

The Aerhauc Tribe stood in a circle around Mozamic's body, which lay snugly nestled in an oval-shaped casket of woven straw, padded with leopard skins and held up by a wooden framework.

The sky above was dark with thunderclouds, angered by the death of The Tribe King's blood-brother. The palm trees hung their heads in mourning.

Mozamic's arms had been placed crosswise against his breast, and a wreath of sweet-smelling, pink flowers had been placed around his neck, unsuccessful in overpowering the sickly scent of death that issued from the corpse. The women of the Settlement wailed funeral dirges as one of the Elders took two stones from a basket, and dipped them in melted tapir fat and oxide pigments. She laid the stones down on Mozamic's eyes, smearing white ash across the tribesman's forehead.

The hunters sworn to him recited a sacred prayer, kneeling.

Oscure recited no prayer. He had starved himself for his vigil, and he had drunk only a

mouthful of water each day for the past three days. He couldn't speak.

Instead, he pulled out a ceremonial kris, made of obsidian, and raked it across his arm in grief, adding to the cuts that were already there. The bleeding wounds stretched across his forearm like sharp, jagged branches, red amongst a sea of black.

It wasn't enough.

Luxyruss

Luxyruss stood before the city of Raj'para, the only city on Ressida. It had once had a population of over one million people, but at the moment, it was completely empty, its eroded walls throwing out long shadows, its once delightful skyscrapers, austere and foreboding.

Gleaming, black, silver, and white high-rises unlike anything in The Kol System towered over insurmountable, hundred-foot-tall battlements of impossibly perfect, grey-white quartz. They used to be almost reflective, but they had grown dusty and chipped.

The city only had only one entrance, a set of stupendous, studded, metal doors the color of soot. Luxyruss knew that the doors were braced on the inside by a thick bar made of the same material, holding back the winds since time immemorial. Apart from the Ighed'bad and certain exiles who had been rejected by society, nobody lived outside the walls. Raj'para wasn't just the planet's only city, but the only place Ressidans lived.

All Ressidans were injected with Shadow Crystals at birth, which remained in the bloodstream and retained Lifeblood, preventing the dissipation seen in other beings.

The doors had failed in their mission, for eons ago, the herald of Raj'para's destruction had infiltrated without arousing suspicion, and the world's greatest threat had simply stepped over the walls.

Luxyruss walked up to the doors and Called Purifire. The sinuous, white blade came into his hands and ignited, zircon flame coiling around it. It had a cylindrical, polished, golden handle embedded with five, blue opal cabochons: two near the blade and two near the pommel, surrounded by short, curved, spine-like protrusions. The sword had a quilted grip pad on the front-edge side of the handle that was made of soft lambskin, bleached white.

The Divinity melted through Raj'para's strong doors and the thick bar behind them, entering the city through a smaller door of his own making. The cutout fell to the ground with a clanging *thud*.

Quite an entrance indeed...

Upon entering the city, he was met with many familiar sights. He moved slowly, passing homes and stores he remembered from millennia ago.

He reminisced about his old life, the memories bitter-sweet. Seeing the market. Happy peasant children. Maidens laughing.

He looked through misty eyes at the pastel houses of the common citizens: square dwellings with flat roofs and wooden posts sticking from their rims.

No one greeted him from their porches. There were no flower pots sitting on the whitewashed, exterior stairways, no mothers hanging up their children's clothes on clotheslines, connecting the community.

His heart ached to see just one youth, kicking a ball across the road. But the roads of the city, which had once been done in grey and black cobblestone, were entirely blackened then, littered with charcoaled bits of limbs, the buildings around them stained black and dulled by smoke and ash.

The buildings drooped more and more as he walked down the main street, as if unable to keep up the facade anymore. They couldn't pretend they were alright before him.

Looking past the commoners' houses, Luxyruss felt his heart drop, and he was gripped by a visceral sort of fear. The skyscrapers ahead, at the center of the city, resembled dripping candles, stone, glass, and steel melted like cheap wax. They had experienced the direct impact of The Theft.

The Divinity prayed that no planet would ever face such devastation again. Prayer was not enough, however.

That's why I'm doing this. I won't let him do something like this again; I can't!

Though the vast majority were destroyed, some of the buildings still remained intact. Amazingly, even some of the skyscrapers near the Fourth Sector in the northwest were undamaged, spared by Skotathis' weakness. They had hundreds of balconies without railings, making it easy to fly around the city. Luxyruss had had them modified in such a way after passing anti-discrimination laws at the beginning of his rule, destigmatizing the use of wings. This modification had turned out to be extremely useful during The

Angelic Civil War, when flying became commonplace, and the skyscrapers, which had been the luxury homes of the nobility, were converted into hospitals for the wounded.

At the northernmost end of the city, was a white Palace with a pale yellow dome topped with a steeple in the shape of The Solaron, wrought from gold. Standing guard before it, were two, white towers with domes of the same pale, yellow color. The castle had no walls, as it used to be surrounded by a luscious lawn that interfaced with the lawns of the surrounding noble estates, palaces in their own right, but at the moment, it was surrounded by a lot of cracked mud, and its paint was peeling off in sheets.

The statue of The Initiator, which used to stand proudly over Ressida's purple-grey peaks, leaned precariously against their remains, its arm broken and its mask cracked. The quartz goliath stood over a series of moss-covered caves that pitted the mountains, but it had started to crush them under its weight. Those pits had been the humble homes of The Ressidans in the early days of civilization, when The Ighed'bad reigned over the plains below and angels were not welcome to walk the land.

As large as Raj'para was, Luxyruss's first destination was close to the city entrance: The Monastery of The Initiated.

Taller than the nearby structures, the Monastery was a long, rectangular, turnstile building made of powdery, white marble, with a large, glass dome at the center, topped with a Solaron forged from black iron, like the doors at the city entrance.

Within minutes, Luxyruss reached it. The Monastery had been a place he had spent significant time in, reading ancient texts and discussing with academics and philosophers.

He gently pulled open the tall, shiny, black, wooden door, which stood between gorgeous, stained glass panels of Chrism, The Initiator, Creating the living worlds and their inhabitants.

Luxyruss' mother and father had been the first Created.

For a second, Luxyruss stood transfixed by the panels, but then he entered, his bare feet padding softly over smooth, brown tile. He was greeted by the winding, white staircase that went up The Monastery's three floors, which encircled and were bridged by The Shadowrise of Raj'para. The bottom floor was home to the chapel, The Shadowrise Garden, the dining hall, the kitchen, and the communal bathrooms. The second floor was taken up entirely by the Monastery libraries, and the top floor was taken up by the Monks' quarters and bathrooms.

The first two floors were lit by lines of oblong, eggplant-shaped, electric light bulbs attached lengthwise to the walls. The lights, about the size of his arm, were powered by a rotor submerged in the underground river that ran below, thick filaments glowing a dark yellow.

The top floor was lit by the glow of Shadowrise leaves, bathing it in a dim but cozy light.

Though empty, The Monastery was still welcoming, the air warmer than the city outside and smelling faintly of myrrh and brown bread, distinguishable only to his incredibly acute, heightened senses after so many centuries.

It's a miracle that the river still flows and the rotor still turns, even after all these years...

The Shadowrise Garden, the most important area in the Monastery, was a large, cylindrical space at the center of the building, with smooth, white walls that only spanned the first and second floors.

The Shadowrise of Ressida was fairly short by Shadowrise standards, but it was still tall enough that the branches scraped the domed, glass ceiling. The uneven floor of the Garden was carpeted in grass, the last patch of greenery on the planet, and smooth, black boulders were purposefully interspersed across the space, serving as seats for the Monks. After The Theft, the grass had been kept alive by The Shadowrise, feeding on the starlight that trickled through the dome, amplified by the tree's transparent leaves. The light was still quite faint, for the dome was thick to withstand the frequent, debris-filled windstorms that razed the planet.

Even when The Monastery had been inhabited, The Shadowrise Garden was always incredibly quiet, an unnatural but serene place.

The light of the Shadowrise touched Luxyruss; face. It was warm, like sunlight.

The Divinity shed a small tear.

It feels like...Luminon.

The old god sniffed back more tears, the fresh smell of grass clearing his head with its cool zing.

I can't get lost in the nostalgia and heartbreak. I came here because she needs me. I must use this Shadowrise... Too many are Twisted.

Soon, Skotathis will set upon her. Premonition showed this to me. I must be ready to grab her hand.

Torran

It had taken several days, but they had built a raft.

It was morning, and they would soon depart. The sky above was a dim, grey-blue, but it would soon be sunrise. The weather that day was cool, but not cold, and the current was gentle—enough to propel them forwards, but not enough to capsize them.

From what the group could tell, they were on one of the islets surrounding The Stareye Isthmus, but they didn't know which one, so they had decided to take off towards the nearest visible island and hope for the best. From the looks of it, it would take a day or so to get there, which would be uncomfortable but doable.

Torran wasn't really worried about the journey. After what had happened to them all, after what they had survived, there wasn't much left to be scared of. The raft they had built was sturdy enough, and they were no longer sailing across the unforgiving God's Anvil.

Torran's mind was preoccupied with something else. Ever since he and Scarolette had washed up on the island, things between them had been strange. They had both undergone a transformation, but neither of them knew what it was, and neither of them talked about it. Luckily, the magic within them had fallen asleep, and although Torran was sure that Jhett knew about their powers, he thankfully said nothing.

Nevertheless, the tribesman's presence made things especially awkward, and though Torran was grateful for his help, he wished that he could have some time alone with Scarolette. He wanted to apologize to her for what he did to her arm, to thank her for saving him, and make his feelings for her known.

He wanted to tell her about his dream, the coming cataclysm.

To have privacy.

But his wants all seemed irrelevant, then. They had to leave the island, to get to The Outpost and then to Starspire. All their energy had gone into escape.

Father, Riane—they must think we're dead. And this man...

Torran had reassured Jhett that he would be a free man in Starspire, that he would be given a great reward for his help, but the Nolite was still guarded around them. He had told them that he was a former galley slave whose ship met with disaster at sea, but there was no way to know if that was the truth. What Torran did know, was that nothing good would come of making the man an enemy, so he didn't press him further, and, if he was being honest, he didn't really feel the need to. There was something in Jhett's demeanor that put him at ease. Perhaps it was the surprising gentleness and civility of his conduct, the unique but subtle sense of honor that he displayed in his actions. This was refreshing for Torran, who had spent much of his life playing politics and fighting wars with men whose treachery knew no limits. It was good to meet someone honest.

Torran exhaled deeply, and put any doubts he had to rest. Whatever Jhett's past was, he had saved them, so he was not their enemy. They got along alright, and he seemed to be a decent person. That was all that mattered at the moment. After all, they were all castaways. Rank, gender, race, and culture meant nothing. They had all endured nature's scorn.

I'll talk to Scarolette when we arrive. I have a lot to say to her, but now is not the time.

The group prepared the raft for launch just as the sun began its ascent and Riize faded from view, the waves shining with reflected light. The clouds glowed a faint blue.

The group's makeshift raft was composed of planks from their two ship-wrecks, tied together with rope from The Sea Star. The mast was a simple board, and the sail was a layering of palm leaves. An oar from Jhett's ship had washed ashore the day before, broken in half, but Torran had already fashioned one from an old plank. They would bring both with them, just in case. They had also kept some of the netting intact and filled it with coconuts, which would be their food and water source for the voyage ahead. Though it wasn't much, it would hopefully be a short trip. Worst-case scenario, they could try fishing from the raft with the nets or use them to bundle up coconut shells to keep afloat.

Everyone went into the woods and relieved themselves, getting their bearings. Then they hauled the raft into the water, climbed on, and set sail. With Jhett's past being what it was, Torran had taken the oar, and Scarolette held the other in her lap.

As the breeze came in and the current began to move them, the group looked on into the distance and into the future, the sky filled with a golden-blue glow.

CHAPTER VI

Adam

Adam woke up slowly. He vaguely remembered being dragged out of the silver mine and thrown into a hole. Then his memory came back to him.

The miner slumped. The glow had left him weeks ago.

It did not matter to him.

All there was, was darkness. The darkness was his, and he was of the darkness.

Adam's holding cell was an immersion of perfect darkness, roots and sharp stones digging into his skin and scraping him whenever he moved. The crumbling enclosure was only about as tall and wide as he was, but it was covered with a hefty, lead grate that was far too heavy for him to lift.

The damp air smelled strongly of earth and decay, and it was hot and suffocating inside the pit. He had not drunk or eaten in days, and he was kept standing, unable to truly sleep, though he was immersed in a tunnel of liquid dark.

It was clear that The Company had had the pit dug especially for him. What was unclear, was why.

Are they going to kill me? Why haven't they killed me yet?

Adam wasn't worried about himself. He was worried about his family. He hoped that they hadn't starved in his absence. He hoped that they had not been punished for his crimes.

He wished he could lift the grate and free himself, but he also didn't feel that he deserved to be free. He was a monster; his family would recoil at the sight of him.

Hell, I'm scared of myself, he thought bitterly.

Adam remembered the bodies—Zarack and the others turned to steam, ash, slime. The miner trembled, remembering the faint, blue light that had emanated from his hands.

They had melted alive.

In waking nightmares, Adam saw their skin bubbling, their blood boiling and eyes turning to jelly as they stood frozen in fear. He smelled their hair burning away as they screamed, their dying wish: for the pain to end.

Adam felt horrible about himself. His existence was a sick joke, a man who had starved just so his family could starve days later, a hero who, by accident, killed the man he saved just minutes later.

He wondered if his family knew what he had done, whether they could still love him afterwards. Then again, he knew that they might not even be alive anymore, and this tore at him.

He couldn't envision them gone, engulfed in darkness, like he was.

However, deep down, Adam knew that even if he could, it wouldn't mean anything. Many times in his life, he had come to a realization that he would quickly try to forget. Death wasn't really darkness. The idea of eternal sleep was a comfort—one for those who were too rational to believe in religion, in an afterlife, but were too scared to realize that they too were holding on to a fiction. He had always been one of those men.

Adam knew it, then. Death was not darkness. Death was nothingness, a lack of experience and a lack of feeling that went beyond even numbness. Death was the end, a snapshot of the world that would never become a memory or a story to be retold. If he died, if his family died, there would only be a flash, and then oblivion. A final moment, and that would be it. They would all be gone...

One day, I will be gone...

Adam cried until his face stung.

I'm going to die here.

At this thought, he curled up into a ball like a babe spinning slowly in its mother's belly. It was not a pit then. It was a womb, a womb of darkness where he could cry about his fate, about his birth into a world of death.

The spinning grew faster, then, a blur. He began hyperventilating, his eyes wild, though he saw nothing.

I'm a child again. I'm a child again, he repeated to himself, trying to offset the panic that had just begun, but his mind raced and he kept saying nonsensical things.

I can't die here! I can't die! I don't want to die!

Adam's mind tormented him, and all he could say was no.

No! No, no, no! No, no, no, no, no!

Adam slammed himself into the cell's jagged walls, beating at them with his hands.

No!

No!!!

Abruptly, there was a grating sound, and light shone down upon him once again.

Having spent days in the dark, he couldn't see. Everything was a burning, pressurized

reddish-black, like someone was gouging out his eyes. The light tingled as it crept across his

face, cold and judgemental. It would have been relieving, like a rag soaked in water, if only it wasn't so chilling. His hole had been uncovered, men looking down upon him from above. He recoiled, suddenly feeling the urge to hide, but he had been revealed to the world like a rat in its hole.

Someone tossed down a cloth, which hit him in the face and snapped him back to reality. Scared, but in too much pain from the light, Adam clumsily wrapped his eyes,

looking through grey fabric. He could see again, but it was fuzzy.

He looked up as a silhouette spoke to him, one of the Overseers' guards. The Overseers

hired guards to frisk the miners and check if they had stolen any ore. He thought he knew which guard was speaking to him, but he couldn't be sure.

"Prisoner, rise; there's someone here to see you."

The miner got up, scraping his cheek against the roots that stuck out from the earthen walls. He hit his temple on a thin, sharp rock as he tried to orient himself.

Adam wobbled for a moment, dazed, grabbing the walls of the pit for support.

"This is the one?" asked a reedy-sounding character. He sounded incredulous.

"That's the one, alright," sighed the disgruntled guard.

"I see. Get him out of there, then," the man said. He seemed annoyed.

"Yes, my Lord."

The guard hurried to do what he was told.

"Lift your arms, Prisoner," he commanded.

Weakly, Adam lifted his arms. The guard promptly grabbed them and yanked him out of the pit, dropping him roughly on his knees. Adam seized in pain for a moment and then collapsed face first in the dust, trying to lift himself back up. but failing. The stones that hid in the dirt were sharp, digging into him.

Comfort was nowhere to be found. Mercy fled.

Adam coughed, though the cough had no force to it. He hadn't eaten in days, rainwater his only sustenance. His ribs screamed from his skin, and his face was sunken and gaunt.

He was a lot like a corpse.

"The man's half dead!" cried the reedy-sounding man.

"He's a murderer and a beast! Why should he get any food?" the guard responded angrily.

"Whatever. Give me a hand," grumbled the reedy-sounding man.

Adam tried to get up, but the guard pinned him down, knee pressing into the small of his back. They were trying to do something with his arms, but he couldn't see what it was, and he couldn't resist.

Adam felt them shove his arms into gauntlets, heard the clicking of ten locks and the jangling of chains. They had put him in a prison without bars, a way to bottle up the chaos within. He wanted to protest, to stop them, but he was too weak to even speak.

My powers are gone. Why are you doing this?!

The guard covered his head in a sack. Adam squirmed, using up the last of his energy to try and get up, though he knew it was futile.

What are you doing? Where are you taking me? Ariel!

Let me go!

He managed to get onto his knees, but could rise no further.

"What are you waiting for?" shouted the reedy-sounding man. " Knock him out!"

A stick broke against Adam's neck, the darkness slowly returning.

As it closed in on him, Adam heard the distinctive clink of coins. Money had been exchanged.

"I trust that you will disclose this to no one," pressed the reedy-sounding man.

The guard lifted Adam up, and threw him across the rump of a horse like he was a sack of potatoes. The miner wheezed, his muscles growing limp.

"I know the drill. Neither of you was ever here, my Lord. There was never a prisoner."

"Good. We ride immediately, then," the reedy-sounding man replied, mounting his steed.

"But my Lord, he's dangerous. Are you sure you don't need an escort?"

"I'll be quite alright, my friend. Tell your masters that the crown thanks them for their generous gift. It shall not be forgotten."

Adam lost consciousness.

Agravius

Agravius' second wife lived in a modest, two-story home in eastern Spring-haven. Much of the white, stuccoed building was covered in ivy, which tiptoed over the foggy, light blue windows and around the shiny, red-painted door with its simple, loop-shaped, bronze knocker.

The first floor had a living room with a large, brown, leather sofa and a small, unused bookshelf made of birch. There was a small kitchen with a humble pantry, and there was a dining room with a large, rectangular table, made from walnut.

The High Empress' room was on the second floor. It was small, and the walls were painted a grey-blue color, with a white, swirled ceiling and a simple, beige rug covering most of the floor. She had a plush, feather bed with red, satin sheets that sat on a fine, but unadorned, walnut frame. A creaking, oaken chair with a red cushion, decorated with golden embroideries of flowers, sat close to a large window facing the east, the thick, red, satin curtains fully drawn to let light into the room. A mahogany nightstand stood next to the bed, topped with a golden chamberstick and a book that Agravius had read for her during his previous visit. A carved, walnut armoire stood at the leftmost corner of the room, holding a modest selection of clothing, as well as a wide array of comfortable slippers. A brass chamber pot sat beneath the bed.

The High Emperor noticed that the room smelled faintly of rose perfume, which was strange, because his wife didn't wear perfume anymore. The scent must have come from one of the maids, who he paid handsomely for their housework and their silence.

The High Empress's abode was cool and slightly damp, but the sun from the window warmed up the room a little.

Agravius laced his fingers together, sitting on a hard, walnut chair the servants had brought up for him from the dining room. His wife sat beside him in her soft, red chair.

Agravius opened his mouth to speak.

"Angelica. Do you ever feel...guilty?"

Agravius knew, even as he asked, that he would get no answer.

Angelica just stared blankly out the window, like she always did. The treatment had made her calm, but it had also made her silent, and dull. For twenty years, she had lived in secrecy, taken care of like a helpless child.

For Agravius, the irony was staggering—an adult child being taken care of, because she could not take care of her child.

It wasn't her fault, really. Agravius had seen it the moment Riane left the womb. Such a beautiful baby... He could see the intelligence in her eyes, that bright blue spark... Angelica had looked down with a morose apathy, not much different from how she currently stared out the window.

She had been ill, an illness brought about by the long pregnancy. It was not a normal reaction.

That does not absolve her, Agravius reminded himself.

He remembered the night of the incident. It was a sound that had woken him, a muffled cry. He had sprung up from sleep, fearing, and finding, the worst.

Angelica was pushing down on her pillow, a cold, blank expression on her face, smothering the baby. Agravius didn't know how long she had been pressing, but he knew that the baby would die soon. Riane's soft skull was misshapen, her eyes bloodshot.

He had seen it when he pulled Angelica off her, his face contorted in an obscene rage. The High Empress looked back at him with blank, tearless eyes, her shoulders slumped. No matter how much he shook her, yelled at her, she did not answer him, even as she was shackled and bound, carted off to The Sagery. The lobotomy they urgently prescribed had stolen any answer from him, but he knew that even if she had spoken, there was no real reason for what had happened. She simply was not herself.

Agravius sighed, the chair creaking. He tried to see what she saw. Her view was partially obscured by the creeping vines that wrapped around the house, but it seemed equally pleasing to her either way.

Still, he would hire a gardener to cut the vines and polish the windows. The High Emperor felt guilty.

He felt guilty for how poorly he had raised his children, how poorly he had treated his wives. He thought about it all the time—how he had failed in the mission that he had sacrificed so much for, how each hard-fought victory brought him no joy when so many people died under his command. When he washed his hands, he felt a slime, a slime that wouldn't go away, and he knew it never would.

Agravius was sure that his wife would never feel that sick feeling in herself. It had been taken by the needles.

But he would always feel it.

He rolled the slime between his fingers, and, with a frown, left the room, leaving his wedding ring on Angelica's bedside table.

I can't sit here like you do. I have an Empire to run...

I have a daughter to raise.

Leafsong

The Stillvein Raleis owned a small, wooden cabin near Beggar's Lake and on the edge of The Forest of Tears. The pine dwelling had a triangular, wood-shingled roof and a square, cobblestone chimney for the fireplace inside, which served as both a cookfire and a heat source.

The simple, arched door was made of cherry wood stained a dark brown, and was bordered by two small, square, open windows with wooden shutters, also made of pine. Two guards stood silently outside the door, watching over the house. They would sleep in the white carriage in which the nobles had arrived, but they would eat inside with the family.

The Ralei family cabin sat in the grass, overshadowed by large pine trees and twisting, leafless maple trees, the glow coming from within the house providing little light in the gloom, which sat like a thick fog over the area. The air was humid and cold, and it smelled of grass and rotting leaves.

It was warm and dry inside the cabin, the fire and multiple candles providing ample light and making the space look much bigger than it was.

On the right side of the cabin, sat a small pantry, and a small, square, wooden table with matching, wooden chairs, just large enough for a family of four. In the middle of the cabin, were four feather beds with bleached cotton sheets resting on simple, pine frames. A small, wooden nightstand with a lit, beeswax candle sitting in a copper chamberstick stood against the back wall of the cabin, and on the left side of the cabin, was a cobblestone fireplace, dusted with soot. The fire whistled and popped, filling the dwelling with the faint and not wholly unpleasant smell of woodsmoke.

Above the fire, hung a pot of chickpea soup, bubbling away, and around the fire were four brown, leather cushions filled with straw. A wicker basket with skeins and thread sat on the left, and to the right, a small, pine bookshelf held an assortment of dusty books. Thick, wooden cross-beams spanned the ceiling, and cobwebs filled every corner of the room, though their makers seemed to have abandoned them.

Sitting in the cozy warmth of the cabin, Leafsong could have never expected what was about to happen, but it happened nonetheless.

The Baroness killed herself that night.

Leafsong was in the kitchen, weaving with her mother, when one of the guards solemnly handed Lady Talassan a message.

The guardswoman was a pretty Luzian who was slightly younger than Leafsong's mom. She had clear, bluebird-blue eyes and wispy, platinum-blonde hair that she wore in a long ponytail. She wore a set of full plate, painted blue-grey, and a messer sat in a studded, brown leather sheath at her hip.

Eyes widening as she read, Leafsong's mother read the message, and, in her grief, drew the knife at the guard's waist and stabbed herself in the heart before anyone could react.

The guardswoman got on her knees, not knowing what to do, trying to staunch the bleeding with the weaving on the floor, but it was pointless. There was no recovering from such an injury.

Leafsong dropped to her mother's side, cradling her.

"I'm sorry, Leafsong," Lady Talassan sputtered. "I'm weak. I'm so, so sorry..."

Leafsong burst into tears, half in denial about what was happening.

"No—you aren't! We can get through this, Ma! Whatever it is, please don't go! Please, don't; no..."

The Baroness died within seconds, leaving Leafsong in shock. Her mother had disappeared from the world forever. It had happened at the most random time, in an instant, and in an almost mundane way.

Leafsong's breath caught in her throat. Her mother's blood was drying to the wooden floorboards as she watched.

The guard, trembling with shock and guilt, opened her mouth to console her, but she didn't know what to say, and so, she did the only thing she could do, and hugged her.

Leafsong screamed in anguish, the woman doing her best to comfort her, holding her lovingly like a mother and speaking softly in her ear, telling her it would be alright. But her words were no good, could be no good. Leafsong cried and cried until no more tears would flow and then heaved dryly, wordlessly against the woman's chest.

The young noble stifled the crying for an instant, suddenly pushing the guard away, and took the piece of parchment from her mother's rapidly cooling hand. She read it slowly, deliriously, as her hand shook violently and the ink bled.

My Lady, I'm sorry to inform you, but your Manor collapsed in an earthquake, killing the Baron, a group of mercenaries he had hired, and many townsfolk. We offer you our deepest condolences. His Majesty, The King of Qeonia, has invited you and your daughter to stay with him and his family in this difficult time.

Many prayers,

King's Scribe, Aurel Markonius.

As soon as Leafsong read the note, the tears flowed once more, and her lament shook the cottage harder than any earthquake could. Hearing the commotion, the other soldiers came in to see what was the matter, but were left frozen by the sight of the Lady's bloodied body.

Leafsong sobbed. It was too much to bear. Blind with grief, she pushed past the stunned guards and ran into the woods behind the cabin, abandoning everything as they tried to pursue her.

She left them all behind; she left it all behind.

Her family had disappeared in a matter of weeks, all evidence of their existence wiped away. She would be just another disappearance, just another heiress among the many, many members of The Ralei Dynasty disappearing from the family roster.

Oh, Ma, Da, Inesa! Why? Why?!

Taking her in, the branches and leaves closed quietly around her, hiding her from view. Leafsong ran and ran—ran until the run was all-consuming.

The new moon was high above the trees, Faal's pink light filtering through the thick, deciduous canopy and dappling the sodden leaves below. The musky scent of decay hung in the air, and the Forest was unnaturally still, not a sound to be heard.

Leafsong plodded along sullenly, the leaves disintegrating into wet mush beneath her.

Faal's light was eventually blocked by a thick web of branches as the canopy grew denser and the woods grew darker.

The young noblewoman paid little attention. She had a splitting headache, and her eyes were puffy, salt-encrusted welts. A while back, she had realized that she should turn back, but she was lost.

At first, Leafsong didn't notice the small, soft, green lights that began to fill the space around her. She just sniffled, watching her feet move as she trudged slowly forwards.

But suddenly, a green blur whizzed past her face and she stopped, startled.

She had reached the center of the Forest, its dark heart and den of mysteries.

Fireflies flitted about the space like green wisps, dancing around a humongous tree, its trunk nearly sixteen-feet-wide and twisted like a coil. Hundreds of feet tall, its ebon surface was marked with tiny knobs, bumps for every soul it contained. Faint swashes of red light periodically shimmered across its surface.

What stood out the most about the tree, was that instead of reaching towards the sun, its branches curved downwards and into the ground, tunneling through the moss-covered soil. Red light streamed upwards from the branches and into its faintly glowing core with an eerie whooshing sound, pulled between sharp, downturned spines and into its crystalline Shadowheart.

This is...the place from my vision!

Leafsong stared at the goliath in awe.

She knew what it was, its significance, but all she knew was from stories. Before her stood a Shadowrise tree.

This makes no sense! All the Qeonian Shadowrise were uprooted and burned centuries ago. So why...

Though it shouldn't have existed, the Shadowrise stood before her in spite of all the historical texts and sacred myths, very much alive.

Something took hold of Leafsong as she gazed upon it. A lust.

Her eyes gleamed an unsettling green.

Not in her right mind, she slowly approached the tree and broke off one of the spines at its base, dripping with dark purple poison.

Not motivated by grief, but possessed by some malevolent power, she watched in horror as she stabbed the spine into the crook of her elbow.

The Shadowrise' famous poison travelled through her veins quickly, her muscles stiffening and her skin stinging.

She called out to anyone, anything that could help her. She didn't know what magic bound her, and she couldn't break free.

No one was there. But still, someone came to her aid.

A voice entered her mind, strangely calming.

This is going to hurt. But I won't let him have you, it told her.

Grab onto the Shadowrise, and don't let go. Let yourself flow into it... Heal the tree, and I promise that you will not die.

Leafsong's eyes washed blue, and the entity took control.

The spirit that had first possessed her could not fight it. She could not fight it.

The young noble took hold of the tree, her essence flowing past smooth bark and through dense wood, her soul overwhelming everything, absorbing the life force of myriad worms that tore through the tree's soft heartwood and ruined it from within, Twisting it.

In less than a minute, it was over. She withdrew her Lifeblood and the Shadowrise soared, Healed.

Though she had done what she was told and her essence had returned to her, the poison continued to spread, finally reaching her heart. Tendrils of wood tore their way through her body, entering every orifice and squirming through her tissue. They were in her lungs, in her brain—her very eyes! She writhed, unable to stop the pain, and then fell still, those same eyes taking on a sheen of glass.

Leafsong died beneath that storied tree, the last member of her family, and the end of a pitiful and cursed line. That girl with a human heart and human blood, that girl who had wrestled with visions beyond her understanding and trembled in the night—was gone. She would never return.

There was a soft hum as the Shadowrise absorbed her soul.

For a long time, there was silence.

Then, there was a wave of blue light, The Shadowheart converting energy into matter and bringing Leafsong back to life, abandoning her poisoned corpse in its confusion, and weaving together a form that was entirely new, never before seen in all the worlds.

Skotathis

Skotathis seethed.

One of The Snares had been Healed, by a young girl no less, the Lifeblood he had collected lost to his opponent. Frustrated and angry, The Adversary broke from the Faalan Shadowrise, punching it and leaving a large dent in its bark. He let out a deep breath and took hold of himself, trying to regain his senses.

He had to plan what to do next. Luxyruss would not beat him. He would never allow that blue-eyed oaf to win, but The Brightest Star had played his cards well this time.

Still, not that well. Skotathis Awareness had alerted him to his enemy's plot in time to intervene with the Healing of the tree. Though he ultimately couldn't stop it, he had killed the girl, and, by interacting through the tree, he had also figured out where The Divinity was.

I know what you're trying to do, Luxyruss... You're trying to Heal my Snares. But that won't be enough, golden boy. I've found you; I drew you in along with the girl. Now, I will hunt you... A single Shadowheart is a small price to pay to finally be rid of you.

Although Skotathis had learned something critical in the interaction, it was still a big blow to lose a Shadowheart, especially The Qeonian Shadowheart. The souls of Avenshra's largest Continental Nation, collected over thousands of years, would begin to slowly return to the environment, Lifeblood beyond imagination wasted. Unfortunately, he didn't have the time to wait for a proper Convergence to try and Twist the tree again. He needed to continue with his plan, maintain his grip on the three remaining Snares.

I will regain control of Avenshra. I've risked too much already.

Skotathis could feel the planets slowly aligning, something only a Power could sense. They were taking the perfect position for an Invasion.

They will fight, but in the end, they will lose. They no longer have The Warriors.

The Coincidence approaches. It's time to take this war to the ground. But first, I'll take care of you, Y'shan.

Skotathis called for M'Cael.

The new leader of the Crystalline attended him, obsidian spikes protruding from wrinkled eye sockets, the same material as his claws. The fallen angel had grown taller and more muscular, and his skin was very pale.

He wore a long, black cloth around his mouth and nose.

M'Cael spoke in a tone like rock crumbling or fire crackling.

A broken man, a thing.

"How can I serve?"

Leafsong

Leafsong examined her reflection in a forest stream. She couldn't tell what was real anymore, unable to recognize herself. She had turned into something new, something that wasn't quite human.

She resembled the dryads of Qeonian myth, the spirits of the wood that served the goddess Tásara. Her succulent skin was a light green, striated with translucent, pale green xylem, and her hair was a tangle of long, rope-like vines, studded with pink flower buds. Her eyes had melted from their opaque, butterfly-blue to a clear, emerald green, and her eyebrows had been replaced by tiny blades of grass.

That wasn't all. She had grown taller, stronger, and, it seemed to her, more womanly, a picture of power and grace. She was now around six feet in height, and she was much more muscular and toned than before, though calling what lay beneath her skin "muscle" wasn't strictly accurate. She had filled out in other unexpected, but equally pleasing, ways.

Leafsong grew out her hair at will, and made it braid itself, gazing into the gently trickling waters.

How did it all go this way? My life was normal. Now nothing is normal...

Leafsong hadn't tried returning to the cottage, heeding the King's blood-stained

invitation. She had remained in the woods, hoping the guards would forget about her and leave. She was at peace, there, the heavy fog banished and the plant life reawakening. The Forest of Tears no longer wept, though Leafsong's heart was deep in sorrow.

Still, she was coming to terms with her grief. Dying had motivated her to live. There was something strange about looking at her own corpse, left to be reclaimed by the earth. Moss and grass grew over her dead self, the decaying body providing them the nutrients they needed to survive.

Leafsong wondered if she was really Leafsong Ralei or someone new. Had the real Leafsong died, decaying before her, or was she the same person, but in a new body? A chill ran through her when she considered these possibilities, but she reassured herself.

He saved me like he said he would. I must trust him.

Regardless of whether or not she was the original, in the days she had spent in the Forest, Leafsong had discovered several strange and wondrous things. She no longer felt hunger, only thirst after several days, and her heartbeat was gone. She could grow "clothes" out of leaves just by imagining them, and, if she spent some of her energy, she could alter her shape and size, make herself as strong and beautiful as she had only ever dreamed of being, though she was confined to human limits. More importantly, she could send her essence through other living things, coaxing them to do her bidding and controlling them as long as they maintained physical contact.

She slowly stroked the fur of a light brown bunny, the rabbit sitting in her lap without fear. Part of her Lifeblood was in the animal, but even so, it was more at ease with her than it would have been with a normal human.

She thought about what had happened, basking in the warmth that now emanated from The Shadowrise.

From all the stories, Leafsong had been sure that Shadowrise poison was lethal, and indeed, her corpse lay beside her, but for some reason her soul had been spared, and the tree no longer gave off a sinister aura. She was certain that whatever had drawn her to it in the first place hadn't given her her life by choice, because when she Healed the tree, she had felt a terrible fight beneath its surface.

Was the fight between the presence in the tree and her savior some sort of spiritual battle? Who was fighting over her, and why? Was her savior the source of the visions? Or was it her possessor? Leafsong didn't know, and she had received no answers.

Nevertheless, the newly Healed Shadowrise was something to behold. Its bark glittered a light green-gold, and its branches had receded from the ground, reaching again for the skies. Its trunk was no longer twisted and coiled; it had unfurled like a spring, the tree shooting to an enormous five-hundred-feet-tall. It towered over the canopy, a mother overseeing her children.

The Shadworise no longer sported vicious spines at its base, and the morbid bumps enumerating the souls trapped within had smoothed out. Its branches had sprouted a cloud of long, frilled, gossamer leaves, and it no longer sapped the life from its surroundings. Rather, it gave back in bright blue pulses, which travelled through the ground in ripples, feeding new life. The withered saplings and drooping wildflowers around it prospered, no longer drowned in shade and suffocated by the unnatural gloom. The tree's transparent leaves seemed to magnify the sunlight, bathing the area in a silken yellow glow that felt amazing on her skin. What had been dead leaf litter was now a meadow, and the stream in front of her had come back to life after what might have been decades, weaving over and under roots, the waters no longer blocked by rotting plant matter.

Somehow, Leafsong knew that this was how The Shadowrise trees had been in the beginning. They had not been named The Shadowrise due to the ghastly, poisonous things they had become. They had once been beacons of light and prosperity, rising from the shadows eons ago to offer life to a planet that was inhospitable and cruel. It had been a name given to them before they were maligned, when people knew their majesty, though it was still just as fitting.

Looking at that natural marvel, it became clear to Leafsong what her duty was.

She would no longer live the life of a noblewoman, waiting to marry, produce heirs, grieve over some soldier husband, and live off of inheritance, like so many other Ladies her age. She wouldn't waste her life as a bargaining chip between houses, and she would no longer stay up all night, scared that she might see another vision.

She was sure, then, that the visions were messages from her savior, vital information she needed to comprehend. No matter how scary they might be, she would listen and figure out her role in the events to come.

She would Heal The Shadowrise and help prevent the coming cataclysm.

But she didn't know where to start.

Luxyruss

Luxyruss propped himself up against the Ressidan Shadowrise, catching his breath.

He was sweating profusely, and he felt weak.

Just as he got his bearings, he felt something move in his vicinity. His sweat ran cold.

The Divinity turned around, half-frozen in shock. Standing there, was a Crystalline, the demon much bulkier than any he had ever seen, much more alive.

He hadn't even heard it, sensed it!

Luxyruss and the demon circled around each other slowly, sizing each other up.

The Divinity summoned Purifire. The demon extended its arm as well.

In a flash of red, a sword appeared out of the hollowness of space. It had come from the ring on its finger.

Luxyruss knew that sword. The golden-orange blade held the shape of a flame. Long and serpentine, a clear, light blue oval of crackled glass sat embedded in its spiked guard. The Fallstreak's oversized hilt was wrapped in soft, white leather, and its small wheel pommel held a white sapphire pommel-stone.

"M'Cael?"

Like tree bark, the ugly thrum of desiccated vocal cords.

"I'm sorry, Brother. I have been Ordered."

"M'Cael! What has he done to you?!"

Luxyruss looked with horror and pity at what had become of his friend. Not a shred of fat was to be seen on The Archangel's frame. His skin was grey as ash and his sparse hair had been cut short—dry, brittle, and white. Spikes made from Shadow Compound protruded from his wrinkled eye sockets, and shiny, obsidian claws had sprouted from his fingertips. He wore a long, fraying, black cloth around his mouth and nose, covering a face that used to belong to a Ressidan's. Obsidian scabs encrusted his scarred back, covering the spots where his wings used to be.

"Be not afraid, Brother. He has perfected me, made me whole."

"No, this isn't right. He's stolen your soul!"

"Come on, Luxyruss... You should know, better than anyone. The light, the darkness—they mean nothing. All this foolishness—over starlight! There's nothing else; there is no soul...only fire and flesh."

Luxyruss eyes narrowed.

The swords of former friends locked so fast, they outsped thought.

And the celestial bodies beyond, they locked as well.

The Coincidence had begun.

Scarolette

The group had been lucky. The island they had seen in the distance was, in fact, The Stareye Isthmus itself, where The High Empire's Outpost was located.

This is great! We won't have to travel from island to island, now. We'll be saved soon!

The raft had made landfall just as the sun began to rise, a thin, periwinkle mantle—a specter. Torran, Scarolette, and Jhett waded through the water and pulled in their craft.

They hurried inland, full of hope and excitement.

However, the group came ashore only to find The Outpost destroyed. What had once been a fearsome military base had been brought low. All that remained were scraps of leather, piles of charred, broken wood, and broken weapons, all covered in congealed, black blood.

Scarolette covered her mouth in shock.

The main fortress, a large, rectangular structure made of yellowed pine sitting on the island's eastern shore, was burned, the walls stained red with smears of blood. The roof was caved in, as if struck by a giant hammer.

They had dreamt of rescue, but had instead come across the unthinkable.

Limbs were strewn about like dice across the gameboard of war, hundreds of corpses lying in heaps on the ground. The bodies lay piled in front of the main fortress and in between the two lines of tents, which stood like traumatized bystanders.

The soldiers' suits of full plate had done little for them. Scarolette had never seen the full brutality of war, always staying behind at camp and waiting for Torran to return, but even she knew that she was looking at something inhuman. What had happened at The Outpost was not a battle, but a slaughter. She saw men and women missing faces, holding their entrails in their hands. Some had no hands, no limbs at all.

The scribe's face grew pale, her stomach overturning. She threw up what little she had eaten, gagging on coconut and acid.

The others just stood there, frozen. Torran's face was black with fear and rage. Jhett's eyes were like saucers.

At the center of the wreckage, lay a hulking boulder—a smooth, melanite egg. The twilight flowered across its gooey surface. It sat in a crater, the ground beneath it branded with otherworldly symbols that had killed the grass.

The air smelled of salt and smoke. Scarolette felt nauseous again, but she was too terrified to even move, swallowing bile along with her fear.

Torran was the first to break free from the grip of shock, prying an enchanted longsword from a lady soldier's dead hand. Jhett followed his lead, picking up a billhook. Shaking, Scarolette picked up a short sword, trying not to make any noise.

"I'm so sorry!" she whispered, trying not to look at the face of the soldier she was looting. His face was bruised, a cake of blood.

Scarolette didn't know how to use a sword, and she wasn't very strong, but it was irrelevant, then.

They all sensed it. The danger.

As if it heard their hearts' fearful beating, the egg began to move. It rocked back and forth and then stilled, wobbly. For a second, Scarolette felt relieved, but then, with a loud noise, the stone split. Cracks foaming with pus began to spread across the eggshell, releasing a pungent sulphuric steam.

From the rock, burst a tremendous scorpion, its rough, ebon carapace crusted in chocolate diamonds. It raised its velvet pincers skywards, bright green compound eyes refulgent with frenzy. It let out a clamoring trill, spitting out a stream of dark grey webbing that blacked out the light, blacking out hope.

Knowing that to hesitate was to die, the group attacked in unison, running at the monster.

The scorpion opened its mandibles and spat at them, hitting both Scarolette and Torran as Jhett jumped.

The torrent of webbing engulfed Scarolette as she tried to avoid it. Torran was caught as well, but he quickly broke free, rejoining the fight.

Scarolette screamed as the Necroscorum scurried towards her and the webbing wouldn't come loose.

But then, she heard the sound of tearing, a crackle. The scuttling stopped. Torran was shouting Jhett's name.

Just as she reached the height of panic, The High Prince freed her, rushing to help Jhett as she pulled herself from the slimy threads.

She found the two men a couple of feet away. Torran was looking up at Jhett.

The tribesman was standing on the scorpion's back. The High Prince had pinned down one of its pincers and Jhett had driven his billhook through its eye, skewering its brain, but the scorpion's tail had gone straight through his abdomen.

The Nolite shrunk, his body falling limp. He remained suspended by the scorpion's barb, held up by dead muscle and cracked thorax.

Torran and Scarolette watched open-mouthed as the tribesman fell still.

Oh my God! Jhett!

No!

Scarolette almost started crying when Jhett's eyelids suddenly unfurled. He breathed in, The Necroscorum's Lifeblood entering his nostrils.

The Nolite lifted his head, his eyes glowing a familiar red. Vortices of wind swirling from his hands, he ascended, pulling free from the poisoned barb.

And then, choking on blood, he fell back down again, falling from ten feet in the air. Breaking ribs and tearing skin, he bled even more, but the hole in his midsection began to fill up, organs regenerating.

Torran and Scarolette rushed to his aid.

Luxyruss

Luxyruss' arms were sore and strained, his left hip sitting partially out of socket. His chest and legs were covered in shallow, stinging cuts, but, miraculously, he had survived an entire minute against a greatsword. Any ordinary fighter would have died in the first or second exchange, unable to overcome the drastic difference in reach, but The Divinity was no ordinary fighter. He had eons of experience and centuries more experience than M'Cael.

If this fight goes on any longer, I'm sure to lose... I don't have the endurance I used to, and I keep holding back, even when I know I shouldn't. He may have been my friend once, but that man is gone—taken by The Tremites. If I don't cut him down now, I'll die.

But dammit, he's my best friend! I don't want to do this! There must be some other way!

Is there...no way?

What am I thinking?! That's right; there's no way! Even if part of him is still in there, even if he's somewhat lucid, Emergence is irreversible. I must kill him, especially if he's still in there. Every moment he spends alive in that form is an affront to his honor.

Purifire, please help me. I won't let him live on as a monster.

M'Cael made a sweeping, back-edge cut for Luxyruss' temple, throwing his sword in long, overhead loops. Luxyruss ducked, rushing forwards, but he was too far away to do anything. M'Cael simply swung through another loop and cut down on the same side.

The Divinity tried to parry, but it was useless, the Theonium flamberge slamming Purifire into his chest, singeing him and sending him flying towards a nearby boulder.

Luxyruss' neck opened, blood spilling. The greatsword had missed his carotid artery and jugular vein, but it had still taken a piece out of his left clavicle, flinging a chunk of bone into the grass.

He growled through the pain, whipping his momentum into a backflip and digging fingers into the dirt to stop himself. Using Synesthesia, he extended his unique, blue Lifeblood through the ground and into The Shadowrise tree.

Cold and expressionless, M'Cael lunged forwards, ready to finish the fight with a thrust to the face, but before he could get in range, roots leapt from the ground and wrapped around his ankles, tripping him.

The fallen angel fell again, tumbling and dropping his weapon, but he rolled out of it silently, tearing roots and reCalling Glorystar. He spun into a cut for The Divinity's left shoulder, swinging with all of his power.

Luxyruss ducked, the giant Fallstreak cutting clean through rock and splitting the boulder behind him in half.

The Divinity flinched, but he overcame his initial shock when he noticed an opening.

Overswing, he noted. *Now's my chance.*

Steeling himself, Luxyruss took advantage of the opening and closed the distance.

M'Cael was slow to react, trying to swing for his abdomen from below, but it was too late, the greatsword's size working against it.

He can't generate enough power to do anything from so close. This is it. I will kill him here.

I'm sorry, M'Cael. I'm really sorry.

The Divinity parried M'Cael's swing with both hands, riding along the flamberge's wavy edge and grabbing him by the shoulder with his off-hand. Pulling M'Cael towards him, he slammed his weapon through the angel's corrupted heart.

Slowly, gently, the sword lit, a single, blue funeral candle. The fire burned a vivid blue, a color that could only be called mercy.

Black blood dripped onto the grass.

M'Cael looked upon Luxyruss for a final time, and it was then that the Ressidan god knew for certain. His friend was still in there. He had been suffering the whole time. Though his face was covered, M'Cael's expression in that moment was distinctly human.

A single tear rolled down Luxyruss' face as Purifire burned away the Tremite infection, killing off the parasites that had turned a man so pure of heart. M'Cael, eyeless, could not weep as the worms died a wretched death and obsidian shattered. Claws peeled away, revealing foul-smelling, wet, white fingers. Vertebrae rearranged themselves with a slow *crackle* and exposed eye sockets lightened to a faint but slightly swollen pink, no longer raked by obsidian spikes.

Luxyruss released his sword and caught M'Cael in a brotherly embrace, not allowing him to fall again.

The Divinity wept, cradling his General as he breathed clean, Ressidan air for the last time.

A ragged breath came and went, and that was the end. M'Cael, The Archangel and First Hero, had died with some small dignity, no longer trapped in the body of a Devourer.

But it meant nothing...

Glorystar Shattered.

Luxyruss didn't bother picking up the pieces.

Absolute

Absolute walked into town a new man.

He was filthy, his feet dry, cracked, and covered in blisters. His stomach growled. He was starving, having had nothing to eat for the last three days. Itchy bumps of dead skin had built up on his arms and legs, and his hair was oily and full of dandruff, a smooth, shiny, grey cap of matted keratin. Grime ringed his neck. His face was harrowed in expression, and his lips were chapped and peeled, his thumbs ripe, and red, and skinned. He had been biting at them, risking infection, just to be able to feel something in his frostbitten hands during cold nights in the hills. Harsh stubble crusted his chin like barnacles would a skiff, and his hair hugged his ears, sticky with wax. He smelled of sweat and his voice was hoarse, but he had committed no sins; he had stayed true to himself and his religion. He had seen what he was leaving behind and recognized it, ready to turn in his unspent coins to the Monastery—looking like a beggar, but feeling like a king.

He hastily passed the vendors' carts, the brothels and the merry inns— sights and sounds of a world he had not been able to partake in or enjoy. Small, silent waves of loneliness washed over him as he passed, but the loneliness faded as his sense of accomplishment grew. The festivities had died down, and the people's demeanor was colder now that the coin had dried up.

The Acolyte smiled wearily. Through sheer willpower, he had persevered, holding fast in his faith where so many others had failed.

Still, he made sure not to make eye contact with anyone. He would not lose track of his goal, right as he was about to become a Monk and a fully realized member of The Brotherhood. He refused to join the masses in their lives of sin.

Nevertheless, to avoid any unwanted temptations, Absolute made his way back to the Monastery utilizing the town's back alleys, which were largely empty. Having spent most of his life locked away, he wasn't overly familiar with the layout of the area, but Perla was small enough that it was difficult to get lost.

Weaving through the hidden network, Absolute turned a corner only to catch sight of the girl he had seen on the first day of The White Week. She was laying on a broken cart at the end of a long, dead-end alley to his right. At first, he almost passed by, but he quickly realized that she wasn't there willingly. She had been badly beaten, and she was crying. Another Acolyte was forcing himself on her, there in the muffled darkness.

It was the kind of scene Absolute had never wanted to see.

The grey-haired Acolyte's blood boiled, but he stayed still, not making a sound. He knew that it would be unwise to intervene, to get involved in a situation like this right at the end of The White Week. Though morally justified, he would nevertheless be breaking the rules, and he was just minutes away from the Monastery, minutes away from the moment he had been preparing for his whole life.

Absolute turned to move on, but he stopped himself. There was no one else around who could help. There was no one to witness the crime.

Absolute clenched his teeth. He was the only one who could intercede.

I won't run away again.

"Hey! You!" he called out, shocked by his own boldness. His voice wavered, and his hand trembled, but he did not run.

The Acolyte didn't even acknowledge his presence, unconcerned. He continued, the girl struggling to break free.

"Hey! Leave her alone!" Absolute shouted.

"Go away asshole!" the guy called back, acknowledging him that time, but still not turning. The woman groaned.

Absolute stepped further into the alley, raising his voice and holding on to his resolve. His voice echoed.

"I'm not leaving until you let the girl go, Brother. Turn yourself in. I don't know why you've done this, but you are not yet beyond the grace of God."

The man snarled.

"I said scram, 'fore I really mess you up, asshole. I ain't no one's brother anymore!"

Absolute's fist clenched, his anger reaching his peak. That anger froze, like steam rising off a snowy, mountain peak, only to be hit by a gust of wind.

"And I said *LET HER GO.*"

Absolute's eyes darkened. The temperature in the alley dropped.

There was a second of crushing pressure, a heaviness. The rapist finally turned to face him, frustrated and angry. He turned like a man reluctantly obeying authority, but his demeanor quickly changed back to the way it was before. Unsure what had happened, but taking advantage of the distraction, the girl kicked him in the neck. Unfortunately, she only landed a glancing blow, and the man grew angrier.

Absolute ran to stop him from retaliating, but he was too far away, only halfway down the alley. The alley couldn't have been longer, then; it seemed to extend endlessly into the dark.

The Acolyte whirled around in a rage, drawing a knife from his hip and stabbing the girl in the pelvis, nailing her to the wood beneath her with a *chunk.*

The girl screamed.

Absolute froze. The girl sobbed, struggling to pull out the knife. She was bleeding profusely, her death all but a guarantee. She let out a final whimper, and then fell still.

The rapist pulled out the knife with a disgusting calmness and turned towards Absolute, sizing him up. He spat, wiping his mouth.

Absolute slowed in his advance as the man adopted a fighting stance, extending the knife towards him. He brandished the bloody knife with the self-assurance of an experienced fighter.

It was an extravagant weapon for a man in rags, a dirk with a smooth, ribbed, walnut handle and polished brass accents. The knife was new, paid for by the Monastery.

Absolute felt like throwing up.

"Should have left us alone, bitchass," the Acolyte complained. "The lady and I were having a real good time…"

He glanced back at the girl, his face conveying an emotion that should have been, but was not, remorse.

"Look at her now. She was so pretty… Damn it."

At the sight of the man's fake sadness, Absolute lost it. He rushed forward and tackled the surprised criminal to the ground, wailing on him and causing him to drop the knife.

The man's nose began to bleed, his eye swelling, but Absolute had no strategy, and he was quickly overpowered, the Acolyte putting a stop to his flurry of punches with a precise blow to the chin. Then he took the top-mount position and began slugging Absolute in the face, hitting him again, and again, and again. Each punch landed exactly, cruel in its exactness.

Absolute tried to get out from beneath the deluge, but his opponent was too strong. He might have been a farmer before coming to the Monastery, or maybe a laborer. Absolute had always been a bookworm.

I shouldn't have intervened. Now I'll never become a Monk… I'll die in this alley! I don't want to die! Please, somebody help us!

No one came, and, to Absolute's horror, the man grabbed the fallen knife off the ground beside him. The Acolyte began to stab for his face, smiling a gleeful, bloody smile. Absolute tried frantically to block, but all he managed to do was shred his fingers on the razor. Seizing in pain, Absolute left himself wide open, and finally, the man stabbed him in the stomach, Absolute coughing up blood.

As Absolute bled out, dazed and confused, his attacker robbed him of his meager belongings, jingling the bag of Liralas over him and laughing. Then, he stabbed him again, stabbing him so many times that Absolute lost count. Blood sprayed.

As the assault pressed on, he retreated into his psyche, the pain receding.

Numbness replaced it, his surroundings dulling to a pale grey-white. Everything seemed to slow down. In that sterile and timeless space, Absolute wondered what had happened to the world that people were so vile. He wondered why it was that he would die this way, never having really loved, never having known his mother or father, or even where he came from. He had never gotten to experience the joys of life, sacrificing all his opportunities to be happy for a grandeur that, at the moment, seemed so far away. He wondered if it was the destiny of all monks to die this way.

Absolute cursed himself for being so impulsive, though he couldn't bring himself to regret it. What he did not know, was that this moment had always been his fate. After all, a hero who abandons the helpless is no hero at all.

It would be a pivotal moment in history, Absolute dead amongst the dirt and cobbles. For trying to do the right thing, he would become nothing more than food for rats.

It would be a pivotal moment indeed, for the son of God is never worshipped for having lived...

The son of God is worshipped for having returned from death.

CHAPTER VII

Leafsong

Leafsong was granted another vision. It wasn't scary, unlike many from before her transformation.

She saw a group of shirtless men swinging training longswords. They were standing in a courtyard, walking on a worn, but beautiful mosaic depicting the constellations, surrounded by old, wooden pavilions. Their starched, light blue jackets hung patiently from the pegs of a nearby spear rack.

It was sundown.

Shining with sweat, the men practiced a couple of stances and group formations and then dispersed, the end of a long day of training. All of them went their separate ways, except one, who stayed behind to put away the trainers and roll the spear rack under the pavilion in case of rain. He appeared troubled.

Leafsong noticed that the man was a Captain, denoted by the silver-hilted arming sword he wore at his hip. His waxed hair was so blonde that it was almost white, and his eyes were an icy pale blue, like cracked glass.

Leafsong's savior finally broke his silence and gave her the instructions she had been waiting for.

This man... You must get to the Imperial capital. Without you, he won't come back. If you do not fight together, this world will fall. Leave the Forest when you wake; remain under cover of night. Go towards The Bay of Scales... The path will become clear to you as you go. You have people to meet and great deeds to accomplish.

The vision suddenly changed. She was standing in the snow, white as far as

186

the eye could see. She was in The Ice Fields.

There, in the sleet, stood another Shadowrise, Twisted.

It is here that you must play your role... You know what you must do. This is how we will stop him—The Fallen Light of Raj'para—my brother.

That thing that possessed me was your brother?! What does he want with the trees, and what does he want with me? You never told me who you are.

For a moment, Leafsong's savior did not respond. Then he replied, only answering one of her questions.

My name is Luxyruss. In your religion, I am God, though I am not a god. I myself am only a man, old and worn, but The Power within me predates all. It was there at the beginning, when She committed The First Sin.

The Power allows me to perform miracles on human soil, but in saving you, I gave up ownership of one of my abilities, an ability that is needed now more than ever. That is a side effect of Emanation, and it's too difficult now to take it back...

I need you to save someone. My only begotten son lies dying in the street. You must save him, bring him back from The Land of The Dead. The Powers were first used to pull and shape Lifeblood, energy made matter. My son's soul drifts away from this world, and though it is unfair to the souls that remain, I need you to bring it back. You must use The Power as it was first used—take hold of pure energy. Please, bring his Lifeblood back down to Avenshra, before it is too late.

Lifeblood? I don't understand.

Shall I...show you? This is what She did.

Though he was planets away, The Divinity touched her psyche. Leafsong's eyes opened, though she remained asleep, lying in The Shadowrise' luminous shade.

The dryad's surroundings wiped to a vacant black. Eyes bulging, she tried to take in the landscape of the vision, but it was incalculably vast. The whole universe lay before her as it was in the beginning—empty. She was seeing the way it all began.

In the beginning, there was nothing: absolute blackness, blacker than any knowable abyss. It was emptiness; it was a hollow darkness, a darkness that had never known the light. It was a darkness that was not only the absence of light, but also the absence of life. It was a pure darkness, isolation, devoid of form or name. It sat resplendent, relishing in its singularity, in its homogeny.

But, at a single, crucial point along the infinite arrow of time, the darkness was disturbed.

From the depths of that tenebrous spacial ocean, which was ignorant, fulfilled in its quiescence, rose a being foreign to the darkness. It was not of the darkness. A being that was total, full of substance.

Infinite substance, in fact.

An Initiator, a Shaper of Paths. Three moved as one, The Powers balanced though they fought violently for dominance—Order, Unification, and Division.

The Initiator had cut through the fabric of the darkness, a golden sword shining in their golden hand, though the darkness had no knowledge of swords.

The being had pierced it.

And everything outside its cold envelope rushed in—a sea of gas clouds, the amnion of Creation.

Absolute

It all fell away around him.

Absolute was gone. Avenshra was gone. Reality unfolded like the peel of an onion.

There was nothing left to see; sight had ceased.

And then, Absolute saw once more.

He was somewhere else, but it was fuzzy at first. Up ahead, he saw a faint light, an omen of death, but there was no tunnel or cave to meander through, just a vague glow beneath a veil of murk.

No "God" greeted him, no heavenly host.

There was a pause, and then he passed through the veil, some unknown force pulling him towards the light, which had grown blinding. It took him in, and spat him back out, Absolute rising quickly through a vacuum of pitch-black darkness.

He should have felt scared, but he wasn't. He felt like he was flying.

With a great warmth and a great joy, his spirit rose with the others, a swarm of red lights, like bees, flitting towards the bubbling, golden orb that floated overhead. Absolute supposed he looked the same as the others, reduced to a tiny bundle of energy, but before he could fully understand what was happening, he was pulled into and through the orb, and there was a silent wave of blue.

As a powerful Emanation, Absolute was given privilege. His corporeal form was returned to him, the Acolyte plunged, naked, into a sea of warm amber. The dense, alien fluid stung his exposed eyes, and it was uncomfortable to breathe, but he didn't drown. He felt out of place, but he distinctly felt that he wanted to stay.

Absolute calmed himself, tolerating the discomfort to look around.

Playful blobs abounded, reminiscent of jellyfish, floating slowly through the aether. They moved with a mind of their own, but where they were going, was anyone's guess.

Inside the wobbling, apatite globules, was a swirling, red mist. Absolute reached out with his hand, curious, and one of the undulating "jellyfish" came to rest in his hand. It was warm, warmer than the aether itself. It almost purred.

Though he wasn't sure how, he knew it was the girl, her spirit encapsulated in a tiny, gelatinous orb. He saw her image in his mind, the way she had looked at him, smiling, that fateful day one week ago, but the picture was fuzzy. Her presence felt weak, her essence slowly losing its character.

Absolute didn't know what was happening or how to help her.

I'm useless till the end.

Before he could move, the orb burst, and the glowing mist that had been the girl spiraled jubilantly upwards through the aether, taking on a vague, humanoid form, and climbing out from the waves.

The ghost of the girl with the tanzanite eyes began to walk across the liquid terrain, leaving him behind.

She had Surfaced.

Absolute tried to follow her, kicking desperately, but it was no use. More than anything, he wanted to see what lay past the water's edge, but something was pulling him down, not by the arm or the leg, but by his energy itself. He was being pulled back down to the land of the living, forcing him to return to the material world and all its woes.

No! Don't leave me behind!

Something tore Absolute away from paradise, the Acolyte swirling down a supernatural drain. He sank to the bottom of the aether, his newborn body disintegrating as suddenly as it had manifested.

Then, meeting some resistance, his spirit blebbed from the golden orb he had risen through a minute prior, and was sucked into a sphere of white light, which lay below. It was the light he had passed through before, clearly visible this time.

Then, to his dismay, the force that was dragging him down began to grow in magnitude. Everything turned into a blur.

Absolute was unable to scream as he was pulled through winding, ethereal branches and liminal spaces, layers upon layers enclosing him again, until, finally, he found himself standing in a small, hollow, wooden cavity.

He was inside a tree.

There was a moment of asphyxiating closeness. The tree was being forced to carry out its standard function, but in a strange and unnatural way. However, the pressure that was being placed upon it was unrelenting, and it eventually gave in.

Surprisingly, Absolute didn't panic. Something about dying and coming back to life had numbed him to the fear and disbelief. He was being jerked around, not left to die, but unable to fully live.

After a moment of awkward silence, there was a *creak*, the tree shaking.

And then the hollow opened like a set of doors. Absolute stepped out onto damp litterfall, seeing a woman, stunningly elegant, kneeling with her hand to the ground. Tree roots wrapped around her arm.

Her skin was green; her eyes were an outlandish blue. But then again, so were his.

He knew she was his destiny the moment he saw her.

Ilidar

Ilidar heard people's voices. They were frantic, but he was frantic too. No matter who they belonged to, he needed to get their attention.

The Captain lay in cold, wet mud, pinned beneath his horse. He had been pinned that way ever since the attack, with no weapons in reach that he could use to cut himself free. To keep himself from starving, he had torn bits and pieces from his horse, whose stomach had been slashed, and he had opened his mouth to the rain when it passed. It was too little, and he hadn't drank in a day and a half.

He had smeared himself in mud to protect his skin from sunburn, and, thankfully, he hadn't taken any sword cuts that could become infected, but the smell of rotting flesh was pervasive, the scent of blood, heavy in the air.

For Ilidar, the worst part of the ordeal was not the smell, but the flies, which wouldn't leave him alone. They had annoyed him non-stop, and he had wasted much of his energy trying to swat them away. They had claimed much of the meat of the animal, making it no longer edible, which was something of a loss, as the weather had been cold, and the meat had lasted for quite a while. The only silver lining was that the decrease in weight had taken some pressure off his leg. Still, seeing what the flies had done to the animal, the guardsman had wrapped his jacket over his head at night to avoid an infestation of his ears, mouth, and nose, but his arms were bitten and red, and any of the bites could quickly become something a lot worse.

Though he had been pinned for a considerable amount of time, The Captain still felt movement in his foot, and though the original pain had been replaced by pins and needles, he could wiggle his toes. His leg was intact and not crushed, and it felt okay otherwise. Deep down, however, he knew that that couldn't be true, and he feared the worst.

Even so, losing a leg was not as bad as losing his life, and Ilidar wanted to live.

All of his soldiers had died, and it was a miracle that he had survived so long. It was a miracle that he had survived at all...

The anguished guardsman tried to shout, to overpower the flickering flies, but his voice was drowned out by their incessant buzzing.

In that moment, Ilidar felt pitiful, as if he was already dead. He only managed a faint "Help!"

The Captain tried again, louder that time, his voice cracking.

"Help me!"

Still nothing.

Ilidar beat at the mud in anguish, losing hope, but he refused to give up. Mustering all of his strength, he prepared to call for help one, last time. He was too dehydrated to try again.

Hoping against hope, Ilidar cried out, straining his vocal cords.

"Somebody please help me!!!"

The voices stopped.

The Captain felt a rush of relief when he heard footsteps approaching, though he remained guarded. Whoever was coming, he would be completely at their mercy.

He prayed that the footsteps belonged to friends and not enemies.

As the footsteps came closer, it became clear that the footsteps belonged to a single individual, not the group.

Good. If they're an enemy, maybe I can overpower them and grab their weapon.

Finally, the footsteps came to a stop.

A shadow fell over Ilidar. It was a woman, though he couldn't see her face at first, the sun in his eyes. Thankfully, the sun was quickly cut off by a passing cloud, and the woman's features eventually came into focus.

Ilidar nearly cried when he saw her face.

Scarolette?

The fact that the voices had belonged to allies was good enough. The fact that one of those voices was someone he knew was almost too good to be true, and Ilidar questioned his sanity.

Am I delirious?

Still, there was no denying it. It was Scarolette.

"Scarolette!" Ilidar cried soundlessly.

The royal scribe stumbled and fell into the mud in shock, but she quickly snapped out of it and hugged him, trying to pull him loose.

"Ilidar? What- What happened to you?! Divinity above—Torran, it's Ilidar!!! We need to help him!"

Another pair of footsteps began to approach. Ilidar's face brightened even more.

Torran?

Torran!

Viktor

Viktor had been imprisoned in the small, dimly lit chamber at the top of The Hemian Royal Palace's western tower. Much of the floor was covered by a thin, red carpet, trimmed in gold thread, which did little to cushion the cold, grey brick beneath. Spiderwebs hung from the ceiling like faded, grey-white, tapestries, and there was dust everywhere.

It was night out, and the new moon was high—the only light in the darkness: a dwindling, beeswax candle sitting in a copper chamberstick, which sat on a wooden dresser containing The Prince's clothes. Next to the dresser, was a woolen bed with bleached, cotton sheets and a red, down comforter. The bed sat on top of a simple, wood frame, and underneath it was a tarnished, brass chamber pot. The chamber's one, round, open window was criss-crossed with rusting, iron bars.

For all its drab smallness, the room would have been cozy enough, if not for the cold air that poured in along with the suffocating, sulphurous fumes from Mount Criant.

Viktor frowned, pacing back and forth agitatedly.

What the hell is taking him so long? He should be here already.

It had been days since anyone had visited the Prince, and no one paid him much attention. The only other person around was the Astrian soldier keeping guard of the tower.

At the moment, the guard was leaning against the red, wooden door at the base of the tower. He had fallen asleep.

Viktor didn't miss the attention. The less attention paid to him, the easier it would be to carry out his plans. It would be problematic if his guest was spotted. He just wished his guest would hurry up.

The Hemian Prince had initially been surprised at the laxity of the Astrian security, but during his imprisonment, it had become clear that The Imperial Army was spread thin. They had won against his father, Falin, by a hair.

That hair had been Torran Xandromen.

In the beginning, The High Sword had been smart enough to be wary of

Viktor, but amidst the chaos of rebuilding the city, it seemed that the man had dismissed him as a threat, eventually forgetting about him entirely.

It made sense. Sunveil was destroyed, its secret weapon revealed, and the nobility had all fallen in line as soon as The Queen was placed under house arrest. Viktor was just a young hostage, left to cough and wheeze. He couldn't do anything. He owned next to nothing.

Or so they thought.

In reality, the Hemian Prince had all the tools he needed at his disposal: a mysterious, black box, a sword, a suit of armor, and a dragon scale that could store a soul. One soul would be more than enough...

Finally, after much waiting, the assassin arrived, stumbling through a swirling, red portal that opened under the chamber window. He had Evanesced.

To Viktor's annoyance, he hadn't seen the assassin come into the city. It meant that he was having trouble seeing heat signatures, a skill he couldn't stand to lose. How the man had reached the tower at such a height using The Travel Spell was beyond him, but it didn't matter, then.

"Your Highness." The man bowed. "I have come bearing gifts... It is done."

The assassin dropped a bag containing the heads of each of the targets specified, cleanly cut. He had passed Viktor's test.

"Your skill, Revangel, is not exaggerated, but you're late. What kept you?" the Prince inquired.

"My apologies, your Highness. I was delayed."

The assassin's response was vague, but although the man's flowery, purple trench coat hid the full extent of the damage, Viktor could sense that he was injured.

Viktor ushered him to sit down on the bed.

"Come, let us discuss the job."

With a crinkling of leather, the man sat, visibly uncomfortable.

Viktor turned, coughing, and rummaged through his possessions, which were hidden under the clothes in his dresser. From beneath socks and undergarments, he produced a chest, carved from obsidian.

The Raishian opened it carefully, producing a glass vial containing a nacreous liquid.

"Is that it?" asked the assassin.

"Yes—water from Judas... It came to Avrenshra in a meteor a long time ago. Beautiful, isn't it?"

"It is, your Highness."

Viktor gently put the vial back in the chest and Drained himself slightly to seal it, making its contents unstealable. Breaking the box would surely break the vial as well.

"It will soon be yours, if you help me. You have passed my test and proven your capabilities. However, you will only receive payment upon completion of the job."

Remembering that the real job was incomplete, the assassin grew uneasy, and although he had done much to prove himself, it was clear to Viktor that he was getting cold feet.

But you can't say no... Without this, your sister dies, and you can't let that happen, right?

"Or, you can just take some coin and leave..." Viktor suggested coyly. "My friend, Lord Elrisain, could pay you right now, and I can find someone else to do the job. It would be a bit difficult, though, seeing as you've killed all the best assassins for me."

Revangel frowned, crossing his arms.

"How do I know you'll come through? Why not sell me out for what I've already done?"

Viktor chuckled, dryly, putting the chest back in his dresser and covering it again with his clothes.

"You don't, but still, I give you my word. The chest will open only once the job is done, and I have no plans to give its contents to anyone else... You're the best I have seen... Think about it. With the water in the vial, you can finally cure your sister! But again, you must see the job to completion."

"This must be an insane job for you to risk so much, and pit me against all these other assassins. Tell me, your Highness—what exactly is completion?"

Viktor paused, pursing his lips.

"I need you to kill The High Emperor."

Leafsong

The man was disoriented.

The Divinity's son looked at Leafsong like she was from another planet, and he wasn't standing straight, as if the ground was tilted beneath his feet.

After a moment of pause, he walked up to her and extended his hand in greeting. He gave her an easy smile.

The roots drew back from Leafsong's arm, releasing her. She took his hand almost instinctively.

"My name is Absolute," he told her calmly. "What's your name?"

"My name is Leafsong," she replied, flustered.

"Leafsong," he repeated, squeezing her hand warmly. "I owe you my life."

Leafsong's cheeks flushed, embarrassed. She turned away for a moment, unsure what to say, but composed herself and turned around again. She turned around only for him to say something outrageous.

"Tell me, Leafsong, what pains you so? Your grace hides it, but I can tell that your heart is full of suffering."

"I—"

"You can tell me," he affirmed kindly.

Leafsong was at a loss. The man didn't even blink. He simply smiled again.

He's definitely not all there. What pains me?! You just came back from the dead! You don't even know who I am or where we are!

But then, why do I feel so...

Leafsong looked silently into his eyes. They were blue.

She began to sweat, warm dew dripping down her neck in the darkness.

He was good-looking. His eyes were blue, too blue. They were unearthly, magnetic.

"Can you feel it?" Absolute asked.

"Feel what?" the dryad blurted, heart pounding. She quickly let go of his hand, but she didn't step back.

Leafsong wasn't sure what was happening. Something drew her to him, like roots seeking water.

The Divinity's son took her hand again, more gentle that time.

"What you have made me. What we have become."

The night hummed.

Absolute leaned in towards her, his face illuminated only by the glow from his blue, blue eyes. The new moon providing no light, and the glow from the Shadowrise was weak in comparison.

Leafsong leaned in too. She didn't know why.

And then, their soft lips locked together. The bond was like hot rivers connecting, consuming each other. Like drinking the sun.

Leafsong had never seen the man in her life, yet it felt right to her. Like it was meant to be. She was meant to be with him, and he was meant to be with her.

They were the same.

And through chance, through luck, they had come together, transcending death,

transcending despair.

They were two halves of a greater whole.

One flesh.

Leafsong didn't worry about anything at all. Not the tragedy she had lived through. Not the visions, or the mission. Not even why he was there: Absolute, the man with the deep blue eyes.

Just a feeling she had never felt before, kissing a stranger, breast pressed against a solar tornado.

Peace.

The apparition disintegrated. Absolute was there one moment, gone the next. His body turned to dust in a flash of blue light.

Leafsong was left reeling, clutching empty air, unsure whether anything that had just happened was real. She felt like she had let go of something, like she hadn't just been holding Absolute, but holding him there.

What on Avenshra?

The Divinity's voice cut through her thoughts like a knife.

Leafsong nearly jumped, mortified and scared of what he would say, but the deity did not chastise her.

Hurry, Leafsong; you must go. My son must make his way alone for now. Make for The Bay of Scales.

Arceon begins to rise.

Leafsong could hardly hear him, her heart pounding too loudly in her head. She realized, then, what she had done.

She had fallen in love with a monk.

She had fallen in love with a god.

Absolute

Absolute jerked, scaring rats.

He was back in the alley, unsure what had just happened or where he had been.

He could still feel her kissing him, lips against soft lips. Soothing.

How did I... What came over me?

Absolute sat up, looking for knife wounds but finding none. His robes were bleached of blood, bright white, and his stomach was flawless, no holes at all. The oil and dirt that had accumulated over his stay in the mountains had been peeled away, his skin as smooth as a newborn babe's. He was completely clean.

That was not all. Absolute had changed at a fundamental level. He was no longer the hunched-over, skinny, awkward-looking weakling he had always been. He had been granted an improved body, his damaged corpse destroyed and replaced with a vessel suitable to receive his father's Power.

It was indeed suitable. His spine had straightened out, years of late nights studying lifted from his back. His hair had a lustrous new sheen to it, no longer grey, but a shiny, silver-white, and his eyes had washed to a glowing aquamarine, irises rippling with concentric rings of blue that differed in shade and intensity. In those eyes, pooled deep wells of wisdom, empathy, and understanding, putting human fears to rest.

Although Absolute was still quite pale and hairless, he had developed visible muscle definition, and his form was very lean, as if carved from living marble. His features had hardened, more masculine and mature, and there was a directness to his demeanor, a confidence he had lacked.

Absolute had not only survived, but become better than he was... If he trained, he could become strong. If he fought for his people, made defending them his purpose, he could become a god.

The resurrected monk looked at the strange sign that had appeared on the back of his right hand. A blue pall connected his wrist to the knuckles of his pointer and pinky fingers, slender at each point. He didn't recognize the symbol, but at that moment, everything was new and surprising.

On his left hand, was a smooth, polished, silver ring, light and shiny, as if composed of solid mercury. Absolute didn't know what to make of it.

Absolute didn't know what to make of his situation at all, his mind sluggish and his surroundings soft and intangible. He was intoxicated, dazed, though he had drunk no liquor.

Reality felt surreal to him as he got up, the cold grit of the material world hitting him like a lead hammer. Swaying, he stumbled across the dark, grimy alley, leaning against the alley wall to steady himself. The rough-hewn, grey brick was almost aggressive in its verity.

Then, Absolute remembered the girl.

He scrambled over to the cart where she had been stabbed, which was draped in a fuzzy sheet of dust as soft and airy as a layer cake. Her skin was dry and sallow, congealed streams of blood running down her stomach. She was nude from the waist down, covered in scrapes and bruises.

Absolute reached out with a shaky hand, touching her limp arm.

She was cold to the touch.

Though Absolute knew, rationally, that she was gone, he jostled her shoulders like a child would, wishing that she would wake up, begging her to wake up.

But it was not to be. He had seen her soul leave the world, enter another.

Guilt ate into him deeper than any rat could have.

Why am I alive and she isn't?! Leafsong brought me back instead of her! I'm not worth it.

I was brought back from death just to kiss a stranger.

This is so messed up... I'm messed up.

Absolute could barely bring himself to look at her, heart stinging, but he forced his eyes, forced them to take in the full consequence of his actions. The girl's glazed, tanzanite eyes were harsh and accusatory.

You did this to me, they spat. *You don't deserve a second chance.*

Absolute squeezed out tears, burning with salt. He wiped his face.

I know. But now it is done.

Absolute lowered the girl's eyelids and covered her. He took her with both hands and carried her. She was his burden to bear. After all, his choices had led to her demise...

Absolute knew that without the coins he'd been given, he wouldn't be allowed back into the Monastery. He wouldn't be allowed to join the Monks' holy brotherhood, and he didn't aspire to it anymore. Not after all that had happened.

The order was a lie; its students were just as bad as all the rest.

And he was one of them. He bore the most blame.

Absolute felt Brother Amalgus judging him, staring down at him from the clouds. There in the half-light, he hung his head. The twilight gleamed, reflecting off his silken hair like a halo.

He didn't know what he had just witnessed, what the afterlife truly was, but he knew he could never be a monk like Amalgus, even in spirit. Though he was outwardly clean, his soul had been indelibly stained. And although he had been wholly submerged in the divine, seeing past mortal veils, he could never again be a believer. His mind had been liberated against its will, thrust like a helpless animal into a world that was masterless and uncertain, without purpose or a reason for being.

Never again could he be innocent or blameless.

He would bury the girl in the desert. It was all he could do.

CHAPTER VIII

Torran

Torran grunted, working with Jhett to lift the dead horse off of Ilidar.

As the horse slid off, they were met with a nasty surprise. Maggots were in Ilidar's leg, so many that their squirming made noise. They plopped in and out of his skin.

Scarolette threw up when she looked.

The High Prince felt pretty queasy himself, but it wasn't the first time he had seen maggots eating flesh, just the first time eating living flesh.

Scarolette had been very brave throughout the journey, but at that moment, Torran saw that she was ghastly pale. The Imperial scribe looked on, mortified.

Jhett motioned to him knowingly.

Right. Let's do this somewhere else.

Together, Torran and Jhett dragged Ilidar into the nearest tent and away from Scarolette, laying him down on a wooden table. Jhett began to press firmly on the wound, removing the maggots like it was the most normal thing in the world.

The guardsman cursed at him, growling, but the Nolite kept going. Ilidar's back arched, and he pressed his fingers into the table, gritting his teeth.

Jhett stopped.

"Bite your jacket. I am sorry, but this will hurt. I have seen this before, and it could become much worse."

After a moment of refusal, the Captain bit down on the high collar of his jacket, and the tribesman continued to press on the wound. Most of the maggots were squeezed out with a *squelch*.

Ilidar screamed, then fell unconscious.

Jhett wiped away the maggots, disgusted.

Then he took Ilidar's feet, and, at his instruction, Torran took Ilidar's shoulders.

"Help me bring him to the water," the Nolite breathed. "The salt will draw out the rest."

Torran did as he was told, ordered around by a commoner for the first time in his life. He just hoped Jhett knew what he was talking about, that they wouldn't cause infection.

The two men hurried Ilidar over to the beach.

Ilidar woke up as soon as his foot touched the water. Jhett submerged the infested leg, massaging it. A good deal of engorged maggots floated to the surface.

Torran gagged, and Ilidar bawled.

"Please, stop! A-how; it hurts!!!"

The men ignored his pleas, though it pained the Prince to hear his friend in pain. They took Ilidar out of the water only after a thorough cleaning.

Scarolette approached, offering Jhett a piece of her dress to wrap the wound, red fabric fluttering in the wind. She had given away so many pieces of her dress that what she wore couldn't even be called a skirt anymore, but she refused to wear anything coming from the corpses, and they let her be.

She he didn't make eye contact.

Jhett took the fabric, but he didn't wrap Ilidar's leg immediately. At his urging, Torran helped pick the Captain up again, the tribesman beckoning to one of the nearby campfires.

Scarolette looked at Ilidar's leg, a mess of bloody craters, half in shock and half-gripped by morbid curiosity. Torran's mind went to a dark place wondering what would become of his friend.

Will he ever walk again?

Ilidar blubbered incoherently, dragging his feet as the men took him by the shoulder and brought him over to one of the logs near the fireplace, letting him rest on a makeshift bench.

The guardsman was not his usual brave self; he had been through too much. When he sat down and saw the wound, he fell unconscious again, the group moving him so that he lay against the log like a pillow.

"Well—thank God that's over," Torran exhaled. "I never knew that what doctors have to deal with is so bad. I wouldn't have been able to do what you did, Jhett, but what you did saved his life."

"Yeah, that was really horrible, but somehow, you knew exactly what to do," Scarolette chimed in. "You could be a surgeon, Jhett, with that kind of skill."

"I am glad that I could help, but our work is not yet done. I must start a fire," the tribesman replied, stone-faced.

"To keep him dry, right?" asked Torran. "Prevent infection?"

"No—well—yes... We must also seal the wound."

Scarolette turned away and retched.

After melting the bloody boreholes with a sword heated over the fire, the group brought Ilidar into one of the tents, his leg wrapped in the singed piece of fabric that had come from Scarolette's dress, which they had sterilized by swinging through the fire.

The tent had a low ceiling and a dirt floor, but it was still pretty comfortable. The Captain rested on a woolen bed, which was supported by a simple, pine frame. They had removed his clothes and replaced them with bear skins from one of the dead officers' beds. The only other furnishings were a sturdy, wooden stool, a steel chamber pot, and a lantern made of glass and steel. The room was relatively warm, the unbleached canvas walls keeping out the humid cold, but the tent smelled of salt and sweat, and the acrid smell of burnt skin made it unpleasant. Still, the tent was in surprisingly good condition, and so were many others.

It seemed that the attackers simply came and went. Where they had gone, however, was a mystery...

Having saved Ilidar, The Outpost's only survivor, Torran, Scarolette, and Jhett worked together to move the bodies of the fallen to the main command tent, stacking them between layers of wood and hay.

Torran took care of the bodies that were in particularly gruesome condition. Scarolette was willing to help, but he denied her.

These are Astrian soldiers. As their Prince, it is my responsibility to put them to rest. You've already done enough.

This is not a sight for a scribe.

Once all the bodies had been gathered, Torran and Scarolette said a quick prayer and then set the tent ablaze, watching it go down. Jhett's eyes glimmered in the firelight, but he said nothing.

By the time smoke stopped rising from the fire, it was already night. Fixing the camp had taken the whole day. Though The Outpost was a significant military installation, it was significant due to its positioning and its ships, not its manpower, and so it had been doable for the group of three, though it had made them tired, and weary at heart.

I have to check on the ships, but I'll do it tomorrow. They're docked all the way on the other side of the island, and right now, I'm too worn out...

The High Prince walked up to the campfire, lit from before, when they had treated Ilidar. A wide, pine log served as its only bench. Jhett walked off towards the beach from where they had come, wanting to be alone.

Torran felt ashamed that he hadn't gone out collecting food with him earlier, but he could barely move after all the abuse his body had taken the past few weeks, and he didn't feel very hungry after what they had just seen. He had told Scarolette and Jhett to eat a portion for him, but it seemed that they too had lost their appetite.

Though the former galley slave said he hated the ocean, it seemed that something about it was inescapable, too familiar for him to ever get too far from it. Torran felt the same way about the life of a soldier. His father had always sent him off to one place or another.

Torran slumped against the log to catch his breath.

Scarolette sat down too.

They didn't talk. There was nothing he could say, nothing she could say... They were both completely exhausted.

The night was cold, silent except for the whistles and cracks from the fire. Scarolette had started it, though Torran hadn't seen her use flint or steel.

The pair stared at it for a while, trying to forget Ilidar's screams, the smell of cautery.

Torran tucked his hands under his arms, shivering. Though he tried not to show it on his face, he was still shaken. Though The High Prince knew the monstrosity of war, nothing he had seen so far had done so much to strike home the stark fragility of life and the senseless, brutal nature of violence, which, like some red-black whirlwind, consumed all in its path and left only bones. The confrontation left him feeling unmoored, searching for security in a vast and threatening world.

Just as he felt himself lose purchase and before he could fall from the cliff, Scarolette quietly leaned against his shoulder. They held each other, both for comfort and for warmth. They didn't bother to think about propriety.

Torran wrapped his arm around Scarolette, careful not to touch the malformed stump of her arm. Miraculously, it hadn't gotten infected, but it looked extremely painful, and he winced when he thought about it.

Torran wished for sleep but it fled from him, and so he watched her fall asleep instead. After a couple of minutes, she finally did, her face relaxing.

Her sleeping form looked peaceful—so peaceful.

Torran drew a quick, sharp breath, his chest tight. Scarolette's eyes opened for a second, but slowly fell closed again.

Scarolette was admittedly gorgeous. Her smooth, straight, red-brown hair reached down to her chest, with long bangs that sat just above her striking, emerald eyes. She had a thin, yet supple body, and a curvaceous figure, with delicate hands and long fingers that produced the finest writing Torran had ever seen. She gave off a distinct warmth, a warmth that carried with it the scent of catnip and spice. It was the kind of warmth that called out to be held, but due to some deeply ingrained inhibition, he did not dare reach out.

Torran knew that, for a long time, she had focused her efforts on gaining his attention, an attention that she already had, but he pretended to be oblivious. All he ever did was give her a few, chaste compliments and admire her out of the corner of his eye. Eventually, it seemed that she had lost interest, dressing in more muted colors and only speaking to him when spoken to, abandoning the chase. Torran knew that it was for the best. He should have felt relieved, but all that he felt when he looked at her was a cold, soft sort of ache, an ache that could only be described as longing.

The High Prince let out a pained sigh. He cursed his fear and his hesitation, cursed himself for what he had done to Scarolette. He had maimed her, the woman who, at one point, had looked up to him in admiration.

Torran's jaw clenched. Every time he thought about Scarolette's wound, he felt horrible about himself. He felt unworthy to be alive for hurting such a beautiful woman, his friend. He had saved her life, and she seemed to have forgiven him, but he still hated himself for it.

What was worse was that he constantly wanted to tell her how he felt, even in this situation. But he couldn't. Every time he opened his mouth to speak, the metal hooks of doubt would dig into his skin, and he would stop himself.

Who was he to ask her to love him? She might feel safe with him, but she could never love him.

Had she really forgiven him? Maybe she hated him, but knew that when they got to Astria, he would be a Prince again, and she would be no one, just a lower-level noble from the outskirts of Springhaven. That must have been why she was drawing close to him again.

No, that was stupid.

Scarolette shifted, letting out a cool breath, her red-brown hair slipping past her shoulder and tickling his fingers.

She didn't open her eyes, but she had woken up.

"What's wrong, Torran?" she asked, quietly.

Torran paused. He had been caught staring.

"How can it be that I'm a Prince, a dragonslayer, and yet you're twice as strong as me? You were just a scribe a couple of weeks ago, yet now I pale in comparison to you... Scarolette, tell me true. Do you hate me for what's become of your arm?"

Scarolette's breath grew softer, then. Her head nestled in the crook of his arm, pressing into his chest. Torran's heart skipped a beat.

She replied steadily.

"No. You don't even need to ask me that."

The High Prince continued, full of doubt.

"But why? I keep asking myself: why would you sacrifice so much for me? You've stayed with me through it all, stayed with me more than my own men or even Ilidar, but I know almost nothing about you. I don't even know about your past, what your hopes and dreams are. Why risk so much for someone like me? No one would have blamed you if you had fled Hemia alone."

"You really can't see it, can you?" she asked, incredulous. She inspected his face for a moment, looking up with those wide, argent eyes.

Torran's muscles tensed. His pulse raced rapidly, chaotically.

Scarolette leaned over slowly, and kissed him. Soft, strawberry lips— beneath them, a blistering heat, barely repressed.

When their lips touched, the dwindling fire revived, sparks showering them, but Torran took no notice. He took no notice of anything but her. It didn't matter to him that her dress was torn, that her nails were too long, or that her hair was tangled, full of knots. All he knew was that he wanted that moment with Scarolette to last forever. He would have been delighted to die right then, then at the beginning of the end.

But finally, she broke away, her eyes red in the firelight.

"Does that answer your question, your Highness?" she asked, breath trembling.

He saw it then. She had feelings for him too; she had never wanted a protector or a friend. She had always wanted more than that, wanted him ever since they had left for Hemia in the first place, assigned to him as his scribe. And even then, though they were both tired, haunted by the shadow of death, she still wanted him.

Torran's eyes watered from the smoke, uncertain whether to make a move. Scarolette pulled at his ragged tunic, crossing the threshold.

In a whirl of movement, they tore at each other's clothing, Torran's heart pounding, breaking ribs. They tumbled to and fro on the ground, frenzied, churning up dust.

Torran hoisted her up, holding her above the ground, and they both gasped, pressing into each other viciously.

Though they had worked doggedly, they felt no tiredness, no pain. Their injuries belonged to another world, one that no longer existed, one which was obliterated.

Scarolette wrapped her legs around Torran's enduring back. He carried her to the nearest tent, where they fell into a pile of soft hay, unable to part. Together, they entered a realm of shared euphoria, of ecstasy, forgetting the horrors they had witnessed.

Torran woke up warm, though there were no sheets or furs on their bed of hay.

Scarolette was still, dark red hair cascading down her perfect body, lifting slightly every time she exhaled.

Torran reluctantly separated himself from her wonderful warmth and padded barefoot across the tent's dirt floor, picking up his clothes off of a nearby stool and putting them on.

Dressed, he peered out from the tent, greeted by quickly fading stars. Jhett was nowhere to be seen.

Torran looked at the fire pit. The flames had been rekindled.

It must have been Jhett, though when the Nolite had done it, he had no idea. Ilidar lay against the log beside it, swaddled in furs like a baby. His makeshift bandage had been replaced with a real one salvaged from the tents.

Torran was suddenly overcome with awe. The tribesman owed them nothing, yet he had accompanied them the whole way. He had saved them, fought for them, and even healed their friend, holding no grudges, though they hailed from The High Empire, the Empire allied with the Nation that had taken everything from him.

I don't care what he looks like, or that Qeonia is our ally. When I get home, I'm going to make the man a Lord. I'll give him whatever resources he wants, I'll make him rich beyond comprehension. If he wishes to seek justice, I'll make it my business as well. He is a real hero, and in his name, I will personally ensure that no man, woman, or child is ever made a slave again. I will meet with Amphitritton and force him to end it all for real, not just on paper.

No more half-measures.

Torran walked over to the fire, stooped down, and roused Ilidar gently.

The Captain sprung up, panicked and unsettled, as if he had just remembered something, but Torran stopped him.

"No, don't get up. You'll hurt yourself."

The man had been out cold since the cauterization, and the group couldn't get any answers from him in his condition the previous night, so his agitation made sense.

"Torran, we must send word! They're coming!"

"That's why I woke you up. I need to know, Ilidar—who did all this?"

"I— I..." Ilidar began drifting off. He was falling unconscious again.

Torran squeezed his hand.

"I need you to stay awake, okay? You need to tell me what happened here if I am to send word. Who did this, Ilidar? The Frosslar?"

' Ilidar no longer stayed awake by force of will.

"The Frosslar? No! These things, they came from the sky! Green beams of light came from the moon! Next thing we know, there were th-these Goblins standing there—hideous monsters with black swords! Knights in full armor couldn't stop them; horses couldn't stop them! They destroyed The Outpost, plowed through my men like they were nothing."

I see... It's just as I feared.

Ilidar grimaced, grabbing his head.

"Oh, man... They killed my men. They killed my horse..."

The guardsman looked at his leg as if, momentarily, he couldn't remember what happened, but he let go of the thought and leaned back again, ready to go back to unconsciousness and healing sleep.

"So they're already here. This is worse than I thought."

Ilidar sprung awake again.

"Wait, you knew about them? What— What are those things?!" he asked, terrified.

"Demons," Torran replied gravely. "There will be more. Seeing that they have hit The Outpost, they're coming for Astria."

"What on Avenshra is happening, Torran? First dragons, now demons! You disappear and then come back with no one but your scribe and that Nolite tribesman, secret knowledge! They said you died at sea! We sent word to your father that you hadn't arrived! No one could believe that you were dead, but we were all beginning to give up hope."

"Scarolette is no longer just my scribe, and that tribesman has been the one thing keeping us alive... Our ship did go down. The entire crew perished."

"What?! You mean–"

Torran cut him off.

"Tell me Ilidar, how is my father? My sister? Are they alright?"

"They were fine the last I saw them, but now, Torran, I'm not so sure. If this is coming for them..." Ilidar was still out of it, slurring his words and asking strings of important but unrelated questions.

"Where did you come from?"

"We came from one of the nearby islands. When Scarolette and I left Hemia and I was recovering from my wounds, I spoke to The Divinity in a dream. He told me that he would bring tragedy upon my crew, that he would set me on some sort of path to stop The Demonium. Just like that, our ship was struck by lightning, and the mainmast would have killed me if it hadn't been for Scarolette. She saved my life but lost her arm in the process. Unfortunately, I got struck by another bolt of lightning, and our ship sank. We only managed to survive because some Spirit saved us. We tied ourselves to one of the pieces from the wreckage and, the next day, we found ourselves on the same island as Jhett, whose ship had sunk a few days prior."

"How are you standing, then?! They say you killed a dragon and fell hundreds of feet! Struck by lightning?! That can't be possible."

"I don't really know what to say. Some sort of magic was afoot when the ship sunk, and it kept us from dying. Although I don't know what has changed exactly, Scarolette and I... Well—we aren't the same anymore."

"What do you mean? And how exactly did you get here from another island? I'm so confu-"

"Listen, I know it's crazy, but right now, I'm just as lost as you. What matters, is that we have to get back to Astria now; we must depart. Rest is good, but if we don't get to Astria soon, we will all starve and die, and without proper treatment, it's not like your leg will get better..."

Ilidar looked at his leg piteously, the skin a single red, melted thing.

Torran changed the subject. "We have to warn everyone that the demons are coming, and I doubt they'll believe it unless we're standing in front of them. We need to tell them what has happened; what we've seen."

The High Prince stood.

"Just rest up for now. I'm going to try and find a dove to send a message to the capital. Then I'll see if I can find us a ship."

One of those birds better be alive.

Flind

Flind scrubbed away at the dirty, grey stone floor of the Temple, using a harsh, brown brush. A brown-yellow mixture of water, sand, and lye dripped down the brush's handle, chapping her already dried-out hands. Her skin split in tingling fissures, keratinized lines criss-crossing her palms.

Though she wished that she had some tallow to moisturize her hands, Flind wasn't afraid of hard work. She had been a hard worker all her life, bowing her head to the floor and scrubbing. She and the dirt had a sort of kinship. And although most of the nuns were unfriendly, helping because the Promises mandated it, they had helped her.

After a day without anything, Flind had been fed a modest meal of pumpkin soup, brown bread, and boiled spinach, and she had been given clothing. The only nun who had been friendly towards her, Xiao-ting, was washing her clothes, unaware that they were stolen. She had been given a set of old nun's garb for the time being, faded and fraying.

To reciprocate, the scullion had offered her services. The Sisters were hesitant at first, but eventually, they accepted. They were warrior nuns, and they spent most of their time training. They tried to stay as grounded as possible, but there was a level of grime that was intolerable, even for them, and that level had been reached a while ago. Though the earth was holy and pure, what lived in that earth wasn't necessarily friendly, and there had to be some hygiene. Up in the mountains, it was difficult to get outside help, so Flind's offer was a rare opportunity.

The Temple was small and secluded, located in a small wood near a bend in The Treasure River. Home to a small host of ten nuns, the building had only five rooms: a dormitory with thin, reed sleeping mats and a privy, a fully-stocked kitchen, a large training area, weapons hanging from racks and pegs, a prayer room—large and dark, with a grey, marble statue of the Incarnation and an army of mung bean cushions—and a small, mysterious room holding the Temple's object of veneration. What object that was, Flind didn't know, and the nuns were divided as to whether they should let her clean there. The mean-looking nun from the carriage ride, Min-ja, had been particularly against it, though she had initially praised Flind for working "close to the ground," and ever they had arrived at the Temple, the nun had been sharp and snappy with her in general, regarding her with a biting look whenever she saw her. Flind wondered whether this was because she was part of the second-lowest caste in The Kisát. But then why compliment her earlier?

Was she insulting me without me realizing it?

The scullion was unsure what could be so valuable that The Veneration Room was off-limits, but she didn't particularly care. There were very few artifacts worthy of veneration in the Lightseeker faith, and most of them had been lost to time.

Guess we'll see, she thought to herself, scrubbing a particularly large spot on the floor. It was a dark brown, and for a second, Flind feared a chamber pot spill had been left uncleaned, but she laughed the idea off.

Even the most zealous Lātists weren't so extreme with leaving dirt alone, and Lātists were generally grittier than Kïsists, who had developed finer sensibilities through their collaboration with The High Empire.

Whatever it was from, the stain was taking a long time to get out, and Flind's hands started bleeding.

Finally, after rubbing her fingers raw against the brush's wooden handle, she finished the training area floor and went on to find Xiao-ting, taking her pail of water with her.

After a brief argument with Min-ja, who could not let the group's decision rest, Xiao-ting allowed Flind into The Veneration Room, fiddling with a set of iron keys. The large, black, iron door opened with a long *creak*.

"Come on in," the nun ushered discreetly, stopping abruptly as she entered. "Bow," the woman whispered reverently.

Flind did as she was told, entering cautiously. She looked around slowly, awed by the sight that met her.

The Veneration Room glowed a warm yellow, thin, beeswax candles burning in standing candelabras ringed with polished, circular, bronze mirrors. Dust hovered in the air like powdered gold, suspended in the quiet.

On a large, trapezoidal, grey block at the center of the room, stood a wooden mannequin in a set of armor.

This wasn't just any armor, but the lost armor of The Incarnation herself. A set of full plate, The Greenscarab Armor was made from enchanted war-beetle chitin. A shimmering, iridescent emerald color, it sparkled softly in the candlelight.

Even to Flind, who was impious, the significance of the relic before her was immediately apparent. However, as awesome as it looked to the eye, Flind doubted its authenticity. Iwidëa was said to have died by a knife to the heart, but the Armor bore no signs of damage or repair. It didn't seem like any pieces had been replaced, either, the whole set covered in small scratches. Enchanting liquid made things a lot more durable than normal, but it didn't make them invincible, especially against the enchanted steel weapons of The Imperial Army.

Haa...and they call themselves servants of Avghe'eah. How did they, who care, forget such an important detail? Religion really makes people blind.

Unless they know it's a forgery?

Nah, can't be.

At best, it's just a very expensive replica, or maybe it belonged to some other famous beetle-rider. It is very beautiful, though... It'd fetch a pretty penny most anywhere, since Luzians wouldn't know it.

"If you could do an extra good job on the floor here, it would really be appreciated," Xiao-ting commented, seeing Flind's reaction. "It really is magnificent, isn't it?" the nun smiled.

"It is," Flind responded, smiling back.

For a Kisist, Xiao-ting was a nice person, but she was still a Kïsist. She wouldn't be smiling if she knew that Flind was actually her enemy. Though Flind did not believe, it didn't change the fact that her life had been destroyed due to Kïsist oppression.

"Min-ja will stay with you for a while," the woman sighed. "She's always been the suspicious type... Just don't touch anything—except for the floor, of course," she laughed.

"Understood," Flind replied, irked, but hiding her annoyance.

I just want to get out of here.

"Great," the nun grinned. "Then I'll leave you to it. The other nuns and I are going to prayer. Min-ja will be in soon, so please bear with her as best you can."

"I see. When I'm done, I—"

"I'm sure you'll want to be on your way," the nun acknowledged, reading her mind. "Your clothes should be dry by now. They're on the clothesline by the east wall. The prayer usually lasts five hours or so, so I wish you luck and safety in your travels. I hope you find new employment."

"Thank you for having me," Flind nodded. "You've been very kind."

Only you have been kind.

"It was nothing!" Xiao-ting grinned. Thank you for all your hard work... Farewell!" she called out, flitting away. Flind knelt down and got to work.

A few minutes later, Min-ja floated into the room and stood there, leaning against an ash-wood bo staff. The scullion ignored her, but the woman's eyes were burning a hole in her neck.

Just ignore her... Ignore her, and finish.

Where do I go from here? Flind wondered, scrubbing away. The lye began to foam as she scoured a particular problem area. *I have no money.*

I really don't know what I'll do, but it's too dangerous here. With nine of the ten nuns against me, it would be risky to stay and pretend, and I'm not about to become a nun, anyway.

Behind her, the nun broke the silence.

"You missed a spot," she chewed, pointing to a spot on the floor that the scullion had already gone over. Flind clenched her fist around the brush's handle, but she didn't protest, going over the spot again.

So you talk, only to be difficult. Talk about ridiculous. You're a nun... Kïsist or Lätist, a Lightseeker's help is freely given. It's one of The Promises.

I only volunteered to do this because I felt bad, not because I had to, you hypocrite.

Xiao-ting was probably the one who forced you all to pick me up in the first place.

Again: "You missed a spot."

Hackles raised, Flind scrubbed over the second spotless spot, opening more cracks in her hands. Blue blood oozed, but she kept working, moving to the center of the room to finish it off.

Sweat dripped down her forehead in beads, but when she went to wipe it, Min-ja interrupted her, her tone sharp.

"Watch out. The statue's right there," the woman clucked.

Flind looked to her right, then over at the nun, visibly annoyed. Her elbow wasn't even close to the mannequin, and the relic was a suit of armor, not a pane of glass. Nothing would have happened.

"I didn't touch it, though?" Flind scoffed.

"You were but a hair's breadth from touching it," the nun insisted. "It's a sacred relic, Girl, not some vase."

Flind had had enough.

"Do you have a problem with me, Sister? Because if you do, you should say it."

The nun's eyes narrowed.

"My problem is that a Lātist is bleeding her filthy blood all over the floor of our Veneration Room, not treating The Incarnation's armor with respect."

Flind froze, standing up.

"Excuse me? Who ever said I was a Lātist?" the scullion asked, her tone sharp.

"In the carriage, you said that The First Promise was "A Lightseeker helps those in need." That's The First Promise in Lātism, but The Eighth Promise in Kïsism. Any real Kïsist would know that," the nun sneered.

"I- I had just woken up and hit my head," Flind floundered. She was angry, but afraid, her lie growing thin.

"Oh yeah?" the nun asked, cracking her staff across Flind's face. Flind fell to the ground, shocked. She daubed blood from her nose with shaking fingers.

"What about now? Do you remember now, floor-maid? What's The First Promise?" the nun demanded.

"It's— It's to always put Goddess above man."

"That's the Seventh, you lying bitch," Min-ja spat. "You really are a Lātist." Flind stood back up, sniffing.

"The Kïsists were the ones who got Iwidëa killed, and yet you look down on Lātists, the ones who toil in the fields to grow your grain. If you don't want me to clean, I'm leaving. We're in Qeonia, not Cairnon, so watch what you do."

The nun moved to block the door, pointing her staff at Flind's face.

"You aren't going anywhere, Afgarŕ," she said, unafraid of the law.

And there it is... Flind shook her head internally. *All that stuff about working close to the ground was bullshit, then, huh? Bigot.*

The scullion picked up her pail of water.

"I'm going to leave, so move aside, Sister. I'll return these items to their places and go. You have no right to keep me here."

"Not before you bow down eight times in apology. You lied, and disrespected The Incarnation's artifact."

"Lady, I've already cleaned your temple, and that was in exchange for a single meal and a wash of clothes. I'm not bowing down to you or your fake armor."

"Fake?" the Sister hissed. "Fake?!"

With a *whir* and a *woosh*, she swung for Flind's head, no longer an insult, but a real blow. Flind ducked, water sloshing, and swung the pail as hard as she could at Min-ja's head, weak wood breaking with a *splash* and knocking her unconscious. The nun fell to the ground with a *thud*—very still, but not dead.

"Ah!" Flind looked at the mess, her bleeding hands, and the unconscious nun. She had no time to get her stolen clothes or put anything away. She had to run—to where, she didn't know.

Anywhere. I just have to get away from here. If she wakes up, they'll beat me, or worse. They don't fear the authorities, and even if the authorities stepped in, they'd charge me with what happened at the Manor.

I have to escape.

But without anything, I...

The Armor. I should take it. I doubt it's real, but even if it is somehow, it doesn't belong in Kïsist hands. They'd have to have stolen it and hidden it here in Qeonia...

If anything profanes the Incarnation's name, it's having her holy armor in the hands of traitors, and it's sat here all this time. If the Incarnation lives, if she really doesn't want me to sell it—the earth can swallow me up like The Baron.

Yeah, that's right. I've gotta take it and run, Flind resolved.

I'll sell it and escape this wretched continent.

Konell

Cold wind whistled past the cluster of tall, red-brown spires overlooking Ashwell Lake. Konell watched as the dark blue waters churned bitterly, polluted with soot and heavy metals. He stood atop the tallest spire, looking down.

You didn't want to swim in those waters, but Konell didn't plan on swimming. He just needed a backup plan in case he messed up the timing.

There was an acrid smell in the air, the faint smell of copper mixed with the stronger scent of phosphorus. The sky was grey, with barely distinguishable clouds, and the rock beneath his boots was wet, and covered in some type of white-green lichen.

He was at least eighty feet up. At such a height, there was little room for error.

Suppressing his fear, Konell jumped from the cliff, feeling it in his bladder. Right before he hit the water, he Evanesced, a cloud of red smoke closing over him like a net. He rolled out of the cloud, reoriented sideways, and held his breath.

Konell found himself in a wasteland where time stood still, overseen by the judgemental eye of a perpetually-setting, red sun.

It was a world devoid of life. No clouds dotted the pale, red-tinged sky, and the desolate earth was cracked like peeling skin. There was no air to breathe, no wind, and no scent on the wind. Silence itself was muffled, buried in hourglass sand. The heat was oppressive, and the air was dry as bone.

I never thought I'd come here again... Guess it's fate, Konell reflected dryly. He found it funny how often he used The Travel Spell without ever seeing this place. Elementals like him moved through a cloud of Lifeblood, a tear in space, but they almost never saw the space they travelled through. When they travelled their usual, short distances, they saw nothing but light.

In ancient texts Konell had stolen talking about Elementals, the authors always treated Evanescence like some sort of unknowable mystery. They acted as if sorcerers could break the rules of the cosmos, and simply appear in a different location at will. The only thing they believed was impossible, was to use The Travel Spell to cross continents.

Konell had realized how stupid they were very early. Whenever Elementals teleported, they would step on something, fall through something, and it was known that momentum was required to travel. That mysterious something was ground and air, just like in the normal world.

The authors often spoke of an ethereal corridor, but acted like Elementals teleported directly, traversing no space. In truth, they traversed no time, small movements exponentially multiplied by the condensation and reexpansion of space-time before them. It was believed impossible to teleport across continents, because no one had ever tried.

This was understandable, as one had to fall a very long distance to escape the shroud, and it required Lifeblood to breathe in the wasteland that followed. One couldn't cover much ground in a single breath.

Thankfully, Konell had ample Lifeblood, though he wasn't proud of how he got it.

Konell was nothing like those Sages and their empty speculations. He had tested the limits, and found out firsthand. Traversing Untime was like diving underwater. When your Lifeblood ran out, you eventually popped back into the real world.

All things float up to the surface, given time.

One had to dive blind, and although the wasteland wouldn't keep you if you had no Lifeblood, to drown in Untime was to appear in front of a cart, at the bottom of the sea or inside of a stone.

Let's hope this doesn't end like that.

Absolute

Arceon blazed across the land, but that didn't stop the pygmy owls from making their homes in tall cacti, or the snakes from slithering across the sands in search of rodent prey. Locusts and other desert insects roamed the skies, looking for edible plant life, and crickets droned.

The sky was a pale blue and the dry air smelled of greenery, the grasses and cacti steadily losing moisture to their surroundings. There was no water in sight, and the rains wouldn't come for several months.

Absolute bit into a locust he had captured.

It was a particularly crunchy locust. It had a pasty, nutty flavor, like earth— or chestnuts, maybe. It was one of the only foods he had found in the Desert, and he had been hesitant to try it, but in the end, it wasn't that bad.

It wasn't that good either.

Nothing in The Basamor Desert was good. It just was.

The mountains were dangerous, and though the Desert had bad weather, Absolute felt that it suited him better. It wasn't as beautiful in person as it had been from far away, blue in the moonlight, but it was peaceful.

However, the point of going there hadn't been to please himself. He had gone to the Desert to bury the girl and find closure. He had gone, so he could understand what had happened to him, what exactly was going on. To reassess his faith.

Or maybe he had gone to repent, to apologize to his master for failing him, for what had happened with Leafsong—his fornication.

To take the burden off his shoulders.

Robes leaving winding trails, Absolute slowly traversed the dunes, hoping to find some shelter. He had gotten pretty far just drinking from gourds, but he would soon need to find a new water source if he didn't want to die of dehydration.

Absolute didn't know the geography of the region, but it wasn't like it was documented either way. No one went to the Desert. The Qeonian superstition was that everything far from the ocean's life-giving waters was cursed, a place of death.

Absolute thought this was nonsense, but he still couldn't shake the vague anxiety...

Though he was on a pilgrimage to nowhere, Absolute had the sense that the destination was immaterial. His goal would become apparent when he reached it. Some higher power was guiding him, setting him on a path that he simply couldn't see yet. Maybe it was God, and maybe it wasn't. Even if The Divinity of The Church and the afterlife that was promised to him didn't exist, he still had some reason for existing. Of that, he was sure. All he needed was direction.

Absolute looked to the sky, searching for a sign.

He was given one. It was bigger than expected.

Haash't

Haash't nearly spun out of the sky, shocked by what he saw.

A human. A human in the middle of The Basamor Desert.

His desert.

It had to be killed! No one could see him! And no one invaded his territory.

He had stayed in the Desert for so many years because it was empty, untouched by humans. It was a place he wouldn't be hunted, a place where he and his family could be safe.

But because of this trespassing human, centuries of ignominy were put in jeopardy. If even one survived the desert, and returned to tell the tale, more would come back.

The Aetan opened his beak.

Absolute

Absolute couldn't believe what he saw.

A golden eagle, a creature of myth and legend, was speeding across the skies.

The last golden eagle, Asteropt'r, had died out three hundred years ago. Its rider had been High Emperor Aeshius Xandromen, the son and killer of the tyrannical Red Meteor.

Like all the other kids in Perla, Absolute had heard tales of the golden eagle that flew across the Desert, but it was just a campfire story, a phantasm seen by lunatics and false prophets.

However, when the eagle's shadow fell upon him, there was no denying it. Overhead, flew a thunderbird, unseen since times of old.

The Aetan swooped down towards earth. It opened its mouth as if to cry out, yet no sound issued from its beak.

Then, there was a hint of gold.

Absolute raised his hand reflexively to protect himself. His eyes washed blue, and the pall on his hand began to glow. He didn't even know what he was doing.

With a *crash*, the eagle's plasma-breath hit a shield of frozen air, smoking light splaying in all directions.

Absolute concentrated on holding the shield together, instinctively Unifying oxygen to form a solid, sparkling, blue whole, but it was difficult. Sensing his weakness, the raptor lunged and bit down, breaking his defense.

The monk scrambled to get away. Lucklessly, the Aetan snagged his shirt before he could put any distance between them, reeling him back in and knocking him down.

The golden eagle towered over Absolute, pride incarnate. It was ten feet tall, with a twenty-five-foot wingspan and long, sharp, black talons that were as long as daggers. Its feathers were a dull, metallic, brown-gold color, with a long plume of hair-like, beige feathers flowing from its head, the same color as the fawn-like spots on its back. The insides of its wings were a similar color speckled with black. Its eyes glowed gold, with thin, x-shaped pupils.

Suddenly, Absolute heard a voice, telepathy. The Aetus Orum had invaded his mind.

Who sent you?! Who sent you to find us?!

"Sent me? What are you talking about? Let me go!" Absolute shouted aloud.

The eagle continued telepathically. It was apparent that it couldn't speak any other way.

Perhaps I was not clear, murderous human. Who sent you?! Does The Red Meteor know we are here? Is that why you have come?!"

"I'm not a murderer; I'm a monk! No one sent me... I- I chose to come here. And Xersus Xandromen—The Red Meteor—he's been dead for ages! It's been three hundred years!"

The Aetan wasn't listening, though Absolute was sure its ears were better than any human's.

Then where did you get that Callring, "monk?" the eagle asked derisively. *Do not try to trick me. I have seen that Callring on one of his Warriors... What, did he kill another one of his subordinates?!*

Are you their replacement? Did he send you to hunt us down? !

And so what if it has been three hundred years?! That man was never normal. He was already far too old before any of this started."

"Callring? What are you talking about?!" Absolute yelled, exasperated.

The golden eagle slammed him into the ground, foot on his chest. The grey-haired monk grimaced in pain.

The ring around your finger, scum.

Absolute's fear surfaced, then. He didn't need pride. He wanted to live.

I don't know; I swear! I woke up a couple days ago and it was on my finger!

The Red Meteor is dead; the world has changed! Please, you've got to believe me! I'll do whatever-

The Aetan was pushed back by a strong gust of wind. It lost its balance temporarily,

taking its foot off Absolute.

Beside it, landed a second eagle, not gold, but silver. A female.

The silver eagle was around nine feet tall, with a twenty foot wingspan and long,

white talons. Her feathers were a shimmering, powdery, steel-blue color, and a long plume of snow-white feathers flowed from her head. The insides of her wings were the same, white color, speckled with black, and she had white spots on her back. Her eyes were a shimmering, seafoam-blue, with thin, x-shaped, pupils.

The Aetus Argyrum nipped at her mate in annoyance. She appeared calmer and more friendly, though it was hard to read the birds' expressions.

I am sorry, human. My mate does not like it when others invade his territory. Especially mages. But I recognize your monk's garb. You monks were the only ones who protested against The Goldfeather Purge... Tell me, what are you doing here?

"I came to be alone, away from my hometown of Perla. A girl I knew there was murdered by a fellow Acolyte, and I couldn't stop him. He killed me too."

How are you alive then? the Aetus Orum asked, a mix of curiosity and sarcasm.

I don't know...

So you are not a hunter? asked the silver eagle, making sure.

"No! Why do you both think that?? The world doesn't even know you exist! It's been more than three hundred years since the last of you disappeared."

The female breathed out through her thin nostrils, a puff of steam.

Child, three hundred years is an eyeblink for us. And how should we know? All that we have is the unchanging desert. Your kind poached us for bones and feathers to use us in their alchemy. All this time, we have been sleeping away the years, staying quiet. Forgive us if we are not trusting...

However, if what you say is true, then that horrid chapter of our lives, brought about by that traitor, Xersus, is finally over. Still, we are just as threatened as we were then, perhaps more so, now that we are the last of our kind. You have endangered us; your trespass will lead others to venture into the Desert.

We cannot allow that. You must leave. Go back to where you came from, and leave us in peace. Tell anyone of our existence, and we will burn your town to ash to guard our secret. We must protect our legacy.

"I'm the one who's sorry. I don't know why I came here, but I know now that it isn't to simply leave. This meeting must be the work of some higher power, some form of providence. Allow me to stay, at least until all becomes-"

The male became indignant, then, his neck-feathers becoming sharper and more fearsome.

That is the problem with your kind, human. You cannot just leave us alone! Die now, since you will not go of your own volition!

The Aetan moved to breathe again, but the plasma went back down, forming a ball and exploding in its throat.

The golden eagle coughed up smoke. Something had stopped him.

Up above, the clouds parted, and there was a smattering of multicolored light. The sand that was touched gave way, a sinkhole appearing in the middle of the Desert. The pit ignited like some subterranean hell, light so hot it burned.

The flames from the pit merged, forming an apparition with eyes of blue, curling eyebrows atwixt in furor. A powerful voice boomed, though it came from nowhere:

"HAASH'T, LUNA'RASE—FOOLISH BIRDS! DO YOU NOT ALREADY KNOW WHY HE HAS COME, YOU IN YOUR WISE, OLD AGE?! ARE YOU SO ASLEEP?!

CAN YOU NOT HEAR THE GROAN OF DRAGONS WAKING, THE RUMBLE OF METEORS? DEMONS FROM THE DEPTHS ARE BREAKING; OUR ENEMY IS RALLYING! YOU WOULD STRIKE DOWN A GOD'S OWN HEIR IN YOUR IGNORANCE, YET YOU ASK ME TO BLESS YOUR OWN CONCEPTION?! HE IS ABSOLUTE, SCION OF THIS LAND—MY BELOVED SON, WITH WHOM I AM MOST PLEASED!!!"

"PROSTRATE YOURSELVES BEFORE ME, NOW; MY POWER IS NOT SO WEAK—LEST I RIP YOU TO SHREDS IN WRATH, LEAVE YOUR HATCHLING ORPHANED UNTO INFINITY!!!"

The birds snapped and cringed like geese at the slaughter, their boldness cowed. They pressed their wings against the ground in submission, recognizing the god of their home world, the god who had brought them to Avenshra. The pall on Absolute's hand glowed vibrantly, then, the terrified monk overcoming his fear, and approaching the burning pit, full of curiosity.

The eagles didn't move. Absolute got a grip of himself, inhaling sharply as the apparition wavered. He was overflowing with questions, ready to have them answered.

The Divinity answered them before he even asked.

"Absolute—my name is Luxyruss. I am your father, and though I left soon after you were born, know that it was not by choice... I left you with one of my servants, Brother Amalgus, to do what I couldn't. He was indeed a brother to me, and he raised you like a father, knowing this day would come."

"Have I become a god?" Absolute asked.

"No. Your mother was human; I have always been more than that. So are you. I came here with a purpose, only to lose sight of it, fall in love as you have with that girl, Leafsong. Your mother Telespora was the most beautiful woman in the world..."

Absolute's heart, which had been rejoicing, dropped, shattering in his chest. His mother was The Queen of Qeonia, but Queen Telespora Ralei had been dead for a decade, and no one would believe him even if he told them. It changed nothing...

"I know you grieve now; this is not what you wished to hear. But you are more important than the both of us ever were... I have a task for you. You must bring them together now, save them in their plight. Your sword will show you the way; I will guide you as long as I draw breath. I had Leafsong bring you back to lead, not love; The Demonium come."

Absolute pushed down his grief, his bitterness. "Bring who together? Lead who, Father? What sword?"

"You will Receive your Fallstreak when the time is right, as will the rest of them. With it, you will help bring together the greatest warriors of our time: The Warriors of Avenshra. As for who you will lead—why, the world, my son! The world! Though you will never lead the Warriors, when all will fall, you will rise."

Oscure

Oscure ordered his men to nock arrows. With a *clatter*, flaming arrows were nocked and drawn, barbed, metal tips pointed towards the approaching leviathan.

A hulking, purple-grey ship was headed straight for The Aerhauc Settlement, slow and ominous. From afar, Oscure couldn't tell how many people it held, a single, fuzzy figure moving about the deck.

Oscure ordered his men to fire. There would be no dealing with outsiders if he could help it. They had cost his Tribe too much in the past.

Arrows flew, falling swiftly towards their target.

Closer.

Closer.

Closer.

Fletchings whistled, dark arrowheads glinting in the sunlight.

And then they moved. The iron arrows scattered, as if an invisible hand had swatted them out of the sky.

The archers broke into a commotion.

"Let fly again," Oscure commanded, silencing them. "Maybe it was wind."

The bowmen did as they were told, but under their breath, they mumbled doubtfully. Oscure had never seen wind do that, but he supposed it was possible.

The second time, the arrows whistled back around towards the beach, the archers ducking for cover. Thankfully, no one was injured. The arrows had fallen short, extinguished in the shallows.

A warning.

That was not normal. However, in recent days, Oscure had come to think that anything was possible.

"It is the will of Madevf, my King; we waste our arrows," proclaimed Ubugo, leader of the archers. "The ship cannot be touched."

Oscure's eyes narrowed.

"So be it. Let us wait for whoever comes. We shall decide whether they are friend or foe when they arrive."

The ship was close, then, visible in all its detail.

It was too small to be a slave galley, but too big to be a fishing boat. Its prow looked like it was made to hit other ships, but, strangely, it had no weapons. It was not a warship.

After an impatient eternity, the strange vessel finally reached the shore, striking sand and slowly grinding to a halt. It would be difficult to get it unstuck.

Do they mean to take us down in one go?

Oscure's men drew their short swords, dull grey, and flared at the tip. Oscure Called Coldspine, his new Theonium chain-mace. The chain lengthened as he raised his sixth finger, where he wore his Callring: a smooth, shiny, black band with translucent, red veins.

With a *creak*, a skinny young Native with brown hair cautiously lifted the hatch in the middle of the deck. Seeing no more arrows, he slowly climbed above-board and walked over to the edge of the ship.

The Aerhauc started, muscles tense.

As the man reached the edge of the prow, about to address the group, the boat was hit by a particularly strong wave, and he fell face first into the sand with a *thwump*.

No one else came out of the boat. The man groaned, extracting himself from the sand.

"Do any of you speak The Universal Tongue?" he asked, painedly.

Oscure wondered whether he should pretend like he didn't, and have his men drive their foreign visitor back to sea like the savages of Qeonian lore. For a moment, he smiled inwardly at this idea, but his mood soured when he remembered the rules of hospitality outlined by The Law of Madefv. He could not shirk that responsibility. This man clearly wasn't an enemy. Apart from looking like a clumsy oaf, he was starved, parched, and bruised. Sending him back to where he came from would probably kill him.

Besides, Oscure was curious.

"I do. Who are you, stranger? And why does Madevf travel with you?"

"My name is Amdryaan, and I'm alone. No one travels with me... I mean you no harm. I come from The Ice Fields. My people were enslaved by The Frosslar, but I managed to escape on one of their boats, and they cannot follow. I'm the only free member of my Clan. If you could give me shelter for a night and some medicine treat my wounds, I will leave on the morrow. I must reach Cairnon and request aid from The High Empire."

So there are slavers in the snow as well...

"Tell me, Amdryaan, you say no one travels with you, but I see that your eyes are red, a color mine become as well. You must be a Beloved of Madevf. Tell me the truth. Who are you, and why did you come here?"

"I told you, no god travels with me. It's just me," the Native insisted. "You shot arrows at me and I moved them. I can't explain exactly how, but one day, these abilities just came to me. Again, I mean you no harm. If you help me, I'll be out of your hair as soon as possible."

Oscure let go of his chain mace, the weapon disappearing in a puff of Lifeblood.

I see. So he's like me; he just doesn't know it yet. But how did he get his powers? Did he also come into contact with a Shadowrise tree?

The Tribe King ordered his men to come and put Amdryaan on a stretcher. It would be irresponsible to drive out a man who needed at least a week of rest and recovery. They would host him until he was back to full health.

I hate hospitality, but he's more interesting than the other visitors with their conversion attempts and noble arrogance. The fact that the ship wasn't full of slavers is blessing enough.

Besides, I have much I want to ask him. I thought I was the only one with powers.

Luxyruss

Luxyruss broke his father's Throne, still angry with Haash't and Luna'rase. It was time to get what he had really come for.

Though Luxyruss was angry, he still smirked as Skotathis' first love died, molten blocks toppling and rolling down the dais at the end of the throne room, the room echoing.

Purifire cut through effortlessly. In the end, it was just dead material, and not worth even a drop of innocent blood. But the mundane, dark grey seat that now lay in pieces at his feet was the reason for all of the world's problems, a thousand years of fighting and an ocean of blood.

Luxyruss shivered, breath floating away as a warm puff.

Though Ressida was deserted, even The Monastery had held some familiarity, some good memories. M'Cael's death had changed all that, of course, but the throne room was cold—colder it seemed, than the outside world—and his bones ached from the strain of the transspacial projection at Basamor. Meeting Torran in a dream had been far easier, though it took careful planning to craft the proper dreamscape. He couldn't afford to show the full extent of his weakness, and although he needed to be honest about the situation with the Astrian Prince, he also needed to show at least a semblance of power and control, or the man, who had never been particularly pious, might have rejected his call to action. Making Leafsong an Emanation and accidentally giving her some of his Knowledge had been risky as well, but she had saved Absolute, and everything was coming together well enough, given the circumstances.

Luxyruss waited for the rubble to cool, and then cut open the throne's hollow base. It was the one place Skotathis would have never thought to look, a short-lived despot sitting The First Throne, all those years ago.

Though cunning, Skotathis had been too vain to realize that he sat above the very power he sought, hidden all those years. Jealousy and greed had blinded him to the monumental presence beneath his feet. His innate desire for power had distracted him, always directing his attention to what lay beyond, and the next unclaimed prize. His sycophants had been equally blind.

Luxyruss felt some satisfaction in that, for all the good it did. Hiding the box under their ruler's ass, he had well deceived them; with this clever deceit, he had made asses of traitorous men.

The Divinity coughed, letting go of Purifire and allowing it to disappear. He could see the statue of The Initiator through the wide, glass skylight that sat at the far end of the throne room, illuminating the space with what faint sunlight came from Arceon.

The statue looked back at him, the mask hiding a face he knew well.

I'm coming to see you... I hope you can forgive me.

You probably won't.

Luxyruss stopped talking to the statue, and—after some sifting through fragments of rock—he saw it: a gold box, stamped with a diamond-shaped symbol. Forming the diamond was a stylized golden eagle—his sigil: The Sigil of the Warrior King.

Luxyruss opened the box, the box that held Avenshra's entire future. Inside was a black

ring, oilslick, and its twin, a gold ring set with a large star ruby. Beside it was an amulet.

The Amulet.

Konell

Konell had arrived in Starspire earlier than his employer could have ever anticipated. It had taken a good deal of Lifeblood, but he had managed it.

Getting into the Astrian capital had been surprisingly easy. There were very few soldiers on patrol. Then again, there was nowhere the assassin couldn't infiltrate with Evanescence. However, to be safe, he had Evanesced into a building on the outskirts of the city to avoid going through inspection by The City Guard, who were posted outside the walls.

With the money the Hemian Prince had given him as an advance, Konell had bought all the weapons and poisons he needed from his contacts in Port Blue before coming, and although he wasn't particularly well-rested, he would at least break into The High Emperor's Palace fully equipped.

It took Konell half the day to get to The Imperial Palace, as it sat at the northernmost end of the city, but, after hours of walking, he finally reached the square in front of the building's east entrance. The sun was beginning to set, and the square was empty.

The sky that afternoon was darker blue than usual, occupied by fuzzy, grey-white clouds. It was as if evening had come prematurely.

The ground was damp underfoot, and the air smelled strongly, dust hovering, suspended, in the humid heat. The suffocating atmosphere was only disturbed by the occasional cool breeze, and Konell's leathers stuck to his skin.

It would rain soon.

Konell looked ahead at The Imperial Palace, taken aback by its elegance in the gloom. Though he had seen the Palace before, he had only seen it from afar during a previous mission with The Guild, and he had never dared come close.

Standing so close, he could say that it was just as impressive in person.

The Imperial Palace was surrounded by burgeoning gardens, white, pink, and purple flowers blooming amongst heavy fruit trees and trellises of creeping vines, listening to the trickle of marble fountains.

The castle was incredibly tall, pointed like a sword or knife, grey, stone brick cutting through the green. It was adorned with a variety of stained glass windows, arrays of sparkling, colored tiles sending brilliant reflections flying. There were long and sharp ones, massive circles done in cobalt, and other, small, blue circles with golden Stars of Astria at the center. Some depicted historical scenes, like the death of The Red Meteor, while others were painted with scenes from mythology and religion, like the fight between The Angelicum and The Demonium.

The exterior facade of the Palace was distinctive, with a large spire extending from the archway of the inner entrance layered over a taller one with a long, light blue strip of stained glass running down the middle and extending from the roof above the arch. The building's scaled, triangular, red roof extended past both spires and into a stone observatory tower topped with a scaled, pointed, red cone that was so high up it scraped the heavens themselves—and—if the rumors were true, many builders had gone to heaven constructing it.

The Palace was protected by a set of four walls connecting four, stone guard towers. The only way in was through one of the large, iron-studded, ebon doors at the center of each wall.

Konell had chosen the east door as his infiltration point, because the gardens there were particularly thick, decreasing visibility between the inner and outer entrances.

The city too used to peace, the Palace's east entrance was manned by only two guards, and although they were still awake, they seemed drowsy.

Konell would be the one to put them to sleep.

Starting his infiltration, he threw down a smoking, poison canister before they even asked him his business there. The men fell down, asphyxiating.

Though the guards might have been good people, they were sworn to die for The High Emperor, and Konell couldn't risk knocking them out only for them to flank him later. Plus, he would need all the Lifeblood he could get.

Konell sucked the Lifeblood from their corpses and did a cartwheel, Evanescing directly through the door.

That's right. I decided this before I left. The guards will oppose me, duty-bound. Even if they're good, I must kill them. I will kill them. Amara cannot die.

The assassin quickly made his way across the interior courtyard, fountains trickling. He crept like a cat through the sweet-smelling gardens, circling around the castle to the front entrance and hiding behind a hedge of light pink flowers. The door to The High Court was guarded lightly as well. There were only four men posted, and they didn't look particularly skilled.

The rest of the soldiers had been sent somewhere, but where, he didn't know.

Whatever the reason, The High Emperor had made a big mistake.

Konell crouched low, ready to tiptoe over, unhitching a second poison canister from his belt. He was about to emerge from the bushes and go in for a sneak attack, when an exotic bird flew out, startling him.

Konell dropped the canister, alerting the guards.

Damn. I guess we're going to have to do this the hard way.

Konell stepped out almost casually, the threat revealed.

"Hey, who let you in here?!" one of the soldiers yelled. "No one gets through the walls until we hear about it!"

Konell grinned, heart turning to stone.

Yes, this is how it's always been...

"It seems your friends didn't keep you in the loop," he smirked. "You should ask yourself whether they really have your best interests at heart."

The guard sprang into distance and swung his sword angrily at Konell, trying to chop him in half, but the assassin bent backwards out of the way, and he missed completely. In the end, he was only successful in cutting a nearby shrub.

Konell Called Tardrown, cutting across the space and creating distance.

"What's that?" the man asked mockingly. "Don't you know those foreign curved swords are no good?"

Confident in himself, though he had just missed, the guard switched directions, aiming for Konell's left shoulder. The assassin caught the sword with his saber's crossguard, twisting the kilij and sliding along his opponent's blade. Tardrown's curved point entered diagonally into the soldier's neck.

Konell let go and the Fallstreak disappeared.

Fall, now.

To Konell's dismay, the man did not fall. The guard gritted his teeth, swinging for his attacker's face, though he was bleeding profusely.

Konell reCalled Tardrown, exchanging three blows before parrying a cut to the arm and changing angles, shoving his sword into the soldier's stomach. He watched the man's eyes widen in fear and agony as the middle of the blade turned to liquid inside of him. The guardsman choked on poisonous tar, intestines lacerated and lungs clogging up.

Konell removed the blade and it was solid once more. A Blood Blade that inspired fear, Tardrown was a disgusting weapon, even in his eyes. But, it was, nevertheless, his—the Fallstreak he had inherited—and fear was a useful tool in battle.

The more terrifying he could be, the better for him.

"I was unaware that my sword's no good. Guess I need a new one," the assassin quipped.

The guard dropped with a *clatter.*

His comrades hung back for a moment, frozen by fear, but they were brave, and the effect was only temporary. They quickly broke free from the fear and ran forward: a man with a mace, another man with a messer, and a woman with a battleaxe.

Konell understood what had happened. Their fear had been replaced by rage. That was good. The more villainous he could be, the better. Rage distracted.

"You piece of shit! How dare you-"

"Venymlash." Konell swung his arm, indigo droplets flying from his fingers. The droplets hit the guards in the face, paralyzing them. They were truly frozen then, black veins spreading across their skin.

Konell walked up to the man with the mace and wrenched the weapon from his hand. Using Lifeblood to strengthen himself, he took out all three soldiers with a single swing.

No need to let them suffer.

Three streams of Lifeblood entered Konell's nostrils as he inhaled. His eyes blazed red.

Hearing a fight, another four guards appeared, coming from the north and south entrances. Konell took them all out with the same mace, gore splattering across the courtyard.

Once he was done, he dropped the mace, and, composing himself, pushed open the wide, wooden doors they had died defending.

Konell strode into The High Court, the famous High Throne twinkling in the darkness.

A group of new recruits to The Astrian Guard stood gathered in front of it, prepared for battle. Commanding them, was a knight in full plate.

The recruits' eyes shone with a light that didn't come from the eerie, blue candles in the chandeliers above, but from a steadily growing panic. They carried a variety of specialized weapons, made specifically for them, but they held them in a white-knuckled grip, legs shaking. To hold such a position, even as substitutes, they had to be very well trained, but no amount of training could prepare them to fight someone like Konell.

Konell pitied them, but he couldn't afford mercy. In fact, their lack of experience was a vulnerability he would have to exploit. After all, he was only one man, without armor or backup. If he was to succeed, he would have to become an object of fear and hate, unbalancing them.

No, it wasn't just that. Konell wanted them to be afraid of him, to hate him, so that they could embody the fear and hatred that he felt towards himself. This was a suicide, a funeral for the assassin that had killed so many and was about to kill more. It was his suicide, but it would cost them their lives, and for that, he deserved to be punished.

Unfortunately, Konell had his sister to save, so he couldn't let himself be captured and tried in a court of law. Instead, he would cut the guardsmen down with as much cruelty as he could muster, so they could punish him in this Court. In this way, Konell hoped that they would at least find some solace, some shred of meaning in trying to stop him, the monster who had murdered their friends. They deserved that.

The knight standing behind them was another story entirely. A tall, muscular, old man with matted, grey hair, light blue eyes, and tan, blocky features, he stood unfazed, watching Konell closely. His scarred and callused hands twisted around the haft of a large, ash spear with an enchanted steel tip, thicker and heavier than any Konell had ever seen. From a loop at his waist, hung an enchanted steel bola connected by bladed chains. It was obvious that the man was an experienced fighter, a veteran who had trained for decades and fought in battlefields for many decades after that. But, for all his experience, the man stood behind the rookies, observing. There was no sentimentality there. He understood what was at stake.

You cold-hearted son of a bitch... You're willing to sacrifice them just to get a read on me, huh?

Fair enough.

Konell pulled out two, black stilettos. Unflinching, he cut his hands with the knives, poisoning each edge in turn. Blood dripped, black acid hissing past fabric and through tile as it fell on the long, expensive, light blue rug leading up to the dais.

Konell walked down the aisle slowly, hands at his sides. The blood-slick stilettos clicked against the ebon pews as he moved, hitting them one by one, the sound echoing across the room.

The knight spoke a silent command, and the recruits advanced, moving in a single file.

It was what Konell wanted. He would finish them all.

I can't have anyone talking. The Prince was explicit—there can be no witnesses.

The first of the rookies swung a glaive at him, but Konell caught it between shiny quillons, bringing it off-target and stabbing him in the forehead. Then, he Called Tardrown, and sliced through the man's torso, mail and all.

A woman caught him in the side with a spear, piercing his liver. Acid spouted from it, the spear-handle smoking, but it wasn't enough. To her dismay, the assassin drew the spear deeper into himself, yelling, and then headbutted her, breaking her nose.

As the woman stumbled back, Konell tripped her, nailing her to the ground by the neck with one of his knives.

Konell pulled the final length of spear through his chest, nearly fainting, and closed up his liver with Lifeblood, but he didn't have enough to finish, and the wound was still open on the outside.

Blood marred the leather of his jacket as the next soldier advanced, punching him right where he had just been stabbed. Konell fell to the ground, gasping, but he kept moving. He pushed against the floor and spun—and—in one fluid motion, he grabbed the man's foot and slashed up his groin, gonads dropping.

The guardsman whimpered, quivering, but he didn't fall. Konell sprung to his feet and stabbed him in the temple to end his misery. Then he threw his remaining stiletto from a distance, striking the fifth recruit in the heart.

The young man looked surprised that that would be the way he would go, not even having fought, but his knees slowly bent and he toppled over as the poison took hold.

Finally, the assassin from Qeonia was face-to-face with the last of the Guard: the old knight who had coordinated the attack.

Konell suppressed his guilt and shame and threw back his head in laughter, reveling in flamboyant death. His dark, deranged laughter echoed along the vaulted ceiling, magnified into a mythic roar.

It was poison, so deep and dark that it drowned everything.

Though the veteran held back, Konell's performance had struck a chord. The man's hands were shaking violently, almost humming with anticipation. It was like he had forgotten why he held back in the first place. He was consumed by the urge, the urge to kill the assassin who had brought his students low.

Do you feel guilty now, old man? What did you see, there in your high tower?

The man's voice was like gravel.

"You bastard... Those were good soldiers. You'll pay for that."

Konell hung his head in what looked like amusement. His voice almost cracked as he issued his taunt.

"They didn't seem that good to me, but maybe you're a cut above the rest... Still, you won't make me pay. Your Emperor dies tonight."

"That's not going to happen," the knight declared.

"Oh yeah? We'll see about that, old man."

Konell moved in.

The guard took a hand off his spear and flung the bladed bola at Konell's ankles, but the assassin let go of his Fallstreak and did an aerial over it, chains skittering across the rug.

Konell swung his sword, Theonium screaming for the old knight's face, but the knight didn't hesitate, spinning his spear around and swinging with incredible speed for his midriff.

Konell aborted his cut, pushing off a pew with his foot and flipping sideways, the soldier's spearhead occupying the space where he had been standing just a moment prior. The man immediately tried to thrust him in the chest as a follow-up, but Konell had learned his lesson with the female guard from before and did a butterfly kick over it. Unluckily for him, he was too slow, and he took a nasty cut down the abdomen.

Konell bit past the pain and used his momentum to roundhouse kick the knight in the face, the armored giant crashing down into the pews.

Konell recoiled, toes broken.

Pulling himself from broken wood, the old knight reoriented himself, cracking his neck and swinging for the assassin's right ear. Konell ducked and Called Tardrown again, swinging downwards in a blistering arc, swinging as if he was trying to crush the man's skull, helm and all. The soldier barred the opening with his spear shaft but Tardrown cut through like butter, indenting his enchanted steel greathelm and bouncing off with a *clanggg*. Helmet still reverberating, the knight didn't hesitate, striking Konell in the ear with what used to be the butt of his weapon and punching him in the face, Tardrown Dismissing itself. Then, he threw the spearhead at Konell like a dart.

Konell used Reflectrica, bending space around him and bouncing it away. The assassin felt a part of himself die, Drained.

I need to replenish myself. Each spell without Lifeblood is a year off my life.

Konell moved to stab the soldier in the arm, but the man had preempted his attack, and he was knocked into one of the pews by a brutal, forward kick. Konell hit his head, nose and lip splitting, but didn't collapse.

The guard wasted no time and drew a sidesword from the scabbard at his waist. He stabbed for Konell's kidney, but the assassin rolled sideways, Evanescing and reappearing on the far side of the pews.

Damn it! I just Drained myself even more. I need to kill him as soon as possible. But I need to be smart...

Think, Konell. Think!

Ah, I see.

Konell hastily lifted an enchanted steel rondel off of one of the fallen guards, shooting an enchanted steel chain-blade from the launcher at his wrist and attacking from a distance as a distraction. The knight, however, saw through this distraction and caught the dart with his sword, yanking Konell towards him. The old man was remarkably strong, pulling Konell yelling through the air and across the room, elbowing him in the forehead and slamming him down into wood.

Konell's orbital bone cracked against the side of a pew, hot, sour, metallic blood filling his sinuses. Dazed, he ignored the stuffy pain in his eye and nose and got back to his feet, Calling Tardrown and throwing a thrust at the guard's face, forcing him to back off for a second. Annoyingly, the knight moved back in as fast as he had retreated, not giving him the chance to breathe.

Luckily for Konell, the knight's impatience worked in his favor, and although he was still reeling from his injury, he had to take what he could get. In his haste, the soldier had forgotten about the rondel, which Konell had hidden in his sleeve.

To the old man's surprise, Konell rushed forward into the attack, elbow pressing his sword arm to the right mid-swing and causing him to miss. The assassin honed in on the knight's soft tissues, placing his left hand against his right wrist, and stabbing through the man's pauldron with a reinforced thrust. The knight shouted, staggering backwards, but somehow, he still managed to cut into Konell's left arm, shearing tendons. His jerking around might have beheaded Konell if the acrobat hadn't ducked.

Konell left his useless arm to dangle at his side and jumped straight out with both legs, kicking the old man in the chest and doing a macaco off what was left of the pew. The last Guard member fell—not quite dead, but soon to be dead.

Blood dripping from his cloak, Konell hopped down from the pew and stooped low, pulling his stiletto from the chest of the young guard he had thrown it at earlier. He dragged it against the ground as he did it, leg spasming, and got up, dizzy. His vision was swimming with stars, though he scoffed when he realized—he couldn't tell whether they were Stars of Astria or not.

The assassin kicked the fallen recruit out of the way and went to finish the knight and get his Lifeblood, but one of the soldiers underfoot stirred. It was the woman. She growled, her neck still pinned to the floor, the blade caught in the soft mortar between the tiles.

She took hold of his ankle and used the knight's fallen spearhead to stab him in the calf, dragging it down like a wide-bladed knife by its broken, wooden "handle." Konell fell to one knee, screaming, but it was just pain. Though she had managed to injure him, she hadn't learned her lesson, and his toxic blood splashed all over her face, killing her.

Konell inhaled, and the wound she had made healed completely, repaired by her own Lifeblood. The assassin looked back at her in sopor, coughing. The woman's eyes bulged.

"You should be one to know—pain is temporary. All I did was remind you," he whispered.

Konell rolled onto his back, breathing heavily, and kipped-up. He would leave the old knight alone and bear with his injuries. The man was sure to die, anyway, and he didn't need any grim surprises. Some minor breaks wouldn't be enough to stop him. Besides, what he really needed more of, was his own blood.

I used up too much blood there with those spells. I was stupid; I should have relied more on my sword; now I'm way too weak! But there's nothing I can do about it now... It'll have to do.

Konell started to second-guess himself the moment he got to the staircase leading to the Imperial suites. It seemed impossible to take another step, let alone make his way up, the assassin reeling.

Maybe I should have grabbed the old man's Lifeblood, just in case. But fuck, I already stabbed him so much, and I'm not walking back there now.

By hook and by crook, Konell pulled himself to the top of the marble steps. He walked across the short hallway, and then stopped to take a breath.

He had reached the fated door behind which The High Emperor, Agravius Xandromen, was hiding.

The young assassin had bought an illicit map of the castle floor plan before coming, and he knew that this door was the only entry to The High Emperor's dormitory. Jumping from the second-floor balcony was the only option for the monarch to escape, but something told Konell that his target wasn't the type to flee that way.

Konell sighed, putting his hands on his knees. The hallway was silent, but he knew The High Emperor was waiting for him.

He was expected.

Konell looked up at the door, preparing himself for the encounter to come, and stood back up.

The door to the monarch's room was ornate but strong, made from walnut wood and secured by three locks. It would be difficult for a normal person to break in, even with a battering ram.

I don't need that, of course... But God damn am I tired...

Konell felt woozy, and not a little bit drunk. He Called Tardrown for what seemed like the millionth time, and sliced straight through the line of locks, three, black bars falling to the ground with a *clatter.*

He pushed open the door, resisted by wind.

Agravius Xandromen was standing in the middle of the room. Modest but spacious, it was overwhelmingly red.

The man was standing beside an artisanal bed with high bedposts, made for two, but used by one. The translucent, white curtains billowed in from the balcony, fluttering behind The High Emperor like woeful phantoms.

The humidity that had defined the day finally let up, thunder crackling and rain pouring. Lightning flashed across the grey-blue sky, curtains set aglow.

Konell adopted a defensive guard with his saber, sizing up the man he had come so far to kill.

The High Emperor was visibly nervous, sweat dampening his light brown beard, but although he was undoubtedly afraid, he didn't make a move to run, or beg for mercy. He just stood there, still in his night clothes, and waited for Konell's next move.

Although Agravius simply stood there in his blue, cotton pajamas, he was holding a well-made sword and buckler, and Konell was no fool. The High Emperor had led his troops through many wars, and, by all accounts, he was an extremely skilled fighter. At the moment, the man stood a better chance than he did in his condition. Konell had lost a lot of blood, with no Lifeblood left to use except his own, and with enchanted steel, Agravius could meet his blade.

God this is stupid...

This is a bad idea. I don't know what The Prince is thinking.

This guy is no joke, and I don't have a lot of tricks left.

But Amara needs me to win...

Here goes nothing.

In a burst of motion, Konell reached into his jacket and threw a poison vial, but Agravius' reflexes were too quick, and he batted it away with a sweep of his buckler. The small, glass bottle hit the wall with a *crunch*, fizzling.

Trying to take advantage of the startle factor, Konell shot a metal dart from his wrist, but the Emperor caught it right before his eye, hand shaking.

The assassin shot three more darts in quick succession, heart rate rising, but The High Emperor intercepted them all with sword and buckler both, cutting them out of the air and slicing at his attacker. Konell engaged, but even though the monarch hadn't seen battle in many years, he put up a hell of a fight.

The High Emperor relentlessly kept up his guard, keeping his shield-hand over his sword-hand at all times and protecting his fingers, exchanging edge for edge and edge for flat. He made a false edge cut for Konell's head, swiftly followed by a sweeping cut for the neck. Then, he swept upwards for Konell's chin.

Konell's blocked, Theonium eating into enchanted steel.

Nothing done, the two men broke apart, reassessing their opponent.

Konell grit his teeth. He was panting already, his grip on Tardrown slippery.

No, he wasn't just panting. He was hyperventilating. He felt an unshakeable dread staring into Agravius' cool, green eyes. Though he had been training to fight his entire life, The High Emperor was much more skilled, and he wasn't letting the assassin's scare tactics get to him.

This next move will decide everything. I have to win!

With a shout, Konell cut for Agravius' shoulder. The High Emperor parried and tried to flip the swords over to strike him with his pommel, but Konell let go of his Fallstreak and threw a punch to the man's side, reCalling Tardrown and swinging for the Emperor's midriff.

This was not enough. The High Emperor broke Konell's knee with a kick, stopping him and parrying his attack.

But it was too late, then. Konell didn't allow himself to feel the pain. He had to put everything into this attack or he wouldn't be able to get back up, knee buckling under him in real time.

Konell improvised. As he fell, he sliced across Agravius' arm in a spray of blood and swung his weight backwards into a touchdown raiz, Draining himself for one last Evanescence.

The High Emperor made a cut for the assassin's stomach, but Konell disappeared before it could hit him, the monarch cutting through a cloud of red smoke instead of his attacker's flesh. Before the man understood the full extent of what was happening, Konell appeared behind him in a kneeling, back-edge thrust. Recognizing the danger, but too slow to stop it, Agravius spun, swinging his sword.

It was futile. The assassin had cheated, using a sorcery not seen on Avenshra for hundreds of years. No ordinary man could have anticipated his next attack.

There was a *crack*; Agravius froze. Tardrown had entered his face, sliding under the bridge of his nose. The High Emperor stuttered, flailing weakly as the blade exploded into sharp tendrils, liquid metal spilling out the side of his skull.

Konell was immediately hit by regret.

Torran

The dock at The Outpost was empty, save for one ship, its hull scorched by fire and its prow broken. It was the only one that hadn't been stolen, still moored to the old, wooden dock by a dry, fraying, brown rope.

Though the dock was falling apart, the ship hadn't been abandoned due to its age. In fact, it was brand new, made of unornamented, dark brown wood, and it had a navy-blue sail, freshly painted with the Star of Astria, white paint gleaming. It was of a strong and light construction, and even though it had taken some damage, it looked seaworthy, at least from the outside.

Though it was plain looking, Torran could tell that the schooner was meant for a General in his father's Army. Most of the lower-ranking officers in The Imperial Army were transported by large, imposing vessels that could accommodate entire platoons, and The Imperial Navy used more specialized warships in its operations.

Body aching and joints popping, Torran climbed up the rope by which the boat was moored, dusting himself off and throwing down the gangplank with a grunt.

He turned, slowly understanding what had happened.

The General who the craft belonged to had made his last stand on the deck, his soldiers fighting alongside him.

Their teamwork had not saved them, bodies sprawled out on the blood-stained planks. Steel was cut. Men had been killed with weapons too barbarous even for animals.

The soldiers leaned against empty barrels, leaned against each other for support. One sat against the mast, as if in peaceful sleep, but his hand covered a large wound in his left flank, failing to hide it and the nearby pool of congealed blood.

It appeared to Torran that the soldiers had died of blood loss while protecting the ship, the enemy choosing to leave behind the damaged vessel in their haste.

Demons sailing with ships made for men... Incredible.

The General stood out from amongst the slain, but Torran didn't know him. His armor was visibly more expensive than the other men's, blued enchanted steel with gold accents, and his hair was grey. In limp hands, he held a longsword with a golden crossguard, denoting his high rank. It had a waisted grip done in brown leather and silver wire, and a gold wheel pommel. He had had his throat torn out, the planks beneath him far bloodier than the rest.

Torran bowed his head in sympathy and respect.

Just then, a flock of unusual-looking seagulls passed overhead, squawking loudly and pulling him from the grisly scene. They were pure white, with sharp, black beaks—an unfamiliar breed. The sky behind them was a flat grey—a huddle of sparse, white clouds fleeing from the Isthmus, as if trying to forget the horrors they had witnessed. Down on earth, wind was nowhere to be found, making sailing difficult, but up in the sky, it was a different story, the seagulls gliding on warm updrafts and calling out to each other animatedly.

The smells of seaweed, salt, and blood mixed together in Torran's nose, creating something distasteful, and the air had a heaviness, a meat to it. Fog hung like a wall before him, a large, amorphous cloud suspended between Sea and sky. It was the only cloud that didn't flee, unfazed by the carnage. Waves of hidden origin emerged from behind the mist and lapped against the smooth, black, pumice-stone beach of the central island, their soft crash soothing Torran's ears, which were too used to swords.

In the fog, Arceon was reduced to a small, blue-white disk, penetrating the fog but not illuminating it. Though it was largely devoid of its usual blue hue, the sun still burned.

Torran covered his sunburnt face, wincing.

Great. What else can you throw at me?

Torran stretched. His back ached, but he had to prepare the ship for departure.

As usual, he was doing the dirty work.

But what can you do? It's not like I want Scarolette doing all this. Ilidar is injured, and Jhett— Jhett's done enough.

Puffing himself back up, the ragged Prince hurriedly moved about the ship, dragging away the bodies and dropping them onto the beach. He would bury them with the others later.

Then, trying not to think too much about it, he inspected the rigging. Thankfully, there weren't any cuts, tangles, or knots, so he went below deck, checking for food, water, and medication. Frowning, Torran came back up, and unfurled the sail.

Luckily, the sail had no tears, and none of the ropes used for steering had been severed, but he had found absolutely nothing below deck, and that was a problem. Only ballast remained, and they couldn't eat ballast.

In the morning, the group had found some grain, boiling it in a tripod with some dried, salted meat, and eating it as their late breakfast. It was a meal that only Ilidar had liked, but it had filled their stomachs. Jhett had found some bandages in the battle-medics' tents, and Scarolette had uncovered half a barrel of fresh water in the main command tent that they had already finished in their thirst.

As if to add to an already bad situation, The Outpost had been struck before it could receive its next supply drop, and it wouldn't receive another for some months. The remaining food and water storage was in the fortress itself, but with the building caved in like it was, it was too dangerous to venture into. Unless they found some secret cache, it was obvious to Torran that they wouldn't have enough food or water for the coming journey, though short. Without water, they would likely pass out before they even reached Port Blue, and though they weren't starving yet, they would be soon if they couldn't find anything else to eat. They were already overwhelmingly hungry and tired from malnutrition, and eating The Necroscorum or the rotting warhorses was out of the question.

Torran looked back up at the skies, sail fluttering audibly behind him. He looked up as if begging for mercy.

The seagulls had come closer, flying lower to the ground. Perhaps they were searching for fish in the shallows, their regular hunt impeded by the unrelenting grey veil.

Torran watched the gulls for a long time, wishing that he too could sprout wings and fly, return home from his years-long odyssey.

His reverie was broken by the growl coming from his stomach. Normally, The High Prince would never have considered eating seagulls, but at that moment, they looked delicious. Unfortunately, he was a bad shot with a bow, and, in the end, he didn't want to harm the birds. They were one of the only friendly creatures he had encountered during his time away. All he had known were rabid dogs, lice, ticks, and firemites—lands of scorching heat and freezing cold—dragons, and monsters, and bloodthirsty men... The gulls deserved to live in peace; they lived hard enough lives, scavenging what little they could.

Just as Torran came to this conclusion, the seagulls proceeded to take a massive, stinking, grey-white dump on him and the ship.

The High Prince stood there, completely aghast, as the deck he had just cleaned and his entire body were covered in guano.

Almost speechless with rage, Torran gasped. He shook his fist indignantly at the gulls, instantly disenchanted with them. During the entire time he had been away from Astria, he had never felt such hatred towards another living thing.

Torran yelled at God, eyes red with fury. He was at his breaking point.

"Would you give me a break?! What the hell did I do to deserve this, you sick fuck?! You like kicking a man when he's down, huh, giving him something good for a night, only to give him this the next day?! Damn it!"

Torran pointed angrily at one of the many, squawking seagulls. He had determined one of them to be the ringleader, his finger trembling in wrath.

"You! Yeah, you! I'm going to kill you, specifically!!! I don't know how, but I will!!! I'm going to kill you and all your friends!!! I'm going to teach you a lesson you fucking piece of-"

Bzzzt!

A streak of lightning issued from his finger, hitting the bird he had chosen as his nemesis and electrifying the others around it. The shocked gulls fell out of the sky—smoking, black puffs. Those that survived turned to fly away, trying to escape.

Torran looked at his finger, stupefied, and then looked back at the gulls, rage distracting him from his surprise.

"Yeah, that's what I'm going to do! You better fly, delinquent buzzards!"

He tried to hit them again with his other hand. He extended his finger as they glanced back, wide-eyed.

Nothing.

The High Prince breathed in to keep yelling, not seeing the dead seagulls' Lifeblood enter his nostrils.

And then, when Torran reached out again, a bolt of lightning cleared the sky.

In the lingering shadow of that flash of electricity, a silhouette bigger than any he had ever seen descended like a thunderhead, the seagulls diving into the ocean to avoid the ultimate predator.

It was a golden eagle, one of the legendary Aetus Orum. The noble eagle broke through the fog, screeching, its mane flapping in the breeze. On its neck, sat a man in robes as white as ocean spray. He was followed by another raptor, equal in size, a bird with lunar, silver feathers, orbed, light blue eyes.

Salvation.

CHAPTER IX

Torran

It had been hours since the news had broken.

But Torran would be the last to know.

The eagles landed in the Palace gardens, kicking up dust. Stray pieces of dry grass spun up in the gale.

Though the eagles were massive, and the commoners had been thrown into a commotion at the sight of them, no one had come out of the castle to greet The High Prince and his group.

I sent out a dove, so they should have known we were coming. What is going on here?

Curiously, hundreds of carriages lined the lawn.

Could it be? Come on, now.

"Great," Torran scoffed. His father was hosting a ball or a banquet. For such events, all the noble families in Astria came to the Palace. The hubbub would bring with it administrative chaos, making it easy for messages to go unnoticed, and the staff would be indoors, tending to the nobility's every need.

They likely don't even know we're here.

Torran hadn't expected much, but he had hoped for at least something, something that said: "My son, The High Prince of Astria, heir to The High Throne, has finally come home after five years at war!" Even a simple pat on the back would have been enough.

But there was none of that. There was no fanfare, no grand welcome.

No one was even there to see to the injured members of the group. Everyone was indoors for the festivities, unaware of their most important guests.

This was not what bothered Torran the most. Torran was more worried about what this celebration entailed. His father rarely hosted gatherings, and when he did, he was usually looking to garner support for something. With The Continental Nations in disarray, there was a good possibility that Torran would be used as a showpiece, a "hero" to inspire the nobility to empty their wallets and volunteer for yet another war.

So you're going to show me off to others without offering me a single word of praise... That's cold, even for you.

The High Prince walked towards the Palace, preparing himself to walk into a celebration.

Though many nobles enjoyed them, Torran had always hated such gatherings. They were tedious affairs. Whenever he attended a ball, he would stand in the corner, talking to Ilidar, or, if his friend couldn't attend due to his duties as a guard, he would try to find an acquaintance to chat with. The music, the artifice at play in every conversation—it tired him. If he couldn't locate anyone he knew, he would grab a cupful of punch and disappear amongst the dancing nobility, a bending silhouette gracefully weaving through the crowd. Then, he would head up to his room and read.

Torran vividly remembered the last ball he had attended, a whirlwind of samite dresses and golden thread, a gaudy tapestry of lies and feigned smiles.

The ball had been a demonstration in luxury.

The banquet that followed was an equally lavish occasion, with ten, large tables and twenty, long benches to accompany them, filled by nobles and commoners alike. The menu consisted of roast beef, roast pheasant, roast swan, chicken, venison, trout, pike, sturgeon, mince pie, soups with cream, clear soups with vegetables, fresh bread, and a variety of cheeses. There were cream tarts, fruit tarts, cakes, fried dough, puddings, and blancmange for dessert. Wine, beer, water, and punch were provided in abundant quantities to wash it all down. Servants in blue-and-white outfits carried in the large, gilded, silver trays, heaping with food, and set them on the large, rectangular, wooden tables, which were covered with thick, cotton tablecloths, dyed a royal blue. and lit by beeswax candles sitting in heavy, silver candleholders.

For all its vast size, the banquet hall was full to bursting, its floor done with smooth, square, brownstone tiles, its walls painted a bluejay-blue, and its ceiling swirled with white. Warm spices hung in the cool air, accompanied by the smells of smoke and roasted meat, and one could catch the occasional whiff of sweetness, the tang of red berries and other fresh fruits.

It was loud, people spraying alcoholic spittle as they talked and picking chicken from their teeth with rolled up sleeves of cloth-of-gold. Torran found this repellant, but still, it was more restrained than other banquets he had attended.

His father had hosted the celebration in hopes of garnering support to build an army and retake Hemia. Normally, The High Prince wouldn't have come at all, since Ilidar wasn't in attendance, but his father had insisted.

Torran searched for someone to sit with, but all his acquaintances were either absent or drunk. Torran didn't drink. Whenever he told people, they looked at him like he was from another world, asking if something was wrong. Torran simply enjoyed having a clear mind. He didn't like the way alcohol made him feel, and more than that, he needed to be sober to deal with the machinations of the scheming rich.

The High Prince walked around, looking for a place to sit. He had stayed in his room too long, reluctant to attend. His half-sister, Riane, was sitting with the noble children at the far end of the room.

Torran glanced over at the opposite side of the room where his father was sitting, feeling strangely left out. Agravius sat with Torran's aunt and uncle on a long, birch-wood bench with a silver, satin cushion and backing. They were talking quietly about something he had no doubt was important. Standing, silver candelabras stood on either side of the bench, holding large, blue candles, dyed with indigo. Though Torran and his father had always had a strained relationship, The High Prince wished he could at least sit beside him and eat like a normal person. Instead, he would have to sit somewhere else, immersed in the nobility's plots.

Torran decided to pick just any seat. Anywhere he went, it would be equally unpleasant. In the end, he chose one of the less crowded tables, a group of minor nobles making room for him and giving him a polite greeting. Torran greeted them back, but didn't engage further. He only half sat down, watching Riane. The usual group of kids was bothering her, taking advantage of the commotion.

For God's sake...

The High Prince was about to go over there and talk to them when Lord Arland approached, taking the seat in front of him. The royal sat back down, piling some food on his plate and pretending to eat.

It'll have to wait.

Lord Arland smiled, his mustache pencil-thin, and his greying, slightly greasy hair combed back to cover a bald spot. He was wearing a grey-green doublet slashed with navy.

"Your Highness. You've grown taller since last I saw you. How is your father?"

"He is well, my Lord, but he's had a lot of work lately. As you know, he's a very busy man."

"I'm sure he is, your Highness. As always, I would be happy to help, make things a little easier. The Lātist embargo of spices must be a big headache for him. The food is already starting to taste bland."

The food was as flavorful as always, but Torran kept his mouth shut. Lord Arland had offered his father his "help" before. The man had been trying to secure the position of High Staff for some time now, but Agravius had already signed a contract with the Fengarden family, who had provided the lumber for the previous line of ships. The trees on Lord Arland's estate were rotten, and he knew that no one would want to buy the ruined lumber. Astria had never been known for its Navy, its fleet too small to outmaneuver foreign fleets and its ships falling apart after only a few years due to the strain placed on them by the surrounding seas, which were particularly rough.

Even if he was made High Staff, Lord Arland wouldn't be breaking any embargos. He had no real interest in building quality ships or getting troops across the sea. By becoming High Staff, he would finally be able to get rid of his headache. If he became High Staff, Arland would lose his estate, as The High Officials owned no land. He would then come to the capital, receiving an enviable salary and ordering the Navy's shipbuilders to buy the lumber. As his subordinates, they would be forced to comply. The money paid for the ruined lumber would then go to his daughter, who would receive the profits and accumulate enough wealth for a respectable dowry.

Torran wasn't about to let the navy sink. And, at that moment, the situation had escalated.

"I'll let him know, my Lord. Please excuse me."

"Yes of course. Thank y-"

Torran broke off the conversation and walked purposefully towards the corner of the room.

Never failing to be a jerk, Benton Valien was holding one of Riane's kittens in the air, dangling it over her head as she protested, trying to grab it. He held it high above the tile floor, suddenly flinching to scare her.

Benton was a tall and muscular kid, second only to Torran in size amongst the noble children, and he had a predilection for bullying those smaller and weaker than him. The High Princess was an atypical child with unusual mannerisms, and she had slightly misshapen facial features from an incident that had occurred shortly after her birth. Due to this, she had been ostracized by her peers, and there was no one her age who had her back. Torran was the only one who defended her, treating her like she was his full-blooded sibling, though they didn't share the same mother.

After all, what difference did it make? He loved Riane like nothing else in the world.

Torran felt his blood get hot. This was not the first time he and Benton had spoken.

If he had been meeting him for the first time, Torran would have said that Benton was a decent-looking kid, with symmetrical features and thick, brown hair, but the Prince knew the boy well, and under that thick crop of hair was a pair of malicious, black eyes that told you exactly the sort of asshole he was.

Riane was just a defenseless little girl, and Benton loved it.

Meowww!

The young noble lifted the kitten even higher, swinging it slowly back and forth. All it would take was one slip for the kitten to hit the floor, and it would be dead.

Torran's knuckles hardened, his fist tightening.

The bullies laughed, Benton going so far as to drop the animal and catch it by the tail. The kitten mewled helplessly, its tail most likely dislocated.

The High Prince loomed over the spoiled brat, a long shadow breathing cold hatred. He ignored his father's words.

Whatever they do to your sister, don't fight. I know it is bad, but... I will buy her a gift afterwards and make it up to her. We cannot afford to lose the support of the nobility.

Torran clenched his teeth.

Forget their support. They're hurting Riane.

Torran's voice reached a gravitic pitch. "Put it down. You're upsetting her."

The teenager turned, smirking.

"Really? It's hard to tell with a face like that," he laughed.

Torran hesitated, turning away for a moment. He could just take Riane with him, ignore them.

No.

Torran's fist collided with Benton's face, sending him spinning into a cream tart.

The High Prince followed up on his initial attack, hitting the noble with repeated hammer-fists to the head, boxing his forehead and ears.

Trenton Valien started yelling, grabbing Torran's arm and trying to pull him off of his bleeding cousin.

Trenton was Benton's best friend and right-hand man. He had a strong build, a freckled face, and a handsome head of reddish-brown hair. Additionally, he was dumb as a rock.

Torran lifted Benton by the collar, and, venting his rage, punched him back down into the table, hitting Trenton with a backfist. The boy stumbled backwards, blinking as blood began to drip from his nose.

Leon Aldridge tried to punch Torran in the kidney, but it was foolish considering his lack of strength.

Leon was a skinny, pale-looking kid who cared more about his curly, blondehair than anything else. He tagged along with Benton and Trenton and sometimes took part in their bullying of the other noble children. An embarrassment to his military father, he wanted to feel strong, even if his enemies were girls or little kids. Torran turned, throwing him over his hip, the boy falling on his neck and rolling across the bench, spilling cups.

The banquet hall went dead silent, save for protests from the brats' parents.

Lady Valien was a haughty woman with a pinched face and a sharp nose. She wore a green, velvet dress and cooled herself off with a silk fan. She looked outraged, though Torran thought she ought to feel ashamed.

Lord Valien was a handsome, if not slightly shady-looking man with long, wavy, silver-brown hair. He wore a blue, velvet doublet, with white frills at the cuffs. Torran couldn't read the Lord at all, but he gave off a vibe of ill will that made The High Prince uneasy. In any case, he seemed indifferent to the situation. The Lord simply daubed his mouth and put down his utensils, done with his meal.

Lord Aldridge was a broad-chested, muscular man in an orange vest with white frills. He had large, muscular arms and a short, thick, brown beard. He looked at his son with a look of unveiled disgust and disappointment, but he joined Lady Valien in calling for Torran's punishment, for the sake of his reputation if not for his son.

Torran looked back at the royal table.

His aunt had her hand to her mouth in shock; his uncle sweat profusely as he looked away. Agravius' eyes were like steel circles, luminous with anger.

Torran's anger gave way to fear and humiliation, which fueled his anger even more. Pulling his doublet tight, The High Prince stormed off, his father looking down on him from afar.

He was sent off to Lonecastle the next day.

The High Prince snapped back to reality.

It's no use dwelling on the past. I have to find a healer.

Ilidar had been out the entire flight to Starspire, and Jhett had fallen unconscious part of the way through. Though the tribesman had healed himself using the same magic as Torran and Scarolette, it was clear that he had been concealing the extent of his injuries, helping others when he was close to collapsing himself.

Torran felt small in front of such selflessness.

I have to find Sigmund. He has to treat them right away!

Torran told Scarolette and Absolute, the monk who had saved them, to wait. It wouldn't do to move the injured before a doctor was even available. However, The Aetans could not stay.

We must return to our chick. We will fly over as often as we can, but our son cannot fly yet, and we need to take care of him.

The three members of the group who were still conscious dismounted and lifted the wounded off the eagles' backs, placing them down as gently as they could.

Torran bowed his head to the Aetans in gratitude. *Thank you for your help. We are in your debt.*

That's right, human, Haash't agreed, flying off first. His mate followed, her eyes smiling at him.

Scarolette and Absolute waved them goodbye.

Going on ahead to get help, Torran ran up to the Palace entrance and barged through the heavy, ebon doors, expecting that he would have to push his way through a giant crowd.

But his entrance echoed in silence.

There was no ball, no feast. Torran's uncle, Velestre Xandromen, was sitting on The High Throne, trying to calm down a throng of nobles.

Why is he in Father's seat?

Torran's aunt, Mereona, sat in what was supposed to be Riane's chair.

What in God's name?

Torran shot a look over at his seat. It was empty, covered in dust, but it was still there, much smaller and humbler than his father's gargantuan slab of rock.

It's still there...

Though another Prince might have suspected treason, Torran knew his uncle too well to fear such treachery.

To Torran, Velestre Xandromen had always borne a faint resemblance to his father, but the two men had little in common. Where Agravius had always been taller and more muscular, his younger sibling was shorter and skinnier. The Lord's eyes were a peacock-blue color—not green at all—and his long, greying, chestnut-brown hair was swept up to look thicker than it was.

What the two men lacked in physical similarity, they shared in integrity. For all of his sonorous getup, Velestre wasn't vain or arrogant, and, in fact, he exhibited an obliging decency that separated him from the majority of The High Court. He was easygoing, one of the few people Torran knew who seemed content with their life as it was. The Lord didn't aspire to rule or gain glory in war; he had more wealth than he knew what to do with. He owned a bountiful estate, enjoyed a happy marriage, and doted on his many children. His daughters were spoiled rotten and not overly friendly, but overall, they were good children at heart. Whether they wanted it to or not, their father's magnanimity had shaped them into better and more caring people, and though they could be mean or insensitive towards Riane at times, they didn't bully or tease her like the other nobles' kids.

The High Prince was immediately struck by a sense of foreboding.

His uncle didn't look happy. His uncle was always happy.

Velestre looked stressed, much older than he remembered, and he seemed to be on the verge of tears. Torran had never seen the colorful, flamboyant man look so drab. The normally carefree and jovial "King of Vineyards" sat a Throne that wasn't his, his expression remarkably grim.

Torran shifted his gaze towards his aunt, Mereona. Like her husband, she too was not her usual self.

Since Torran's mother's death, Mereona Xandromen had always been the center of attention. She knew all the latest gossip, and the Ladies of the land, both young and old, looked to her as a trendsetter in fashion. She was, admittedly, gorgeous, perhaps the most beautiful woman in Court, with statuesque features, olive skin, long, voluminous brown hair—which hung in ringlets—and playful, melted-chocolate eyes. She enchanted every man she met, both single and married, but, strangely, no one except Torran was looking her way at the moment. She wasn't giggling with her maids, whispering something unbecoming in Velestre's ear, or teasing noblemen, smiling at their wives with perfect teeth.

She was a picture of dismay.

After a moment of unfamiliarity, the crier announced Torran's presence; the entire courtroom turned to look at him.

The nobles of Astria stood up from their pews, a flutter of silk, velvet, and sable. For all of their colorful trappings, their faces were solemn and unusually devoid of guile. The atmosphere was dour, and there was a sense of urgency in the Overseers' voices as they convened with his uncle, trying to tell him something before the room fell dead silent again. Sigmund wasn't there with them.

Torran stood still, unsure what was going on. The Lords in the audience twirled their facial hair nervously. The Ladies covered their faces with their fans as they whispered fearfully amongst themselves.

Something had happened. Something terrible.

Velestre's voice was hoarse.

"To- Your Highness? I-"

Why would they all be gathered here? And why are they all so...

Torran suddenly realized what had happened.

Without a word, The High Prince ran down the aisle and past his uncle. He sprinted past the guards and up the steps that led to Agravius' room.

Torran reached the doorway to his father's room and came to an abrupt halt.

The High Emperor lay inanimate atop his plush, feather bed, virtually afloat in a pool of blood. It soaked through the sheets, which had been pulled over his face.

Though it might have seemed strange for a royal, Torran had never really thought about his father dying. Having lost his mother, Juliana, at the age of six, Agravius had always seemed like an enduring figure in Torran's mind. He thought that his father would forever be there to guide him, even when they disagreed. After all, he was a man who had survived countless wars...

Looking at his uncle's face and the reactions of the nobility, Torran knew that it should have been immediately obvious to him what had happened. However, in that instant, the death of the great Agravius Xandromen had felt impossible...

Such words meant nothing to the world. Though Torran's mind rebelled against it, the impossible lay realized before him, starting to rot.

The High Prince stood petrified in the doorway, silently trying to get a grip of himself. Not noticing him, the Palace physician and Overseer of The Public Health, Lord Sigmund Jiralt, tried his best to assuage Torran's sister and prevent her from running over to their father's corpse.

Unable to bear the anguish of watching Riane scream and cry, Sigmund offered The High Princess anything he could to console her—a sweet, a song, a story—but of course, it was no use. She was too old for such distractions, and this was no trivial loss. This was something she had to process.

In the end, Sigmund realized that all he could do for Riane was to hold her close, so he knelt down on the floor and hugged her, comforting her and blocking her view of the gruesome scene with his large frame.

Sigmund Jiralt was roughly six-and-a-half-feet-tall—taller than Torran—but he stood slightly hunched over, with drooping shoulders. His long, straight, cordwain-brown hair was combed back behind his ears and over his neck, and his eyes were a dark lapis-blue. Though he had nice eyes, and he wasn't going grey, or balding, he wasn't the most physically attractive man, with pale skin, dark red lips that were much too narrow, and a large, beak-like nose. On top of that, he was thin and gangly, with a long, craning neck, and there were always red spots on the bridge of his nose from the use of spectacles.

That said, Sigmund was one of the kindest and most caring people Torran had ever met, and he was, without a doubt, one of the brightest minds in The High Empire. His knowledge of biology, medicine, and sanitation was extensive, more extensive than many of The Sages, and he used that knowledge to ensure the public health.

That was not all. In Scarolette's absence, Sigmund took care of The High Princess and was in charge of her education, as he had been with Torran when he was young. In truth, he was more of a father to the Xandromen heirs than Agravius had ever been, but he was only a Lord, and a servant of the crown, so he did not overstep his bounds.

Those bounds didn't exist anymore. The Overseer cried as well, hugging

Riane tighter. After all, he was grieving too. He and The High Emperor had been best friends.

Overcoming the initial wave of grief, Torran let go of the doorway and entered the room, the wooden door frame settling with a *crack*.

Hearing his entry, Sigmund looked up, and the two men locked eyes.

The Lord's initial look of unfamiliarity softened into a warm, but tearful look of recognition. He gently shook Riane's shoulder, alerting her to her brother's presence.

"Look, Princess! It's your brother," he whispered.

Riane looked up at Torran, eyes awash with tears, but then she buried her face again in the Overseer's soft, dark brown robes, sniffling. She didn't run to meet him, though he had been away for many years.

In other circumstances, Torran would have felt hurt, but he understood.

"Sigmund."

"My Prince."

"Who did this?" Torran asked.

Sigmund's eyes widened.

"An assassin, your Highness! They killed off most of the Guard just to get to your father; he—"

Torran raised his hand, cutting Sigmund off.

I understand... You can tell me the full details later. Let's not rehash what happened in front of Riane.

Getting the message, Sigmund took the girl's hand and wiped away her tears.

With a sigh, The Overseer stood up and walked over to the balcony, closing the curtains and darkening the room. Then, he led The High Princess out of the room and into the hallway, leaving Torran with his thoughts. Though she was reluctant at first, Riane followed quietly.

"Come, Princess. Let us give your brother a moment alone."

Torran walked up to the bed and peeled back Agravius' temporary shroud. He knelt, taking hold of his father's cold, limp, hand.

Though he wanted to desperately, Torran refused to cry. He held it in— that terrible aching feeling—his eyes burning with salt. He had to be strong, though he had little strength left.

His father's face was a gaping hole. Torran didn't want to look at it. There was no nose, the Emperor's brains soaking into the mattress.

Torran held on to his father's hand as long as he could, but it was too much. He pushed himself away from the bed, nauseous.

The High Prince vomited, though he had barely eaten in the past week. He threw up bile into the glazed, blue ceramic pot that held his father's favorite dracaena.

Torran knew, then, knew that it was all for nothing.

His father's hand would never again be warm. He would never feel it pull him close or hear the word "congratulations." The thing that he had fought for had disappeared, fled from his grasp. All his life, his father had never been proud of him, and he never would be.

Leaving Riane with a nearby guard for a moment, Sigmund ventured hesitantly into the room.

"Your Highness, is there anything I can do? Maybe I can give you..."

In the court below, Torran could hear Lords and Ladies chattering incessantly. They weren't sad, so much as intrigued, or frightened.

"What dreadful business! What sort of monster could have done such a thing? Do you think it was the Frosslar?"

"I've heard they've been causing trouble, but those snowmen would melt here in Astria!"

"I heard it was a Monolid thief, come for gold and silver!"

"You dolt, the Monolids only care about their precious tree."

"The High Prince has returned! I thought he was lost at sea!"

"He had people with him? Who's the girl? I don't remember him taking a concubine."

"He brought a Nolite to Court! Can you believe-"

"I heard the assassin was a phantom, dressed in gold—the ghost of Aehsius Xandromen!"

"This is an omen; The Xandromen Dynasty..."

"My Prince, I have a tea with ginger root that could help clear up the nausea... "

Swirling emotions filled Torran's head. He started feeling dizzy as his ears stuffed up, ringing, and his blood boiled.

He couldn't stand the gossip of nobles. He remembered how they had spoken about his mother, years ago.

I heard she ran away with her lover and had another child! That's why he killed her. Of course, being The High Emperor, he'll never admit it.

She was always fooling around with other men. It's no surprise to me, Deary.

Torran's voice became unimaginably deep.

"ENOUGH!!!"

His outburst brought down a thunderclap, shaking the very foundations of the Palace.

The entire castle fell quiet; the Court hushed. Even Riane, standing in the hallway, stopped crying for a moment.

"Sigmund, bring Korac here, now!" Torran demanded.

The High Prince knew that he was being overly harsh, but he couldn't help it. He needed to restore order, and quickly.

"My Prince, I can't; you see-"

"Never mind! You, what's your name?" Torran asked, beckoning to the guard standing with Riane in the hallway.

The soldier looked at the Prince confusedly, pointing at himself in disbelief at being directly addressed.

"Me? Bethel, Bethel Perrin, your Highness."

Bethel Perrin was a tall, earnest-looking young soldier with a long face and short, brown hair.

"Bethel, you are now my Lieutenant. Go and find Korac. Have him tell The High Sword to return our soldiers from Hemia, and tell him to cancel the resupply at The Outpost—it's gone, having suffered an attack by what can only be described as demons. Then, tell him to call upon The High Sage. The man's sat in his Monastery too long."

"Your Highness, K-"

Torran continued, cutting the Lieutenant off so he could finish getting out all of his thoughts.

"He should be ready for a funeral followed by a coronation. When you are done, choose two squadrons from The City Watch. Under your command, they will temporarily act as The Astrian Guard."

The newly promoted Lieutenant simply stood there, mouthing words he couldn't speak.

"What is it, Lieutenant? Spit it out!" Torran shouted, frustrated.

"K-Korac is dead, Sir."

Oh.

The Prince's anger dissipated.

"Has he been replaced?" Torran asked calmly. "How did these nobles hear what happened, if there were no doves sent out?"

"Y-Yes, Highness, he's been replaced. Sage Cindis Cato is commanding the Rookery for now."

"Then relay to him the messages I gave you and tell him to send them immediately. That is all; you're dismissed, Lieutenant."

"Yes, Sir!" the Lieutenant shouted, speeding off to do what he was told.

Torran turned.

"I'm sorry, Sigmund. I didn't think that the assassin would have killed The Palace Dovekeeper as well. I shouldn't have cut you off like that."

"It's alright, your Highness. We're all overly emotional right now."

The High Prince covered his father's face again with the sheet.

"That's true. We should leave this to the coroner... If you can, please tend to my friends downstairs or send a doctor you know; they're still weak and injured from the journey over. I need to talk to my sister."

"Yes, your Highness."

The Overseer quickly went to treat Torran's group, patting Riane on the head before heading downstairs.

The room empty, Torran walked over to where his sister was seated in the hallway. She was sitting on her hands, her eyes red and puffy, and her cheeks stained with tears.

Torran daubed her cheek with his hand, smiling at her, though smiling was difficult, at the moment. He had missed her.

"Did you miss me?" Torran asked.

Riane scrambled to her feet, hugging him. That was her answer.

261

The siblings embraced for a long time.

"Where were you?" Riane asked, voice scratchy from crying.

"Trying to get to you," Torran responded, giving her another, small smile. Out poured more tears.

"Were you scared?" he asked her.

"Yeah." The High Princess sniffed, wiping her eyes and nose. "Were you?"

"I was. But you don't have to be scared anymore."

"Okay."

"Come, let's go to your room and have the servants bring you some food. Right now, I need to talk to Uncle and calm the Court... Eat and get cleaned up. I know it doesn't seem that way right now, but it'll all be alright, okay? It does no good to stare at this when Father's already in a better place. He wouldn't want us to see him in this way... When you're done eating, tell the servants to gather your things. I'll have Uncle Velestre take you with him to Springhaven for a while. Though I'm taking command, now, you'll be safer there."

"I don't want to; I want to stay with you!" Riane protested, crying.

"I know," Torran replied sympathetically. "But, with Father gone, you'll have no family here other than me, and there's an enemy coming that I must fight. Sigmund and Scarolette will be busy too. Though I wish that I could, right now, I can't be there for you, and The High Court isn't a place where you can survive on your own. It's full of dangerous games, the people that compose it each more petty than the next, and if I lost you—"

Riane hugged Torran again, squeezing the silence into him.

"You see?" Torran smiled, meekly. "I don't know what I'd do."

"But— But I don't want to be alone! Can't you come with me, let The High Sword take your place?"

"The High Sword is only skilled in war... He has no idea how to run an empire, only make one... If I could, I would, but right now, I have things I need to take care of. I promise to keep you safe, Riane. I'll always keep you safe. It's just that, right now, I'm not a safe person to be around."

"I know, I'm just— I'm just so sad! Father was a good man! Why would anyone want to kill him?!"

Torran looked down at Riane and her overly trusting eyes. For a thirteen-year-old, she still seemed like a little girl. Then again, he hadn't spent much time with her. He hadn't seen her grow up. To him, she would always be his little sister, a younger sibling to return to. He was unable to reconcile the existence of the present Riane with the one in his mind. For the past eight years, his life had revolved around the military, his mind entirely focused on stratagems and swords. For a long time, he had thought returning to the Palace again wasn't in the cards, stripped of his rank and title, but, through effort, he had risen to the rank of Corporal and succeeded in his first mission, bringing him back into his sister's life.

Maddog Rebels had attacked Goldenknife, the local militia no more useful than a knife of soft gold.

An exemplary student, Torran headed the mission to retake the town, capturing the insurgents without any casualties. At twenty years old, Torran Xandromen, the son the High Emperor disowned, had become a military hero.

When the news spread, Torran was finally asked to return to the capital after three, long years of penance for the mayhem he had caused at the banquet. Unfortunately, during that time, he had little opportunity to see Riane or Ilidar. Agravius hosted another banquet, and at that banquet, he was offered a chance at redemption. Given back his title, Torran believed that those three years of hell had been but a prolonged and brutal lesson in duty and responsibility. He thought that he had pleased his father, that he would finally get to catch up with Riane, take his place in Court again. Instead, he was tasked with reconquering the Hemian cities surrounding Sunveil and bringing The Second War of Unification to a close. That same evening, Agravius gave him command of The Fourteenth division and Scarolette as a scribe and assistant.

It took him another half a decade to return home, only to find his father dead and his city threatened.By that time, his Riane was all grown up, and he had missed it all.

Torran held back the tears for a second time. He held them back desperately, almost violently. Though The High Prince was unsure if it was because of her condition. or because she had been under the same sort of delusion he had, his sister didn't seem to understand.

Agravius waged wars. His enemies were too many to count.

There hardly needed to be a reason.

Finally lucid enough to think rationally about the situation, Torran looked back at his father and decided to look for evidence. Though the coroner was a well-respected man, Torran was unsure whether he could be fully trusted, especially when the stakes were so high. Whoever was responsible for The High Emperor's murder was clearly rich, and the Prince refused to lose his father's killer due to bribes. There was no limit to how unscrupulous people could be.

Breaking from Riane after a long hug, he went back into the room and searched the floor around the bed for clues. Then he searched Agravius' person, and, after no luck finding anything in or on his clothes, Torran's eyes came to rest on his father's tightly clenched fist.

Did he...

Though it hurt his heart to do so, Torran broke his father's fingers out of rigor mortis to reveal the only clue that had been left at the scene of the crime.

In the Emperor's hand, lay a scrap of cloth, striped with dark blue and grey.

He must have torn it from the assassin.

Though it was only one, measly piece of evidence, it was all the evidence Torran needed. Even with the fabric wrinkled, crumpled into a ball, Torran could still see them.

The Qeonian colors.

Jhett wasn't the only one Qeonia had wronged.

Viktor

The Moondrake nymph fluttered in, snaking around iron bars and through the open window.

Even with his heat vision, Viktor couldn't see it. It had become invisible, an ability only nymphs of the species possessed, with the exception of queens. Their feathers were special—bending light and hiding them from predators.

Viktor hadn't seen it, but he had heard it.

This particular nymph was queenless. Viktor's pet, it knew no other master, so the Hemian Prince had no need for ravens or mourning doves.

Viktor's voice was soft.

"Here, Ziphra; appear."

Feathers shifted and the winged reptile was visible.

The feathered, silver serpent hovered before him, her small, silver wings flapping quietly as her tail dangled down. She was carrying a message.

Ziphra's milky, blue, faceted eyes rested on Viktor's hand in apprehension.

The Prince pet her, thanking her, and then sat on his bed, ushering her to land on his knee so that he could detach the message from her neck.

The Moondrake flew over.

Carefully undoing the wax thread, the Hemian Prince detached the small, rolled up piece of parchment from Ziphra's neck, petting her for a while longer before moving her over to the spot next to him.

The feathered snake coiled up against his leg, purring softly. Still, her blue-diamond eyes rested on his hand, waiting for more.

You're too much.

Viktor pet Ziphra all over, thanking her thoroughly, and then unfurled the parchment, the feathered reptile falling asleep.

That's right; rest.

The Prince of Hemia read his message.

"It is done. Have payment ready. I will come soon to collect.

-Konell"

Viktor broke into a scalene grin.

Perfect. Good, good...

How do you like that, Torran?

Do you feel my pain, now?

No, of course you don't—not yet.

To feel what I feel, you'll have to lose everything...

But that's okay. There is still time.

The Raishian looked over at his dresser.

As for the assassin, I was thinking about just giving him the vial and letting him go, but such talent shouldn't be wasted.

Viktor took the obsidian chest out of his drawer and opened it. From within, he retrieved the vial, priceless water held in fragile glass.

Yes, that's right. I'll keep him.

Come, Revangel. You shall have your payment.

In fact, I think you'll receive more than you bargained for...

Luxyruss

Luxyruss had one more visit to make before he could return to Avenshra.

He wasn't sure if he wanted to go through with his plan. He wasn't fully prepared to make another sacrifice. He had so little left to lose, that even small things were becoming extremely difficult to let go, and this was no small loss.

But all of humanity would depend on it. He had to give his champion all he could. It was the only hope against Skotathis.

The Divinity slipped The Armorring, the Callring, and The Amulet into his pocket, concentrating.

Luxyruss Jumped.

Luxyruss Converged on a planet unknown to any living astronomer, a planet that was hidden from Skotathis and his Demonium: Euter, The First Sphere, which lay in the grey wastes outside The Kol System. A glimmering, gold ball resting in a dark, dusty void, much of Euter's surface was covered by the amber-colored aether, swimming grounds for thousands of souls. At its south pole, mountainous strips of land surrounded a white sand isle, impaled by a towering, granite peak, which jutted like a stake through the planet's lonely heart. At the base of the clean-cut, pepper-black mountain was the mouth of a large cavern, which emitted a rolling, guttural sound.

Matching Karibidone's moods, the weather was often somber. The mountain's west face, carved with a long staircase to the top, was slick and dark, still sodden from recent rain.

Luxyruss looked up in awe and sorrow.

The planet's sky glowered a burning, smoky red, the rippling, Lifeblood atmosphere held in place by Karibdione's aura. This Lifeblood mantle provided the light that Arceon couldn't at such a distance, but it was dim and morose, not happy like sunlight.

After all, how could it be? It was the light of the dead.

Atop the granite mountain stood The House of The Initiator and the capstone of Kenon's awful prison. Though there was a mountain between them, She could feel its every move, The Primordial wreathed in chains of icy cold. In defiance of its grim purpose, Her white, peristyle mansion exuded a haunting elegance. Ivy ran up its sparkling, marble pillars, which rose like white fountains from the ink-colored rock.

He would meet Her there.

As Luxyruss crossed The Beach, achromic white sands were swept up by gusts of wind, blowing into his face.

The Dohrnae emerged from the aether behind him: the red ghosts of every living thing—faceless, mercurial, humanoid forms walking across the sands. The shambling specters marched dutifully into The Cave only to be sucked into the abyss, a never-ending supply of food to satiate Kenon's hunger, keeping him placated and limiting his power. Like bugs, they were drawn to the swirling, white light issuing from the cavern, oblivious to the fate that awaited them. Some probably were bugs, led to die again just as they had died before, a cruel joke that only Luxyruss, in his desolation, could see some twisted humor in. They would drop hundreds of feet only to be snapped up and digested.

Luxyruss pitied them: that shambling procession of souls, but he knew they weren't fully conscious. They were only remnants—a vestige—the life forces of people, animals, trees, insects, fungi, and microbes—creatures from all of The Living Worlds. Their erasure was the price of Creation, a debt owed to the cosmos' original and eternal ruler.

Had Luxyruss not remembered, he wouldn't have felt so bitter. But it had been different, a thousand years ago. Shadowrise trees brought back the dead, the mercy of an anguished Goddess who realized her mistake too late. In days, or decades, they would return; it mattered not. No one was ever truly gone.

Skotathis had changed all that. The Adversary of all life, he invented death in a deathless world.

Now, only The Powers were immortal.

Looking at his thin and wrinkled skin, the cavern entrance glowing before him, Luxyruss knew that one day, he too would perish. Human life could be prolonged, skirting the brink, but there was a limit—a limit he would eventually hit.

Each Emanation had taken much from him, and, if he went through with his plan, he would no longer hold enough of Unification for his Lifeblood to stay intact.

He would no longer be a Power.

Though he wouldn't have had to die if it had not been for Skotathis, after nearly two millennia, it was fair. He had lived for centuries longer than he should have, a god escaping death while his followers were Devoured. Why should he be exempt? Because She didn't want him to die?

She was a thief, and his life had been stolen from It, along with the rest.

No—someday, he would join The Dhornae in their march into The Cave, into oblivion. His Lifeblood would be stripped of its character and reclaimed. He would never return.

There would be a justice to it, a justice proclaiming that, in the end, all living things were created equal. Nothing was valued; everything was recycled.

But must It reclaim what It owned? Are we not allowed to exist?!

Luxyruss clenched his teeth and walked past The Cave, leaving that ever-lasting funeral behind.

I wish that I could, but— I cannot save them... They are already gone.

The Divinity scaled the sheer mountainside, the narrow, granite staircase, slippery and unforgiving. He clutched the mountainside with a white-knuckled grip, holding on for dear, dear life as the winds hounded him, pouring through his threadbare robes. His nails cracked, caked with dirt, but he continued along the grueling way, huffing and puffing.

You could help me, make this easier, but I know that you're angry.

Your anger is righteous; I cannot deny.

By the time Luxyruss made it to the top, sleet poured from the moody sky, like frozen light.

She was standing outside, waiting for him.

Skotathis

When Tethered, Skotathis seemed to lose himself.

There were so many souls entering him that it was hard to stay present.

The Snare's roots dug into his arms, neck, and ribs, every point of contact like electricity. Muscles grew and bones hardened, his body overflowing with vitality.

At that moment, Skotathis had so much Lifeblood in him, that if it wasn't stored in The Shadowheart in his chest, anyone he touched would be vaporized on contact.

In such excess, Lifeblood became a drug. He felt an overwhelming feeling of pleasure, his back arched-to-breaking, and his eyes swirling, no specific color, and not focusing on anything in particular.

But the high wore off quicker and quicker each time, and that day he felt cheated, the pleasure evaporating in mere moments. Just as quickly, the pain was back—he could feel her diameter pressing against his skull, pulsating against the insides of his horns. The Tremite Queen pulsed, throbbing colors shifting.

The Tremites had allowed for the creation of The Demonium, turning what were once fragile, mortal beings into something more: a new species that gave up their sanctity in exchange for invincibility—an unpierceable, unmeltable hide. One only had to be willing to spill a little blood, accept the parasite into their body.

Tremite larvae could mutate any living thing, fundamentally altering its genetic structure, and putting it under the direct control of the Queen.

The Queen had approached him first, that day, long ago. She offered him her help on the condition that he became her host, brought others. Skotathis accepted the bargain, but their relationship soon became strained, the Queen growing too rapidly within him.

Come from desert pools, the Tremites had never known such an abundance of food. For eons, they had survived off of Arceon's weak rays, absorbing Lifeblood directly through their skin. Starlight did, after all, carry Lifeblood, as did food and water. However, the Lifeblood they received this way was very little, and they had never known the sort of bounty brought to them through willing and unwilling hosts. Being very strong mentally, Skotathis eventually managed to suppress the Queen, subjugating her and forcing her to hand over complete control of The Demonium. Using her ability to produce psionic waves, he could Order The Demonium to do whatever he pleased, but the price of this power was constant pain. Still, he refused to let it go. The control it gave him wasn't the only boon the Queen's presence granted. His new body had allowed him to survive The Theft and all the trials he met in his journey. His greatest failure, The Theft had taken everything from him, but it had also given him something back. That pittance would now help him take a big step forward towards achieving his destiny and becoming King of The Kol System. Granted Elementality, he had expanded his Lifeblood, dissolving part of his Power into it and turning all of his soldiers into temporary Emanations with immunity to Therius.

The Adversary stopped brooding and got up from beneath the Faalan Shadowrise, pulling the roots out of his skin. He had taken his fill and so had the worm.

Skotathis knew he shouldn't feel glum over the loss of such short-term gratification. It was time to celebrate. Soon, he would claim his birthright.

Even without The Qeonian Shadowrise, he had more than enough Lifeblood to send in his armies. He would take on The High Empire, and crush it under his heel.

The Adversary looked at the force he had amassed as The Demonium gathered in Windswept Valley, the largest flat surface on the dark side of the moon. Monsters made for war stretched out as far as the eye could see, a seething ocean of horns, claws, and teeth. Five hundred thousand demons stood divided into ten batteries, each fifty thousand strong.

The first four batteries were composed of Goblins, Threshers, Shadowbats, Penumons, Unicorns, and Beasts, and were to be sent to Sunveil under the command of Scelis, a Goblin-Thresher hybrid embedded with a Shadowheart and Risen to the rank of Archdemon.

The fifth battery was composed of Goblins and Necroscora and was to be sent to The Stareye Isthmus.

The sixth battery was composed of Goblins, Salamanders, Shadowbats, Threshers, and Pneumons—as well as his latest creation—and was to be sent to The Shattered Crest.

The seventh battery was composed of Goblins, Threshers, Pneumons, and

Shadowbats, and was to be sent to Ríodad.

The eighth battery was composed of Goblins, Pneumons, and Shadowbats, and was to be sent to Lauhapell's Peninsula.

The ninth battery was composed only of Goblins and was to be sent to The Crumbling Bluff.

And finally, the tenth battery was to be composed of a small group of Drozers, and sent to The Ragged Coast.

Though Skotathis already had a massive army, he knew that more dragons would awaken from their slumber, and The Threshers would produce Crystalline to add to his ranks once the fighting began. He had even made some of the more powerful demons into substantial Emanants of Division, endowing them with his aura, amongst other combat advantages.

That was not all. He still had a trump card up his sleeve, a weapon that brought entire planets to their knees...

Stotathis gazed smilingly upon his proud horde. More demons than he could name were arranged in ranks before him, kneeling before his Throne.

He knew that once they touched ground, some of those ranks would fall apart, crazy for Lifeblood, but he hadn't created The Demonium to be a disciplined force. They were meant to be the embodiment of chaos.

Some would be lost in the Pyrocast, but, being an ability he had created himself, and a recent creation at that, this was acceptable.

The only loss he wouldn't accept would be to lose to Luxyruss.

Skotathis sauntered over to the edge of the sheer cliff face, his voice echoing against the stone, reverberating through the cloudless sky.

His mistress, Lilith'in, stood with him, her slender, black fingers wrapped around his shoulder. Half Ressidan, half demon, she was the only truly independent member of his ranks. She had once been his friend and his betrothed, but things had changed over the course of years of war, and they had remained an unmarried couple. However, due to his affection for her, she had been spared from the ugliness and constant pain he and the others felt. He had Purged her of the Tremites immediately after her transformation, leaving her with only the best of each species. She suffered no infestation, and she never would.

Skotathis put a hand around Lilith'in's slight waist, and raised his other hand to silence the raucous crowd of soldiers. Though they might have once been pacifists or prey animals, over the course of centuries, the majority of them had lost their minds entirely to The Tremites, reduced to their crudest, most base impulses.

Of course, I can always Order the reluctant few to obey.

In the distance, Avenshra hovered, a large, glowing, blue globe.

"Brothers and sisters—with the power we now possess, Avenshra is ours for the taking! We will destroy The High Empire, and we will do so together! Now, remember, Hemia is our ally in this fight, and so is Whitereach, so spare any Raishians and ice giants you meet. As for the rest—our enemy's beloved followers—I leave them to you! You can go wild! For this is our kingdom come, the time we've been waiting for! Our earthly followers pray for our return, eager for the coming fight. Go forth now; let us answer their prayers!"

Skotathis raised both hands skyward as black wings poured from his oilslick back, his eyes, quasars.

"Give them hell!" he snarled.

With that, The Adversary breathed in Lifeblood and waved his hand, Casting The Demonium down to earth in a titanic, green fireball.

Luxyruss

"Karibdione. It's been a long time."

Goddess was ravishing—red eyes, dark blue hair—skin like porcelain. The form she had taken was thin, but supple, and the rain revealed what lay beneath Her white, lace gown.

It was obvious to Luxyruss that this was by design.

Karibdione blushed at him girlishly, Her eyes glowing a deep, rose-red. She lowered Her voice to a tone that was purposefully sultry, Her gaze seductive, but The Divinity saw a dark furor hidden beneath, a war raging inside Her between a loneliness beyond human comprehension, and an anger that was all too human.

It was an ire he had rightfully earned.

"Too long, Lux. I've been waiting for soo long..."

Karibdione feigned despondence.

Luxyruss smiled inwardly, but remembered who She was and what She was doing.

"I'm sorry, my Lady," he apologized.

"I know you are. It's been nearly a thousand years, and—after all—I'm 'your Lady.'"

Goddess pushed forward, Her blouse soaked though, though he knew it didn't have

to be. The goddess slid Her hand up his arm, Her countenance wanton as she brushed Her fingers against his chest.

She was playing games with him, and he had just arrived. The Celestial was bored.

"Come, Karibdione. You know why I'm here, what I've been through to get to this point. Let's not run in circles. Time flows by like a rushing river."

Karibdione crossed her hips, sighing lewdly.

"Oh, yes... A rushing river. I know exactly what you mean. Why don't you come inside, where it's nice and warm?"

"I cannot stay."

Luxyruss knew what She wanted. "You are my Goddess, Karibdione; I cannot—"

The Celestial grew like a shadow in the afternoon, Her skin turning to a shimmering, golden-black. She revealed Her true, alien form to him, the form he couldn't bring himself to accept, so many years ago.

Beneath Karibdione's beautiful transformations, was not a human or angel, but an eyeless alien with a forehead crowned with three, golden horns—a trident. She had long, sharp claws and a spiked, frilly tail, and where Her mouth should have been, there was a set of vibrating, ridged chords. Goddess hands zapped purple lightning, fueled by a stream of Lifeblood that came from the large, white crystal at the center of Her chest—the heart he had broken.

As quickly as she had grown, she shrank down again, returning to her human form and slapping him.

"You can't what, Luxyruss?! Ever visit the Goddess you supposedly worship, talk to her for once?! Give her a night of comfort after a thousand years of solitude?! You don't even pray; you don't even think of me, treat me like I'm nothing!"

She was shouting, then.

"I am everything! Yet all I do is sit and rot on this wretched planet, sit above that foul creature and its lascivious gluttony, all to ensure you, and your beloved human race, can live out your fleeting lives! Your kind wasn't even at the peak of evolution when I touched ground on Ressida, the evolution I set in motion! And this—this skin I wear—you can't possibly understand what it's like!"

The Goddess grew more aggressive.

"My Creation made you—your mind, your body! It is mine if I will it! I made The Living Worlds! You only live, because I will it! What say should you have, Luxyruss?! Are you a god?!"

Luxyruss bit his cheek.

"N-No, my Lady," he answered, head bowed.

"No. But you left anyway, broke your wedding vow and fled like a thief in the night, that night so long ago... All because you—the wisest of all the angels—couldn't bear to see my true form, to love an Ioen! Even after I took on this form, gave you eternal life—Bound The Void: an enemy you yourselves Awakened—you left, cheated on me with that mortal, human bitch, Telespora and had that grey-haired bastard of yours. You had your day and now that that day grows dim, you've come to ask for the ring back, treat me like some alien slut for feeling lonely! I AM GODDESS ALMIGHTY—CHRISM, THE INITIATOR!"

Human tears flowed. Karibdione's face contorted in anger.

"You know how easy it would be?" she asked, her voice but a whisper. "I could just wipe your soul from that body, feed it to the pit!"

Luxyruss' heart was racked with guilt, his holiness disposed of like garbage. The grandeur of "The Divinity" was no longer there. His grey hair dragged against the rock, skin sagging.

She is an alien and The Creator. I cannot be hers, no matter how human she may seem!

"I lost Creation to protect your people; I gave you my power to protect

274

Ressida, and all its ungrateful inhabitants! But if I destroy you now, I will never see another soul, Bound how I am..."

Goddess' tone softened; She wiped away the tears.

"I will give you one last chance, Luxyruss. Come with me; give me something in return, or leave me with nothing, leave with nothing, leave—as nothing."

Luxyruss complied.

Flind

Flind couldn't escape.

The nuns were furious with her. She had stolen their sacred relic and dishonored their Temple.

The Greenscarab Armor was surprisingly light, but it wasn't very flexible, held together by a mix of brown leather and bronze mail. The lack of flexibility restricted her movement, slowing her down.

The suit was incomplete without the helmet, which she had been forced to leave behind after the chin-strap broke, but she had risked her life to get it, and there was no turning back. Even incomplete, it would still be worth a lot—if she could survive.

Selling the Armor on the black market would let her go anywhere she wanted. The average merchant wouldn't recognize it and would gladly pay; She just had to lose the nuns in the forest and get to The Bay of Scales.

Flind cursed.

A week hadn't even passed, and she was on the run again. Worse, her powers had left her, though she didn't know where they had come from in the first place. All she knew was that when she had woken up in the nuns' carriage, they were gone, and there was a ring on her finger.

The nuns who had begrudgingly picked her up were now chasing her, and they had emptied their entire armory to do so, carrying enchanted bronze kunai and wearing enchanted steel urumis as belts.

Or at least, they had sent their Sisters. The five that were after her now weren't the women she had met, but the others, who had been out at the time. Their order's best fighters, they were elites amongst elites, and they were gaining ground fast, though Flind had had a huge head start.

Flind wished she could say that she would be forgiven if she was caught, even if she had taken one of their relics. Most Lātist nuns were kind and compassionate, and would forgive crimes of necessity. And although it was very convincing, Flind was certain that the Armor was not the real thing, merely a well-made recreation. After all, why would such a famous Cairnian relic be kept in some no-name shrine in Qeonia? It didn't make sense.

But Kïsist nuns weren't against violence.

In fact, it was their calling.

Flind stumbled, pushing off a tree and continuing to run. They were quicker than her in their loose, dark green robes, their movements lithe and agile. Flind's footsteps clunked as she half-ran, half-stumbled through The Forest of Tears.

This whole plan is ridiculous. What was I thinking?

I'm just a maid and a scullion, not a skilled fighter! They're hunting me down like an animal!

A throwing knife barely missed Flind's ear; an urumi whipped out to sever her neck, but she ducked, the blade wrapping around a tree trunk.

I'm going to die! I should never have stolen from them!

Flind heard more urumis fly and spun around on instinct. In a puff of red, a copper-colored war pick appeared in her hand, catching three different urumis and redirecting them around her.

The weapon had a thick, crooked spike for a point, jutting from a square face, with a pyramidal stud at the back to add weight, though the weapon was supernaturally light. It was truly a beast of a weapon, but two urumis still got through, shaving skin off her cheek and nicking her wrist, the vicious cut barely missing her radial artery.

Blood dripped, and—for a moment—nobody moved. The Forest was dark—cold and still—tall pine trees huddled together. The ground was soft underfoot, and the grass was very sparse.

Behind them, the trees broke ranks to form a small clearing, where the light green grass was thickest, partially obscuring large, grey rocks.

Riize was very large that night—a full moon—and it lit the clearing up, revealing the secret dances of shiny, white moths. The air was cold and smelled heavily of pine sap and dew, the sky a dark blue-purple.

Snapping back to reality, Flind tried to pull the war-pick free and fight back, but, for whatever reason, her movement made the weapon heavier. Giving up, she let the weapon go, the pick disappearing into thin air, and causing the nuns to lose their balance.

One, pinch-faced sister recovered more quickly than the others, pulling a throwing dagger from the brown, leather sash around her chest and using it for close quarters combat. She rushed at Flind with the intent to kill, aiming for her face.

Shit, shit, shit! I'm going to die! No!!!

The blade was halted millimeters from Flind's left eye, her assailant pulled up and into the canopy by a moving branch. The nun had been speared through the spine.

The other Sisters immediately spaced themselves out, whipping their urumis around their body and creating a radius of flashing steel. They looked for an aggressor, finding none until another tree branch came.

Urumis snapped, their wooden foe cut to pieces.

Unfreezing, Flind got back to running, but one of the Sisters noticed, diverting her sword-whip to catch the scullion by the ankle, and drag her back into the clearing.

Flind clung to mossy rock—all she could grab. A root took down her pursuer within seconds.

Seeing this, the other three nuns abandoned their previous strategy and formed a triangle, back to back. Before they could fully assume the formation, a leaf-like khandjar took one of them in the right buttock, a ferocious dryad running in and springing off of the lodged knife. The green lady flipped over the screaming nun's head as her leafy dreadlocks took hold, and threw the woman into a nearby oak. In that same motion, she spun, knocking out the remaining two nuns with a split-leg kick that broke orbital bones and noses.

The dryad didn't move to retrieve her knife. The lime-green dagger had disappeared in a vaporous cloud, Dismissing itself just like the pick that had appeared in Flind's hands a moment earlier.

The dryad bent over, catching her breath.

Wow... She's...gorgeous, Flind thought to herself.

Catching her breath, the dryad walked up to Flind and reached out her hand, coming into the light. Seeing the woman's face in its full clarity, the scullion stumbled backwards, doing her best to contain her shock.

She recognized the woman.

"Hi, my name is Leafsong," the woman chimed. "Do I know you?"

My La– What happened to you, Leafsong? You've turned into a plant?

This is crazy! This is all so crazy!

What am I saying?

Things have been crazy.

It's fine. After all, after what I did, it's probably for the best that she doesn't recognize me.

Yeah, this is good.

Flind wasn't particularly surprised that Leafsong didn't recognize her. Even if the noblewoman had known her face when she was a maid, she probably didn't know her name. That was the way it was with the wealthy.

It seemed that Leafsong didn't even remember her face, but the young heiress had undergone a dramatic Transformation, and Flind hadn't recognized her either.

I guess it's only fair.

Hesitant, the maid took the dryad's hand. She would have to start lying— about everything.

Though she had done what she did to save the woman's sister, Leafsong was no longer the same, no longer human. She had become dangerous, and if she found out who Flind really was, her life would be at risk.

Flind bit her lip. The dryad was dangerous, but she had no one else to turn to. The nuns might come back for her...or worse.

She quickly came up with an alias.

"Leafsong... Thank you for your help. I'm Fiona, Fiona Brunei."

"Are you okay?" the dryad asked, concerned. "Why were those women attacking you, and what is that Armor?"

"Honestly, it's a long story," the scullion answered sheepishly.

Viktor

It was on the twelfth toll of The White Bell that The Demonium arrived.

All day, Viktor had been sitting patiently in his tower cell, waiting for what his Lord had promised.

Hearing shouts, The Prince of Hemia looked out from his barred window to see the sky brimming with pillars of green light. Astrian soldiers drew their swords in fear as arcane symbols were branded into the ground, the marks of a Pyrocast.

Being a devotee of Skotathis, The Lord Defiant and The Adversary, Vitkor knew well enough what that meant.

He was going to be rescued.

With a *fishhh* the pebbles around the soldiers' feet began to levitate.

And then, like meteors, demonic flames fell upon them: Goblins with their black steel swords, Threshers with their Epidemions—thousands of them—in their midst—Shadowbats and Beasts.

Viktor had never seen such bloodshed.

Soon, the ground was covered in a layer of blood, inches deep, baptizing newly made Crystalline. The people of The High Empire were forced to confront the enemy of their god.

The Prince's attention was drawn to a fireball bigger than the rest. It fell roughly a hundred yards away from his tower.

A Unicorn.

The Unicorn was a pot-bellied, quadrupedal demon with a clubbed tail designed for collapsing joints, and smashing in finely-painted breastplates. An ill-made creation, its head was largely taken up by a massive, peeling, grey horn, and its back was covered by rough, obsidian armor, a rhinoceros mutated into something even more formidable.

Smelling blood in the air, the eyeless thing flared its six, slit-like nostrils, shaking its head wildly. The smell threw it into a frenzy, and, within seconds, the living battering ram began rushing towards Viktor's tower.

For any other man in his situation, this would have spelled death. But for the imprisoned Prince, this was the perfect opportunity.

Viktor didn't panic. He sucked in Lifeblood from below, and prepared to make his escape, placing his hands on the chamber floor in a crouch. He felt the fires of the world falling into his Reach again, the earth at his command.

With a *crash*, the Unicorn rammed the tower along with the soldier guarding it, its real target. The red-haired knight was pulped to mush in an instant, and white-painted bricks encapsulated the bovine creature in a salvo of bleached clay.

As the tower broke in half and fell, Viktor used the momentum to Evanesce.

He reappeared, rolling, in front of a squadron of dumbstruck Imperial troops, The Draconid around his neck absorbing the Lifeblood of the dying. The dragon-scale necklace glowed, a red-citrine chip pinched between two pieces of etched, enchanted silver.

With the carnage around them, the soldiers expected Viktor to join the side of Astria and fight for mankind, proving his renewed fealty to The High Throne. They expected him to fight The Demonium.

Instead, he led them.

Skotathis

Skotathis looked through The Chronoccul, which was pointed at Avenshra.

The hulking telescope was made from enchanted black steel, consisting of a wide seat and a tube as long as a man and as wide as a round shield. The tube ended in an obsidian lens, which focused the light into a pair of binoculars connected to a Shadowrise-wood helmet. Behind the telescope, sat a honeycomb of obsidian panels, polished to a mirror sheen. The whole setup sat on a rotating base, managed by a system of black steel gears, and operated with an array of levers wrapped in light blue squid leather.

The Chronoccul had been built on a clifftop to the west of Skotathis mountain throne, the space dedicated solely to the machine. The seat was smooth and made of metal, uncomfortable, and the air smelled of oil. Occasionally, a cold wind would freeze the gears together, but the area was good enough for his purposes.

The Adversary couldn't actually see detail through the telescope's murky, glass lens. It was merely a way for him to anchor his focus to a specific point in the distance. Knowledge did the rest, The Power of Division's cosmic awareness allowing him to see the world and its happenings in real time.

Skotathis grinned, watching his Emissary lay waste to desperate men and despairing women, Astrian Stars snuffed out by a blade not seen in a thousand years.

Beasts roared like hairless lions, the thousand-eyed demons gnashing their teeth and taking on whole squadrons at a time. Terrible Shadowbats flew overhead, smokescreens pouring from the sacs on their wings. They carried soldiers with greathelms into the sky only to drop them again indiscriminately, eliciting a shallow splash of blood. They reminded him of hawks, dropping turtles whose shells were too thick.

Though all were fierce, the most fearsome fighter on the field was, by far, his Emissary.

Viktor Eridion wore his father's skeletal, Theonium Armor, and he held the Tainted blade that had once belonged to The Red Meteor, impure capillaries spreading through the Fallstreak's candle-white surface. With a *vwoom*, the Lifeblood of the vanquished was severed, and then absorbed into the three, parallel, black stones in the sword's hilt, trapped forever. It was a blade that turned men into ashen, grey statues, brittle as starfish left to dry in the sun.

Bloodweep—the blade with the red edge.

The Adversary sat on his throne, pensive, thinking over his next command.

Which of The Continental Nations should I invade first?

His mistress, Lilith'in, floated towards him, her smooth, aubergine skin glistening like soap.

Lilith'in was very tall for a woman. She wasn't quite as tall as him, but she was the only one on Faal who dared to look him in the eye. She was the only one who could have dared—dared to use her wiles on a man who had burned his homeworld to ash.

Most days, Skotathis would have readily given in to her seduction. She was monstrously beautiful, with straight, sleek, raven hair that poured down her back from between a pair of slender, obsidian horns. Her eyes burned a bright green, like sulphurous fire. Her back was ridged with thin, interlocking plates of obsidian, and a long, lissom tail whipped feistily over her heart-shaped ass, ending in a heart-shaped, obsidian isoscele.

The Demonium would stare at her with a salivary lust whenever they saw her, and even a normal human would have been instantly enraptured by her. But that day, The Adversary resisted her temptation.

The time of conquest is approaching; I must prepare.

Seeing him brooding, Lilith'in let out a wry smile, small, white fangs resting on plump, purple-black lips. She stroked his horned head affectionately, her tone provocative.

"What's wrong, my King?" she pouted.

Skotathis answered curtly, ignoring her advances.

"That fool, Luxyruss... I can't feel his life force, but I can't feel The Archangel's either. I fear he has survived somehow, that he's plotting against me... The Amulet is still beyond my reach."

"Come on, Skotathis... For The Blackest Night, you sure worry a lot. He's so old; he's got to be dead! Plus...if he was alive, we'd be in big trouble right now."

The succubus lifted her knee and placed her foot on the throne's armrest. Running her hand along her lover's leg, her tail unraveled, isocele tickling his cheek.

"Why don't we have some fun? The plan proceeds smoothly. And look—we're alone..."

Skotathis pried her hand away.

"Maybe— Maybe later. I'm not in a good mood right now. Something is off, and I just know that man managed to survive... I have to consult my library, meager though it is. I need to figure out his plan. Why don't you tend to your whores and let me think? After all, that is your role in all this."

"Woww! You'd rather "consult" some dusty old books than lie with me... Okay, then, good luck with the necklace; though you don't need it anyway. With the power you have already, there's no way he would beat you, but I think I will "tend to my whores.""

Skotathis got up dismissively, shooing her off.

"Yeah, yeah; just go already."

The demoness Called Dragontail with a sigh, the yellow whip falling into her hand with a *swish*. She took a black steel syringe from out of her belt pocket, and filled it with Tremite larvae from a large, glass vial. Frustrated, she walked off, returning to the wails of human women.

She was off to bring forth a new generation of demons.

Lilith'in

The birth slaves wailed, as they always did.

Lilith'in ignored their cries.

Bound tightly by Shadowthread ropes and kept in cramped, dirty, black steel cages, they were stacked one on top of the other, exposed to the elements and unable to move an inch. They rarely had time to rest, if it could be called rest, and their only moment of freedom was during labor, a labor that was both agonizing and fatal. Human women weren't meant to give birth to things with horns, and nature rebelled in gruesome fashion.

Lilith'in watched with despicable excitement as a group of Goblins marched up the hill to pay the slaves a visit. They were the third group that day.

Anyone with a shred of humanity—of goodness in their souls—would have been mortified, sick to their stomach with revulsion. They would have covered their eyes in horror.

But Lilith'in didn't bring her hands up to her eyes as the demons dropped their loincloths and the women began to scream. Instead, she put them between her legs, and relished every moment of it.

Oscure

Oscure ate his dinner on the sun-bleached, wooden patio outside his Hut.

A tropical beach sparkled in front of him, the cool, turquoise waters of The Sea of Glass continuously trying to reach past the line they had previously set for themselves in the sand. They headed past the little, grey rocks and over broken seashells to destinations unknown.

Arceon was a pale white-blue, sunlight playing off of the undulating waves, and the air smelled of ripe coconuts, the sweet-and-sour scent diluted in sea spray. A pink conch shell with a pearlescent, dark blue interior sat steadfast in a pool of water, abandoned by the Sea in a sandy depression. Hermit crabs crossed the white sand beach, trying to keep a low profile, but their own, colorful shells gave them away, and the children of the Tribe watched them with curiosity, offering them new houses, only to fall crestfallen at their rejection.

Squawking gulls made wide circles overhead, looking for fish, and the palms behind them rustled in the toasty breeze.

A salt-encrusted, makeshift wooden pier extended from the beach and into deeper waters, where handmade nets sat marked by floating coconut shells, used as buoys. Sharp, black mussels crusted the weathered support beams, and if one walked those creaking boards, they would see the shadows of small fish in the water.

The Aerhauc Settlement was a small, but lively community. Women brought in fruits and herbs from the forest in large, wicker baskets and men carried water from The Snake River in old, wooden pails, hanging from strong, wooden poles. They carried the food and water past a group of hunters, who headed into the jungle holding stone-tipped, ironwood spears.

Fishermen carried in nets of mussels and fish, fresh-caught, and gave them to the mothers of the Tribe, who cleaned them and threw them in a pot of bubbling, red stew spicy enough to melt straight through the cast iron.

The village Elders, a wizened group of women with long, grey dreadlocks and rheumy eyes, sat in the shade of the palms with a group of toddlers, keeping them occupied with stories and poems while their parents prepared the meal.

Unperturbed by the heat, a group of older children played together, their skin glistening with sweat as they kicked a scuffed-up, brown leather ball across the shore.

Oscure smiled, remembering his reckless youth. He had played like that with Mozamic...

At some point, the children lost control of the ball and nearly knocked over the pot of stew, which got them chided by the cooks.

Oscure chuckled, sighing.

His guest *slurped*, pulling him from his reverie.

Amdryaan, the Tribe's strange visitor, had recuperated, so he had invited the man to sup with him.

That had been a mistake.

Though the Native was friendly, and very gracious, he ate like a wild thing. Oscure rubbed his eyes to make sure he was seeing the number of dirty dishes he thought he saw. In the course of half an hour, the man had eaten a whole day's worth of fishing, hunting, and gathering.

Across the table from him, sat an earthenware mountain. Amdryaan had consumed not one, but three bowls of afang, crayfish, honey, and waterleaf soup, a big plate of steamed tree pulp and mashed tubers, seasoned with chili peppers, a whole basket of fried plantains, and a tiger shark chutney with mango slices as garnish. He had washed it all down with a honey alcohol, flavored with tropical flowers.

Oscure looked at his plate of roasted galjoen. He had barely eaten any of his fish and the maize, horned melon relish, and fried plantains beside it, while the foreigner had devoured everything in sight.

He came from the barren Ice Fields, and he was really thin... Still, isn't that a little too much?

"Your Majesty, the food is delicious!" Amdryaan mumbled, stuffing his face. He looked like he was about to cry tears of joy. "I've never eaten so well in all my life! You have my thanks."

"Then eat well," the Tribe King replied. He gave the tribesman an obliging, fake smile, peeved.

Not recognizing his host's annoyance, the Native continued to dig in.

Knowing it was futile, Oscure tried to catch up anyway, grumbling under his breath.

Hospitality...

Oscure smiled. Now that his visitor had finished eating, he could finally have a real conversation with the man, explore whether he knew anything about the powers they shared. He was curious why the Native possessed a Callring that was only bestowed upon Beloveds of Madevf.

"Now that we have eaten, I would be interested to know more about your story, Amdryaan. We Beloveds are exceedingly rare, but you do not seem to know what you are. What is your power?"

"I don't know anything about "Beloveds," but a couple of days ago, I became able to control metal."

Oscure asked one of the village women to bring him some stew, giving the bowl to Amdryaan.

"Breathe," he instructed.

"Um...okay?"

Amdryaan breathed in quickly, his eyes suddenly glowing red. Though the tribesman didn't know it, he had instinctively extended Lifeblood from his olfactory and gustatory nerves, smoke-like energy travelling in a line to connect with the protrusions, and form a larger whole.

The stew darkened, as if spoiled.

"Now, see if you can move my fork," the Tribe King instructed.

Without delay, the iron fork flew into Amdryaan's hand.

The Native put down the utensil, his eyes still glowing, but a little more faintly.

Oscure took off his Callring.

"Now, try moving this," he challenged.

Amdryaan stretched out his hand, trying to move the black-and-red ring, but it was clear that it wouldn't budge. Sweat began to drip down his forehead.

Move it, if you can.

Pull with all you've got.

The tribesman gritted his teeth, hand shaking. The table started to shake in turn, but the ring was immovable.

Knives and spoons lifted off and began flying around the pair in circles, like planets orbiting a miniature sun. They spun faster and faster, getting to a speed that could even pierce Nolite skin.

The people of the Tribe stared, transfixed.

Eventually, Amdryaan's eyes faded; the silverware slowing in its orbit and dropping to the floor.

Oscure smiled, reassured, and put his Callring back on.

"Very good. I did not think you could do it, but I wanted to make sure. This ring is one with me, made of a metal more valuable than most cities. If it could be taken so easily, that would be an issue. You will learn soon... You shall have one too, in time."

"What was that?" Amdryaan asked, overflowing with curiosity. "What does breathing have to do with my power?"

The Native gulping in air like an idiot, Oscure smirking.

"I'm breathing now," he blabbered. "Nothing's happening."

"You have it all wrong, my friend." Oscure smiled.

He took the tribesman's latest plate of food and breathed in, corn greying. Eyes faintly glowing, he beckoned to Yeyemba, asking her to fetch one of the nets, full with the latest catch.

The fish had stopped moving, out of air, but only a few minutes prior.

Oscure nodded to her apologetically. "Thank you, and tell Gambuko I'm sorry."

Smiling, but confused, Yeyemba went back to her chores.

He'll be mad after spending all that time fishing. Oh, well.

Oscure breathed in again, increasing his Lifeblood. His eyes blazed red.

He raised his hand and harnessed his abilities, the abilities granted to him for fighting and defeating Naraklar. He had practiced as much as he could, intuiting out some basic functions.

With a motion, Oscure surrounded the entire Settlement in darkness, blacking out the sky and erasing the waves.

The children, who had been playing in the sand, paused, amazed at the sight, though they had seen it before. The adults muttered, their eyes fearful, but the trust they had in their Tribe King was evident in their composure.

Amdryaan watched in wonder and awe.

After a few moments, the Tribe King's eyes faded back to brown, and the light was allowed to pass again without detour, everything returning to normal.

"You see, my friend, it has little to do with breathing. It has to do with sacrifice. I had to lose someone closer to me than anyone, fight for dominance. It is the way things have always been... All power comes at a price—ours most of all."

Torran

Torran dreamt that he was ahorse, Sunveil looming before him—The City

287

of Red and White with its perpetually overcast sky.

He was reliving the last day of The Second War of Unification.

Torran remembered how his steed's shoes had scraped the malnourished earth, a hundred thousand soldiers taking the rear, all under his command. Behind them, rolled dozens of wooden oxcarts, heaped to the brim with food, the red-brown cows that pulled them mooing unhappily. Behind them were more carts, carrying medical supplies.

King Falin Eridion had sent a dove to Starspire a week prior, offering surrender. The walls of Sunveil could repel any direct attack, and a siege would be too costly for The High Empire, so terms had been agreed to. The High Emperor had decided that Torran and his force would bring food and medical supplies to the remaining people of Sunveil, saving them from sickness and famine. The city had been hit with The Yellow Plague, and with so many noble houses smashed and holds destroyed, Agravius wouldn't let innocents starve when peace had been made. He had sent his son and his troops in an honest show of peace. Torran was eager for the war to be over, so he hadn't questioned the decision.

When Torran's forces arrived at the gates of Sunveil, there were no soldiers manning the towering, white walls, only a couple of peasants peering out over the battlements, cloaked in tattered, brown rags. Starving magistrates, along with peasant men, women, and children, shivered outside the city's entrance. Many were sick—all looked like skeletons. They watched the approach of the Imperial forces with eyes that were sunken and hollow.

When asked where the royal family was, the magistrate at the front of the group explained the situation.

He was an old man, with a long, grey beard and fearful eyes, which had turned pink from poor health, and though Torran had been fighting Raishians for half a decade, he felt sorry for him.

His voice hoarse and raspy, the magistrate told Torran that The King and Queen of Hemia had died of the Plague, along with their son Viktor. After that, The Bloodred Battalion had committed suicide to accompany them to the afterlife, a custom that was mandated by their code of honor.

"Your Highness—please accept our surrender. We are the only survivors of this bloody conflict. It is solely the sick who remain within the city, along with whatever healers we have who are willing to treat them, and some lower-ranking soldiers distributing whatever rations are left. Though we have escaped The Yellow Plague, I fear some of us may yet fall ill."

Torran knew he had the means to help the survivors, but something felt off about the situation. He had never heard of the Battalion swearing an oath. In fact, if he recalled correctly, they had originally started off as a group of mercenaries known as The Red Riders. Even more dubious, was that the royals would die, while their magistrates survived. Avenshra hadn't seen a plague capable of killing entire cities since the time of Xersus Xandromen. Even the accounts of such plagues were suspicious, and Falin Eridion was always a clever man, one who wouldn't perish so easily to disease. The thing that roused Torran's suspicion most was that there were no pyres burning, even though there must have been many bodies to cremate. If anything, the sky was clearer than usual. He didn't hear the wails of sickness, the screams of organ failure.

But the Prince's sympathy won out in the end, clouding his judgement. He pushed down his suspicions, eager to return home to see his father and his little sister.

"I accept your surrender," Torran confirmed. "You will have as much food and medicine as you need, and you shall not be harmed. Now, tell your people manning the walls to open the doors, and I'll have my battle-medics assess the situation."

"Open the doors!" The High Prince called up to the battlements. His men approached with the carts, but, strangely, the survivors didn't reach for food.

The children began to cry, the women too. The men sat with dead eyes, like fish without oxygen.

The doors to Sunveil remained closed, the magistrate strangely silent.

"Why aren't you...opening them? Open the doors," Torran commanded.

"I-I can't do that, your Highness," the magistrate answered gravely.

The earth began to have a seizure.

Blocks shifting, the city walls began to quiver. The peasants manning the battlements nearly fell to their deaths.

Torran drew his sword, putting it at the old man's throat.

"What treachery is this?! Tell me what's happening, or I will cut you down here and now! The fate of your city rests on what you say next... Why can't you open the doors?!"

The magistrate hung his head, and began to sob, tears rolling from his eyes.

"I'm sorry, your Highness. He made us do it."

Torran didn't get the chance to follow through with his threat. Mount Criant—the volcano that had been asleep since Sunveil's founding—exploded in a burst of magma, rock, and smoke.

"Retreat!" Torran cried. "Retreat!!!"

His men looked at him in confusion, but then left the oxcarts behind, running for the nearby crags.

The magistrate fell to his knees in apology.

"I'm sorry..." he whispered. "I'm so, so sorry."

With a *crack*, the mountain's south face crumbled in a prodigious eruption. The sulphurous, black column was dispelled by hideous, orange wings.

Falin Eridion, the self-proclaimed Brimstone King, sat atop the largest dragon to ever exist, alive after all.

But Dragons are supposed to be extinct!

That dragon—it's Flameheir!

I thought Aeshius killed him himself! How is he still alive?

Still—there's no mistaking it; the legends tell it true.

"Get to the cliffs!!! Run!!!" The High Prince bellowed.

Like a blistering umbra, the dragon swooped down. Flameheir, last of The Firetongues, seared a line of red through the middle of the city, through everything in his path.

Torran vaulted off of his horse, and rolled to the side, diving, the fire lighting up the linens under his armor without even touching them and carbonizing his horse.

Falin Eridion cackled wildly as he burned through both his people and Torran's people alike and took out the entire supply line in a single sweep— armored knights, shrieking children, mutilated oxen, and stinking, roasted cabbages, propelled in all directions like a macabre pyrotechnic display.

Torran ordered his archers to aim for the dragon's wings in an attempt to ground it, but only some stopped to carry out his orders, and most missed. The few arrows that hit glanced off the lizard without even touching it.

Just then, Torran heard shouting coming from atop the walls. The "peasants" took off their cloaks of rags to reveal suits of shiny, red plate. They took out crossbows and fired, covering for others, who were busy rolling ballistae up the parapets.

The Prince shuddered as warhorns sounded, titanic doors opening to release The Bloodred Battalion, an army of Hemian elites fifty thousand-strong.

Torran tried desperately to get away, but the dreamscape changed, and all of a sudden he was hanging off The Firetongue's horn, a recreation of the wild gambit he had made to save his men.

The dreamscape changed again, and to his chagrin, he was sitting atop the beast, which was no longer Flameheir, The Red Dragon, but Haash't, last of the Aetans. In the sands below, were one hundred and fifty thousand Goblins, loosing barbed, black steel arrows at the bird, while loading more.

And then he was falling like before, falling towards the tall, ashen cliff that had both shattered him and saved him.

However, it was different this time. For a moment, he was a girl with green skin, hair of vines. Then he was a tribesman, maybe Jhett, falling towards a hostile, blue ocean, an Oceantongue staring imperiously down at him.

And then he was himself again—only, not himself, but something greater. A clawed necklace burned around his neck, red lightning from the volcano's plume striking him.

That time, he didn't crash. Molten, red metal coiled around his body—cold torment.

Torran heard a voice, at the same time both masculine and feminine. It was the voice of his god, Luxyruss, and another.

"Claim your place. The fight nears, and so does destiny... Take these gifts. Untold thousands have died for them; you may yet be unworthy. But alas, the enemy makes their move. Prove your loyalty and fight for me. Fight for this world. You will face your Ordeal when the time comes, and She will decide what you deserve. But for now, you must fight with what I have given you."

Torran righted himself, invincible, his fist breaking the ground on impact and the shockwave pushing the demons back.

Lightning pulsed in his slate-grey eyes as The Acheron Armor solidified—a sleek, jet black with gold ruts and silver, spiral accents. Its long, prominent, oval pauldrons were scored with three, red grooves, red like open wounds. Its midnight surface glimmered like oil.

Torran raised his hand, bejeweled with two rings—one gold, one black.

And the air rippled, the demons recoiling.

Torran woke up to a cry of fear. Scarolette held the covers to her breast, eyes wide.

"Torran? What are you doing?!" she cried.

The High Prince was back in his room in The Imperial Palace. He was standing on top of his bed, completely nude.

Around his neck, was The Amulet. And on his fingers, twin rings.

In his right hand, Torran held a golden sword, gemstones glowing as bright as his eyes.

His purpose had been made clear to him.

He claimed that sword readily, that sword and its forgotten past.

The sword of The Warrior King.

CHAPTER X

Torran

Torran sat resplendent upon The High Throne, his turbulent, grey-blue eyes shadowed by a shock of ash-blonde hair. Now The High Emperor, he wore a black velvet doublet, double-slashed with silver, and he had a silver Star of Astria pinned to his chest.

Torran stood. "Be seated," he ushered.

The nobles sat down, a thousand shades of finery.

"Lords and Ladies of Astria, as you already know, my father, Agravius Xandromen, The High Emperor and ruler of The Continental Nations, is dead. He was killed in cold blood by an assassin in the night. This shall not go unpunished... Though we often quarreled, my father was a just man and a strong leader, and his loss will be felt by many across the world. And although he fought many wars, he was not a warmonger or a tyrant. He entrusted the rule of each of the four Continental Nations to the local, ruling Dynasties, allowing them as much autonomy as they desired. He trusted that the leaders of the world shared his dream of peace and harmony. This trust was his undoing, for one of our greatest allies is responsible for his murder."

Torran unraveled the scrap of cloth he had found on his father's body, revealing it to the Court. Emblazoned upon it, was The Theic Eye, the sigil of The Ralei Dynasty and the symbol of Qeonia.

"The Ralei Dynasty left their coat of arms as a message—a declaration of war! They sent the assassin who killed my father!"

A shocked hush fell over the Court.

"That is not the only message that I have received of late... When I was at sea, I heard a voice. That voice was The Divinity. He gave me a revelation... God told me that our enemies would strike, but I arrived too late to save my father... That was not all he told me. He told me that our enemies have been conspiring against The High Empire for years, that they are in concert with The Adversary himself! They will lead The Demonium across Astria and its ally Nations, aiming to finish what was started a thousand years ago—crushing The High Empire and bringing bedlam to our motherland. This is The Great War foretold in The Book of a Thousand Deaths, a supernatural threat unseen since the time of The Sufferer. We must defeat Qeonia and repel this Invasion like we have all the rest!"

General unrest took hold of the court. Lords and Ladies whispered to each other.

They must think I'm crazy...

"When I was told, I didn't believe it either. I didn't want to believe it, dismissing it all as the hallucinations of a castaway. But I have seen the demons with my own two eyes. I fought and killed The Red Dragon, Flameheir, returned from death. They're real, and others can uphold these facts. Soon, these abominations will appear all over Avenshra. The Outpost at The Stareye Isthmus has already been destroyed, and the monsters responsible are making their way towards Starspire! I know this is a lot to ask—asking you to believe such things—but during my journey home, I faced near endless suffering—all so that I could return to you, my countrymen. I ask for you to sacrifice for me, as I have sacrificed for you, and join hands with me in this fight. Please—help me prevent this cataclysm."

The Emperor's call to action was met with a clamor, every man and woman wrestling with the implications of what he had just said. Some were inspired, others were doubtful, and yet others were afraid, thinking panickedly of ways to escape the coming chaos.

To Torran's relief, some of the more loyal nobles quickly stepped forward to affirm their loyalty, bringing back some measure of calm to the Court.

Lord Horace, Knight of The Grey Dawn, unsheathed his sword, Greyblood, and offered it on bended knee.

"Your Grace, we would fight the very sky if you willed it. If they be demons, so be it. We'll be demons as well—your demons. You have my sword and my men. And if The Divinity wish it so, you have my life as well," he declared.

"Qeonia has overstepped its bounds for the last time!" shouted Lord Baldwin, shaking his fist. "We will help you punish them, your Grace!"

"Those Ralei traitors! How dare they take our Emperor! And now, they take demons into their ranks... By my bones, we shall destroy them!" proclaimed Lord Juliaard of Keystone, indignant.

"The Demonium must be stopped. We cannot survive another Invasion. Though some may doubt, I've already heard enough. Your Grace, let us stop these Qeonian traitors and cast out The Adversary once and for all," spoke Lord Breakway of The Holy Light. He knelt before the throne, dignified.

"Though we might not be able to offer many men to fill your ranks, we can feed and clothe the Imperial forces. Your father helped our family many times... Allow us to do this much for you, your Grace," spoke Lady Weaverwill, nervously clutching her arm.

Father... You really were a good leader. Look at these people.

Torran felt moved. He hadn't even expected this much, but he had to remain stolid, and serious. The Lords and Ladies of the Court, silent, or speaking, had all pledged their fealty to The Xandromen Dynasty and The High Throne. And although he had hoped for volunteers, the nobles were duty-bound to support his cause.

I would rather rule by love and not fear, but The Demonium come. To hesitate now is to die. Good or bad, these nobles didn't fight in the War. I'm the one who bled.

It's time they repay me for all the wealth they received...

And what's there to think about? If the demons breach the city walls, they'll have to fight whether they like it or not. Better to be scared and prepared than ignore the threat.

"Lords and Ladies, I am truly grateful. You are the first, brave souls, to pledge yourselves to the cause. But the room is awfully quiet. Do the rest of you not remember your oaths?"

The remaining nobles began to sweat, wringing their hands. Out of hundreds of Houses, only four had stepped up.

Lord Holden was the first to voice his concerns.

A middle-aged man with greying, dark brown hair, and a pair of nervous, blue eyes, he was the type of vassal who only provided assistance when mandated to do so, never wanting to get involved in any sort of social conflict or political dispute. This was not due to a low social standing or a lack of money, but due to a lack of resolve in anything except contesting the decisions of the High Emperor and his Overseers. He moved and spoke with a characteristic speed and agitation, as quick to recoil from the convictions of others, as he was to raise his concerns.

Normally, it would be praiseworthy for a Lord to put the wellbeing of his family first, but Lord Holden didn't seem to be such a family man. In Torran's opinion, Lord Holden was the type of man who was quick to poke holes in the ideas of others without offering better ones of his own—a personality that sprung from doubt and insecurity.

"But your Highness—"

Now is not the time, you imbecile!

I have to assert my authority. If I'm not harsh with him here, others will follow, and the city will fall.

"I am now The High Emperor, Lord Holden, for want of a crown. You will address me as such. Now, what is it?"

"Your Grace, our Army has shrunk in size... Hemia is in ruins, and Cairnon is still recovering from Civil War! Even if what you say is true, you can't truly be asking us to risk our lives and those of our men in fruitless war against Qeonia!"

I know all that! But this is what The Divinity said, and he's only ever told the truth.

It's what we must do!

Torran walked slowly down the dais, arms extended to each side. The Amulet seared his neck.

"Do you doubt me, Lord Holden? Do you have so little faith in your Emperor, the word of your God?"

"Come now, The Church... It's not— Your Grace...with no evidence, how can any man believe?"

So it's still too unbelievable. What about this, then?

Torran touched his hand to his heart, the black ring on his pointer finger turning to a cascade of black metal. Like midnight oil, The Acheron Armor slid over his clothes and around his body. He breathed in, the ever-flowing Lifeblood of The Amulet entering his irises.

There was a taste to it—faint, but ever so nuanced—like a suffusion of cherry.

He did all this naturally, easily. The elder artifacts had connected with him the moment he had Received them, and there was nothing he needed to learn. Their function was as intuitive to him as that of his organs or limbs. They were his.

Concentrating, Torran raised his hand to The Qeonian banner, one of the four National banners hanging at the end of the hall, and Reached, lightning striking with a *zap*. The crowd got down, Lord Holden stumbling backwards.

The High Court watched in awe as the dark blue tapestry of The Theic Eye burned, curling up and turning to fissling shreds.

Torran's eyes blazed red, his voice resonant.

"See me, and know that I am your Emperor—The Emissary of your God! You shall obey. Qeonia shall pay for its sins."

The Lord knelt, trembling.

The young Emperor turned to the rest of the Court.

"Qeonia was given sovereignty as were all the other Nations! It doesn't matter how many troops we have; demons march as we speak! Even if they did not, even if after all you have seen, you still will not believe, it is required by law! Amphitritton Ralei must pay for his crimes. No matter how powerful, no Nation can avoid the judgement of The High Empire."

The Emperor glanced bitingly at the cowering Lord, his mordant gaze sweeping across the room. "To the doubters like Lord Holden, I pray that you wake up to what's happening, and prepare for the battle ahead, or when it is over, you may leave Starspire without lands or titles; it makes no difference to me. To all who remain loyal—I swear by The Divinity and all The Four Heavens—we will foil The Adversary's plot! I shall avenge my father's death."

Konell

Konell and his sister, Amara, lived in an abandoned building at the edge of Beggar's Alley, marking the divide between the dwellings of the poor, and the whitewashed houses of the well-to-do. It was a tall, skewed, rotting, wooden building with a broken, wooden door, held closed by a rusty chain. The roof held on to just half of its drab, blackened, wooden shingles, the sun, the only source of light in the building for the few hours a day it was available. The inside of the building was dark, and smelled of leather, vinegar, and the cold must of black mold.

The lowest level held the old and the infirm, who lay moaning on the floor in makeshift beds of rags. Black widows dangled down from the ceiling, landing on their heads.

The second level was home to homeless families, the few healthy beggars that lived on their own, and a group of scrappy, orphaned children that ran a pickpocketing game.

The third level was relatively clean and empty, but it was by far the worst of the levels. The space was monopolized by a group of violent thieves and murderers who demanded tribute from the levels below. They spent their days sitting around a cracking, wooden table, playing cards, reclining in their creaky, wooden chairs, and drinking wine. No one dared oppose them.

No one except Konell, that is. The young assassin had killed three of their men, including their original leader, the day he and his sister arrived at the building. After that, the siblings had lived undisturbed in the attic—a cold, drafty set of crumb-covered floorboards with minimal furniture. They only had two, wool cots, two, iron chamber pots, three, wooden boxes and a linen, which served as a dining table, and three candles in copper chambersticks.

Konell had patched the hole in the roof with some poor-quality lumber, and cut a window into the east-facing wall, a hole that acted as a trash chute, and was covered with an oiled leather flap.

The siblings' room smelled a lot better than the lower levels, but it still carried the scent of sweat and vomit, and was only marginally more pleasant than the lower levels—more spacious—but still hard and uncomfortable.

The criminals dared not disturb them for fear of Konell's magic powers, and none of the people in the lower levels had ever seen their faces, for Amara never left the room, and Konell never used the door. All they saw was the occasional emptying of a chamber pot down the trash chute. After the first load had been dumped and splashed into the exposed sewers below, anyone trying to catch a glimpse of them would have had enough good sense not to try again.

Konell came into the room with a *puff*, a whirl of red light.

He peeled off his garb, his body healed, but his leathers stained with blood.

Amara was sleeping awkwardly on her cot, her breathing irregular. She tossed and turned, restless.

Konell watched grimly. *She probably has a fever...*

Amara was a petite, sixteen-year-old girl with long, straight, black hair and trusting, brown-grey eyes. Though she wasn't much younger, Konell had always been fiercely protective of her, taking care of her.

Lying in her makeshift bed, anyone could tell how ill Amara was, her skin jaundiced and her face gaunt. She was extremely thin—thinner than she had ever been before, even when starved—and she wouldn't take food or drink. She hadn't gotten up to use the privy in days.

The last time she woke up was to vomit blood.

Konell shivered remembering. His grip tightened around the vial, the vial that he valued more than his own life.

Yellow fever had taken Amara soon after they took residence in the building, and he had done everything he could to cure her. Without a cure, she was bound to die in a few days.

Nothing he had tried worked, his sister getting worse and worse.

At least, nothing until now.

Though Konell was badly injured, his heart rejoiced knowing that he held the cure that would change everything. If the legends were true, Amara only had to drink a couple of drops of the water from Judas, and she would be saved.

He had brought her a whole bottle of it. Death wouldn't claim her early—at least—not if he had anything to say about it.

He had done what he had to to get it. He had killed The High Emperor—started global war—all to save a sick, peasant child.

Konell knew it was wrong. He regretted it, but he wouldn't take it back even if he could. If he was to be judged as evil, thrown down to hell forever, then so be it. He didn't care about himself. He didn't care about the world. But Amara...

Amara was his only family. No price was too high for her.

Amara stirred, smiling groggily, though she had been alone, and in pain for many days.

"You— You're back... I thought you might have listened to me, and left for good, this time, but you came back... How long has it been—days?"

"About a week," Konell sighed.

Amara touched his cheek. Her hand was not warm.

His sister's face darkened.

"I know you know that I'm going to die... Let's not pretend, Konell; it'll only make it harder on us both... You should leave. Live your life and let me die. There's nothing left to try, and you've sacrificed too much for me already. You don't have to live like a criminal."

"Too late. You are worth it, and I won't leave you to die. Drink this, and be saved."

The assassin took out the vial and showed it to her, swirling the water around. The alien liquid began to glow, albeit faintly.

"What is that?" Amara asked, half-curious, half-afraid.

"The cure," Konell stated seriously, handing her the bottle and pressing her fingers closed around it.

"Where did you get this?" she questioned, her eyes interrogating him. There was hope there, but also dread. She knew the type of work her brother did. She was really asking a different, more terrible, and more dangerous question.

What did you do to get this?

"I sacrificed a little bit more," Konell grinned, trying desperately to see past the darkness, to hold himself up and out of the mire until she took the first sip. The cost had really been steep.

"I trust you, but are you sure it's safe? What do you mean by 'the cure?'"

"Just drink it, please. Trust me."

Hand trembling, Amara unstoppered the vial and drained it slowly.

At first, there was a moment of heart-wrenching inactivity.

And then Amara smiled wide, the whites of her eyes etiolating. She flexed what little muscle she had left, strength returning, and looked at him, surprised, and in disbelief.

Konell touched her forehead. The fever was gone.

The assassin shed tears of joy, his sister finally free of disease. They hugged.

Suddenly, there was a loud hiccup, and Amara fell back down, giggling. Her pupils were dilated.

Eyes narrowing, Konell snatched away the empty vial, holding it up to the thin ray of light coming through the trash chute. There was a white, powdery residue clinging to the glass.

Konell tasted it, his eyes flying wide. He threw the bottle across the room in a rage, the vial shattering.

What he had given his sister, was not just a cure.

It was a drug. His sister was high.

The Prince of Hemia had tricked him, adultering the water, and making his sister an addict.

Konell Called Tardrown, and flew out the door.

Adam

Adam was unmasked and forced to kneel, the back of his knee jammed in by the butt of a halberd. He confined his gaze to the floor, but in his peripheral vision, he saw a hoof.

The guard beside him was not human.

Seeing the swirled, orange, marble floor, he immediately knew where he was, the identity of his captor.

He had been brought before The Brimstone Chair by Lord Elrisain, Agent of The King of Hemia.

Lord Elketh Elrisain was a reedy-sounding Luzian with long, straight, brown hair that shone with the slightest bit of grease, a grease the man seemed unable to wash out. He was clever, with the eyes of a crow, and the voice of a fox, but he was surprisingly loyal—always willing to get his hands dirty for his King—and he wore a long, stained brown overcoat over a set of clothes that looked far too shabby for a Lord, though his wallet hung heavy at his hip.

Adam knew Elrisain and his dealings, and he had been to Court many times in the past. It had always been unpleasant, frequented by a pack of vultures.

This time, it was swarming with demons.

The King spoke. From his youthful voice, Adam could tell that it was Viktor, the son of Falin and Fegara Eridion. He had met the boy when he was just a kid.

He remembered feeling sorry for him.

How is he King?

Didn't Astria win? The High Sword told the Company to keep mining...

I don't understand.

Why am I here? For all they know, I'm just a miner... Is this some sort of test?

Does he know something?

"Look upon me, prisoner," The King commanded.

Adam didn't want to look up, afraid that he would be recognized, afraid that it would all be real.

What on Avenshra is happening?

The demon guard whacked him in the spine with the flat of its blade, but still, Adam did not look up.

"Please tell me he isn't deaf," the monarch sighed.

"No, Sire; he is as I told you," insisted Lord Elrisain.

"Very well, then; bring them in. Maybe he will respond to that."

A few seconds later, Adam heard the approach of familiar footsteps, the scared, but unmistakable voices of his wife and children.

He heard the shifting of iron links.

No.

The King spoke to Adam's guard, a Goblin.

Tall and muscular, it had an oblong skull, and steer-like horns that were banded with rainbow colors, and glowed from within. Those horns were connected to its glowing eyes by deep, channel-like grooves, leading to red scleras criss-crossed with rainbow-colored membranes. A long, slimy, bright green tongue protruded from its eight, large fangs, and its forehead was adorned with a trident-shaped, obsidian growth. Its shoulders were encrusted in the same material, organic pauldrons fused to tough, shiny, grey skin, a mosaic of microscopic, obsidian tiles.

The demon's forearms were lined with small, curved spines, a glowing green, as was its back, and it was covered in green, fluid-filled blisters. Its chest was armored with interlocking plates of obsidian, and it had sharp, black claws.

Though its form was barbarous, the Goblin was restrained its demeanor, and it wore a war skirt that looked like it was woven from cobwebs. It carried a serrated, black steel falchion in a light blue sheath at its hip.

"You—Lor'gran, isn't it? Bring me the ears of the little one there, the boy. Our prisoner seems to have lost his; maybe that will help him."

Adam's wife got in front of the child, screaming as the demon hesitated and then unsheathed its weapon, its obsidian hooves *clip-clopping* against polished stone.

Lor'gran

The intelligence of The Demonium ran on a spectrum, and was mostly based on luck during their mutagenesis. Some had a remarkably high acuity, able to come up with complex thoughts, and speak multiple languages. In these demons, the Tremites had failed to take full control, either due to a biological defect, or the host's overwhelmingly strong will. Others could speak their native tongue and could follow basic commands—mostly controlled by the Tremites, but still retaining some level of consciousness and understanding. The majority of the demons, however, were little more than animals. Reduced to their basic instincts, they only followed Orders from The Tremite Queen, hungry for slaughter and burning with lust. Without a target to destroy, they would tear each other apart, clawing, biting, and raping anything that moved.

Lor'gran had been unlucky. Unlike the Archdemons, who had been granted a name and the ability to act independently once Risen, he remembered the name given to him by his mother at birth, and he retained near-complete autonomy over his actions. A rare anomaly, he could speak the tongue of The Ighed'bad, The Ancient Tongue, and even The Universal Tongue. He was also quite skilled with a sword. A thousand years ago, he had been an anomaly amongst his people as well, a progressive, almost enlightened individual, who kept himself under control even when the sulphur reserves dwindled, and his people slowly lost their minds, locked outside the walls. He was not abnormally bloodthirsty or filled with lust, but, like the ones who were mindless, he had been Ordered, his autonomy discovered by, and distasteful to, Skotathis. Forced to follow The King of Hemia's every command, he did what he was commanded to do without question.

The petulant, young monarch's words echoed in his skull.

Bring me the ears of the little one there...

Lor'gran cursed himself as he reached for the boy, his nerves hijacked. Muscles fired against his will, the worm squirming around in his neck and head, strong enough to possess him, but too weak to erase his guilt.

Adam

Adam and his wife, Ariel, had been blessed with three boys: a seven-year-old with straw-colored hair, a four-year-old with curly, light brown hair and wide, dark brown eyes, and finally, a six-month-old with wispy, white-blonde hair, and blue eyes.

The King meant to harm the baby.

Adam immediately looked up. His wife and children stared at him in shock, hardly recognizing him in his malnourished, battered state.

"Wait!" he cried, his voice hoarse. "Please, your Majesty— I heard you; I'm sorry. Please don't do this! Don't hurt my child!"

"So the prisoner has ears after all," Viktor laughed. He turned back around in his Chair to face the old, bedraggled miner, motioning for Lor'gran to be at ease.

"Tell me, prisoner—why are you here?" he asked, though Adam was the one in the dark.

"I— I don't know, your Highness," the miner answered truthfully.

"You don't know?" asked the King, his tone low, and mocking. "You must have done something to be imprisoned."

"I— I killed some men..." Adam admitted. "It was an accident, my King; I've been cursed."

"Oh, God!" Ariel gasped, sobbing.

Adam couldn't bring himself to meet her eyes.

The King shook his head.

"You have not been cursed, Adam Akris. You've been blessed, blessed with a power that most could only dream of, a power that many would kill to possess."

"I never wanted this power... How—" Adam's voice became but a whisper. "How can my family love me when I've become such a monster?"

Viktor looked down almost empathetically.

"You're not a monster, Adam. You're an Elemental—a sorcerer unseen since the time before The Goldfeather Purge. Unfortunately for you, others were by your side when you came into the element of Radiol, The Blue Fire hotter and more dangerous than the lava of Mount Criant. You are not at fault."

"If I bear no blame, your Majesty, then why am I here? And why do these- These things guard you, man your castle?! Any man would know who you are, my King, but the last I heard, Sunveil was occupied by The Imperial Army. Have we gained independence? Are we free from The High Empire?"

"Intent does not affect guilt. Manslaughter is still a crime, and it is written that any crime of such magnitude warrants death. My friend Lor'gran here is one of the servants of The Lord Defiant, and yes, we are free, free because of him and his forces. I am now the acting King of Hemia, though The High Empire doesn't know yet, and I intend to keep it that way. They believe that we are currently under the stewardship of The High Sword."

What the hell is going on?! What does this mean?!

How can you trick an entire Empire?!

"Your Majesty, I respect your beliefs as a Fïamegian, but this is madness. Why am I here? If I am to be executed, then— I mean... The Book of a Thousand Deaths, it-"

""The Book of a Thousand Fools" is a fairy story, written by men under the instruction of another twisted, old man, drunk on power. It was a fiction, where The Divinity was a benevolent god who made Avenshra in his likeness, The Adversary a monster from the pit who corrupted Creation. Do you really believe that this "Adversary" would fight for hundreds of years, all so he could come to kill us all? None of it is true. Skotathis is The Adversary's true name, and he too was once an angel, but he was betrayed."

Adam bit his tongue. To misspeak now, was to lose it.

Viktor, like his father before him, was an adherent of Fïamegianism, a heretic religion that rejected all that The Church stood for.

Unlike Astria and Qeonia, which largely believed in The Divinity, most of Hemia—or at least, The Raishians of Hemia—believed in The Adversary, who they called The Lord Defiant. In their alternate version of history, The Adversary was indeed an angel and a servant of The Divinity that Created Avenshra, but the similarities stopped there. In their retelling of events, The Divinity wasn't the benevolent god he was portrayed to be in The Book of a Thousand Deaths, but a selfish demiurge known as The Lord Oppressor. This "Lord Oppressor" forced humanity to toil blindly in the cold dark of The Early World, building great, wooden towers in his honor.

Pitying the people, The Lord Defiant descended from the heavens, and, with the help of some of the other angels, gave humanity fire, lighting the night.

But when humanity, not knowing how to contain the flames, lost control and burned down one of the towers, The Lord Oppressor threw The Lord Defiant into the wreckage along with his followers.

Rather than dying, The Fiamegians believed that The Lord Defiant's sins were burned away, leaving him spotless, and without fault. And though he and his followers were horribly scarred, they were reborn as heroes of mankind, with power equal to that of The Lord Oppressor.

They claimed all this based off of The Burned Book, an ancient text supposedly written by The Lord Defiant himself, and given to his first believer, Atrometus. A black tome stamped with The Forked Flame, it was their holiest relic, but being not much more than a lump of coal, Adam doubted its validity, like he did with most holy texts. Few had ever flipped those blackened, illegible pages, and those few had passed on centuries prior.

Was the story true? Was The Adversary innocent?

Why burn the book if it spoke the truth? Was their Lord not spotless?

Why purify his book in flame, if it was already so pure?

The Fïamegians told a very convincing lie, but Adam didn't buy it. After all, The Burned Book was not a book for saints or martyrs. It was an excuse for the wicked-at-heart to put down their morals, and live only for themselves.

Though the King readily embraced cruelty, flanked by demons, he was still a young man. He didn't quite have his father's eyes.

And although he couldn't be sure, around his arms—Adam thought he saw strings.

Adam swallowed his misgivings and didn't say the things his devout, but timid wife was too afraid to say. Unwilling to die for any religion, he pinned his hopes on hope, on the monarch's underlying humanity. Though martyrs were honorable, his children were too young to die a martyr's death.

He would become the martyr for them.

"Your Majesty, if you believe it, who am I to question you? I do not contest the justice of my sentence. I deserve to die for what I've done. Still, I beg you not to kill me, not for my own sake, but for my family. Without me, my wife and children shall fall into further poverty, and be forced into the mines. The mines swallow men whole! I beseech you, my King, do not punish them for what I have done!"

The King slowly closed his eyes, and then opened them again.

"Do not despair, Adam. I wouldn't have kept you alive, brought you here, if I didn't have a task for you."

"What would you have me do?" the miner asked, worried what he might hear.

The King smiled, pearly whites flashing.

"Now you're asking the right questions, Akris... I want you to fight for me. I can't teach you how to fully control your magic, and I don't know why you became an Elemental, but I do know how powerful Radiol can be. In the coming weeks, I will wage war with Astria, and the full forces of The Demonium fighting under my banner. I will tear The High Empire to the ground, and have revenge against my father's murderer, Torran Xandromen. I'll already have the military strength to fight on an even playing field with The Imperial Army, but your sorcery is worth thousands of demons. Fight for me in the coming war, and your family will be kept warm, safe, and fed here in the Palace; you have my word."

My family— Ariel and the boys will be able to eat!

But fight for him? Ariel was always the religious one, but to fight with demons...

No. I can't kill anyone else! It's too horrible! These powers are not meant to be used!

But what choice do I have?!

Adam wished he could refuse, but his family was on the line. If the Hemian King was telling the truth, his loved ones would be provided for—truly provided for—and that was the best he could ask for, given what he had done.

He deserved nothing but an open grave. Still, he hesitated, restrained by his morality. That same morality damned him as he looked across the Court, raising his head once more. His wife stood in scared silence, flanked by a pair of Goblins, his children crying and pulling at her hands. They pulled at her as if begging her to run away, but she knew as well as he did—there was no running away from a king.

"I... I'll do it. If you spare my family, I will fight for you."

The King clapped his hands.

"Great; that's what I wanted to hear!"

He turned to his scribe, a frail-looking, bespectacled man in beige robes. He appeared to be a prisoner like Adam was, one of the few Astrians left alive after the Prince's successful coup.

"Let it be known that Adam Akris, citizen of Hemia, is fully pardoned of his crimes, on the condition that he fights for me in the coming war."

Adam knew that that pardon would mean nothing, even in the future. Viktor was not a legitimate King, and Akris wasn't his real name. Thankfully, the man didn't recognize him.

He might kill me here, if he thinks that I'm a threat.

Adam's real name was Plutarchus, not Akris. He had been the scion of a great house, set to inherit a vast fortune and a name that had once been both honored and respected. Years ago, if you asked anyone which noble house sat second in line to the Hemian Throne, you would hear his namesake mentioned. His father, Essol Plutarchus, had been the Agent of Commerce for Faalaran Eridion.

Back then, Adam could have never imagined that he would be forced to work as a miner, as a soldier fighting beside hideous demons.

But that was back then.

His namesake no longer mattered. Now, he was nothing more than a weapon in the hands of a tyrant.

Though Adam was sure that his powers would be used for evil, his family would be spared the indignity they had suffered for so many years. There was no room for pride, for morality. He couldn't say no. He couldn't reveal himself.

Pleased with the "negotiation," The King addressed his Agent.

"Thank you, Elketh. Your information is always useful, but it was especially good this time. You will be well compensated... Now, if you could please see to it that the woman and her children are taken care of. Then, remove Akris' shackles and have him bathed and fed. "

With a few words and a clicking of locks, Adam was free, his family led out of the room. He had been spared, and so had Ariel and the boys.

But at what cost?

Flind

Leafsong led Flind to a forgotten glade in The Forest of Tears. At its center, was a tree bigger than any the Monolid had ever seen.

A Shadowrise Tree?

Why does it look like that? It looks like—

The dryad put her green hand up to the tree, almost caressing it. Its slender, toothed leaves seemed to speak to her, the restless, fluttering tongues all gossip.

The Baroness smiled.

Flind shivered. She knew not what was being said. She didn't want to know.

It was a little cold, but Leafsong didn't seem to mind as much as she did, and she debated whether or not she should run while the woman's back was turned. Leafsong Ralei, daughter of Stillvein, might not have recognized her, but Flind wasn't about to take any chances.

I shouldn't have followed her in the first place.

The dryad spoke, her voice soothing.

"When humanity was in its infancy, The Shadowrise were the only things that lived, and they numbered in the thousands, branches reaching further than the clouds, across worlds and throughout The Four Heavens. There were so many of them, but they were corrupted... They used to be beautiful, healthy and without flaw, until Skotathis of Raj'para, the one The Church calls The Adversary, Twisted them. They used to be good... Now it's my mission to return them to their original state. I came here seeking answers, and my God has been forthcoming. But you have not."

What?

"If I can behold the true nature of the universe—" Vine-hair flew outwards, taking Flind by the throat.

"Huk-"

"Then it's only right that I should understand yours."

The vine began to constrict around the scullion's larynx. She tried to bring back her magic weapon, to make the dryad stop, but she couldn't. She still didn't know how.

Flind saw some irony, there in the lightheadedness. She would be killed out of revenge for her own revenge.

Or at least, that was what it seemed like, at first. The woman didn't know.

"The fate of the entire world depends on me, my mission, and I won't abide deception. Tell me the truth. Where did you get that suit of armor, who were those women, and what did you do to anger them? What is your real name, "Fiona?""

She doesn't recognize me; I was just another maid! But what do I say? How do I explain my powers?

She knew that I was lying. But if she could read my mind, she wouldn't be interrogating me like this.

"I-"

Leafsong cut her off. "Before you even consider lying, trust that I will know. The trees know men's hearts better than they do themselves."

Flind doubted that. *I'm not a man.*

For all her resistance, the scullion was getting desperate. She began to see stars, then flashes of light. She had little air left.

You've got to think, Flind! Think!

Right, she doesn't know that I know who she is!

"Alright, I'll tell you—" Flind choked.

The woman's grip loosened, but not by much.

"My real name-huk-is-Flind Baodin! I was a nun-hmk-of The Temple of Iwidëa Exalted."

Leafsong loosened her grip entirely and allowed Flind to speak clearly, but the green noose was still coiled around the scullion's neck.

Flind swallowed, her vision not quite right. Leafsong's eyes appeared to glow blue.

No, they were glowing...

"Go on."

"I— I took the Armor from the Temple because I'm actually a Lātist. Iwidëa was a Lātist, one of the greatest heroes of her time, but when she died, her Armor was smuggled over to Qeonia by the nuns you fought. But the Armor isn't theirs! They're fanatics who pray for her to grant them strength, Kïsist zealots who do not know Avghe'eah and think that Iwidëa would support their violence! Iwidëa's Armor is said to bring victory to the faithful in Cairnon. If I can go there, I can be a symbol of hope! My people have been hunted down and imprisoned, and many of them have been executed! I alone can inspire them, help them fight back! That is why my "Sisters" hunted me, though they hated me even before I betrayed them. By infiltrating their cult, stealing back the Armor, I have reclaimed what was never theirs to begin with. That's why I ran."

Leafsong released the maid, the noose slipping away. She looked inspired, but she was still cautious.

Flind felt bad, but her lie had worked.

So much for magic trees.

"I see... I'm sorry," the dryad apologized. "My mission is just too important, and I don't know who to trust. Right now, I'm headed to The Bay of Scales. We could make the journey together. What do you say?"

What are the odds?

Flind decided to accompany the woman to the Bay, though she knew she would regret her decision.

I'll just have to lose her there.

"Sure. Let us journey together."

Amdryaan

Amdryaan crept out of his guest hut, unsure what was happening. He had heard the clangs of metal in the night, faint cries, and dull thuds against wood.

The sounds of a struggle.

Scared of what he might find, but compelled to help those who had taken him in, he tiptoed his way along the narrow, wooden boardwalk between the dwellings. He walked past the neighboring huts, but they were empty, belonging to the hunters who had left a few days prior to hunt. They wouldn't return for at least a week.

Amdryaan walked past the next line of huts, peering in, but strangely, they were empty as well. No one slept.

Fear growing, Amdryaan kept tiptoeing along until he was behind the line of huts closest to the beach. He hid behind one of the structures and looked across the c-shaped Settlement.

A group of Nolites from another Tribe was silently prowling the area, skulking in the shadows. They were wearing leather armor covered in palm leaves for camouflage.

Though they were well hidden, Amdryaan could still see them, even in the dark. He saw them by the iron in their weapons, the iron in their blood. Unlike the Aerhauc, they only had five fingers.

The men snuck quietly into the huts and pulled out their inhabitants, muffling their screams with a hand to the mouth and a club to the head.

Slavers!

The slavers were merciless and cruel, using thick nets and hefty, hardwood clubs to capture as many of their fellow Nolites as they could.

Amdryaan watched in horror as one of the Elders of the Tribe resisted and was cut down with an enchanted steel machete. Archers hid in the jungle beyond, enchanted steel arrows ready to catch any stragglers.

The slavers took only the most desirable members of the Tribe—strong men with bulging muscles, mothers with wide hips. The others were cut down before they could make any noise.

The beach was littered with bodies.

Amdryaan tried not to throw up, biting down and into his anger.

All these people... How dare they!

His eyes widened when he saw Oscure.

Oscure was trapped in a net on the ground, spun from Shadowthread, and weighted with lead balls. He was at the feet of a group of slavers in front of The Tribe King's Hut. Looking down at him, was the leader of the slavers, a man in a dark green, leather jerkin and a deep red headband. He watched, intrigued, as the leader of the Aerhauc thrashed inside the net. The Shadowthread was having some kind of magical effect on him, the Beloved of Madevf wobbling between human and inhuman forms. One second, he was the man who had offered Amdryaan hospitality—the next, he was a monster, floundering on the ground and pressing its back against the ropes.

His wife lay dead beside him, stabbed through the chest. The sand beneath her body was a sticky red.

Oscure! Queen Kilanjara!

Dear Goddess! How can they do this to their fellow Nolites! Do they have no humanity?!

Amdryaan looked around for some champion, some hero or martyr who could step forward, and put an end to the atrocity. But he was the only one left, unseen amongst empty huts.

I'm afraid, but I have to intervene.

I can't believe I didn't hear them sooner... I'm so sorry!

Please forgive me.

Amdryaan breathed in, and the Lifeblood of the dead came to him, though it was hard. He tried not to think too much about it.

I wish things were different, but I need all the power I can get. The dead are already gone, but the path of the living can still change course. I must act.

With a jolt, a machete flew from the leader's grip and into Amdryaan's hand, the whole Settlement made aware of his presence.

He sucked in more Lifeblood, taking advantage of the slavers' confusion and pulling swords from their sheaths, the weapons floating aimlessly around each other in the air before being crushed into a ball. He sent the ball flying out at the men, breaking and reforming it, scattershot hitting disperse groups of enemies only to come together and home in on specific targets, following them like living lodestones.

A poisoned arrow came whistling at Amdryaan from the right, but he ducked, conserving magic, and then propelled the machete in his hand towards the bowman's neck, the blade spinning.

The archer barely dodged, the machete shaving off a piece of skin, and lodging in a wooden support beam.

One of the slavers had used the distraction to flank Amdryaan, coming up from behind, but without even turning, the Native yanked the man's beard toward a nearby hut by its metal decorations, the other hand pointed in the opposite direction, trying to dislodge the machete from before.

It was too late; another arrow came.

With a glance, the tribesman redirected the arrow into the bearded man's back, causing him to trip and fall face-first, breaking his jaw, and falling unconscious.

Amdryaan recoiled at his own violence, but he forced himself to snap out of it, pulling the machete out of wood, and back into his hand. He turned, ready to face more arrows, but the leader of the slavers had decided to change tactics.

In front of him, were a boy and a girl, kneeling in the sand. The little girl had short dreadlocks, coated in ochre, and the little boy had close-cropped, nappy, black hair, and a flat nose. They were both maybe six or seven years of age.

The girl had two black eyes, and the boy's smile had become a tesselation of white and black, bone and empty space, his lip split. He had tried to protect his sister against full-grown men.

In the children's eyes, was a placid kind of fear—a fear borne from trauma and shock that was soon nothing more than glass—obsidian. They didn't scream or cry, but looked down blankly at the ground. They simply knelt in the cold, dead silence, and remained there, petrified.

Amdryaan knew those children. Their names were Ritsi and Mobo. He had met them and their parents just days before. They had greeted him awkwardly, but they seemed like nice people.

Looking to the right of The Tribe King's Hut, he saw them for a second time, decapitated outside their dwelling.

Amdryaan's blood chilled, a river of ice.

The leader of the slavers called out to him in a tribal dialect that he was unfamiliar with. Though he didn't speak his language, from the man's tone, he knew what the man was saying.

Move, and I kill them both.

Slowly, hatefully, Amdryaan knelt in surrender.

His form finally stable, Oscure pulled and tugged at the net, Shadowthread between his teeth. He desperately tried to escape, but he was weak. In The Universal Tongue, he begged Amdryaan to repay his debts, to save the children from slavery.

"Don't let them be taken like the rest! Let them die free; kill them if you must! Amdryaan!!! You are dooming them to a fate worse than death!"

Amdryaan refused.

"I'm sorry, your Majesty...I can't. They're just kids."

The Native hung his head and closed his eyes. The slavers had him right where they wanted him. He would be dead soon.

He hadn't saved anyone.

One last arrow came, centered on Amdryaan's left ear.

Before it could hit, a shadow stretched across the sand, moving up the ramp and down the raised platform in front of the stilted Hut. It unglued from the ground, taking human shape.

Oscure.

With a roar, The Tribe King tackled the archer targeting Amdryaan, the bow discharging. The two men fell off the platform, the Fivefinger's head dashed against a nearby cookpot, breaking his skull with a *slosh*.

Oscure pushed himself off of his victim only to turn over, Amdryaan yelling when he saw the arrow. It had discharged into the Nolite's arm, poison quickly spreading.

The two children watched with eyes too haunted to be those of children.

The leader of the slavers drew a knife from his belt, ready to kill Oscure. But he was blinded by anger.

Eyes dark, Amdryaan threw the machete in a bitter arc, slitting the man's throat. The blade returned to his hand, dripping red.

Amdryaan trembled.

Seeing their leader fall, the archers loosed arrows, retreating, but Amdryaan reversed their projectiles, eliminating them.

He looked around, seeing only bodies.

The Native kicked at the sand.

Dammit! Dammit!!!

In the chaos, the other slavers had gotten away, taking their captives with them.

It was too late to save them. He didn't know the jungle well enough to follow, and he didn't have the time. He had to help Oscure.

Enemies bleeding out around him, Amdryaan ran up to fallen Tribe King, raising the machete. He had to chop off his arm and stop the spread of the poison.

The dying man's hand shot up to stop him.

"No. No, my friend. This is not the end of the Aerhauc. Survivors have yet remained; these children live. Save them; flee with them now to your high-masted ship; more will come. My hunters are too far to return now, if they are even still alive. Head to the Trialoim; they are our allies. They will care for the children, help them remember us, even if our Tribe disappears. If I lost my hand, I would have no reason to live. I am a leader, a protector. Or at least, I was... Now, I am unworthy of the name King. The last time I fell, I awoke a creature—a being of darkness. I managed to fight it due to the love I held for my Tribe, for my beloved Queen, Kilanjara. Today, I woke to see a kukri stabbed through her chest... No more. I will not wake to anymore nightmares. Madevf does not love me; I see his hate. Let me escape him, this mortal form, and rest."

Oscure fell still, his head falling to the ground.

I'm sorry, Oscure, but I can't let you die. These are your children, the blood of your ancestors... Who am I to deliver them from evil and leave you to rot?

Unsure if it would work, Amdryaan channeled Lifeblood into his arm and slammed his hand into Oscure's chest, the red smoke pouring out and into the

Shadowheart.

Hoping against hope, he watched for movement.

Then, suddenly, Oscure coughed, straining. He crawled onto his elbows, looking at him with a look of surprise. Behind that surprise, was not amazement, or even gratitude, but terror.

"You frozen fool! I am not to be saved! What have you done?!"

What do you mean?! You're alive!

The Tribe King muttered grimly to himself, back arching.

"I will not let you take them. I will not let you use me as your vessel. I will not— Amdryaan—take them and run!!!"

Amdryaan edged away as The Shadowbat took over Oscure's mind, conquering his body. The three witnesses of The Tribe King's death were thrown back across the beach by the unfurling of six, massive wings.

The Native hit the sand with a grunt, the children rolling.

Slowly getting up, Amdryaan watched, enthralled, as a stream of pure Lifeblood pierced the heavens like a bolt of crimson lightning, tearing through the clouds and hitting the Shadowbat head on. He watched as The Adversary himself anointed his chiropteran servant, Risen to the rank of Archdemon. He couldn't tear his eyes away, completely transfixed.

This— It's the work of Itat! Goddess save us!

After a flash of blinding light, the sky darkened again, and The Shadowbat lumbered forward, its skin shining dark blue in the gloom. Smoking, red light welled in the empty pits that were its eyes, its muscles swelling, and the spirals on its arms ignited, lighting to a bright scarlet.

As the Shadowbat grew larger, The Tribe King fought against his spiritual eviction, his face pressing out of the demon's skin only to disappear again. At one point, his voice came through for a moment, suppressing the demon's.

"I will not— By Madevf, I will not— I will not—"

Resistance was futile, and Oscure's weak, but valiant opposition ended in a mere instant. His presence disappeared, a language like no other shredding through Amdryaan's mind.

QIE MADEVFRE?! NIENAN EXISTATEHO, FOLERVEF! the demon bellowed. Its snarl was like a hurricane, a thousand deathly voices as one.

In a stupor, the tribesman walked up to the children and grabbed their shaking hands, trying to drag them away from the danger, but they wouldn't budge. No, it wasn't that they wouldn't move—they couldn't move. He couldn't move either, completely paralyzed with fear.

What is this monster?! We're going to die!!!

The Shadowbat expanded, becoming much taller and much bigger than it was before. Long, obsidian talons shot through its fingertips, pulling Ritsi and Mobo through the air and into its open palms.

Amdryaan felt powerless as the Archdemon Drained them, taking years off their life through Lifeblood osmosis. Oscure-then-Naraklar leered at him, the children immutably chained to the souls of their deceased family, their ancestors. They squirmed, kicking, as what had been their King slowly killed the last two members of his Tribe.

I have to do something—anything!

Oscure—these children...I won't let you take them!!!

Amdryaan's eyes blazed red. Throwing away his cowardice, he rushed forward, an ululating cry. Drawing the weight of Avenshra's swirling, cadmium core into his hand, he hit the demon with a tremendous punch, breaking its grasp.

The children fell coughing into the sand.

"Run!" the tribesman shouted.

The children obeyed, finally present enough to flee. Though they didn't speak his language, they understood.

Amdryaan cursed at fate—he had been manipulated into a devilish plot— facilitating the Rise of a foe that could kill angels. Like an echo across centuries, the demon cackled, though it had no lips, no teeth, no tongue.

SHASH NAS FILIARO, ET KULFI TRIBNAL, HOMTRIBINE, QOEN NARAKLA NO MONOSU FORAIA! SESMARI QOS SHASHEZ ET NILIMAGINO ARCEO TERID DE SHAID!

QOEN—IE CANDASAR'ILIO—SHES VANDER KARKELALEHO XON DAYI DIEM—E VANT ARRIREVE—PREPEYEN DE MORTIALHICAR!!!

The demon's shadow grew as big as the sea. It released its aura, the sands, water, and trees all protesting.

And then, it wrapped its wings around itself, Shadowsplayed across the waters.

CHAPTER XI

Karibdione

Karibdione allowed herself to dream, escaping to happier times. She found herself in the Palace gardens of Raj'para.

The Palace gardens were relatively small, but there were many flowers in a wide variety of hues—blue thistles, red poppies, and anemones of purple, red, and white. Grey, cobblestone footpaths cut through plots of rich, dark soil, abutting walls lined with fragrant cypresses. On the edges of that cobblestone footpath, sat simple benches of white marble.

Karibdione breathed deeply. She was sitting on one of the benches, drawing in a sketchbook.

The air was cool, with the occasional warm, summer breeze. Light blue bumblebees zipped about, held precariously aloft by tiny wings, and the sky was the same, light blue, fluffy, white clouds floating lazily across the sky's great, open dome. Luminon had started its slow descent, donning an evening gown of hot pink and stunning violet.

As the sun set, a man approached. He looked at her, the gardens, and her work.

The man spoke.

"Tell me, my Lady—what are you drawing?"

Karibdione looked up, brushing the hair out of her eyes. For years, she had come to that same place, but it was the first time someone had noticed her drawings, as well as her figure. She had found many suitors in those gardens, suitors who had never spared so much as a glance at her work, at the beauty around them.

"Oh, you know, flowers..." she smiled bashfully.

"Flowers? My Lady, a woman as pretty as you has no use for flowers. They drop dead at the sight of you."

Oh. He's the same as all the rest... It can't be helped, I suppose. It's how they were made.

"Hush, my Lord," she breathed. "You're embarrassing me."

"Do not be ashamed, my Lady. They are still quite beautiful. You're quite the artist... Tell me—are these plants native to your world?"

"Sorry?"

Karibdione's pencil stopped. The flowers stared back at her accusingly. She was being stupid.

Or maybe, she was just bored. Maybe she had been looking for a man.

The flowers were indeed beautiful—roses, lilies—flowers that didn't exist on Ressida. She could always make an excuse, say they were pictures from her imagination. That wasn't far from the truth.

But he wouldn't believe it. This man wasn't like the others.

My world?

"Come, my Lady, don't play the fool... I know a fellow traveler when I see one. The Kol System is not so vast."

Karibdione went white with shock.

He's been to other planets! Could it be that he's—another Ioen?

The Lady looked at him, wide-eyed, mortified by how easily he had understood her. Then she noticed his eyes. They were a gorgeous blue.

No, they glowed.

He was not another Ioen. She knew exactly what he was. Who he was.

"I only ask because I've never seen such flowers before...on Ressida," he clarified.

It's The King's son. The younger brother.

Karibdione hadn't known who he was at first. She had given Knowledge to her son. It was a critical loss, but Slippage was unavoidable with Emanations.

The Prince smiled, thinking he knew her mysteries. A man in his thirties, he had a lush, brown beard, a straight nose, and creased hands. He wore an understated, brown velvet doublet, slashed with navy, and at first glance, she had mistaken him for some farmer Lord, but Y'shan Xandren was no farmer. He was a shepherd of men, and he carried a Power that she had once possessed.

Thankfully, Knowledge was not all-encompassing, and her memories were not as sharp as they used to be. She handed him the drawing, feeling somewhat childish as something stirred within her.

He took it gently, admiring her artistry.

There was no artist better than her, no designer more deft of hand. On his right hand, the man wore a golden ring, a Callring. It was of fine craftsmanship.

She pretended not to recognize her work.

Y'shan Xandren... Why did you come back?

And what is this strange feeling?

Can I really be attracted...to a human?

"You are very wise, your Majesty. I am from Avenshra. I was the only one amongst my people who understood the Shadowrise."

"Avenshra must be beautiful," he said, taking the revelation in stride. "Sadly, I never got to visit. In my exile, I travelled The Living Worlds, searching for enlightenment, but I had to return."

"Did you find it?"

"Enlightenment? No. Maybe it was on Avenshra. That would be ironic," the Prince chuckled, his expression wistful. He gazed out into the distance, or maybe beyond it.

Then, the man took a handkerchief out of his pocket and held it in his hand, frowning in concentration. In the space before him, the air coalesced into a fragile rose. He plucked it from the garden of clouds, and gave it to her, a rose of smoking ice.

He had never seen a rose before, but he still knew what one looked like, in all its three dimensions.

Knowledge.

Unfortunately for him, Karibdione hadn't told him the truth, and her secrets were much

greater than his Knowledge. She wasn't really from Avenshra.

She had never seen a rose, as a child. She had never seen with eyes.

"Would you dine with me this evening, my Lady?" Y'shan asked. "It's not often that I meet someone as worldly as yourself. You must have travelled quite far to get here."

You couldn't imagine, Karibdione thought to herself.

My world ended as yours began... It was just another Neuron. It made no difference to Him.

I had to make a life in this cruel hell... I had to make life, alone in a wasteland of dust and gas.

Your world was built from the bones of my world, the brimstone squeezed into planets, the fire collapsed into stars. It was so crude that it shouldn't have worked, but the Lifeblood had a will of its own. It didn't want to diffuse again, and lose its chance at sentience. It evolved to remain whole...

I never thought that it would be so beautiful.

"I would be honored, your Highness."

Luxyruss

Luxyruss tossed and turned, plagued by his one, recurrent nightmare. He remembered Ressida and pined its loss.

Luxyruss could hear Skotathis screaming in the central square, the Element of Therius tearing him apart.

With a low hum, the sky above Raj'para opened in a massive portal, concentric circles of blood-red smoke. An open wound in space and time, Luminon jutted from the gulf, flames burning up the city in an explosion of ash and smoke.

Try as he might, Skotathis couldn't steal the sun, fully make The Connection. He only held it for a second.

But that was all it took.

In a single second, the entire city was destroyed, the sky illuminated with a yellow light.

And then Luminon disappeared forever. The planet froze.

In shock and terror, the armies surrendered to Skotathis.

Luxyruss fled, taking refuge in the night.

And Goddess wept for the fallen.

Luxyruss had never slept with another woman.

Telespora had been everything to him. His infatuation with her had even made him abandon his Goddess.

But Karibdione was Goddess, and, as such, everything about her was superior to any woman he had ever known, including his wife.

Though Telespora had been dead for two decades, Luxyruss felt guilt creep in on him for what he had done. He turned underneath the covers.

Back turned to him, Karibdione lay sleeping. She gave off a soft, feminine scent.

While human, she lived as a human—at least, as close to human as she could get, but Luxyruss was not at ease.

All was calm.

The Divinity didn't know if The Initiator saw him watching her, if she could read his thoughts. He hoped she could not, but there was no way to tell.

Luxyruss sighed, ashamed of himself. He looked at Karibdione in lust one moment and in horror the next. He had slept with Chrism, The Initiator, slept with her even though he knew what she was. They had been going for days, the Goddess knowing that the Transmission would only buy her a few nights with him. He had to leave before Skotathis found out the truth, located the Celestial and her Primordial prisoner.

Luxyruss trembled, remembering every thrust, every spike of pleasure. He shivered, remembering the three-horned, eyeless thing beneath her skin, but he tried to dispel the memory.

For a moment, the thought of pregnancy struck him, but he laughed it off.

Still, something transcendent told him that what he had done was wrong, wrong at a universal level. He had made a choice, continued, and all for her entertainment. He had lost all illusion of spirituality so she could savor human pleasure, so that he could be free of his guilt.

Luxyruss' mind was awhirl with the consequences of his actions. He just wanted to lie there and think, but Karibdione woke up again, and took him into her hand.

Luxyruss spasmed.

This cannot be allowed. I have defiled all that is sacred. I have taken God and made them man.

Who am I to pray to, now?

Goddess had her own religion, but Luxyruss knew not her god.

Her people had called themselves The Receivers of Dreams. They worshipped Ün, The True God and The Dreamer, a being so vast that each of his Neurons was a universe itself. Their belief was that everything that happened in the Neurons was part of one, big Dream, and The Dreamer, though asleep, was lucid. His consciousness scattered across infinity, he rarely gave individual Neurons his direct attention, but he could nevertheless exert his influence.

According to Karibdione, her people's leader, known as The Grand Receiver, was appointed directly by Ün and granted The Authority, allowing him to build a paradise for his people. Though the Receiver was powerful beyond measure, he was killed in battle during The Invasion of The Saïonan, a conflict with an alien race that destroyed and consumed Neurons like a disease of God's body.

In death, The Grand Receiver's Whiteheart broke into three pieces, fragmenting The Authority and giving rise to The Powers of Unification, Order, and Division. In the aftermath, the pieces containing The Powers were collected by those who had survived, and forged into a sword, giving the wielder The Authority and title of Grand Receiver. This turned the tide in the war against the invaders, and allowed the Ioen to reclaim their home, but before they could celebrate, their Neuron collided with The Kol System's Neuron, and both they and their enemy perished in the collapse.

All except for Karibdione, who escaped with her unborn child and cut through space and time with The Sword That Split The Night.

The Divinity had held that sword in battle centuries ago, but by then, it was long empty. And if The Dreamer could indeed speak, he had never heard his voice.

Perhaps it was because he had never invoked the God's name. It was difficult to have faith in something so impersonal.

His people, The Ressidans, had worshipped Karibdione and called her The Initiator, who set all life in motion. The Goddess lay beside him, and she was already beyond his grasp. To pray, then, to The Dreamer—an entity so vast —was completely unimaginable.

After all, what were human beings to an entity like that? Surely they were as small as ants—smaller, even. All mankind had ever worshipped, was people, or at the very least, aliens.

When Karibdione fought The Void and disappeared, the citizens of Raj-para didn't lose faith. They went on to worship his mother and father instead, Solomm and Luteana Xandren, calling them The First Man and The First Woman. Given mandate in the form of The Sword, which Karibdione dropped in the struggle, they ruled over the planet with unquestionable authority, though the weapon no longer held the real Authority. Calling themselves The Completionists, the devotees of House Xandren made it their mission to perfect the Creation Goddess couldn't complete, adopting the symbol of The Solaron—a pointed, red pall representing the balance of Powers.

After eons of experience, Luxyruss knew that that pall leaned heavily toward one side, and there was a fourth, bastard Power that stood above...

He had been worn down, bearing that asymmetric weight for too long. He had wanted comfort. He had been attracted, as any man would be, but he was not just a man.

I have to tell her to stop. We've done this long enough.

This isn't right.

Doubts still plagued him. Luxyruss was unsure if he was throwing away the only comfort he had left, or perhaps, he was trying to rationalize his weakness.

But isn't she the judge of right and wrong? She Created them. She Created these bodies, spurred our evolution. Telespora was merely a human, another, wretched soul swirling mindlessly in the belly of the beast below. Karibdione will always sit in this house on high, the last of the Ioen.

There is no justice in this life... There is no such thing as sin.

But if that is true, then why do I feel such guilt?

Why do I hate myself?

Luxyruss removed her hand.

Who am I kidding? I know this is wrong. This was never meant to be.

Sin goes beyond religious morality. What we have made here—it goes beyond all that.

I must repent...

But to who? A God asleep?

The Divinity stood and put on his underwear, feeling like a child in the presence of their mother. That bothered him more than he could say.

The marble was cold beneath his feet.

Without having to look into his eyes, Goddess knew that he was leaving, and that time for good. She looked at him as if asking why.

He didn't know himself.

"Stay with me," she begged.

Luxyruss retrieved his robes. He wrapped them around himself tightly, tying the rope around his waist.

"You know I cannot. You know who follows me."

Karibdione persisted. "We can take him on, together."

"You know that isn't true—not anymore. You can't leave without letting the barrier fall. If he no longer faces the threat of Lysis, Kenon will break his chains, and do far more damage than Skotathis ever could. You must keep him well-fed and subdued... Do you forget what he can do? Do you forget why you Bound yourself here in the first place?"

"I Bound myself, because I thought I would be Bound to you." she whispered. "Luxyruss, I am Bound, but Skotathis... We can— Luxyruss..."

The gods' eyes met. Tears were welling in her eyes. Luxyruss' eyes were uncomfortably dry.

"Please. I want more in life than pleasure; you know that. I want more from you than that... I've just been so bored, so alone. My existence is meaningless in solitude..." The Goddess smiled weakly, lips quivering. "I know that I'm not human, can never be human, but I just wanted to— I love you," she breathed.

"I wish that I could love you," he replied.

Luxyruss Jumped.

Nemkri

Nemkri Laolin was an angler, and a simple one at that.

The old fisherman was hard and coarse, as if carved from salt. His hands were scarred from the lacerations of nets and lines, and his eyes were those of an osprey. His skin was like brown leather, and he had more years on him than any of the other sailors in The Bay of Scales, but for all his experience, he had little to show in the way of success.

He didn't have a family; he didn't live in luxury. He was just a peasant—a man who respected the sea and thought that it respected him. However, The Three had not been answering his prayers, and neither had the sea, and so he had starved for three days.

Nemkri's faith was waning. He needed to bring a fish to port, or he would starve again.

The Three will answer my prayers; they have to.

I've been loyal to them and to the sea.

Please, please, great Neraids—let me have something to eat, even if it is some small fish! Mermëa, I beg you—stir up the depths; pity this old man.

But The Ocean Neraid wouldn't have it, it seemed. The skiff rocked as listless waves passed by, apathetic. The Ocean did not hunger. It would always be full.

Nemkri's stomach growled. He could feel his ribs through his skin, but he didn't let it faze him.

Don't think about it. Don't think about it. Come on, Nemkri—just one fish.

Nemkri steadied his boat.

I guess this spot is just as good as any.

As he had many times before, the angler lay out his nettle-hemp line, the stone sinker taking the hook down, and into the depths below. He lay back, line in hand, and waited.

He had been forced to resort to hand-lining, as long-lining wouldn't take him deep enough for what he was looking for, and he was down to a mere one-and-a-half hooks—one snapped, both rusty.

He was trying to catch black sea bass, so he had attached a clam, their favorite, to his one, intact hook, but he didn't have much line.

Neraid-forsaken string! It better reach.

Black sea bass were deep-water fish, and though they were aggressive fighters, they were common year-round. One just had to coax them from the depths. He hoped his bait would be appealing enough.

After half an hour of waiting, the sun began to make its way down the horizon, and Nemkri still hadn't felt a nibble.

It seemed that even the deep-water fish had abandoned him, or maybe his spot wasn't as good as he had thought it was. It was chilly.

Nemkri cursed his bad luck, and the arrogance of the sea, hot air whistling through parched lips.

Suddenly, there was a tug. A real tug. Whatever he had caught, it was big.

Is that a bass? No...

Squinting, Nemkri caught a glimpse of something in the water, a flash of metallic, purple-blue scales.

That's not a bass! It's a sailfish!

I've gotta act fast; I just hope the line will hold!

Nemkri let his catch draw line, allowing it to exhaust itself a little, but he couldn't let it get too far. There wasn't enough string for that, and he was an old man. He had to bring it back quickly.

A plan quickly formed in Nemkri's mind, the elusive genius of excitement. He would let the sailfish draw line, then let it pull the ship, repeating the same game until the fish tired out. It was the only real option.

Nemkri had never caught a sailfish, the sigil of The Ralei Dynasty, and though he had no idea how he would end up doing it, his heart was set on bringing the glorious specimen to port.

The problem was that the fish was too strong. It kept swimming forward, pulling the boat, and even after several reels, he sensed no frustration coming from below. It was as if it had taken the hook for fun.

Nemkri didn't realize he was being reeled in, not the other way around.

To his dismay, the sailfish began to move even faster. It was very strong, and definitely heavier than anything he had ever caught. It would be too heavy for him to lift—heavier, even, than his boat. It wouldn't tire any time shortly, and he had no harpoon.

The skiff accelerated. Faster. Then, even faster.

Suddenly, fish of all sizes began flying from the water, some flopping into the boat. Nemkri secured them all as best he could, surprised, but his hands were full, and he still couldn't reel in any line.

I have some fish, now; I should cut the line. The sailfish must have stirred them up! To do that, it must be truly enormous...

But blast, I can't just let a fish like that get away!

The creak of wood told Nemkri that he was being foolish, but he couldn't help but dream.

All men must have a goal. Mine is to catch a truly big fish.

This is the biggest fish I've seen, and so— Starvation be damned, I'm bringing it in!

The line began to create its own wake, fraying slightly.

Mermëa protect me, this fish is enormous! Please—let my line stay strong.

I have to get this sailfish, even if it takes me all night! It'll be worth hundreds of Liralas at market, and I'll live like a king! Yes. I can kill it and secure it to the boat, bring it to port that way.

I'll be the most famous fisherman this side of the coast!

Yes, that's what I'll do...

What providence! The Three have answered my prayers after all!

Nemrki redoubled his efforts, making a concerted effort to reel in the sailfish. He sensed that there was less resistance, then. That pleased him.

It's getting tired.

"Come to me, fish. Come to Nemkri, fish."

The old angler pulled harder, hoping that it would bring the fish up higher, but instead the line went slack. He nearly fell overboard from the sudden loss of tension.

The boat slid a few more feet, then stopped.

Hook or line must have snapped.

"No! Mermëa... Ah, blast! Blast!"

"That huge fish... No..."

Nemkri pulled in his broken line, deeply saddened. He had lost the catch of a lifetime.

A fish so splendid, lost...

The reeling was easy work, then. He was a failure again.

What a joke.

The fish that had fallen into the boat would have to be traded for more line and a new hook, and so, he would starve again, after all. He probably couldn't even afford to eat just one.

Nemkri pulled in the last bit of string. He felt like he might cry.

But when he saw the end of the line, Nemkri gasped. It wasn't broken. The hook was still there, a clump of seaweed hanging from it, crawling with ocean bugs.

"What in God's name?"

Seaweed doesn't pull like that, and those gorgeous scales... If not a sailfish, then?

Nemkri hung from the edge of the skiff, and stuck his face in the water. It was cold, chilling.

He ignored it, scanning the depths, and searching for what he had caught. What he saw shook him.

Scarolette

Scarolette bustled about the archives, trying to track down a book on magic.

The Palace archives contained only one bookshelf, but that one, long bookshelf held hundreds of ancient texts—more wealth than any merchant could hope to make in their lifetime. The dusty, birch-wood bookshelf held tomes with spines of leather, paper, and even gilded metal, titles known and unknown. The colors stretched across the room like an accordion of muted hues, the space lit by a small, ring-shaped, brass chandelier with candles that sat in pink-beige, tulip-shaped, glass enclosures. The ceiling was painted brown, and the floor was made of mahogany. The cool, dry air was musty, and smelled of old wood. Dust coated everything.

Scarolette's nose itched, but she didn't mind too much. The room was peaceful and quiet.

Most of the books in the collection were merely esoteric pieces of memorabilia accumulated by the old High Empress, Lucretia Xandromen. It was no secret that The High Empress loved to read, especially mysterious, arcane literature. She cared for the books more than her own children, dusting them and sorting them well into her late seventies.

Scarolette knew that she too would have to learn to love reading, as writing was beyond her capabilities after losing her arm, at least, unless she learned calligraphy with her left hand. Starting again from scratch would be difficult.

It wasn't just that. After all that had happened, after all she had seen and done, writing seemed pointless.

Scarolette didn't know her place in the world anymore. She and Torran were—she didn't know what they were. Things had been awkward. And Jhett was in a coma.

All she knew, was that they had experienced some bizarre physical changes, and she wanted to find out what they meant.

I need to learn more about these powers.

Scarolette pulled out another old tome, admiring the silver elements on its black, leather cover. Though its spine was brittle, dry and peeling, it held together well.

Blowing off dust, she opened it.

The book was made of thick, bark moth-scale pulp, and not the thin wood pulp from The Wildlands that trade had provided in the last century. The pages were discolored, and parts even appeared to be scorched, but the fancy writing was mostly legible.

Though educated in The Old Tongue, Scarolette still had some difficulty reading the title.

"Ettes Elementales Dismaeolean, et Magoxiphon, eles Alagre Antiqiaren Elderef... The Elements of Dismaeol, The Fallstreaks, and Powerful Elder Artifacts," she interpreted.

This is it! This is what I've been looking for!

If only it wasn't in The Old Tongue. This is going to be a drag to translate.

The author noted was Sage Asdroel Saranderom. The book was written in weather-resistant Moondrake blood, dull, silver letters jumping from the page, and it was clearly expensive, but Scarolette had never heard of any Sage by that name.

Moondrake blood was often used as ink, allowing for effortless, flowing writing and calligraphy. It was Scarolette's favorite, or, at least, it had been.

Moondrake blood was, overall, a very useful substance. It was used in candles to prevent flickering and flare-ups and it was also used in the quenching of Moondrake-bone weapons. In recent times, farmers had found a way to make artificial nests, raising Moondrakes in a similar way to how beekeepers raised bees, fumigating the hive and drawing blood from the reptiles while unconscious. But Moondrakes were hard to find in the wild, and even harder to catch and raise, their queens and nymphs literally invisible to the naked eye.

How did they get Moondrake blood so many years ago? They must have been really rich.

Scarolette flipped to a couple of pages in, finding clusters of strange symbols, circles with notched lines through their circumference. She assumed that they represented words, some sort of cipher, but she didn't have the key. Sketches of various hand signs and body movements accompanied the symbols.

Though the cipher looked complex and the hand signs were unintelligible, the majority of the text was in The Old Tongue. The passage she had turned to was titled "Dismaeol."

Scarolette read, slowly.

"Dismaeol is the language of sorcery. The sorcery I speak of is not the magic seen in fairy stories, creating something from nothing, nor is it alchemy, changing lead into gold. Dismaeol is, quite simply, the language of trade, a language that the Universe itself understands. When you use it, you make a trade with The Living Universe, but instead of paying in coins or goods, you pay in Lifeblood—your own, or another's.

Lifeblood, what people call the "soul," is the spark that animates every living thing, an ethereal fluid that pervades tissue and wells within the heart and brain. A form of energy like heat and light, it is the essence that was imprisoned in you during the act of Creation, as it has been in me, and all of humanity.

Our Creation was not a gift, nor was it an accident. The Lifeblood of the world is stolen, and the Universe yearns to have it back. So if you ask for a stone, it will bring it to you, no matter where it must find it. If your Reach is great enough, it will allow the trade. Reach is not the only limiting factor. Translocation heavily depends on how much you can offer, how much Lifeblood. The energy trade must be equal.

Though Elementals are undoubtedly the most dangerous fighters, their greatest limitation lies in the availability of Lifeblood. Even the most prolific killer would be hard-pressed to kill enough people to have a constant stream of Lifeblood, and most Elementals are not murderers. Though Lifeblood can theoretically be stored in the material of each Element, we are currently limited in our understanding. Of the four Primal Elements: Aegis, Therius, Solitus, and Haskaleon, only gemstones representing Solitus and certain liquid cocktails representing Aegis have been successfully used for storage. Complicating things, only Elementals can see Lifeblood in its diffuse form.

But Lifeblood is something all possess. So why isn't everyone a sorcerer, an Elemental?

The answer is simple. The Universe only operates in magnitudes. The common man's troubles lie in the foibles of daily life; the sacrifice isn't nearly great enough. Only the greatest of sacrifices are enough. The greatest sacrifices are those made in selfless regard for others' happiness and wellbeing. Such sacrifices often involve putting one's life on the line.

There is a darker truth beyond this, for the Universe always deals in opposites. Selflessness is not the only road to Elementality. Those that sacrifice others for their own selfish needs can also become Elementals. After all, the life of an innocent is a hefty price to pay.

Extremes of both selfishness and selflessness in the presence of a fragment of The Power of Order will trigger a permanent transformation, known as Elementality. Once Elementality is achieved, one must keep themselves in check, as sorcery can be used for good or evil. The Power only cares about balance. It cares not if justice prevails.

There is an additional caveat to Elementality. Like how the peasant man in Qeonia cannot find chili peppers, and the peasant woman in Astria cannot find cinnabar, so too is a sorcerer limited in their selection. When one makes a great sacrifice, they pass a threshold, an extreme of selflessness or selfishness that The Power, when nearby, takes notice of. Whichever Element was present at the time of the sacrifice will become theirs, and they will be Bonded to it forever. Bonding can take anything from seconds to days, as the nature of the process is fickle. However, once Bonded, Elementals cannot be harmed by their own Element like normal human beings, and they have a natural affinity for controlling their element, even without knowledge of sorcery.

Dismaeol is a man-made language, an imprecise construct used to ask for the right things and lower risk, but knowing it isn't strictly necessary. Dismaeol is useful, because wordless sorcery wastes some Lifeblood in interpretation. Just as a Raishian man looking for a tailor may accidentally be directed to the nearest brothel, one is not always understood, and so Words of Calling must be learned if one is to fully master the art. This book contains all of the Words of Calling known to date. I have encrypted them so that no one may speak them foolishly and without guidance. If you wish to learn the art, you should go to The Sagery.

That said, every Elemental should know the following two words.

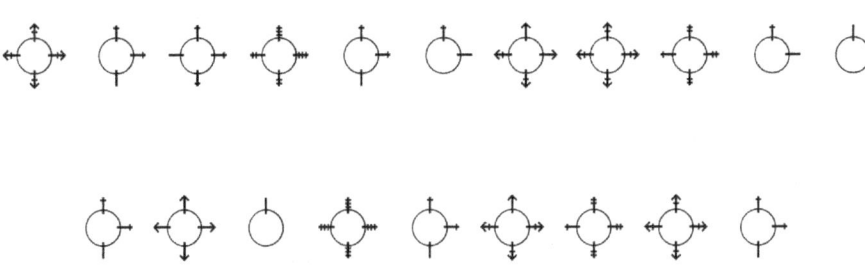

These are The Travel Spell and The Protection Spell.

The Travel Spell allows the user to disappear from one place and reappear in another of their choosing, but it is limited by sight and requires momentum. In exchange for Lifeblood, the Universe allows the speaker passage between two points. In between those two points, no one knows what happens, but traveling through the ethereal corridor is not the same as normal travel. The distance is magnified. The momentum it would normally take to travel five feet would be enough to travel twenty-five feet in the ethereal corridor, though excess momentum can carry through over short distances.

The Protection Spell allows the user to deflect weapons and spells by warping the ether around their body. Though nothing can get through, this spell is limited by the user's reaction time. One must start the warp as soon as a projectile nears, for failure to do so will lead to injury or death. Some attacks are too quick to be deflected in this way.

Scarolette skipped some pages, and saw one titled: "The Fallstreaks."

Though the Words I have given you are quite powerful, sometimes, they prove insufficient. Skill at arms is of utmost importance to the warrior, but it is of equal importance to the sorcerer. Sometimes, charms like *The Protection Spell* are not enough to block incoming attacks or subdue the enemy. This is problematic, as spells require an Elemental's full concentration in the moment. While a spell is being cast, there is no time to draw one's sword, swing one's hammer, or throw one's spear.

This is why The Fallstreaks exist. Originally forged from Sailsteel, Fallstreaks are weapons that are supernaturally light and sharp. Instead of being carried, they are brought forth with Callrings, though the name "Callring" is somewhat misleading, as Fallstreaks are not summoned, but manifested from Lifeblood.

When Called, Fallstreaks appear in the sorcerer's hand at will and in an instant. Beyond convenience, they are superior to ordinary arms in strength and durability. They hold an edge remarkably well, and they are impervious to rust. They can even repair themselves after bearing the ravages of war, healing from scratches, cuts and dents as if forged from living flesh.

Before the advent of sap-hardened, or "enchanted," steel, Fallstreaks were effectively unstoppable on the battlefield due to their supernatural properties, and they were even able to cut through steel, with enough force. Conflicts, whether political duels, or territorial skirmishes, could be won near single-handedly by those who owned them. Since being gifted to humanity hundreds of years ago, Callrings have been worn by kings as a symbol of their mandate, used by warriors as weapons of war, and brandished by criminals as a token of strength, instilling an almost irrational fear in all who see them.

However, Callrings are not made, or even found. They seek out their owner. Though a Callring can appear on anyone's finger at any time, they seem to be attracted to Elementals, and it is rare to see a non-Elemental wearing one. This is not to say that a non-Elemental wielder cannot use a Callring, but it does not happen often. After all, The Fallstreaks' purpose is to be used in magical combat.

Sages who study this subject claim that the Callrings' search for an Elemental wearer is a symbol of divine providence. Yet others argue that the rings seek out those in need. Still others argue that The Fallstreaks were advanced technology meant to combat knights in full plate so as to level the playing field between The Continental Nations, travelling autonomously through ether to balance the Nations. I fear that we shall never know. The only known fact is that the rings appear *mysteriously, and once they appear, they're there to stay.*

Though The Fallstreaks are extremely powerful weapons, with the fashion of wearing rings amongst the rich, it is hard to measure the true size of The Fallstreak Arsenal. From my research of stories, myths, and legends, I believe that there are around twenty-two Callrings scattered across the world, worn by both Elementals and unsuspecting commoners, but this is merely conjecture.

Scarolette moved to another page titled "Elder Artifacts."

Though we were born around that time, many of my peers misunderstand The Goldfeather Purge, believing that it was a cull of the golden eagle population. However, The Goldfeather Purge was actually a cull of Elementals, and the golden eagles were killed off to fuel the cull. The noble Aetus Orum were stripped of their bones and feathers to create a metal known as Rapterium, an alloy of copper and a special kind of gold in Aetan tissue resembling soft bronze. Though weak compared to iron or steel, Rapterium was valuable, not due to its edge, but because it nullified sorcery. Xersus Xandromen used the metal to kill The Warriors and solidify his rule over Avenshra in the years leading up to his death. What made the Purge so tragic was that the eagles were highly intelligent, sentient beings, and he slaughtered them all.

Amdryaan

The icebreaker was a hulking, heavy-looking ship. It was made of an oily, purple-brown wood that was almost black, its prow longer at the bottom, and sharp—allowing it to break through the ice of The Ocean of Ŭlrihh and ram enemy ships, though it wasn't built for war.

The boat had one, large mainmast, strung with a light blue sail painted with The Cold Tooth. It had very little on it, and there was next to nothing below deck. The Frosslar rarely left Whitereach, and there were few whales in recent years. Though the ship was simple, and mostly bare, there was a small cabin for the captain, with a black, scaled wooden roof and a small, glass-paned window, which was unusual, as The Frosslar didn't mind the cold.

Inside the room, was a large, rectangular, wooden table covered with rolled-up, parchment maps, and bolted to the floor with iron nails, a hammock made from bear skins hanging from the ceiling. A jacketed, glass and steel lantern sat on the floor, holding whale oil, and a brass chamber pot sat beneath the hammock.

The underbelly of the ship could only be accessed through a small, tightly-interfacing wooden hatch in the middle of the deck, the seams lined with wax. The crew's quarters contained another ten hammocks, made of sealskin and paired with iron chamber pots, as well as a small, round table with four wooden chairs, bolted to the floor. The floor below held the ballast and bilge.

The boat's interior smelled of oil, rust, and mildew, but, thankfully, it was warmer and drier than it was outside, the air surprisingly humid and chilly that night.

The icebreaker moved noiselessly through the waters, as if one with the sea, hugging the coast as Amdryaan searched for The Trialoim Settlement, but so far, the jungle appeared uninhabited. No fire's smoke or fishing party could be seen anywhere.

Ritsi and Mobo sat in the cabin, but they wouldn't talk to him, only responding to offers of food, and they were less than enthusiastic about eating it.

Amdryaan didn't blame them.

Those poor kids... Their parents are gone; their friends are gone... They're just as alone as I am.

No; they still have their allies in other Tribes, and I am not the last of my people. I must remember that, show them the face of hope, even after what they saw. I must hold on tight to my own hope.

Amdryaan wished, then, that he could speak their language, even if they wouldn't talk to him. He wished he could comfort them with some familiar words. The twins had seen their hero die, The Aerhauc Tribe King corrupted and turned into something alien, inhuman.

Though Amdryaan hoped to unite the children with people who spoke their language, what was more important was that there was no food or medicine on the ship. Finding The Trialoim was as much about keeping his promise to Oscure as it was a necessity, and he was becoming more and more anxious. Unless they found The Settlement soon, they would have to go into the jungle to forage.

That didn't change the fact that Amdryaan wished he had a treat for the kids. He remembered how his mother had made akutag for him in the summers, a sweet that made him forget his sorrows. With one spoonful, he would forget all about the jeering of the other boys and how weak he was compared to them.

Again I am in a position of weakness. This land is not my land.

Even for the children, who know this place better than I ever will, the jungle is too dangerous to venture into alone. We need the help of experienced hunters.

Amdryaan climbed on deck, and walked over to the larboard. He peered through the murky darkness, spotting what may have been cookfires, but they were a ways away.

If we do not find The Trialoim tonight, we'll sleep on the ship. That is all that we can do... I'm not afraid of the sea.

Sienna

Captain Sienna Heratus of The Imperial Army ordered her archers to aim for its eyes.

The Sixteenth Division was one of the strongest Imperial Divisions, comparable to the famous Fifteenth Division cavalry and the respected Twenty-second Division headed by Captain Merle Rustedsword. The Sixteenth Division had about fifty members in total, headed by a squadron of elite fighters including The Captain, her Vice-captain, Rosie Ellenwell, her Lieutenant, Dame Andrea Qaris, and her three sworn knights, Dame Isla Wayland, Dame Veronica leTeaque, and Sir Maxwell Nerron. Or at least, it had been, as Veronica and Maxwell had died to The Seadrake's first attack.

"Die, you fucker! We're The Sixteenth Division; you're just a dumb fish!"

Purple-blue scales were dislodged as arrows missed, but the keen-eyed Andrea found her mark, The Seadrake's eye squirting vitreous.

Dame Andrea was a slender young woman with neck-length, wavy, dark brown hair and sharp, dark green eyes. She wasn't very strong looking, with bony legs, a sylphlike waist and wiry arms, but she shot a bow better than most men and never shied away from battle.

"Yeah! That's what I'm talking about!" The Captain shouted. "Let's go ladies; nock arrows!"

Gotta hit it where it's weak. Come on, now—we just took your eye; don't be timid. Show us those teeth.

The Oceantongue slithered towards the Perlan seawall, hissing. It threw its weight backwards, tail scraping the sand and punching a hole through the barrier.

The dragon's dark blue fluke went through brick like an awl through leather. Stone flew, slamming a knight in shining, silver armor against a nearby house, plaster cracking. The woman detached from the wall, her short, wavy, pink-white hair spilling out as she fell to the ground, bleeding from a large gash in the back of her skull. Her greathelm rolled loudly across the cobbles.

"Rosie!" Sienna cried.

Not you too! We've already lost Veronica and Max!

As she ran to her Vice-captain's side, Sienna heard The Seadrake swing its tail for a second time, the air whistling. She moved to get out of the way, but it was too late. Desperate, she threw up her arms to stop the blow.

With a resounding *crack*, The Seadrake broke her elbow, sending her spinning across the cobblestones, her face hitting the ground with a *thwack*.

Dizzy and bruised, The Captain rolled, grunting, up to the foot of a hooded figure in green. Beside her, stood a woman in Armor like dark emerald.

Flind

Perla was a small, coastal town between The Bay of Scales and Sandkeeper Ridge. There, one could easily charter a ship to the capital, as Clearwater was less than a day's journey away. Flind had been there before when she was young, but only once.

The more traditional houses in Perla were whitened with quicklime, and topped with blue, domed roofs. The main throughway was wide, and ran along the town's iconic seawall. Merchants and peasants alike had set up inns, shops, and brothels along the side of the road, bringing significant wealth to the town's small population, which numbered at around a thousand people.

The streets of the town were done with grey stone and brown mortar, and there were flowerpots in every window, the cobbles littered with broken pottery from unlucky houseplants. The road to the town was downhill, with every alley leading to the beach, like tributaries to a lake, but the alleyways were dark and winding, and people generally stayed on the main roads. Unfortunately, the streets were often crowded, people pushing past carts, barrels, and vendors' stands, and street markets drew crowds of peasants in fine linen and cotton clothes, better off than many in The High Empire. They bought their produce from travelling farmers, many of whom came from Stillvein, merchants from foreign lands yelling over them from their colorful stalls, sunlight passing through fabric ceilings and dappling the grey stone with colored shadows—vibrant stripes and checkerboards. The whole place smelled of sizzling meat and fresh fruit, and the friendly atmosphere was inescapable.

Also inescapable, was the cold, dark shadow of The Monastery, which sat at the town's east end. Only Acolytes of The Church of The One-thousand-and-first ever left the building, save for a few ordained Monks who went to the bank in preparation for The White Week, and the abbot who sometimes met with the local farmers. Flind knew that a few of the denizens of the city were Acolytes who had defected during the previous White Week, men who had gone from monks to brothel owners, scholars to homeless men walking around with their begging bowls, robes more brown than grey.

Flind followed Leafsong down one of the town's larger roads, which led to the beach and a crumbling portion of the seawall, dark green moss growing in the cracks.

The Perlan seawall was made of purplish-grey brick, fifteen feet tall, but rising only five feet above the edge of the road, with the town sitting at a higher elevation. This setup allowed the inhabitants a view of the gorgeous, blue waters of The Goldflight Ocean, while protecting them from that same Ocean during hurricanes and other storms.

Unlike the usual hustle and bustle, the street was weirdly empty, a large, wooden cart broken down on the right side of the road, its wheel broken. Shuttered brownstones and whitewashed houses huddled in fear, the streets empty, save for litter from the day's street market—flour, fruit peels, breadcrumbs, and small fish half-devoured by stray cats. It was chilly out, but the air still smelled strongly of mandarin oranges and salt, and there was a faint whiff of ozone, a precursor to lightning.

The silence was broken by desperate shouts. The docks were torn up, ships sunk. A giant, purple-blue serpent towered over the dilapidated seawall, a group of female fighters manning the embankment, bows and spears in hand. They were struggling to hold the monster at bay, the only thing barring it from destroying the rest of the town.

No wonder everyone's hiding.

The Oceantongue was nearly forty feet long, and when it raised its body up, it towered at an imposing thirty feet in height. It had a serpentine body, with overlapping blue and metallic purple scales coated in a thin layer of iridescent slime. Seaweed was lodged in the crevices, the dragon's underbelly lined with off-white, bony plates. The Seadrake's fluked tail ended in a bony point, the same color as its underbelly, and it had a sinister, downturned, beak-like mouth full of teeth like clear needles. It had a dark green, snake-like tongue, and its grey-blue gums were crawling with whale lice. It looked down with eyes the size of saucers, glowing a sulphurous yellow. One of those eyes had an arrow sticking out of it.

Flind froze, shocked, as the dragon swung its tail, and a knight in full plate was sent flying, rolling towards her and her companion.

The knight looked up at them, raising her hand in warning, then fell unconscious.

Flind didn't know why, but seeing warrior women strewn about like reeds made her angry. Very angry.

Flind's breathing grew heavy. Red vapor began to steam off the dead, seeking her out.

And then Lifeblood filled her lungs, entering her eyes. She felt her powers return.

Leafsong was about to help the injured woman up when The Seadrake breathed pressurized water upon the barrier, finally splitting it in two.

Brick shot out, but Flind stopped it in its tracks, crushing it back together. The stone fell to the ground as a pile. Flind reanimated it, sending it at the half-blind eel as a stone hand, closing around the monster's throat.

Leafsong brought the knight to shelter behind the broken cart, and came back to help Flind as the dragon broke free, growling.

Flind's ring flashed, the pick she had Called before appearing in her hand. It was a war pick with a spike like a stone tooth.

I think I'll call you Stonetooth. Yeah.

Flind looked at Leafsong. Leafsong looked back, knowingly. Then, they turned towards the Seadrake.

Though it wasn't theirs, they would take this fight.

Let's do this.

Leafsong touched the ground, and her eyes washed blue. The knife she had used against the nuns jumped from the mantis-green ring on her finger.

The dryad ran towards the breach, Flind making a bridge out of the fallen stone. She ran across the floating rocks, vaulting over the dragon's head.

Yelling, Leafsong landed on The Seadrake's head, but its scales were slippery, and she was unable to stab it in time. Making the best of a bad situation, she slid down the dragon's back, dragging her blade through flesh and piercing its swim bladder.

Losing her balance, the dryad fell into the water, writhing in the salt. The Oceantongue turned to bite her.

Seeing this, Flind sprinted down the street and jumped over the seawall, rolling across the sand.

Not if I can help it.

The scullion spun and hit the monster hard in the stomach, sending it sliding across the beach with a hole in its armored underbelly. It swung its tail at her, but she did an assisted sideflip over the attack. Flind dropped her pick, blocking the dragon's return swing with a column of sand, and depleting her Lifeblood.

Suddenly, the Seadrake spat a jet of pressurized water at her, peeling skin from her arms as she protected her face. Blinded, she didn't see its tail come in for a third and terrible swing. It hit her in the head, breaking her skull with a *crack.*

Leafsong slashed at the dragon's scales to no avail, screaming, calling her name, but she couldn't move. The dryad was being crushed, the constrictor holding her in a vice grip.

Flind's brain was bleeding, and she couldn't get up. Clear ooze that might have been blood was pouring from Leafsong's damaged torso.

The Oceantongue screeched, transparent teeth refracting light. It opened its mouth to shatter the seawall entirely, shatter the women warriors in all their armor, tightening its grip on the unfortunate dryad.

But then, there was a *thrum*—the thrum of a bowstring—and an arrow went through The Seadrake's mouth, sending out a festoon of glaucous blood.

Ilidar

Ilidar woke up in a cot. He had been undressed, save for his undergarments, and his leg had been bandaged. Beneath the muslin, was a salve of honey and various spices.

Just by the smell, he could tell that he was in The Palace Infirmary. It was the sterile sweetness of mint masking the acrid scent of Cairnian herbs. It was the smell of vulnerability and false promises, a smell he didn't like.

Ilidar had only ever known the barracks. They were the only home he could remember, and he missed that home dearly. He wanted to see his men again, but he was too numb to attempt such movement yet.

The injured Captain looked around.

The Infirmary was as he remembered, though he had only been there a few times for minor training injuries. Though it was a relatively small room, it was well-equipped, and thankfully, few people had had to go there over the years. Four, woolen cots sat in a line, supported by hardy, wooden frames. In between them, sat two, oaken nightstands, one topped with a green, glass bottle of Rejo, its red, wax seal hanging broken from the lip, and an unfilled, silver chalice sitting beside it.

Rejo, or strongwine, was a bright red, medicinal spirit made from grapes, red apples, and cherries. Used as an anaesthetic, the bottle was half empty, which was strange, considering how few patients there were, and how potent the alcohol was.

On top of the other nightstand, was a silver chamberstick with a stubby, tallow candle, and a worn-out copy of The Book of a Thousand Deaths, bound in brown leather.

The walls of the room were a flat brown, and the ceiling was painted white. The floorboards were made of quality mahogany, but they were thin and warped, sounds audible from The Palace Kitchens below. Opposite to the cots was a long chest of drawers, topped with squirming jars of leeches, bottles filled with dry leaves, and tins containing various powders.

Ilidar looked to his left. In the next cot over, lay Sir Reginald Drye. He was wounded. At the knight's side, was a wheeled, wooden cart with vials of medicine, scissors, clamps, needles, and thread.

Ilidar wasn't sure why the knight was there. The man no longer served in combat, and he was too good to be injured by some greenhorn during practice.

Sir Reginald had been Ilidar's mentor in the arts of sword-fighting, wrestling, and tactics. He was a warrior who had spent the past twenty years teaching, and one of the best sword-fighters Ilidar had ever seen, but he was retired.

In his prime, Sir Reginald had been an incredible soldier, leading offensives across The Continental Nations. When he stepped down to a supporting role, Ilidar became his successor, but his promotion was more due to pedigree and preparedness than extensive combat experience. If Sir Jonathan Pillair hadn't been so averse to playing a leadership role, Ilidar might have remained a Lieutenant, but the legendary knight had no interest in anything except fighting. Ever since The Battle of Snowpack, Sir Jonathan hadn't been the same.

That being the case, Ilidar had left Sir Reginald in charge of The Astrian Guard in his absence, with Dame Isabel Loret as a second-in-command, but the assignment was a hollow task. Even diminished, the Palace still had a small army of guards left, and The High Emperor was well-liked, at least in Astria.

He hadn't expected anything to happen, especially to Sir Reginald. Nevertheless, Sir Reginald was next to him, heavily bandaged. Several rounds of muslin wrapped diagonally across his chest, soaked through with blood.

How was he injured?! What happened?!

His squadron was the last resort in case of attack... The soldiers I left were good, but they were still new. They were only supposed to act if The High Emperor was in immediate danger. That means—

Ilidar stopped. His whole body shook.

He remembered what Sir Reginald had said to him the night before he left for The Outpost.

This is a bad idea, Ilidar. Stopping The Frosslar isn't as important as protecting his Grace. You know that. Don't take so many troops.

Come on, Drye! Where will he be assassinated? Between his office and his bedroom?! There hasn't been a threat to his Grace in years, and I need the men if I'm going to fight the ice giants. They're dangerous.

Ilidar, our duty as members of the Guard always comes first. We must remain vigilant. Even if we're ordered to, we mustn't leave the crown unprotected. Don't you remember your oath? What would your parents say?

They're dead, so it doesn't matter.

Ilidar held his head in his hands.

Well, I remember it, the Knight continued. *I forsake the pleasures of the flesh.*

The Captain's ears began to ring, his mind aflash with the memories of his failings.

A brothel frequented by the upper class. It was only one night, a night where he felt like he would die if he was not wanted. So many years of taking care of himself and his appearance had yielded no results.

Yes, Ilidar! Right there! the prostitute screamed.

She had heard his name for the first time a few minutes prior.

Oh, Ilidar!

I forsake the fruits by sickles threshed.

A tavern in the central square, a place he would go with his friends, or without. The Winter Angels never came along.

Pour me another ale. I'll be spending the night.

You shouldn't be drinking Ilidar. You have responsibilities.

Oh, lay off, Drye! It's just a little wine.

I forsake the fear that grips man's heart, and so from pain my soul does part.

A battlefield, clouds of smoke and sprays of blood...

Do you remember those words? If his Grace dies, it'll be a disaster. If we die, it means nothing.

Maybe you don't value your life, Drye, but I'm not just some nobody to disappear from Avenshra. It would mean something to me.

The cacophony quieted. Ilidar's face was immersed in shadow.

Horrified by what he did not know but only vaguely suspected, The Captain tried to stand, to wake Sir Reginald, but his leg was very stiff, and it was hard to move.

I need to know what happened. I need to —

He grabbed the nightstand, trying to turn himself so that his legs would hang over the edge of the bed, but the sheets slipped, and he fell off of the cot with a *crash*.

Ilidar felt crusted skin split, fiery ooze wet against his bandages as stitches tore.

"Ahow!"

Lord Sigmund Jiralt rushed in.

"Captain, your leg is severely injured! Please don't move!"

The Overseer helped Ilidar get back onto the bed, struggling with the guardsman's weight.

' Finally, they managed.

Ilidar sat awkwardly on the wrinkled sheets, holding his injured leg. It hurt a lot.

Sigmund clicked his tongue. "You've ruined the stitching. I'll have to redo it. Stay still."

The Lord hurried over to the nearby cart and grabbed some disinfectant, a needle, and thread. Then, he undid The Captain's bandages.

Ilidar looked at his red-black leg as he would another man's.

My leg — it's destroyed! Oh, God!

The cold needle went in, Ilidar steeling himself against the pain that followed.

The Captain growled.

God, I hate this helplessness! What the hell is going on?!

Slowly, the pain grew more tolerable, allowing Sigmund to more easily do his work.

"Sigmund — The High Emperor — is he alright?!"

The Overseer paused. His expression was grave.

"I'm afraid not... His Grace was killed, an assassin in the night... The Guard fought bravely, but the attacker was unstoppable. If I hadn't gone to The Sagery for an errand, I—"

The Lord turned his head, wiping tears on his sleeve. The two men had been friends for over thirty years, but Sigmund couldn't cry for his friend, Agravius. He could only mourn the loss of the esteemed "High Emperor."

The Lord composed himself, but Ilidar was wholly in the grip of shock. The Overseer's words barely registered.

Sigmund's voice wavered.

"Judging by the wounds inflicted on your men, the damage they did, the assassin was a truly terrible fighter. I've never seen such barbarism. They even killed The Dovekeeper. Somehow, Sir Reginald managed to survive. At least that's good news..."

Ilidar remained silent.

I've failed. I've been dishonored.

I should never have left. I should have been there, posted more guards!

He glanced over at Sir Reginald, the man's breathing erratic.

The Overseer spoke.

"I fear that his chances of recovery are slim, but after all he has done for the crown, his Grace felt that it would be only right to try and revive him. Unfortunately, Sire Reginald has been unconscious ever since the attack, and there is little hope he will remember what happened, even if he wakes."

"What about the Princess? Tell me that at least she is-"

"Safe," the Overseer nodded. "She hid in her wardrobe when the fighting started. It doesn't seem like the assassin even looked for her. However, his Grace is sending her off to Springhaven as a precaution. She will stay with her uncle."

"Has The City Guard been deployed? Has the assassin been found?"

"The City Guard is out searching, but no—not yet. That said, the suspect bled quite profusely. I doubt that they made it out of the capital alive, and with so many soldiers searching for them, sooner or later, they'll be found. Someone must know something."

"What about Hemia? Has there been any news from The High Sword?"

"With Korac dead, everything is a mess. It was foolish to have only one Dovekeeper, even if it allowed for greater secrecy. His replacement says that The High Sword has written back, that everything is progressing smoothly with Sunveil's reconstruction, but I still have a bad feeling about it. The last time dragons roamed the skies—well...it is an ill omen."

Konell

The assassin Evanesced.

Demonic blood ran, splattering the floor.

Bow-shots and longswords all missed, as Konell skirted The Bloodred Battalion and flouted the Palace's security measures. He had to keep Viktor's royal guard off his back. The Bloodred Elites in their cinnabar-red banded mail wore no helmets, so he took out some shurikens.

I'm not here for you.

Throwing stars span, entering exposed throats.

Should have worn gorgets, you fools.

The assassin Evanesced again, a portal opening in The Brimstone Court. With an inward thrust and a swish to the head, the Goblins guarding the throne were relieved of duty, Theonium passing through their obsidian shell and to the goop beneath.

Konell walked up the dais leading to The Brimstone Chair and extended his sword. The King of Hemia sat back relaxedly, as if the sword was nothing but a harmless feather.

Konell pressed Tardrown's edge into the Raishian's taut neck. The monarch looked up with wide eyes, mock innocence.

"What have you done to my sister?!" Konell asked, his tone deadly.

"I upheld my end of the bargain," the monarch answered, matter-of-factly. "I cured your sister. Why did you kill my guards?"

The assassin pressed down harder on the Fallstreak, blood beginning to trickle.

"I'm asking the questions here! The Water was not pure! What did you put in it? What else was in the vial?! Tell me before I slit your throat, Princeling! I know you drugged it."

"Well...theriac," Viktor laughed. "I only use the finest ingredients. I am a King, after all."

"You— You gave my teenage sister opium?!" Konell shouted, growing shrill. "Opium?! I will kill y-"

The Raishan King kicked him in the chest with unnatural strength. The assassin was still dizzy when a backhand slap sent him sprawling.

Konell got up, swinging Tardrown, but The King of Hemia had Called a sword that could meet his blade. It was a sword that was instantly recognizable to anyone on Avenshra—a sword of tyrants.

Bloodweep.

Theonium clashed.

Viktor looked down on Konell with deep, red eyes. There was fire in those eyes.

Konell looked up, pupils as black as a taipan's mouth.

He swung for Viktor's ear, but the King parried, shifting the bind. The monarch headbutted him, tripping him with a well-placed foot and disarming him.

Viktor kicked the assassin in the ribs, sending him sliding across the polished floor.

Konell tried to get away, but more Goblins came to the scene, restraining him. He resisted, cursing, but he couldn't break free. The spines on the creatures' forearms dug into his clothes.

"Settle down, Revangel. I'm not going to kill you," The King assured him calmly.

"Like I'd give you the chance!" the assassin spat.

Konell grabbed the demons behind him with poisoned hands, trying to shake them off, but the poison merely dripped down their obsidian hide.

"Must be strange, feeling powerless. Your toxins have no effect on my soldiers. Your magic is useless. And your blade..."

Konell tried to Evanesce, but he had no momentum. He managed to break free from one of the demons, rolling, when the King issued a stinging cut to his right arm with a long, gold-bladed knife. The red doorway that had just opened sputtered and faded.

Viktor kicked Konell again, dodging the acidic blood that flew from the assassin's lips. The blood fizzled, pitting the marble floor.

Stepping over the puddle, Viktor knelt, pinning the assassin down, and removed the smooth, black band from Konell's finger.

"...is mine to command... Nice Callring," Viktor mused.

Konell's tears salted the floor. Viktor smiled, walking back towards his throne.

Snarling, Konell chased after the man, but the demons grabbed him again, punching him.

With a *crack*, Konell lost three teeth, bone skittering against tile. Then, they took Konell's arms again, the youth swaying. He saw stars, about to faint, but he gritted his teeth.

The monarch sighed, cleaning his knife with a red, silk handkerchief as he walked back up the steps. He sat back down, in a position of power again.

"What did you cut me with?" Konell sputtered.

"Rapterium. You won't be able to use any sorcery for a while... Marvelous, isn't it—how easily it shuts you down? I've experienced its cut as well... I know how it feels—when even Lifeblood cannot save you."

The assassin trembled with rage.

"You— You took away my powers?! You'll-"

"I'll make you an offer. Attacking the highest court in Hemia, you are now an enemy of the state, and your sister needs a constant supply of theriac to live, a compound more potent, and more expensive than regular opium—more expensive than anything you own. However, if taken regularly, there are no side effects. After all, I wanted your sister to have the best..."

The Raishan King smiled, coyly.

"If you work for me, your sister will live in luxury, and she'll have no problems if she just takes her medicine. So tell me, how am I in the wrong? Your sister was cured of The Yellow Plague, when she should have died."

"You lied to me—made my sister an addict—and now you ask how you're in the wrong?! I'm a criminal for what I've done for you! You took everything from me! How are you not in the wrong?!"

Viktor didn't answer, the demons breaking Konell's fingers open and replacing Tardrown's Callring with another, golden ring made of Rapterium.

"As I was saying, I am now your sister's only hope. Theriac withdrawal is as deadly as The Yellow Plague, and twice as painful. With The High Emperor gone, and our man in the Imperial rookery, I'm planning to move on Astria in the coming weeks, a plan that you helped me set in motion. If you fight for me, your sister will be kept safe in the Palace and given a constant supply of theriac. She will know a life she could have never even dreamed of, for I am a benevolent ruler. If you do not, I can always cut out your tongue and send you to The High Court to be tried."

"That's not a choice."

The monarch's tone hardened.

"Well it's the only one you're getting, assassin. Should I throw your Callring away, let you be executed like the criminal you are? Or will you be my general in the fight to come? The choice is yours."

Riane

The caravan headed to Springhaven was a line of four horse-drawn carriages, and two carts, guarded by two squadrons of mounted soldiers. The carriages were new, and painted with pastel colors—orange, pink, blue, and purple. The carts were drawn by large, brown horses, which were guided by cart drivers dressed in brown leather.

The carts and carriages hugged The Astris Run, almost precipitously close, but the grassy hills to the right had not been trampled down in that area, and The Riverlick Pass grew narrow, people accommodating nature, rather than the other way around.

The first carriage was for Velestre and his advisers. The second, carried Riane's cousins, and the third, was for Riane and her aunt, Mereona. Riane was surprised that her aunt had stayed with her, rather than her own girls, but the Lady's sour mood made her wish that she hadn't. The last carriage carried the servants.

The carts carried the food necessary for travel—fresh produce and bread for the nobility, paired with exquisite wine—and for the soldiers and servants, salted meat, biscuits, and water in barrels.

Riane was sweating. Summers in Astria were usually hot and dry, but that day was suffocatingly humid.

Riding the blessedly cool breeze, the song sung by crickets, flies, and bees was barely audible over the river's rushing waters. The smell of sweat and grass was pervasive.

The High Princess would have felt bored if she wasn't so sad. She curled up as much as etiquette would allow, wood digging into her.

Dad...

The inside of the carriage was spacious, but simply furnished, with two, wooden benches bolted to the olive-painted walls of the compartment, which were decorated in gold scrollwork, and the floorboards were made of the same oak as the benches. Dark green, wooden window shutters sat on either side, held up by shiny, brass latches. The road was bumpy and not as well-maintained as it could have been, but the procession was slow, so the ride was relatively comfortable.

Riane was about to fall asleep, when she was woken by a loud sound.

It was the sound of wood breaking. The caravan came to a stop.

She heard shouts coming from outside.

"Aunt Mereona, is everything alright?" Riane asked, concerned.

The Lady put down her fan, listening more closely. Then, she leaned back again and closed her eyes.

"Yes; everything is fine. I wouldn't worry, Princess, one of the carriages probably just broke a wheel."

"Can that be fixed?" Riane wondered aloud.

"Of course, child, what do you think?" her aunt replied, almost scoffingly. It seemed the heat was getting to her. "Our family is the richest in the world. Do you think we wouldn't have spare wheels? What a silly question!"

Riane felt stifled. Riane felt stupid.

Mereona kept cooling herself off with her silk fan, not offering her niece one, though The High Princess was boiling in her repressive, white, linen dress. Riane wished that she could take it off, the balloon sleeves bunched up under her arms, and the collar clinging uncomfortably to her chest. Though it was pretty,the material was rough and itchy.

Just our luck. It's so hot today, and a broken wheel... What a mess...

I wish Torran hadn't sent me away.

Minutes passed, but the caravan was still at a standstill. When no one came over to report on the situation, the Lady became impatient, opening the window and calling out. Still, no one came.

The soldiers should be outside. What are they doing?

A rumbling came from down the road, officers calling out orders, soldiers forming a line.

"Auntie, do you hear that?!" Riane asked panickedly.

Nodding, Mereona opened the window latch, looking outside the carriage. She called out, wary. Torran's new Lieutenant answered her after a couple seconds of commotion. His face was shining with sweat.

"Lieutenant Perrin, why have we stopped?" Mereona asked. "What's happening?"

The Lieutenant looked afraid.

"My Lady! The guard has formed up in front of the caravan! We're under-"

A barbed, black steel quarrel interrupted him, going through the wooden shutter and into his ear canal. Blood dripped from the Lieutenant's nose, body left standing as his skull bloomed like a fetid rose, spattering the Lady with gore.

Mereona pushed herself away from the window, speechless, then screaming.

Riane didn't scream. She no longer paid attention to the danger. She had withdrawn from it all, no longer fully present. She didn't want to be. The High Princess began to twirl her hair, pulling some out.

The twirling became more and more frantic. She pulled out a whole lock, then several.

The Lady fainted, hitting her head and shaking the carriage,

Riane was brought back to reality by the nigh melodious clash of black and silver steel, the high, metallic note of weapons unsheathed challenging the brassy scrape of falchions against parched earth. Within seconds, the sound devolved, and all she could hear was the splurt of serrations against flesh. Steel ate steel in vicious cannibalism, human and inhuman animals seeing each other again for the first time in hundreds of years.

Riane finally noticed her aunt's bruised forehead, reacting.

Oh my God! We're under attack!

Riane ran to Mereona's side and tried to lift her up, but the woman was too heavy. She was about to use the main door to get out, dragging her aunt along, but, just then, the carriage splintered against a black steel battleaxe; the door buckled.

Drooling outside, was a Pneumon.

Ten feet tall, top-heavy, and muscular, The Pneumon was an imposing demon. With a barrel chest and a dome-like head, it was covered in bumpy, green-brown skin, which sloughed off its face in oily flakes. It had a puckered, sphincter-like mouth, and its back was lined with short, downturned spines. The monster had inflated itself to a preposterous size, bearing resemblance to a bullfrog, or perhaps, a pufferfish.

The creature looked down at Riane with wide-set, unintelligent eyes, and, without a sound, made a grab for her ankle.

Riane avoided it, but its claws nicked her heel and took her shoe. She scrambled towards the other door, but the Pneumon began to inhale air, drawing her back towards it.

The High Princess grabbed hold of the carriage floor, anchoring herself, but her clothes were dead weight, and she had never been particularly strong. She was losing her grip, about to fly into the demon's hands, or worse, its mouth, before it was accosted by Sir Donald Jendry, The Sun Warrior—her uncle's sworn knight.

The suction gone, Riane fell to the carriage floor, looking at her savior in a mix of gratitude and relief. The knight's messy, black hair was full of black blood, his skin, scarred and leathery. He wasn't the most handsome of men, with a porous, strawberry nose and slightly sagging jowls, but he had a set of beautiful, light blue eyes surrounded by crow's feet, which had earned him his nickname. Although he wasn't particularly comely, his loyalty to the crown was strong, and he was a legendary fighter. Famed for his noble deeds, Riane prayed that The Sun Warrior could kill the demon that so dwarfed him in size.

The demon turned to match the knight; Riane crawled to the back of the carriage. Her aunt was still unconscious, a pile of rumpled, pink silk.

The Sun Warrior got into a high stance; the Pneumon got into a low stance.

The monster swung upwards for Sir Donald's torso, but the knight redirected the cut, slashing the Pneumon across the face, and deflating its head. The telltale iridescence of enchanted steel was revealed by the light playing off the sword's fuller.

Oh, Divinity—I'm scared! Please kill it!

Riane pressed her back against the carriage's left door, cracking it open. She wished that she could take her aunt and escape, but they were at the river's edge. The Nation's largest waterway, swimming across was too dangerous.

There was nowhere to go. The lives of the two noblewomen rested firmly in Sir Donald's hands.

Fighting valiantly, the knight threw a flurry of slashes at his opponent, forcing the Pneumon back. He stabbed it in the cheek, but the monster remained standing. Though it couldn't breathe, black blood squirting from the wound, it was upright, fishy eyes bulging. To Riane and the knight's dismay, the wounds healed at a supernatural speed, skin crawling together. In mere seconds, it could breathe again.

Losing hope but refusing to give up, The Sun Warrior continued to fight.

The Pneumon swung its axe around its head and at Sir Donald's left shoulder, but the knight sidestepped, what would have been a lethal blow, glancing off of a masterful hanging Guard. Riane remembered seeing Ilidar practice the move, but she didn't remember the name.

The knight then made a cut for the demon's temple, successfully getting its left eye. The creature stumbled, grabbing the carriage to avoid falling over. It swung its weapon wildly, carping, but within seconds, its eye had healed as well. However, the injury had taken longer to close than the one before.

With renewed malice, the Pneumon hit the knight in the face with the butt of its axe and then made a brutal, downward swing for his right shoulder. The soldier blocked, sword pointed skywards. Pear-shaped pommel in line with his eyes, his stance was strong, but the crossguard of his sword was not enchanted, and the fire-axe cut through the steel. Unchecked, the axe blew through the knight's enchanted steel plate, severing his trapezius muscle and collar bone and driving him down to one knee.

The Princess threw her weight across the carriage floor and kicked the demon in the back of the head, trying to distract it and save Sir Donald, but she simply bounced off of its inflated body, hitting her ear against one of the benches.

Cartilage stung, her ear ringing.

Ignoring her, the Pneumon stepped on Sir Donald's knee, dislodging its axe, and prepared to deal another blow.

The Sun Warrior was not resigned to his fate. He was about to try another Guard, the determination in his eyes giving the Princess renewed hope.

The demon proved the falsity of that hope, a swing from below with the butt of the axe sending the man flying into a nearby squadron. Then, the creature reached into the carriage, and grabbed Riane's aunt, who had just woken up, throwing her to the ground and leaving her to the other demons.

In a craze, a group of Goblins tore off the woman's arms, then her clothes. Riane watched in horror as they surrounded her limbless aunt, but the Pneumon only made a sucking sound, a sound that might have been laughter.

Riane screamed, kicking its hands away as it went to grab her as well. In a moment of pure and visceral terror, the creature caught her foot, claws tearing the sleeve of her dress. Desperate, the Princess threw herself backwards, falling out of the carriage and rag-dolling into the Run.

CHAPTER XII

Torran

The funeral procession for High Emperor Agravius Xandromen stretched across the city, a gathering of tens of thousands of people. It seemed like every last inhabitant of Starspire had come to pay their respects to the dead monarch, who was being transported in a closed casket covered in a roughspun shroud of cloth-of-gold. The shroud was richly embroidered with red and green Stars of Astria done in shiny, silk thread, and it sat on a mahogany palanquin carried by The Winter Angels, who had finally returned from Lonecastle.

They had gone to get strong for their Emperor. They returned strong enough to lift him.

The Astrian Guard was followed by The High Sage, The Cardinal Sages, The Sages of Starspire, swinging censers, and the new High Emperor on horseback. Then came The High Council and any other nobles who chose to be a part of the procession, followed by a throng of commoners wearing the darkest clothes they owned, dark browns and dark greens. The sky above was a dark grey, the clouds trying not to weep, and the air was humid and cool.

The High Emperor would be marched over to The Basilica, where he would be entombed, laid to rest.

The march would take hours.

The Court wore black, the color of mourning. It was pouring out, and there was no gossip, no idle chatter.

The Cardinal Sages, clad in long, hooded, white robes, walked slowly down the long carpet with their ceremonial, gold censers, encrusted with diamonds and burning anise-seed oil. Fragrant smoke filled the room, soft footsteps echoing.

They were followed by The High Sage, who wore long, white robes with cuffs that were much too big for his arms, cloth dragging on the floor. Contrary to what one would expect, the head of The Church was only around ten years of age. This High Sage had been newly elected, and his outfit was not his size yet. Nevertheless, he stood before all, carrying The Imperial Crown on a blue, velvet cushion—a silver circlet holding a drop of black aventurine, cut from the same stone as The High Throne.

Its center was as black as Torran's grief; its sparkle was frightening.

Torran knelt on the dais. The carpet and some of the tiles had been replaced, but apart from that, he had saved as much coin as he could for true necessities. Gold couldn't be thrown around carelessly with such disquiet amongst The Continental Nations.

Though the repairs to the room had minimized the damage done by the assassin, new tiles could never hide the fact that Astrian blood had once seeped into the mortar.

Torran looked up at the frescoes on the ceiling, The Divinity standing in His Cloud, surrounded by angels. It felt like he was watching him.

This is the moment. I never wanted this, but here I am.

Father... I wish you were here.

The head of The High Sage approached, walking up the dais.

Torran knew that the boy was just a figurehead for The Council of Monks, but he couldn't really argue with the practice of appointing child Sages. The Book of a Thousand Deaths stated that children were the purest and closest to God. Still, it was strange to kneel before a child in veneration.

The High Sage raised his skinny arms high, invoking holy power.

At first, he appeared to be a normal boy, with brown hair, brown eyes, and a fairly average build. There was nothing striking or authoritative about him, and the voice that had offered Torran condolences at the funeral was naturally high-pitched.

But there on the raised platform, something changed. The boy's voice deepened, eyes washing to an all-too-recognizable blue, glowing near-imperceptibly in the sunlight. The air felt heavier, then, The High Sage's every word falling with the weight of a hammer.

Torran looked up and into the boy's blue, blue eyes, hands shaking. He could never forget

those eyes. The frescoes weren't even close to the truth.

I will disturb the strings of fate... I will make you powerful, but The Power will not come from me.

"Divinity, hear our prayer. We raise this man of mortal flesh to the title of High Emperor—Ruler of The Continental Nations of Astria, Hemia, Qeonia, and Cairnon, and Protector of The Ice Fields. May he stand strong, always. Watch over him... Watch over us all."

Like I'm supposed to feel safe with The Divinity pulling the strings.

Torran closed his eyes, and the Crown was placed upon his head, cold metal. The nobility bowed.

The High Sage's eyes changed back to their original brown, his tone lightening.

"Torran Xandromen, firstborn of Agravius and Juliana Xandromen, and heir to The Xandromen Dynasty—rise. You have been granted The Divinity's blessing. Rise as a new man, and lead Avenshra into the light."

So it's done. I hope you got what you wanted.

Torran stood. He had been crowned High Emperor.

Though he didn't want it, the world had been given to him, pushed on him by a god who wasn't a god, just another father placing the weight of the world on his child.

The world was his.

His to repair.

Leafsong

The Sixteenth Division barracks was a long, rectangular, one-story building made of mulberry wood situated at the west end of Perla, just far enough from the sea to prevent wood rot, but close enough to quickly respond to emergencies. The structure had a smooth, flattened, triangular roof, and three sets of windows on each side. Two, unlit lanterns hung above its main door, and sketches of wanted criminals were tacked to its splintering exterior, offering rewards for their capture.

The barracks were surrounded by an unsteady-looking, spiked, iron fence and a small yard, with sparse clumps of grass poking out from the sandy dirt. The backyard housed an old, worn-out, humanoid pell made of straw and wood, and a dusty, leather glove lay abandoned and stomped into the dirt. A large, wooden outhouse sat at the rightmost corner of the lawn—wide, tarnished, green, copper pipes going through the seawall and draining into the Ocean.

The building's interior smelled of wood, lanolin and sweat, and the air was humid, warm, and slightly salty.

Leafsong's nose still felt dry.

The eastern portion of the building held a modest kitchen and a pantry with barrels of wine, salted meat, water, and dry biscuits. The floor looked like it had been recently swept, but the occasional bit of sand or blade of grass still jutted through the cracks between the floorboards.

The western portion of the building held an infirmary—four, straw beds with cotton sheets, and a wooden cart carrying medicine and bandages.

The middle portion of the building held twelve, woolen mattresses, dressed with cotton sheets and sitting on wooden frames, as well as a mulberry weapons rack with twelve, well-kept arming swords, twelve longswords, and two recurve bows strung with gut string. All were well oiled. There was also a large, round, mahogany table at the center of the room, covered with maps, and a set of pegs on the leftmost wall to hold Dame Isla's prized bow. Under the beds sat sets of enchanted full plate, coated in lanolin.

Leafsong sat on one of those beds, watching Flind sleep. The Monolid's navy-blue head had been shaved of curly, sorrel bangs, bones set in place. Stitches crawled like centipedes across the back of her skull, and her arms were wrapped in muslin. Underneath the muslin, was a yarrow root tincture.

The Division healer, Jaquelin Faberlin, had gotten Flind into a stable condition, and Leafsong had sent her essence into skin and bone, drawing the energy out of any microbes that might have gotten into the wound through Lifeblood osmosis. There were other soldiers who still needed medical attention, and the infirmary was full, so the scullion had been moved.

Leafsong felt guilty. Flind had sustained such severe injuries trying to help her, thinking she was going to die, but she had healed with supernatural speed, no scars at all. Flind's scars would last a lifetime. Thankfully, hair would eventually cover those scars if left to grow, but Leafsong was ashamed at how easily she had failed, the consequences of her failure.

I was the one who got Flind into this mess. She could have taken it down, if only I hadn't missed my first attack.

This incredible new body is no excuse for fighting skill. I don't know any martial arts and I'm not a soldier. All I have is athleticism and intuition, and so far as I know, Flind doesn't know much about fighting either...

Why did we think that we'd be able to beat it?! I'm just a messenger and an arborist; Flind is a religious devotee; neither of us was supposed to approach that Seadrake! We were just playing at being heroes...

The dryad was approached by the true hero of the day, Dame Isla Wayland, a woman she admired.

A couple of years ago, Leafsong's father had told her all about Dame Isla, as he had been present at Court when the King knighted her. Rumor had it that she was so good with a bow, she could shoot enemy arrows out of the air.

"Hey. Are you doing alright?" the knight asked. The other soldiers had glared at the dryad, giving her the silent treatment, but the Dame was friendly.

"Yes..." Leafsong answered demurely. "Thank you."

"That's good," the Dame said softly. She unlaced her leather wrist and finger guards, and hung up her bow. The ironwood longbow was elegantly carved, bejeweled with labradorite bijoux.

Dame Isla's hair was dyed an exotic blue to match the stones. She was fetching, with an athletic figure, gentle, brown eyes, and a freckled face. Leafsong realized that she was staring too much when the woman flushed, smiling sheepishly.

Though the Dame was smiling, her face was pained. She had lost friends that day.

The knight brushed the hair out of her eyes.

"You were very brave to fight that monster. I don't know why you are the way you are, but I apologize for the way the others have been acting. If the two of you hadn't been there, the town might have fallen."

"Thanks. I can't say it didn't hurt, but I understand. Seeing the supernatural is shocking, and people are scared of what they don't know. Anyway, it was you who really took the creature down, Dame Isla. You're the one who deserves the credit."

"I appreciate you saying that, but honestly, I should have made the shot sooner, even if it was a dragon... I was too slow, and because of that, my comrades died."

"Slaying a dragon is no small feat. I wouldn't blame yourself."

"That's true, but the glory of victory is nothing compared to the grief of loss."

Dame Isla's doleful face suddenly changed to embarrassment.

"I forgot to introduce myself. How do you know my name?"

"Are you kidding? You're the youngest female knight to ever be knighted! Every girl in Qeonia knows who you are! Plus, your bow makes it pretty obvious."

The Dame became even more embarrassed.

Leafsong offered her hand, and Isla took it.

"I never introduced myself either. I'm Leafsong, Leafsong Ralei."

The knight's eyes widened.

"Wait—you're Baron Agamus' daughter?!"

"Yeah."

"Wow; I'm so sorry! Our Division heard news of the earthquake just last week. How did you escape?! And...why do you look the way you look, if you don't mind me asking, my Lady?"

"My father sent me to the countryside, and—well, it's a long story, but I'm no longer a Baroness, and I'm no longer a Ronari. Though it may be hard to believe, I was granted this form by The Divinity, and I have a mission to accomplish, one that leaves no room for marriage or childbirth... I've made my peace with how I look and what happened to my parents. I've finished grieving and I'm trying to move forward."

363

"I see..." the Dame responded. Her tone was disbelieving but polite. "What sort of mission?"

Leafsong sighed.

"God told me that my destiny is to Heal the Shadowrise trees of Avenshra. My companion, Flind, is a religious devotee as well, but not of The Church; she's a Lātist. Although we have separate goals, we've been travelling together. Our plan was to part ways here at the Bay. I need to get to Starspire, and she needs to get to The Swampgreen City, but we have no money, no ship, and we're in a hurry. Now that Flind's unconscious, I'd feel bad if I just left her here. To tell you the truth, I wasn't very nice to her when we first met."

"Is that so? You fought well together."

That is true. We did make a good team, and she has powers. They might be different from mine, but she would make a good ally.

"Our Division is heading to Clearwater tomorrow. Given its unprecedented nature, The King wants us to give him a report of the attack. Why don't the two of you accompany us, my La— Leafsong?" The Dame suggested. "Being his niece, I'm sure The King would offer you and your friend passage, even if you've changed. His Majesty is a spiritual man. If your mission was given to you by The Divinity, he'll definitely listen to you. We can vouch for you as well, since we all saw you fight."

Leafsong considered the woman's offer.

"I already declined his first invitation, but I guess that that could work. Uncle Amphitritton has always been good to my family. Still, I don't know what he'll think of me now that I look the way I do... This isn't some small change. There's not much choice, though... We'll go with you, then," Leafsong responded, unsure.

"Great. I will tell Sienna." Dame Isla squeezed Leafsong's shoulder reassuringly, walking off.

The woman stopped, turning.

"Oh... And don't worry so much about the way you look. You still look beautiful," she winked.

Leafsong flushed a green so dark it was almost black.

Riane

The Astris Run sat in its own, miniature canyon, the soft, dark brown earth eroded to make way for water. Pebbles and stones stubbornly stayed at the river-bottom, even after the dirt had left them.

A steady flow of corpses floated downstream, half-torn by enemy halberds, body parts bobbing up and down. The pinguid chum was thick as tar, and sat on the surface like oil, red-brown mush clumping together and breaking apart, flashes of blue only visible when the human fluid was bashed against the rocks. Large, chipped, grey boulders stood out from the run like the teeth of a comb, caressing the river's silken hair and removing the sticky, bloody gum that frothed and bubbled in the tumult.

The odor was unbelievably bad, and the air reeked of iron. To the left of the channel was a gorgeous field of yellow flowers, producing a stark dissonance. Daffodils carpeted the entirety of the west bank, small, deciduous trees interspersed amongst them. On the east bank, lay a dense, dark forest—The Athaponn Wood. There were no man-made landmarks or signs of settlement to be seen, cicadas unrelenting in their loud, and nigh on irritating, thrum. Arceon was at the apex of its ascent, a bright white-blue, with a sky the color of ice, and populated by fluffy, sheep-like clouds.

Riane coughed. The river had punished her, but she had survived. The irony was that it was all thanks to her dress. The garment had snagged on a rock, The Princess hoisting herself out of the Run, and onto dry land, albeit without most of her clothing.

She had been lucky, as the rocks near The Yellowsweet Fields stood at a knee in the river where the current slowed considerably. There, the waterway was only three feet deep, and only six feet lower than the surrounding land, but she had only gone over to the nearest bank, as she had little energy. She would assess whether or not she should cross once she got her bearings.

The other victims of the attack weren't as well-to-do. A steady flow of Astrian soldiers passed her by, looking at her with eyes that cried out: "Help me!"

But they were already dead.

Riane retched. Her dress was a wet red-brown. There was nowhere to wash off, and the odor alone made her want to vomit, but she was grateful, at least, that she had survived.

In a daze, she shuffled along the right bank, heading back towards Starspire, or where she inferred Starspire was. Dangerous or not, it was the safest place she could go with her uncle dead, and she had to warn Torran.

The demons were already there.

Unfortunately for Riane, she had never really paid attention during carriage rides, and the last time she had been out of the city was when she was five.

The High Princess tried to find a landmark or sign of settlement, but there was nothing to see. She wished her aunt Mereona had lived.

Head throbbing, she remembered the demons pulling down their war skirts. She would never forget what she had seen.

I can't.

Riane sobbed, taking a moment and sitting in the soft dirt. Cradling her legs, she sobbed for a long time, rocking, sobbed until the chum dried, and her outfit became so itchy that she had to take it off completely, leaving her with just a cotton shift, underwear, and stockings.

She hadn't gotten very far from the rapids when she heard shouts.

In her mind, Riane heard the Lieutenant's head explode. Beside herself, The High Princess half-jumped, half-climbed up the left bank and popped her head quickly over the margin to see who it was, spotting a pollen cloud speeding through the Fields.

Are those Lieutenant Perrin's men?

Riane listened for words she recognized, hoofbeats. Instead of words, she heard growls; instead of hoofbeats, she heard scratching.

Riders. But whose riders, and what kind of horses are they riding?

With a gust of wind, the pollen was blown away, revealing the source of the commotion.

The girl was right; she had heard riders, but the riders weren't human, and their mounts were not horses.

Those aren't the Lieutenant's men...

The riders in the Fields had thick, banded horns like twin rainbows, giant horns, which grew more than a foot out of their skulls. Under those horns, tympanic membranes pitter-pattered, listening.

They were listening for someone, or something. Riane shrank lower, trying to stop her heart from beating so loudly.

The Goblins licked their lips with slimy, green tongues. They stretched, as if sore from a long ride, shiny, grey skin appearing between the plates of obsidian armor fused to their chest, arms, and legs. Like the ones from the attack, they each wore a war skirt and cape, which seemed to be woven from cobwebs. Sheaths swung at the monsters' hips, the protruding hilts of black steel falchions, well-wrapped in powder blue leather.

The Goblins dismounted, letting their mounts take a look around. When the creatures returned to them, nudging their hands with spiked snouts, they let them sniff a tiny, women's shoe, dark blue leather with The Star of Astria stamped into the suede, revealing the natural, light beige color beneath.

Riane instantly recognized the shoe as the one she had lost, the one that had ripped off when she was attacked by The Pneumon. She had lost the other one in the river.

Thank God the cobbler who made those shoes was such a crook. His cheap shoes were well worth the money, after all. I only wish he made them to fall apart completely after use. Then, I'd be even more grateful.

Written about in The Book of a Thousand Deaths, the large, reptilian steeds of The Demonium were called Salamanders. Their skin was dark and coarse, like black sand, and rough, bumpy, white calcifications grew from their heads like mold. Their eyes were as big as oranges—glassy, pitch-black orbs— and their long, flat, pink tongues hung loosely from their wide mouths, like dogs. They resembled Gila monsters, or, more accurately, marine iguanas. The lizards had been saddled with seats made of the same strange, light blue leather as the Goblins' sheaths.

Curious, The Salamanders sniffed the star-stamped shoe and then snuffled around with their many nostrils.

Oh, Divinity! They're looking for me! Those things are trying to track me!

Noiselessly, Riane hid, sliding down the embankment and pressing her back against the concealatory drop. So close to the river of blood, she hoped that the creatures couldn't get her scent.

The Princess' heart refused to quiet as the Salamanders stopped at the edge of the Fields, the Goblins following. They stood directly over her, looking past her flattened form and down at the river.

Riane held her breath. Thankfully, the demons hadn't noticed her.

However, before she could breathe a sigh of relief, some water began to drip from her dress, rolling downhill like an uncooperative toddler running from its mother.

No, no, no, no, no! Please, stop!!! Stupid water, you're going to get me killed!

The trickle of water kept going, but just as the sunlight was about to hit it and refract, the Goblins turned around and got back in the saddle, the shining droplet left unnoticed.

And with a *scrape* and a *clatter*, the demons disappeared.

Riane gasped for air, relief hitting her in a euphoric wave. Though it smelled vile, air had never tasted so sweet. She hadn't been discovered.

One thing she found strange, however, was that the Goblins hadn't cared about her footprints. She had left quite a few near the Run.

Maybe their vision isn't very good, or maybe, where they come from, people's footprints don't last... I don't know, but I have a feeling that those creatures...they really don't know how things work on Avenshra.

Well, thank The Divinity for that.

Though the monsters had left, Riane stuck diligently to the river bank for the next half hour—stuck to the dirt like a dirty starfish until she felt safe enough to look over the edge again. Praying that she wouldn't meet with horrors, the Princess peeked out, seeing no one, and then looked over at the opposite bank.

Deciding that Sprighaven was most likely on the other side, she slid down the slope and ran across the wet stones, twisting her ankle a little, but making it over in one piece.

They shouldn't be on this side of the Run, and I think Starspire is actually on this side...

Torran will recognize me, even like this; I'm sure of it.

I just hope Starspire is on this side...

Skotathis

Skotathis met with Viktor in a dream.

His Emissary spoke:

"My Lord, the preparations have been made. I have found my Generals, and I've procured the materials you requested. Hemia awaits your arrival."

"Good, good... Once I have recovered from this latest Pyrocast, I will make the Jump."

"I see," Viktor replied. "Have The Demonium taken Springhaven yet, my Lord?"

"No; not yet. Unfortunately, they didn't Pyrocast inside. It's a little disappointing, but even after so many years, Pyrocasts aren't easy to aim, especially when they're split into multiple locations... It is of no matter; we will take the city soon enough. Without Fallstreaks, my creations are unstoppable, and I don't believe the Springhaven Xandromen's have Callrings. I will keep giving Orders. With some impetus, The Demonium will breach the walls."

"Yes, my Lord," the Raishian affirmed, kneeling.

"Just remember, Viktor, our actions must be swift and decisive, now more than ever. I'm counting on you."

The Adversary looked down at the kneeling King.

"Yes, my Lord. Your will is word; you know that. Anything you ask of me—it shall be done."

The Adversary smiled, inwardly amused.

"I know. Just make sure your two "Generals" get ahold of themselves. They need to become skilled fighters in a very short amount of time."

"I understand. Don't worry, my Lord, I will see to their training personally."

"Glad to hear it... Till we meet again, my Emissary."

Skotathis left the dreamscape in a whirl of black smoke, opening his eyes. He was sitting cross-legged beneath The Shadowrise of Faal.

Skotathis Evanesced, reappearing at the bluff of a deep crater. The air smelled of rotten

eggs and the hard-packed earth crunched beneath his feet.

The crater housed a small city, sheltering it from the dust storms that regularly swept the moon's red-brown surface. Army camps were set up in the soft ejecta at the crater's rim, keeping the warlike Demonium out of the city, and out of trouble.

In that city, lived The Seranum, the last angels of Ressida. Aeons ago, they had sworn an oath to Kenon to become Devourers, but the difference lay only in semantics, and their rainbow swords had never seen use.

We didn't have a choice back then.

The Seranum were not the regal Ressidans of the past. They had gotten old, their hair white, and their skin, pale and sagging. They constantly moaned and groaned about their ailments, hunched over Shadowrise canes as The Workers tended to their every need. The bitter, fallen angels wore the same finery that they had worn back in the day, but the satin and brocade had faded, and their gold and silver rings had lost their luster. They walked around in togas that used to be green, keeping their wings folded behind their backs. They did this no longer out of politeness or class, but in order to hide the fact that they were losing their feathers. The feathers that remained were grey and dull.

Skotathis' wings used to be a pastel, baby blue, but that was before he had met The Tremites.

Though their eyes were clouded by cataracts and they could hardly move around, the ailing nobles still held the same arrogant and conceited attitudes they had espoused on Ressida. Even though the life that they lived was worse than that of most Astrian peasants, barely scraping by on the desolate Red Moon, they thought they were special. But, as unpleasant as they were, they were the last of his people. He would protect them. After all, they had taken his side in The Angelic Civil War.

He was their King.

The Adversary looked down at the makeshift settlement with a certain pride, sighing.

The angels' square houses were made of red mud-brick, and they were clustered around a pool of rusty, brown water, which was also surrounded by the same mud-brick. Pine-green, algal scum floated on top of the water, a food source that The Workers would skim off the top and boil into a thick porridge, which tasted faintly like pecans.

You know, I might just miss this place; even if the water's rusty and the weather's bad. I guess that's how it always is, though, how it feels when you've got to leave the place you've lived for a long time.

But destiny calls... And who am I kidding? This place is a living hell. I'll be glad to leave it.

Skotathis clenched his teeth, looking out at the lunar horizon.

To the west of the city, bubbled Lake Melpheor, a large, bubbling, grey basin heated by

hydrothermal vents. Bright yellow sulphur deposits formed a ring around the Lake, Tremite larvae proliferating in the heated, chemical bath. The tiny, black worms coated the Lake's entire surface, each no larger than a speck of dust.

Skotathis had used the Lake to build up his ranks, throwing in anything from living people and animals, to bugs, plants, and even fossil bones, plucked from The Living Worlds. Though nothing had ever surpassed his greatest creation— Flameheir, the giant red dragon he had made with a tyrannosaur skull—his recent work hadn't been too shabby.

The eel did quite a bit of damage... It definitely slowed that girl down.

And I never would have thought one of those blue air-bags would do so well with a rose bush. Just goes to show that I should have some fun with my recipes...

Skotathis chuckled snidely, gazing across the griseous waters.

I can't wait to see the look on their faces.

A couple of miles out, were the dusty expanses where one could find the black steel deposits—volcanic plugs that poked out like blackheads from the moon's rusted face. The metal had been forged into weapons that shattered Lifeblood, a temporary scattering of the energy that made it easier for The Demonium to absorb. This quick absorption wasn't only convenient, but a big advantage in battles with sorcery, as Elementals could only use whole souls.

Past the deposits, which were mined day-and-night by The Workers, sat The Amber Ocean, which was really just another lake. The freshwater tarn was the city's main water source, and the cherry-red Ironridge Mountains encircling it were the home of the flying squid, a type of large, filter-feeding fish that ate the microorganisms in the air, its helium-filled flight bladder carrying it across the jet-black sky. The Workers would shoot down the squid with arrows, frying the meat for The Seranum, using the bladders to carry water, and making weapon wrappings and other products out of the animal's skin.

The Workers were dutiful creatures, the most tame of The Demonium. Tall and muscular, they could cause damage if they wanted to, but they didn't. Like the rest of the demons, they had no need for food, only water and sunlight, and their hide made them resistant to Faal's dust storms, but unlike their more monstrous brethren, they didn't have large, glowing horns, or sharp, obsidian claws. They were humanoid, but with pachycephalosaurian features, their hard, domed skulls surrounded by tiny, horn-like growths, with rough patches on their shoulders. Their skin was a brownish grey, like unfired clay, and their wide eyes glowed a pale blue, a color that, amongst the Tremites, meant sleepiness, calm, or relaxation.

Before they had been reborn as demons, The Workers had been members of a more aggressive species, but on Faal, they did whatever The Seranum told them to without question, silent and dejected. Like the Ighed'bad, their minds were too weak to resist the parasites, the prideful Shang'hachar of Focale turned into beasts of burden built to withstand heavy labor.

I would feel sorry for them, but all they ever did was butt heads.

Skotathis Evanesced again, finding himself in The Talkingtree Forest. He walked

past the hundreds of trees that were not really trees, limbs twisted at unnatural angles, nails at their feet crusted with dark red sap.

He stopped once he had found the one he was looking for.

The person he was looking for.

Viktor

Viktor's new Generals were escorted to the Amphitheater by a squadron of demons, their footsteps amplified by the structure's curvature.

It's like I can see everything around me by sound, The Prince noted. *I could probably hear a firemite fart.*

Goblins forced the two men along, Revangel dragging his feet while Akris moved along without resistance.

Leaving them to him, the demon guards took their stations around the perimeter, though Viktor didn't anticipate any escape attempts. The men weren't always immediately compliant, but they knew that if they disobeyed or fled, their families would be killed in retribution.

Though Viktor was blackmailing the both of them, he planned to give his Generals the best equipment he could provide, as they were his most powerful fighters. He had commissioned new weapons and new uniforms for the pair.

Viktor rolled Konell's Callring between his fingers as his Agent, Lord Elrisain, laid out the new equipment. There would be no training swords, no padded gambesons or protective masks.

What better way to develop confidence than through real danger?

"What is all this?" the assassin asked, his tone sharp.

"You mean: "What is all this, "your Majesty,"""" Viktor corrected.

"Yes..."your Majesty,"" Konell spat.

This one... His spirit's still not broken. It will be soon.

"All this, Revangel, is for the two of you."

"This must be a trick, "your Majesty." Why would you arm your two most powerful foes?"

"I wouldn't flatter yourself. You may be Elementals, but neither of you is a threat to me, and you know why that is. I'm giving you all this, because it's time to begin your training."

The Raishian King picked up a Battalion-issue short sword—a silvery, Moondrake-bone flyssa—and tossed it to Adam. The man nearly lost a pinky trying to catch it, but he caught it nonetheless.

"Akris, I assume you've never held a sword before. Am I right?"

"Uh...yes, you're right, your Majesty."

"Well, we're going to have to teach you how to use one. This should be easier for you than learning how to fight longsword, as you shouldn't have any preconceived notions. A short sword isn't a two-handed weapon, and it's nothing like a pickaxe, so I'm hoping your form here won't be as bad as your longsword form undoubtedly will be."

The King of Hemia reached into his pocket.

"Before we begin, put on this ring. It'll ensure everyone's safety. The metal it's made from will prevent you from using your sorcery on accident. Konell here is already wearing one for other reasons."

Adam put on the ring, afraid.

Don't worry; it won't hurt you.

The assassin skulked nearby. With his thermal vision, Viktor could see that the man was growing angry, his temperature rising. The monarch paid him no attention, asking Adam to get into a short stance and modeling the position.

"Hand above your right knee, left leg perpendicular to the rest of your body." He used his foot to shift the miner's foot into the proper angle.

"Perpendicular, like this. Good. Now bend your knees, and straighten your back."

"Now Revangel-"

Konell tried to goad Adam to anger.

""King" Viktor here has really made you his dog, hasn't he, friend? Why don't you beg for a treat, now, "Adam Akris," lick his boots?"

I knew the man would be difficult to teach, but his sister is in my hands... Why isn't he cooperating?! He killed an Emperor to keep her alive, and now he does this?!

Does he think that I won't kill her? I mean—I won't, but he should have no reason to doubt me...

Before the miner could get drawn into an argument, Viktor walked over and slapped the assassin to the ground.

"Watch your tongue, Revangel, before I have it removed. If you act out again, you'll have to watch Amara endure ten lashings with the cat-o'-nine tails."

"No!" Konell cried.

"Yes!" Viktor responded, kicking him in the stomach. The assassin groaned.

"Are there anymore complaints?! No?! Good! Now, both of you, get your uniforms on and pick up your weapons, and under no circumstances take off the ring I've given you. It's time you learned how to fight, and I don't mean a bar fight or a contract. I mean how to fight on the battlefield. Once you've mastered the basics, I'll teach you how to use your magic, but only then, and not before."

He turned again to Konell, who was wiping away a nosebleed. "What are you waiting for, smart-mouth? Let's move!"

But there were more complaints.

"This is nonsense," the assassin scoffed. "I could take you on any time of day, so you took my sister for leverage. That's the only reason you're still standing, coward. I know more about fighting, about "magic" than you ever could!"

"Really? That's great! Make it twenty lashes, then. I'll tell poor Amara who brought them upon her before we begin, so you can learn your lesson. A-fourteen-year-old girl, she's sure to understand."

"Screw this; I will kill you!" Revangel shouted, running at him.

Even after I humiliated you in the courtroom, you still have no idea who I am.

Viktor reached into the bucket of snails sitting under a nearby table and threw them to the ground, inhaling their Lifeblood. Then he kicked the bucket over to Konell, stopping him in his tracks, and nearly tripping him.

The assassin paused.

"Come on, then! Try me!" Viktor shouted, settling into a strong stance. Adam, who was caught in the middle of everything, backed away, worried.

Konell took off his ring, throwing it at Viktor's face, but the Raishian caught it, to his chagrin.

Then, the young man reached into the bucket of snails and took some out, crushing them underfoot.

Konell's eyes blazed red.

Without a moment of hesitation, he threw out a Venymlash, but Viktor diverted the poison with The Protection Spell, the area around his hand distorted like a mirage. Then, he brought his fists together in an upward motion. Tiles flew, detaching from the theater floor and hitting the assassin in the chest as he rushed in. Konell yelped, flying over his captor's back and falling hard into the theater's black limestone seats, bruised.

The King turned, looking down on him.

"Are you done?! Now get your stuff! I feel no shame for having outsmarted you—especially now, where you buy your sister undeserved punishment! You buy her lashes so you can make your little snide remarks! Your stupidity brought you to this point; you've done this to yourself! I'm trying to teach you how to be an even more skilled fighter, and you complain! Whatever—you've got to deal with it, or Amara won't get her medicine today, either. I'd hate for her to suffer twenty lashes without a painkiller."

Konell growled in rebellion, but finally he submitted, hitting the ground with his fist.

I'll find some excuse to postpone the girl's punishment till after the battle with Astria. If he survives, I'll forgive him and "spare" her.

I'm not a total monster, but I can't let him know that.

Viktor threw the ring back at Konell, bonking him in the nose. The ring fell to the ground with a clink, spinning loudly. Eventually, it stilled, the assassin slowly picking it up.

"Now, put your ring back on and wait for further instructions. If you ever defy me again; Amara dies. I've been very lenient with you so far, given you my grace. I even humored your little attempt at violence. Now, you will learn a different kind of fighting, more advanced magic."

"And you, Adam..."

Viktor turned.

"Pick up that sword; don't leave it in the sand like that. I'll make you a man of war."

CHAPTER XIII

Skotathis

The woman he sought was nailed to the ground by her feet, long, rusty, iron spikes keeping her from being taken away by the wind and sand. Wisps of dry, peeling skin hung off of her branch-like arms like cicada shells, her ears upturned like dried apricots. Her bony limbs were pronated against their natural range of motion, and the desiccated muscle that covered them was as brown as mahogany.

The woman's mouth was drawn into a grimace, teeth crawling with tiny, black beetles. Her hair was a dry mummy-red, and much of her rubbery, wrinkled face was splotched with a faint, irregular, pink birthmark. Her empty eye-sockets were like two pits, but she wasn't dead. She had been skinned alive and plastinated with Shadowrise sap, a single tree in a petrified wood.

Just as it does with steel, Shadowrise sap hardens things, makes them last an eternity... But I see that you've learned that already, Mother. How do you like immortality now?

Though they were disfigured and ugly, the woman's ears still worked. She heard Skotathis' footsteps. Blind, she didn't know they were his footsteps.

"Help," the woman croaked. Her lips cracked at the edges.

"Help."

"I'm sorry, Mother, but I can't," The Adversary responded almost sympathetically.

Luteana Xandren wasn't conscious enough to understand that it was actually her eldest son who was speaking to her, the man who had punished her in brutal fashion for not supporting his claim to the throne.

Good thing I only need your subconscious...

She tried to move her arms, creaking, but they were too stiff, too gnarled to move.

Again: "Help."

"Stop being silly, Mother; The Process is irreversible; you know that. But I wouldn't help you even if I could... Don't you remember?You betrayed me," Skotathis reminded her, his tone infantilizing.

In desperation, the talking tree learned a new word, his mother's vocabulary growing slightly larger.

"Please," she begged. Her tone was pleading, almost recognizable as human. Skotathis' tone was cold.

"No. Your treason brought you here, Mother, and for your sins, your body will stand here until there's nothing left but rusted nails."

The Adversary threw back his arms, boastful. "But rejoice, for I am a loving god. I won't leave you here to see all that—at least, not the part of you that matters."

Skotathis Called Lighteater, the crystal machete rippling with zebra stripes of color. It was not a Fallstreak, but a Devourer's Sword, a sword The Living Universe produced from memory out of Lifeblood. As such, it required no blueprint, no Callring that could be lost or stolen.

"Please!" his mother crowed, vocal cords rattling.

The Adversary shook his head, brow furrowing.

"You're just like The Tremite Queen, constantly moving around inside my head—constantly blabbering! You don't even know what it is you're asking for! You don't even know what you're talking about, do you?"

The talking tree stopped talking.

"That's what I thought," he retorted. With an effortless swing, Skotathis cut down the tree and decapitated his own mother, her head falling to the ground.

He blithely picked up the severed head and threw it over his shoulder, holding it by the hair like a thief would hold a sack.

Luteana continued to move her lips—begging, pleading. Skotathis continued walking, paying her no mind. Like every other crime, any remorse he should have felt was eaten away by the Tremite, the horrid thing moving, always moving.

Time to find out where you really are, Luxyruss. You always were a mama's boy... There must be something she knows, someplace I haven't thought to look. I'll glean all the insight I can glean from this eggshell of a head and find you. I can't keep looking over my shoulder.

Skotathis Evanesced once more, securing his mother's head in the crook of his arm.

As he left them to their suffering, the hundreds of other trees trembled and groaned. Faces contorted in agony, they reached out, as if searching for release.

Amdryaan

When the icebreaker struck ground, The Trialoim fortified themselves within their enchanted, wooden walls, equipping atlatls with throwing spears.

Amdryaan put his hands up in a sign of surrender.

I really hope they don't attack.

"People of The Trialoim—please listen to me! I have children here! I've come with children from your sister Tribe!"

I should've expected this, especially since they probably know what happened to The Aerhauc by now. If they attack the ship, I'll be dead before I can say "sealskin." Those spears are just whittled branches, and my powers don't work on wood. I won't be able to get below deck in time.

They probably think I'm a slaver. I need to show them the kids before I become a human pincushion.

Amdryaan took hold of Ritsi by the waist and lifted her. Then he did the same with Mobo. The children called out to The Trialoim, waving their arms. They spoke in a different dialect than they had spoken in The Aerhauc Settlement.

To the tribesman's great relief, the bristling atlatls were lowered.

Finally, we found them.

Amdryaan threw down the gangplank. The doors to the Settlement opened; the children ran down the platform. They ran off the icebreaker and away from him as fast as they could—like they were running from a plague.

Somewhere deep inside, this hurt Amdryaan. In their minds, he was a harbinger of loss.

But I tried to save your village. I was just too late... I tried to save your Tribe King, but it was too late. The attack wasn't my fault, was it?

The children's relatives came out from the huddled masses beyond the walls. They took them into their arms—hugging them, kissing them. Aunts and uncles, grandparents and cousins, they mourned the loss of their sister tribe, the children's loss of innocence.

Amdryaan walked down the gangplank as well. He wasn't sure if he should even be there.

Members of the tribe came forward, moved. They touched his hands, offering him gifts, and praising him in bits and pieces of The Universal Tongue. Outwardly, Amdryaan smiled, but inside, he was full of woe. He wondered if they could feel the blood rub off on their fingers, if they knew the sort of man he was.

You are all blinded by your compassion, your grief... But I know the sort of man I am... I corrupted Oscure.

I had great power, granted to me by the divine, but I couldn't save The Aerhauc.

It shouldn't be this way... I'm Amdryaan, son of Kanis Winterlove... I should be a strong leader who stands for hope. But that's not how it is...

These people... If they can give me food, I will take it. If they can give me shelter, I will take it.

But their praise... I don't want that.

Once I resupply, I'm leaving for Cairnon, and then, The Ice Fields. I will go to rescue the imprisoned. I'm leaving The Ice Fields so that I can return stronger than I was before.

Seeing it from the inside, The Trialoim Settlement was a small but well-fortified beachside village—a cluster of sturdy, square huts with triangular roofs. Made of grainy, brown palm wood, they held fast, even so close to the sea. The community was surrounded by twenty foot walls of the same material, each "board" consisting of what was, in essence, an entire tree, glimmering with enchantment. The source of the enchanting liquid was unclear.

Beyond the walls, were makeshift ramparts made of cecropia wood, which stood on whole, whittled cecropia saplings, lashed together with reeds and grass, and connected to long ladders.

Tanning racks laden with exotic skins and raised, wooden spits holding up fish, tapirs and wild boars stood at the center of the Settlement flanking a large, wooden table, used for communal meals. Nearby, iron cauldrons rattled. Food—bathed in colorful spices—was cooking.

Beyond the table, was The Tribe King's Hut, made of black palm wood. It stood taller than the rest, with a triangular, thatched roof made of banana leaves, and a wide balcony. The structure balanced on thick, square, wooden stilts, suspended over a hill of packed sand. It could only be entered by climbing up a set of winding, wooden stairs to the right of the dune, and its entrance was barred by a solid, wooden door, unlike the welcoming, open entrances of the other huts.

The Settlement itself had two entrances, guarded by wooden double doors. Past the southern door, a dusty footpath had been carved into the jungle—a water route.

Amdryaan breathed in deeply, sighing.

The sands below his feet were a greyish-brown, and the sky above was a pale blue, filled with fluffy cumulus clouds. The air that day was warm, with a gentle breeze, and the water in front of the Settlement was a pretty, light blue that caught the eye, but the scenery was not as vibrant as that of The Aerhauc Settlement. Behind him, waves rushed again and again across the black, stone beach, fading to a sort of background noise over which birds of paradise could be heard. Above these sounds, came the occasional shout of criers at the door and the blast of a large, conch shell horn, which was used to mark the passing of time.

Though the Settlement was full of activity, The Trialoim were not as loud or as lively as the Aerhauc had been. Children helped their mothers with tanning and cooking, while men skinned the spitted animals and prepared fresh-caught fish. With a low *creak*, the doors opened to let in a group of spear-fishermen, who carried sharp sticks made of ironwood, and smiled at the village toddlers as they marveled over the latest catch. Though the men projected confidence, the doors were hastily shut behind them, and Amdryaan saw fear hiding behind their happy faces.

Their neighbors had just been attacked.

Descending the spiral staircase, The King of The Trialoim came down to meet his visitor. Fairly unassuming, he had a soft voice and dun, watery eyes, but he cut a sharp figure in his tribal regalia, wearing blue robes, adorned with gold thread, and a cylindrical, red hat.

One of the only Nolites in the tribe fluent with The Universal Tongue, he greeted Amdryaan warmly, ushering him to sit at the central table. His subjects followed suit.

"Traveler, my name is Zawichi, and I am the King of this tribe. What is your name?"

"Amdryaan," the Native answered.

"Amdryaan... My advisors have told me what you did for the children. You have done us a service we can scarce repay, but we will try. Come sup with us. I wish to hear your story."

Amdryaan smiled weakly. "Okay," he replied, doing as he was told.

He wasn't sure where to begin.

Jhett

At the edge of sleep, Jhett heard his wife's voice.

Jhettisquan... Open your eyes.

Jhett!

The tribesman sprung up. A maple headboard creaked behind him.

He patted his chest, frantic, trying to find the wound he had sustained fighting The Necroscorum. He was looking for the hole in his heart, but it was gone—all gone.

Jhett itched like he was covered in army ants, an army with a hundred thousand legs. Neuronic tendrils of pain and irritation travelled along his ribs.

What?! I thought— I thought I was dead...

No, wait a minute... I— I think I healed myself. I was awake, helping the others, and then...

But how?

The tribesman's memory was fuzzy. He remembered almost nothing after The Necroscorum's attack, a stinger like Fvedam's fist bursting through his chest. The spiked barb had pierced him, going through skin, and then his spine, liver, and heart. He remembered falling down to the dust, his back torn to ribbons against the demon's shell, though he was a Nolite, and Nolites couldn't be cut. The Tribes of The Wildlands had known that forever, using percussive weapons to bludgeon their opponents into submission. Even in death, Nolite skin didn't completely break down, remaining as a net of yellow-white fibers, hard as teeth but flexible, resembling a tamarind husk.

How am I alive? How is this possible?

Jhett looked around. He was in a lavish room, more lavish than any he had ever seen.

It had been so long since he had had a well-made ceiling above his head, that he thought he was dreaming.

But I'm not dreaming... I couldn't have imagined a room like this if I tried.

Am I dead? Is this some other world?

Jhett had been born in a hut of wood and straw. When he was older, he had slept in the open air with the other warriors of the Tribe, huddled in bivouacs of bark and sticks. When he was a galley slave, all he had known was mud, rotting wood, and isopods.

He had never, ever seen such a room. The walls were painted a rich, chocolate-brown, and the ceiling was swirled with white. The floor was covered almost entirely by a soft, beige rug, and he lay in a feather bed with shimmering, beige-colored sheets, feather pillows, and a deeply-colored, red, silk canopy hanging above, which was embroidered with bees done in gold thread. A standing, rectangular, gold-framed mirror stood on the left side of the room just past the wooden door, which had a polished, silver handle. A few feet in front of the bed, sat a chest of drawers, topped with a white-and-blue vase with purple flowers inside, freshly cut. The chest had been placed in front of a glass window with brown, wooden shutters, the flowers and sunlight helping to ease his mind a little.

To his right, was a wooden nightstand with a small, glass bottle of water and a silver candle-holder, though there was no need for additional light in the bright, sunny room, and there was no candle to burn.

When Jhett looked out the window, he saw only bushes. He listened for the sea.

He thanked his ancestors when he heard it.

Since he had escaped the galley, he had been reveling in his ability to walk, run, and jump unimpeded, but there was still a handicap he couldn't escape, a handicap the merchants had shackled him with: he needed the sea to relax—needed it more, even, than when he had lived in The Aerhauc Settlement.

Maybe I'm just broken... the tribesman mulled.

I know that I should be scared of the ocean, but after seeing what I have seen, it no longer holds any fear for me. I've already dredged its depths, seen its nightmares. The worst terrors lurk not beneath the sea. They sail above.

Jhett balled the sheets up in his hands, taking a deep breath and cracking his neck.

The room was warm and dry, a pleasant change from the sweaty damp of the galley. There was a sweetness in the air, coming from the flowers in the vase, and beyond that, he smelled the stronger, more rugged scents of leather and musk. At the end of the day, however, what most pleased his nose, was that the air was fresh.

Hearing a thump from the floor above, Jhett glanced at the ceiling. At the leftmost corner of the room, was a solitary spiderweb, a tiny, black spinstress working tirelessly on a web doomed to be swept up like all the ones before.

Wearing only a pair of cotton underwear, the tribesman removed the sheets from his body, a crackle of static, and turned, slowly placing his feet on the carpet.

Jhett gasped as his feet sank into the softness.

Everything was alien to him.

This is...a little difficult.

Though the tribesman was well-rested, he was thirsty. It felt like he had swallowed a barrel of salt. He reached for the bottle on the nightstand and drank it greedily, but it was contemptibly small.

The Nolite sighed, wiping his mouth. The mattress compressed beneath him.

It seems that the nobles found help, and took me with them like they promised. That's the only explanation...

As Jhett came to this conclusion, the silver door knob turned, and the room opened.

Eight, gorgeous servant girls entered in a flutter, carrying feather dusters and other cleaning appliances. They wore elegant, black outfits, with white, lace aprons and white, lace trim. Though their outfits were ostensibly cute, they wore heavy, iron bracelets whose significance was unknown to him.

When the maids saw Jhett standing there, half nude, they all scrambled out, giggling. The tribesman was confused.

Do they not see The Brand?

A couple of minutes later, four handsome, male servants came in the girls' stead, bringing him new clothes. They were led by a tall, Luzian man in a gold doublet. The man had coiffed, shiny, brown hair and a chiseled jaw.

Like the women, the male servants wore beaten metal bracelets on their right wrists. Jhett slowly understood what that meant. Although they looked well-fed and healthy, wearing neither shackles nor chains, they weren't free. The bracelets were too small to come off, and they had been enchanted to prevent rust or breakage.

Eschewing words, the servants began to clean. Their leader put Jhett's garments on the bed in a neatly folded pile: a cinnamon doublet with bronze, spiral embroidery, a pair of brown, cotton trousers, a black, leather belt with bronze studs, and a matching set of shoes, made of suede.

Jhett had never worn such luxurious clothes in his life. They looked like something the merchants would wear, and that was off-putting, but he couldn't complain.

"Where am I?" the tribesman asked.

The lead servant answered him, his tone cool, but formal.

"You are in a guest room of The Imperial Palace under the hospitality of the new High Emperor, Torran Xandromen. His Grace has asked The Overseer of The Public Health, Lord Sigmund Jiralt, to attend you. The Lord will be with you shortly to explain everything."

"Please cover up," he added. "The girls were sent in to clean your room."

With that, the male servants left the room as well.

So Torran rules the world now... the tribesman considered. *This is all so strange.*

Jhett got dressed. At first, he put his new belt on backwards, but he got it right the second time around . He wasn't sure why the leather had so many holes when only one of them fit him well.

The tribesman stretched. The clothing was comfortable, and the bed had been very plush and stable, admirable qualities in a bed, but it was a challenging transition for him, going from slavery to luxury, and his body ached.

Thinking about the past, Jhett's wrists and ankles began to hurt. They were truly scarred, more scarred than his arms and neck, which had been scarred on purpose. The scars ran deeper than even he could see.

I swear that I will put an end to the slave trade. No longer will Nolites live in fear.

Wherever my brothers live in chains, I will break those chains and make them men again. And when I am done—when I am done—I will put an end to The Fivefinger Tribe and The Quorkorath forever.

Yes, that's what I'll do... I will find my family and then return to my Tribe, return in glory.

Those men who brought me clothes, they were servants, practically slaves—so were those women. That's why they wore iron bands around their wrists, though they bear no scars. They live lives of subservience.

No more. From now on, I won't let them do anything else for me. The Continental Nations may have a different culture than The Aerhauc Tribe, but Torran promised me that he would help me put an end to the slave trade. Now I see that I can'tjust end the slave trade; I must end forced servitude altogether. I will try and convince Torran to let them go.

He said that he would give me anything in his power, reward me for my help. His power now is close to limitless, and I know what I want. I'll return this world to a world of honor, a world where the Law is followed.

The Aerhauc didn't take servants or prisoners of war, as sparing an opponent would dishonor them. Likewise, the killing of innocents was a crime worthy of exile or death, as, under The Law of Madevf, all wars ended on the battlefield. To spare an opponent in battle meant that the warrior didn't have the courage to take their opponent's life, or their opponent was too weak to pose a threat. An opponent who no longer posed a threat was pathetic and as good as dead, and to hesitate out of fear made one a coward. Killing outside the battlefield showed that the warrior wasn't strong enough to fight their opponent face-to-face, winning through trickery or surprise.

Jhett knew shame well, having been a galley slave for so long; he knew dishonor. But he would never break The Law of Madevf.

With a creak, the door opened for a third time.

A man, who Jhett assumed was Lord Sigmund Jiralt, walked up to him as he finished tying his shoes.

"Hello, Jhett. My name is Sigmund Jiralt. I'm his Grace's Imperial Advisor and The Overseer of The Public Health. I took care of you while you were sleeping. Though I didn't see anything, he said that you suffered significant trauma to your chest, and you've been asleep for the past three days... How do you feel?"

I feel...very strange, but I am happy to be alive. I thought I was dead. Your work must be blessed by Madevf."

"Thank you, but I'm afraid I did very little. You came here in a coma, but there wasn't a scratch on your body. I've never seen anything quite like it. You did have some swelling, but I lowered it. It was hard to inject fluids or bloodlet anything from you, as your skin is quite thick, but I managed. If you feel any pain from the procedures, let me know."

None of this makes any sense. I remember it well—I was cut; I was pierced. Now this man says he pierced my skin as well.

"How did you get through my skin?" Jhett asked, his accent thick.

"Ah, that. I used an enchanted needle. I had never used one before, but the stories of its effectiveness were not exaggerated. If Sage Shakar can be believed, your people's skin cannot be cut by anything except enchanted steel, obsidian, and diamond. Anything less will bend or break against the Nolite epidermal shell."

Obsidian... Diamond...

"I must say, your fluency in The Universal Tongue is quite commendable, Jhett. Tell me—where did you acquire such a skill?"

"I... I was a galley slave, rowing for a Qeonian merchant ship. I heard the merchants speaking on deck and so I learned as well."

The Lord stopped.

"Oh... I'm so sorry. His Grace, High Emperor Agravius, outlawed the slave trade years ago, but with the rebellions of The Second War of Unification, he wasn't able to enforce the law."

Jhett ground his jaw, brushing stubble.

"If he created a law but did not enforce it, then I do not understand him. In the end, I simply do not understand this place. What are all these things in the room, what is an "Overseer," and why were the girls who came in afraid of me?"

"Afraid of you?" The Overseer of The Public Health puzzled. Then he laughed, understanding. "Our land is full of things I'm sure you've never seen, but many Astrians are in the dark as well. Most peasants have never seen the kind of riches The Xandromen Dynasty has... As for the servant girls, it wasn't fear that made them leave. You got out of bed without any clothes on, and, well—can you blame them?"

"I do not understand."

What are you talking about?

"Don't worry about it, friend. They can't see what I see. You weren't trying to be indecent. I see that you're a married man from the triangular scars on your neck, but the girls would have had no idea. Our customs differ from yours, and there are bound to be some misunderstandings, but I think you will find that we are all similar in the ways that matter... Anyway, allow me to lead you to the dining room so you can eat. You must be starving. Once you've regained your strength, I'd be glad to show you around the city if you wish. That way, we can learn about each other's culture. Oh, and by the way, Jhett—please don't take anything people say to you to heart. I know it will be difficult, but the people here are largely ignorant about The Wildlands. Even I haven't seen them in person, and many of my medicines originate there... All I know about your people, I know from the books I've read."

"I do not know how to read. My people are not interested in writing everything down, as yours are. I have never read a "book.""

"Well... To be honest, you haven't really missed anything," The Overseer chuckled dryly.

Scarolette

Scarolette found Torran in his father's solar. She had only been there once before, when she had started her employ.

She didn't remember it being so cozy.

The room was warm, dust motes shimmering in the sunlight. Though it was small and cramped, filled to the brim with rolled-up parchment, it had a quaint allure. The air smelled of jasmine, which flowered behind the tall, yellowed, leaded glass window at the back of the room, white-pink blooms hidden behind fine, diamond-shaped cames.

No wonder his father loved it here. It's so comfortable...

The High Emperor's love for his solar was well known. Outside of Court or the occasional outing with Riane, he had spent the majority of his time holed up in his study. A sharp mind with a strong work ethic, Agravius worked tirelessly, if not obsessively, on his research, though no one knew what that research was about. He had kept it under wraps, getting all his books and scrolls delivered by The Sagery. And if the Sages knew what he had been up to, no one had revealed anything.

He must have spent a lot of time here, even during the War. Look at all these scrolls! So much parchment... What was he even doing with it all, eating it?!

Scarolette remembered when she had first met The High Emperor. Per Sigmund's recommendation, she had been assigned to be Riane's instructor in reading, writing, and etiquette. The day she was interviewed, the room had felt cold, The High Emperor a dark, imposing, almost faceless figure, sitting in his chair. But coming back from the War, the solar seemed small—too small for an Emperor—almost like a broom closet. She wondered why she had seen it differently.

Scarolette smiled when she saw the pictures tacked to the room's overburdened, wooden shelves. Drawn in bright, expensive colors, were rainbows, clouds, bees, and flowers—Riane's scribbled daydreams.

Scarolette felt a warmth in her chest. She had become something of a maternal figure to The High Princess, guiding her in the areas the girl's deceased mother had been unable to. Unfortunately, she had had to leave Riane behind when she was sent off to Hemia.

Poor Riane; I hope she doesn't think I avoided her...

Torran sent away before I even got the chance to see her, but I guess it's for the best... She'll be safer in Springhaven, and we'll see each other soon.

During the War, Scarolette's duty was to keep up correspondence with the crown and act as Torran's Imperial scribe. As such, she had travelled everywhere with Torran and his soldiers. Wherever the Company went, she also went, sending periodic updates to The High Emperor about the campaign's progress. At the time, she hadn't thought much about her selection for the job, but after everything that had happened, she suspected the old monarch had chosen her for reasons beyond mere competence.

Though he was already twenty by the time he left, The High Prince hadn't taken an interest in any of the noblewomen in the Court. Scarolette was a noblewoman, just not one of particularly high birth, so it made sense. Torran had little good to say about the many marriage partners The High Emperor had invited to the Palace, but he always had a compliment ready for her, even during the worst campaigns, even when he was injured and the company lay besieged behind shaking walls.

Scarolette's father, Lord Adiel Verana, had sent her to The Royal Academy in Starspire to get a proper education, which meant that she was, for all intents and purposes, an acceptable, if not optimal, match for the Prince. She had been single for a long time as well, and at the time when she received her position, her mother, Adeline, had seemed all too interested in setting her up with someone. In Lady Adeline's eyes, any man with so much as a gold tooth would do. Adiel's Imité addiction had put the family in a difficult position. However, when the earnings from the first month of tutoring came in, Scarolette helped her parents escape their financial pitfall, and they stopped pressing the issue. In fact, both her mother and her father had stopped writing to her altogether— at least, for the few months that it took for The Lord to gamble their house back into poverty, but by then, Scarolette had had enough of the manipulation and cut ties with her parents. She had been deeply hurt.

Scarolette had broken contact at the start of the War, resigning herself to the fact that she would be single forever, but even without her mother's constant nagging, she had found herself developing an attraction to The High Prince over the course of the campaign—fantasizing about him, even. Sometimes, she looked back and imagined that her mother would be happy, but then she remembered that the woman wouldn't be happy for the right reasons.

Thinking about the past, Scarolette became increasingly skeptical of the Emperor's choices, the real purpose of her journey with the Xandromen heir.

Did he know that we'd eventually fall in love? Was this destined, something prophesied in this unfathomable mess of scrolls? And, if so, what happens now? What happens now...

Scarolette looked at The High Prince, hardly believing that just days before, they had lain together, two castaways with no one else to turn to in their despair.

Torran stood behind his father's desk, peering into glass as it glowed, sunbeams trapped in faded honey. He was still, hands folded behind his back.

Poor Torran... His father's dead, and he had to comfort his little sister, too... I can't even imagine...

We came here for peace, but found another hellscape waiting for us.

"Scarolette. Thank you for coming." Torran's voice was terse. He didn't even meet her eyes.

For what seemed like a very long time, The High Emperor simply stood, saying nothing. Scarolette felt her stomach tighten. All the emotion she had seen, all the affection he had shown during the ordeal they had been through was replaced by flat affect, or so it seemed.

Scarolette had heard that tone from him a couple of times before. It was his protection from pain, one which came out when he didn't want to deal with the horrors of war, the horrors that had been forced upon him by his father. Torran had seen friends die in brutal manner—events that should have broken him—but when it came time to grieve, he simply clenched his teeth in an unsmiling, dead stare.

Torran was bottling it all up.

I wish he'd open his heart to me, let himself be vulnerable for once. But by nature, he is invulnerable, and he won't grieve in front of me. I suspect he will never grieve at all...

"Torran, are you alright?" Scarolette asked, breaking the silence.

I'm here, Torran. You can talk to me. Just say what you need to say.

"Scarolette..." Torran's voice trailed off.

The young High Emperor met her eyes, stepping away from the window. He looked
distracted.

"I... I just wanted to tell you something. I'm leaving for Qeonia on the morrow."

"What?!" Scarolette shouted. She lowered her voice. "Torran, you just got back, and you're not even in the shape to fight, are you?! I mean—you'll get killed out there! Can't you send one of your Generals in your place?! Does it have to be right now?!"

The monarch looked like he was about to laugh. This upset her.

Torran smiled a depressed smile.

"I would do anything for you, Scarolette, but what do you suggest? Which Generals? I see no one I can trust, no one who can help. The High Sword is busy rebuilding Sunveil, and Ilidar can't even stand. My armies are diminished, pieces moved around the board so much that their heads are spinning like windmills. All the while, the Nations plot to overthrow The High Empire! The assassin hasn't been found; The Outpost is gone! Not to mention the demons at our gates."

The High Emperor sighed, stroking his jaw.

"Scarolette, you of all people should know that I want this to end. I want us to be together, for our relationship to grow like normal people's, and I think you do too. If there was any other choice I would make it, but there is no other choice! The Divinity himself has placed his faith in me, placed his faith in me because he can't fix this mess alone. I have to do this."

Torran turned away from her again, aggrieved. He faced the window, his posture crumpling, but he didn't send her away. He didn't send her away, but he refused to cry in front of her. He wanted someone to hold, but did not take hold of her.

Torran's eyes were haunted, his voice low, and wavering delicately.

He spoke.

"Does it not anguish you, Scarolette? That this life cannot be changed? That there's no choice, but to live and die in this world just like those who came before us? How can people stand to live in a world without truth or meaning?"

Scarolette swallowed, putting together the right words. She reached out, trembling, and then put her hand on his shoulder, not as a caress, but as reassurance. This did not call for seduction or sweet, carnal comfort. This was slate—dark grey—stone eroding under a waterfall of bad emotions. She had to be pure, in both thought and intent.

I must respond with the greatest truth I know.

"There is always a choice, Torran. Just because we're all born to travel the same path doesn't mean that we can't walk it differently from those who came before. Of course, I wish that things were better. After all, everyone wants the path to be longer and not shorter, not rougher, but smoother. Everyone wishes that the scenery was more beautiful and that problems would not arise along the way... Then again, if things were perfect, one might wish for challenge, for hardship, given enough time. But wishing changes nothing. The world is unfair."

Scarolette wanted to embrace softness and not hardness, but instead, she hardened her resolve, and kept going.

"Every time you take a seat, stop moving down the path, you succeed with no rebellion. The brambles close in around you, forcing you to walk a straighter, shorter line than you originally had. It is wretched; I agree. But would you rather sit and wait? For how long? Is an eternity enough? Would you rather cry?"

Torran jumped slightly.

Maybe that was a little harsh.

Scarolette kept on going, digging deep.

"And would you really want a universal truth? Would you want to know the same thing as everybody else? Would you really want some meaning handed to you? What if it's disappointing? What if it rings hollow for you?"

She stopped. "We only get this life—as many years as are handed to us. It's unfortunate; I know. But it's our choice to use those years, or throw them away. It's our choice to become the people we want to be."

Torran looked into the slowly melting glass and embraced the wastes.

"Haa... But it isn't our choice, Scarolette—not really. Every one of us has obligations. It's not just the world that's unfair. It's desire. Man can't choose what he feels, and what he feels is more powerful than what he wants. I tried to draw my own path, years ago. I tried to cut through the brambles, find meaning for myself. But the world didn't want me to. I tried to do the things I wanted, the things that felt right, and I was punished for it. So I changed to suit the world, but when I changed, my punishment didn't end. My father didn't once praise me, even after five years of fighting, after wasting my life doing what I hate. I could have walked away, then, pushed through thorns and pain to be free. But now, he's dead, and God himself tells me that I must continue doing what I hate, or my countrymen will die. It makes me feel horrible, but what should I do? Scorn God, curse my countrymen, throw away my obligations? How could I live like that? How would I live with myself? If doing what I want is tantamount to evil, then what choice exists?! The choice to feel horrible now or feel horrible later?!"

"No, Torran. It's not just you. Everyone chooses their own path in life. Some are born with power, and it's honorable for them to use that power to help others. But just like our lives are limited, the power of a single person is also limited. You're not responsible for everyone. You can't save everyone. Your first obligation is to yourself and to those who mean the most to you. I'm not saying you should throw your duty away. I'm not saying this world is great, or even good. But I think you should rely on others. Ask for help along the way. You don't need to shoulder such a heavy burden by yourself... If God himself can't carry such burdens alone, why would you be able to? "

"I— I don't know," he breathed.

Scarolette continued.

"Now listen. There's a book that I found, a book that explains some of the mysterious things that have been happening to us. There are encrypted passages within the book that I believe will teach us how to use magic. If you can bring in some Sages to help decode it, we might be able to understand our powers. We might be able to fix everything and restore peace."

The High Emperor turned abruptly to face her, almost angrily, but he wasn't angry. He was anguished, a look of sad exasperation written on his face. He was on the verge of looking down on her for naïvete, but he did not. He was arguing with himself, more than he was with her.

"Scarolette, who do you think we are?! We're caught in a cataclysm, a cataclysm even The Divinity can't stop, and you think we can "fix everything," "restore peace?" There's nothing we can do..."

Torran pinched his nose bridge with his fingers. "You probably take me for some maltheist, lost in nihilism." He leaned against his father's desk and brushed the hair out of his eyes, one with the gloom.

"Scarolette...you need to understand. You didn't see what I saw. For you, the War was writing messages, crying as you delivered bad news. Surviving in the wild is one thing. Surviving war is another... When I returned from Lonecastle, my head was filled with delusions. I believed that I was a master of the sword, that I was unstoppable in battle. I was the perfect cadet, and I dreamed of heroism and grandeur, bolstered by my one and only victory in Goldenknife. I captured a group of starving rebels, armed with sticks and farmer's knives, and thought I was ready for war..."

The monarch's tone grew bitter.

"You weren't there when we launched the assault on Ravenshear. You stayed in your tent, writing to my father. I charged into battle, breaking away from my squadron... I knew all the cuts, every obscure move—but it didn't matter. I thought I had gone through hell, those five, long years, but I had seen nothing. There, on the battlefield, I saw men gutted, screaming for their mothers. In the first few minutes, I was beaten close to death, completely incapacitated... My squadron pulled away from their position to come to my aid. Five men died for me, the sixth reaching the battle-medics before succumbing to blood loss. I was their Prince, you see... My father had given me back my title, and suddenly, my life was worth more than theirs. I wasn't their hero. I wasn't even their friend. I was nothing to them. They died for me because it was expected."

"You took the city!" Scarolette interjected, shaking.

Torran's voice was cold and sure.

"No, I didn't. The city fell, but I didn't contribute anything at all. My incompetence cost those men their lives. Their lives paid for my own, an unfair trade... You ask me why I refuse help, why I act alone. Maybe now you understand. I can't bear that debt. I have no choice but to fight."

Scarolette balled up her fists, balled up all her good and human feelings. She knew she sounded childish, but she responded anyway.

"I'm sorry you had to go through all that. It must have been very difficult. No one should have to face such hardship. But even if the world is crumbling once again, you aren't looking at the good that remains. We killed a demon; we found out that the golden eagles are alive! We gained powers which can help us in the coming conflict, if we can only find out how to use them. We found each other... We made new friends—powerful friends who are willing to fight for what's right. If you say you must fight, so be it. You're The High Emperor; we will follow you. But at least, do not fight alone."

Scarolette looked at him, breathless, feeling ridiculous, but compelled to do everything she could to cut through the cold, the dense layer of fog that had solidified between her and Torran.

"You need to let go of this darkness! In the dark, it can be easy to forget what we have, but darkness only hides what is there; it can never take it away! We're back home after five, long years! Your sister has grown up into a beautiful, young girl, and she'll be safe and happy with her cousins in Springhaven! You get to see your best friend, Ilidar, every single day! He and Jhett have gotten treated, and are going to pull through. There are many reasons to despair. But there are many reasons to count your blessings. You're now in the highest position in the land; you can make changes your father couldn't..."

Scarolette flushed.

"And don't make it out like sleeping with me is bad either, because we both know it isn't," she added, hot embarrassment.

Damn it. I said I wouldn't do this, but I can't say it doesn't hurt my pride a little.

The High Emperor looked up, shocked. Not backing down lest she become totally ridiculous, she shot him a coquettish grin, her eyes a clear green.

Torran flushed, emerging from the dark.

"Yes—the past couple nights have been really...nice," he whispered, his cheeks pink.

The Emperor frowned.

"I'm sorry I raised my voice at you. I shouldn't have done that. You're right—about everything. Things are bad right now, but I shouldn't get lost in negativity. I am now The High Emperor, and I can't be reckless. My father's greatest weakness was letting his emotions guide his rule. I can't just leave in pursuit of my own revenge. If we're going to pay Qeonia back, we're going to do it right. I won't die carelessly, and I won't take my men with me to the grave, not if I can help it. I'll call a meeting with The High Council to prepare a proper strategy."

Thank goodness, Scarolette thought to herself, relieved. Though the weight could not be taken off his shoulders, she had at least helped him avoid disaster. And though she had given him the best counsel she could, he would have to choose his path alone.

I can't decide for you... I only hope that you'll make the right choice.

"Thank you, Scarolette," the High Emperor murmured, his eyes shining. He pulled her in close, kissing her hair.

Scarolette smiled. He felt stronger, then, more sure, though she couldn't fully let go of her misgivings.

The couple kissed, their noses touching briefly.

Torran broke away. "Thank you for reminding me what I stand to lose."

Flind

What a horrible morning... I've got a splitting headache.

Flind touched the back of her ear, her arm aching.

It was both hot and sore, her eyes nearly swollen shut. She looked through the narrow, puffy slits, surroundings shadowed by her long, dark eyelashes. She was in someone else's bed; she could tell by the smell—lanolin, salt, and sweat.

Though Flind was awake, she hadn't fully taken a hold of her senses yet, her mind jumping from theory to flimsy theory. She didn't remember having slept with anyone, but lanolin was used for keeping weapons and armor clean. Had she gotten drunk; slept with some hunky soldier passing through town? She had always found soldiers attractive... But then why was she so injured?

That would explain some of this, but nah, I would never do that; would I?

Had she been hit by a cart, or something? The last thing Flind remembered, was that she had gone to market to buy a duck. Cook was going to prepare a nice meal out of it, brine it in honey and mead, and serve it for dinner.

Yeah, I must have been in an accident! But where am I now?

Maybe I'm at The Manor nursery...

Yes, I must have been hit by a cart! Damn those cart pullers!

With a rustle, a shadowy figure approached, looming over her.

Flind opened her eyes a little further, seeing braided hair.

Green hair. She had never known anyone with green hair.

Could it be the Mistress?

No, it can't be the Mistress.

Who is this person? How did they dye their hair that color?

"Where am I? What's happened to me?" the scullion asked, groggy. She tried sitting up, but couldn't.

Flind was getting scared. The figure remained unspeaking, and she felt dizzy.

"Stay away, whoever you are!" she pleaded. "Please, stay back!"

The figure spoke. It was the voice of a young woman, kind and gentle.

"Flind, calm down. Do you recognize me? It's Leafsong. You got injured in the fight and broke your skull."

"Lady Leafsong?!" Flind sputtered.

There was a fight?! My skull is broken?!

The maid began to panic.

"I beg your pardon, my Lady, but was the estate attacked?! Are you alright; are your parents alright?! The Baron and Baroness—did something bad happen to them?!"

"No, the estate—" Leafsong broke off. "Wait a minute—why are you asking me that? And why are you addressing me as "my Lady?" I never told you who I was. And why do you speak like you know my parents?" The woman's tone was suspicious, almost repulsed.

Flind was at a complete loss.

"Uh...Lady Leafsong, not to be impolite, but I work for your parents, so how could I not know them? How could I not know you? Perhaps you don't know my face, but I clean the Manor and help the cook. You must have seen me at least once before? Anyway, even if you don't know me, I know you. What I don't know is what happened. I don't remember any sort of fight, and I can't really open my eyes. And maybe I'm not seeing right, but your hair looks green right now. I must be hurt pretty badly if my vision's so messed up..."

The young heiress didn't respond.

"Lady Leafsong, are you still there?! My Lady!"

Please don't leave me alone! I don't know what's happening to me!

Why are my eyes so bruised?! Who broke my head?! And how?!

And I can't believe you don't know who I am... You must have seen me at least once... Am I that forgettable?

Flind was going crazy; no response came. Then, two fingers touched her temple, and the amnesiac fog cleared.

Flind's memories returned to her, reforming the fragmented whole. In a flash of lights and colors, she began re-experiencing all the lost time. Because she was a Seer, Leafsong experienced it all with her.

As the memories passed, Flind's confusion was replaced by dread. She had killed the woman's father, destroyed The Ralei Manor and then lied about it all, acting like she was a stranger to the Baroness and The Stillvein Raleis. She had pretended to be a Lātist fanatic, a key player in The Third Cairnian Civil War.

I said I was...

Flind's lies fell apart like rags. She was at Leafsong's mercy.

Ilidar

Lord Sigmund Jiralt opened the door, wheeling Ilidar into The High Council meeting.

Apart from The Overseer of The Public Health, The High Council was composed of Lord Sheru, The Overseer of Finance, Lord Millington, The

Overseer of Agriculture, and Lord Sïdermann, The Overseer of Smithing.

Lord Sheru was a thin man, with discerning, dark green eyes, close-cropped, reddish-brown hair, and a receding hairline. A set of small, round spectacles with gold frames sat at the tip of his long, thin, nose, attached to his neck by a gold chain. Though he was one of The High Officials, the Lord was very frugal, and he worked very hard to properly manage the crown's finances. He wore beige, cotton robes that made him look more like a monk than a Lord, and his fingers were always stained with ink. His glasses were probably the most expensive thing on him. The man carried his ledger with him everywhere, which was barely held together by a cover made of beaten-up, dark brown leather. The book left a trail of wood pulp and leather dust everywhere he went, a sort of breadcrumb trail that one could use to track his movements through the Palace.

Lord Millington was a calm man, with long, wavy, golden-brown hair and clever, brown eyes. He wore a bluebird-blue doublet, double-slashed with gold.

Lord Sidermann was a short, but handsome man, with a stubbled face, coiffed, dark brown hair, and honey-colored eyes. He wore an ochre, corduroy doublet and a pair of brown, cotton trousers.

They were already discussing the plan of attack.

"...and then we change the sails to purple. The Qeonian navy..."

There was a break in the conversation. Ilidar's wheelchair squeaked.

Torran looked up from the map tacked to the large, circular, wooden table at the center of the room, his eyes bloodshot. The High Council Members stood, acknowledging The Captain's arrival, then sat back down in their chairs.

Though Ilidar was his old friend, the Emperor addressed him in a formal and authoritative tone. He was doing everything he could to show strength.

He needs to in such a time of war...

"Captain Inverniquist—thank you for coming. Lord Jiralt, would you be so kind as to help the Captain to his seat?"

"Of course, your Grace," The Overseer answered. He wheeled Ilidar up to the table and helped him into his chair.

"Thank you," The High Emperor said. Sigmund nodded.

"Now, gentlemen, what were we discussing again? Oh, yes...subterfuge. High Staff, why don't you go over your plan for the naval assault again? Now that Lord Jiralt and the Captain are in attendance, I would like to hear their opinion as well."

Ilidar had seen The High Staff a couple of times, but he didn't know him very well. In charge of The Imperial Navy, the High Official was usually at sea.

Ilidar met the man's eyes.

The High Staff was a proud, boot-faced man in his early fifties. He wore a well-starched uniform: dark blue, with gold-tasseled shoulders, but his bulging gut stuck out from under the fabric, and his overgrown, curly, grey hair was unruly and matted. His jowls sagged, a perpetual frown on his face, but for all of his pomposity and bluster, he was not a man beyond reason. That reason simply took a long time to set in, and involved a lot of loud, booming protestation.

The High Staff didn't seem to like Torran's suggestion, but he went through with it anyway.

"Very well, your Grace," the man coughed. He picked up a piece from the table—a ship, painted blue—and placed it at home port on the map. He began tracing the path he thought the Astrian ships should take for the assault on Clearwater.

"To reiterate—under this plan, our ships would hug the northern coast, then skirt Saharr. From Spider Crab Point, we would cross The Sea of Sāltrimorix and make our way to Harcrome's Point. We would then send in a small fleet of ships with purple flags as a distraction. Thinking it's a pirate raid, The Qeonian Army would man the seawall, and The Qeonian Navy would move in on the threat from Banshee Cove. In The Qeonian Navy's absence, we would send the majority of our ships to Banshee Cove. From there, the Army would unboard and move in towards Clearwater from the south, reconquering every settlement along the way to the capital."

What?

Ilidar was not on board with The High Staff's plan.

"Your Grace, The High Staff's plan shows a blatant disregard for both The Code of Combat and the value of The Imperial Army. Not only is it a

401

dishonorable move, based on deceit, but it would send many of our best soldiers to the unnamed graves of pirates. For the plan to succeed, the soldiers sent to Harcrome's Point would have to number in the thousands, and for the assault to last long enough to draw out The Qeonian Navy, our men would have to sacrifice themselves. They would die horribly—regardless of victory or defeat—and that would be if, and only if, the enemy took the bait. I cannot in good conscience advocate for such a plan of attack, and that's not even because it's immoral; it's because it's wasteful. There are so many threats to The High Empire right now that to lose so many men would be catastrophic! Gentlemen, we can't go through with such a risky plan! We must consider every option. The Book of a Thousand Deaths rightly states: "Those who sign a declaration of war sign it in their own blood." It's obvious that this mission would be a bloodbath, and we're already bleeding; there's not much blood left! My apologies, High Staff, but I fail to understand how you could come up with such a foolish plan!"

Offended, but trying to maintain his composure, The High Staff gave his response to Torran instead.

"Your Grace, The Astrian Guard is one thing, but The Imperial Navy is quite another. The Captain here is young and inexperienced, and he doesn't see the bigger picture. Sending the ships in any other direction would mean more time spent sailing the open ocean. That would mean more time vulnerable to storms, sea creatures, and actual pirates! It would be suicide! All the other options are worse! Maybe he thinks we could take the path from The Outpost, down Lynrāva's Belt, and then, to Pear Point. I've considered this as well, but Mount Criant has been spewing lava into the waters, and raiders ride along the coast, so that's not an option anymore. There would be nowhere to rest, and even if we made it safely to Pear Point, we'd have to march up the entire length of The Mountain Track, running us out of supplies and tiring our men. Even disregarding such barriers, it would take weeks, by which time, Qeonia would be ready for us."

Good thing that wasn't what I was suggesting.

I won't have my men die just to protect your ships and your pride. How did you even think of such a plan? Has old age gotten to you?

"I know, High Staff, and I completely agree that that would be a bad option. But in your fear of open ocean ventures, you didn't see the third option here. The distance between The Spider Crab Peninsula and Banshee Cove is almost the same as the distance between The Lauhapéll Peninsula and The Lips. We could sail inland on The Mermëan River, make our way up The Mountain Track, and make double the time overland. We would sacrifice none of our soldiers as a distraction, and we would still take the city, albeit a little more slowly. This would preserve our national honor and take advantage of our strengths. Astria isn't known for its Navy; it's known for its Army."

The High Staff's eyes flew wide.

"Captain Inverniqist, how dare you! The Navy-"

Torran cut him off.

"Lord Jiralt, what about you? What do you think?"

"Well, as Overseer of The Public Health, I have to lean towards the Captain's plan. Though I understand where The High Staff is coming from, and I respect his experience, the Captain is right that there will be many casualties. And although the Captain could have been less confrontational in his response, I believe it would be better to risk casualties than to guarantee them."

Torran decided.

"Then, we will go with Captain Inverniqist's plan, High Staff. I now see flaws in your plan that I was admittedly too tired and too angry to see before. We must minimize loss of life. The Demonium are coming, and we can't waste men or morale. In the end, this will be a ground assault, and I cannot favor the Navy over the Army."

"But your Grace!" The High Staff protested.

"High Staff, I understand your fear. However, we cannot afford to be cowardly in our approach. We must be both smart and bold. If The Imperial Navy faces significant losses, I will compensate you directly so that you can rebuild your ships, but my decision is final. We will take this approach."

"As you wish, your Grace," The High Staff harrumphed.

Ilidar smiled inside.

Torran stood up for my plan, even though I have less naval experience.

"Captain Inverniqist, in the absence of The High Sword, I name you Adjunct

High Sword. Once your injuries have healed, you will lead The Imperial Army in this offensive, and when The High Sword returns from Hemia, you will step down."

The Captain bowed.

"You honor me, your Grace."

"I'm glad. Now, are there any other matters to discuss?" Torran asked, looking around the room.

No one spoke.

"That is all, then. Everyone but Ilidar may leave. I wish to speak with the new High Sword alone."

The High Council members left the room. Ilidar lifted himself out of his seat and wheeled his way over to The High Emperor's side.

"Long day, your Grace?" he asked.

"Long day," Torran replied tiredly.

"What would you have of me, your Grace?" The Captain inquired.

The High Emperor rubbed his face with his hand.

"You can drop the "your Grace" now, Ilidar, come on. I just wanted to know how you're doing. How long till your leg heals?"

Ilidar scratched his head.

"Well, I fell out of bed in the infirmary, so the wound had to get restitched. It'll take at least another week or two to heal," he guessed, sheepish.

"Damn." Torran turned to brood, leaning over the carved table. A bead of sweat dripped down his face.

"Are you alright, Torran? I mean, with your father?"

"I'm fine. Everything's fine; yeah. Just a lot of stress. Nothing new; nothing I can't handle... Your leg, though—that is bad news. I know that a couple days ago, we were all half-dead, but the assassin has put us in a very bad position. We have to hit back at Qeonia, and hit back now. Allowing this rebellion to continue unchecked will only give the other Nations their own bright ideas. Naming you High Sword, I thought you would recover soon enough to lead the attack, but that might not be reasonable. I shouldn't have spoken so soon... If your leg isn't healed by the time we have to leave, I'll lead the attack myself. I'm not fully recovered yet, either, but I'm in better shape to fight, and the men need to follow someone they know, not some Court vulture."

Ilidar was about to ask Torran how he planned to deal with The Demonium, but he thought better of it. The dark circles under The High Emperor's eyes were darker than usual, muscles twitching involuntarily. He was coming unhinged.

"Torran-"

"Yes?!" The High Emperor stammered.

"Are you sure you're alright?" Ilidar asked,

"Yeah, I'm fine. Just tired," Torran replied. Ilidar wasn't sure he believed him.

The Emperor rolled up the map on the table and put it away, revealing a carving on the surface of the table. It was a stylized "S."

Torran smiled, seeing that Ilidar had noticed it.

"Reminds me of the good old days..." he breathed.

"We caused so much trouble... We were so young, back then..." The High Sword thought wistfully.

"Do you remember when we knocked over that statue?" Torran asked, his face lighting up a little.

"Yeah!" Ilidar laughed. "Your dad was so angry."

Torran grinned.

"Yeah... I know it was grandfather's statue, but in the end, it was just a lump of stone. He turned so purple I thought his head would explode!"

Ilidar chuckled, scratching his chin.

"My parents gave me such a hard time about it. But they were always going on about something or another," he commented.

"At least your parents paid attention to you. My father was always busy..." Torran's remark was casual—perhaps a little too casual.

The High Sword's voice became somewhat bitter.

"Maybe, but it was pretty annoying. When you went off to Springhaven, they were always going on about "duty," how drink and sex were some terrible sin, that I shouldn't talk to girls or go out with friends. I had to be the perfect soldier, even at fourteen. Fortunately, they no longer have a say."

"Divinity, man; they died in battle!" Torran shook his head.

"So?! It was what they wanted. And you knew how they were."

"Yeah, I guess, but still," Torran murmured.

"Then again, you probably wouldn't understand. You've never shown any interest in girls or drink. You never approached the women that flocked to you over the years. That's what makes the present situation so surprising... Speaking of which, have you finally done it with Scarolette?"

"What?!" Torran asked incredulously.

"You know—did you sleep together?" Ilidar asked, unabashed.

Torran's face went white.

"That's personal!" he cried.

"Oh my God, you totally did!" Ilidar teased.

Haha! Too funny...

Torran immediately turned a bright red, whispering.

"Alright, alright; we did it; just lower your voice. That's private."

"You're so lucky," Ilidar sighed exaggeratedly. "Every time I tried my luck with her, she just laughed it off. I think she liked you from the start."

Torran

Torran's embarrassment faded. Ilidar was a huge lothario, but he offered women little.

In name, the man was Captain of The Astrian Guard, but he was still a soldier, with few possessions, and a family name unknown to anyone outside of the military. It was easy to see why he had no luck.

When he wasn't fighting, Ilidar was at Court. No matter how good he looked, he wasn't nobility. Through many failed dates, Torran had found that the primary interests of most Astrian noblewomen were money and status.

Maybe his luck will improve, now that he's High Sword.

Like Ilidar, Torran was not a schemer, but he had been educated in the ways of the Court by his uncle, Velestre. Agravius was already handing him political responsibilities at twelve, responsibilities he was not ready for. As a child, all he had wanted was for his father to do something with him, but his father was always busy, and his mother was dead. His sister lived in her own little world.

As much as he ridiculed his father's rage, Torran had felt awful about breaking that statue. He hadn't done it on purpose. He was just a kid who wanted to play. That day, he had pestered his father to teach him sword-fighting, but the man said no, and so Ilidar volunteered in his stead, to a predictable end.

As punishment, Agravius sent Torran away to Springhaven, the first of many forced absences. Torran's uncle was a good man, and there was no better teacher in politics and etiquette, but The High Prince's stay in Springhaven was no bed of roses, and he returned to Astria only two months later.

Torran remembered his father's anger.

You kissed a servant! A peasant girl, a servant, and you're locking lips with her?! You're The High Prince, heir to the Throne! It's good to treat our subjects well, to care for them, but this girl is a nobody! You shall not see her again. She is a commoner, and you are a Prince! Remember your place!

The young royal had lashed out tearfully.

I'd rather be a nobody than a Prince nobody cares about!

Torran hid his trauma, plastering on a smile. Loneliness had always plagued him. Even his sister had had company as a little girl: three, bright-eyed kittens, a present from Agrvaius to his favorite child. She used to bring them everywhere, pushing them around in a light blue stroller, pretending they were her babies. For years, she was their caring mother, and though Torran loved his sister, he had no desire to play house with a bunch of mewling kittens. He wanted his father's acknowledgement, words of praise.

His father only gave him words of reprimand.

Agravius had never praised Torran's sword-fighting. Though The High Emperor had been a great fighter in his prime, as he grew in years, he began to look down on violence as a crutch of the uneducated. He could see art in the beauty of the blade, but not the art of crossing blades, and he never gave Torran the affection he desired. In fact, no matter how talented his son became in any one area, Agravius never saw it as an accomplishment.

Torran cleared his mind. He looked again at the carving on the table, feeling a pang of nostalgia. His childhood was fraught at best, but it was the only one he had.

"Ilidar, you try your luck with every woman you meet!" he razzed. "You've been combing your hair since you were ten years old!"

"Not every woman," The High Sword corrected him. "Just the good-looking ones. But alas, I have little success. I think they're jealous of my looks," he quipped, flashing his teeth.

Torran laughed, but it was strained.

"Not in the state you're in right now," the Emperor asserted, allowing his mirth to fade.

"Don't worry about anything else right now; just focus on getting better... And no more accidents, okay? Promise me."

"Sure," Ilidar responded.

"Good. Then you too are dismissed," The High Emperor stated, patting his shoulder. He went to finish cleaning up the war table.

Ilidar turned his wheels and began to maneuver himself towards the exit.

Torran swiveled, calling out.

"Oh, and Ilidar?"

The High Sword turned.

"Yeah?"

"Thanks for caring. You're a good friend," Torran smiled.

Ilidar

Ilidar retired to his chambers, happy to be back. When his horse fell on him, he thought for sure he would die. He never thought he would see his bed again.

Ilidar's room was as small as every other room in the barracks. His bed was a woolen cot with undyed, cotton sheets and a feather pillow. There was a dirt-laden, rectangular, straw mat at the foot of the bed, and an oaken nightstand with a brass chamberstick on top, which held a small, beeswax candle.

The High Sword's one luxury as an officer was a small, square window with oaken shutters, which overlooked the old, mosaic courtyard on the Palace' east side, a training area where he had spent hundreds of hours.

A breeze blew in, Ilidar digging his hands into the mattress and really sitting down. There was give, but then there was the feeling of solidity from the bed frame beneath him. It was nothing like cold mud.

The newly appointed High Sword let his head hang back, breathing deeply.

The air was cool and dry, smelling faintly of dust, salt, and old straw, and although the scent was brusque, it was a familiar smell, a pleasant smell.

The floor of the room was made of oak, marred and scratched, and the ceiling was but an array of solid, oaken beams. On the right wall, was a strip of wooden pegs from which Ilidar hung his jacket and sword, which sat in a dark brown, leather sheath dangling from a leather strap. The sheath was capped with silver to match his arming sword's crossguard, a polished silver that deviated from the steel of the standard issue, denoting his rank. The sword was outdated, as Ilidar was no longer a Captain, but The High Sword. However, that didn't matter much, as the rank of High Sword was denoted with platinum.

If I just polished everything, no one would know the difference.

A gold buckle gleamed from under Ilidar's bed. Straining against his wheelchair, he reached down and took out a large fightbook, bound in light brown leather, and fastened with a leather strap. The dust-covered tome was titled in gold lettering—"The Seventeen Guards" by the famous Guy Phero.

Moving his lush, white-blonde hair out of his eyes, Ilidar inspected the book's fine craftsmanship, as he did every time. The plates were drawn in incredible detail.

For such frugal people, his parents had spared no expense, the drawings filled in with indigo and scarlet, gold and silver leaf, a book commissioned from one of the greatest sword masters in the land.

As much as he had resented their conservative stubbornness, Ilidar loved his parents. Within months of their death, he began drinking regularly, wasting his first time with a prostitute. Though the pleasure was undeniable, the experience was disappointing, and it only made him hate his life more. He hadn't really liked drinking. He hadn't really wanted to lose his first time in such a sad way. What he had thought was hate was really just the anger of a teenager who had been forced to be chaste, to be serious. His parents had spent so much time fighting, that the War had been everything to them. They couldn't separate themselves from the military life, even to raise their son, guide him in all the most important areas.

In the end, Ilidar was a guardsman, and his parents had left an indelible mark on his soul. No matter how he tried, he would never be able to completely get rid of his sense of duty, fully melt his stiff, moral backbone, only soften it. As much as he liked to flirt and joke, he wasn't a player, and he had never had any meaningful relationships. His careless attitude was, ironically, just an act, and the women he met saw through it after only a couple hours. He couldn't let loose.

My idea of fun is reading a dusty old book, a book for soldiers and scholars. What woman would care about that?

I really am a loser.

Ilidar smiled. *Oh, well.*

He flipped to the pages illustrating the different Guards, reading more as a distraction than anything else. It always paid to reread the plates, to notice the discrepancies between his form and the proper form, and it was always good to think of new moves to use in fighting. His parents had given him the book when he had become a Corporal, and, since then, he had studied it thoroughly.

According to Ilidar's father, the fightbook held all of the plates from the Astrian longsword tradition, but The High Sword doubted that. There had been centuries worth of sword masters, many of them poor, their works lost to time. Still, it was pretty comprehensive.

Ilidar touched the gold leaf, feeling its slight graininess. The first guard was Tower Guard.

In this Guard, you are strong. This is your castle, and no one may take it from you. Show

them the folly of facing a student of this noble art.

Then, there was Crown.

With this Guard, you protect your head, turning your crossguard into a crown—a crown of victors and kings.

Lover's Guard

With this Guard, you hold your beloved sword close to your body, avoiding the

bind. When the opportunity strikes, you attack, thrusting outwards and into their face.

Ilidar smirked, hearing Ryan Pabodam's familiar voice. The youth had deepened his voice, imagining what Guy Phero had sounded like.

Lover's Guard

You hold out your long, hard sword, and thrust deep into the enemy.

The guardsmen laughed.

Now that I think of it, that's Ilidar's favorite Guard, but he only uses it on other dandies! God knows they're rare enough on the battlefield! A man has to find relief somewhere!

Not true! Ilidar countered. *I had your sister in the bind just yesterday. She was impressed with my swordsmanship!*

Shut up!

Ilidar snickered childishly, remembering his friends and their childish humor. Then he remembered that they had all been killed, killed by an assassin in purple robes. They weren't great fighters, renowned across the land, but they were brave men, dutiful to the end. They had been dispatched in mere seconds.

Ilidar hadn't been there to protect them. He had taken only the best with him, and though he cared deeply for his friends, they were just lowly foot soldiers.

Ilidar returned to his reading, trying to forget.

Seeker's Guard

With this Guard, you discover your enemy's motives and enter the bind. This is the Guard of a man who seeks a fight. Make your intent clear, and thrust outwards with both commitment and strength.

Cloud Guard

With this Guard, you hold the threat of death over their head. If they dare to stand before you, bring your sword down like a bolt of lightning; show them the heavens' wrath.

Rose Guard

With this Guard, you protect your beauty and honor, holding your enemies at bay. They

cannot get past your deadly thorns.

Dragon's Tail Guard

With this Guard, you will sweep them off their feet, a crude swing from below, the swing of a dragon's mighty tail.

Fisherman's Guard

*With this Guard, you lure in the fish. If they take the bait, pull your sword
up and out of the waters, catching them with your blade.*

Serpent's Guard

*With this Guard, you lean back in wait, flying outwards into a thrust full of anger
and venom.*

Crescent Guard

*With this Guard, you will swat away their arrows, and knock aside their spears.
You are like The Twin Moons—no weapon may reach you.*

Compass Guard

*With this Guard, you judge your opponent's intent. When they attack, you shall
find their sword like a compass finds a lodestone, meeting their blade and hitting
your target without fail.*

Archer's Guard

*With this Guard, you take your aim. When the opportunity presents itself, shoot
outwards like an arrow, ensuring victory.*

Oil Guard

*With this guard, you make yourself a slippery customer. The enemy will seek to
harm*

you, but they shall not find you.

Pabodam laughed.

Use Oil Guard and Lover's Guard together and you're in for a good old time!

Ilidar wanted to laugh. Instead, he felt a tremor of dread run through his
body. The words of the dead echoed through his mind, through a maze of dark
and hollow halls. They moved through the labyrinth of misery, of depression.

Death is the end. There is nothing after it. Someday, I won't exist...

No!

Don't think! Just read!

A page tore, a blasphemy against the arts, but Ilidar threw himself back into
his reading. In the book, were fictional characters. No matter how many sword
cuts they took, they stood smiling, immortalized in ink.

I won't exist.

No!

Scarab Guard

With this Guard, you threaten your enemy, horn lowered in a charge. No one can stop

you. Ram through their defenses and make a powerful thrust.

Raptor's Guard

With this Guard, you watch your enemy intently, ready to take flight. When they move,

you strike, like a bird of prey.

Scorpion Guard

With this Guard, you will threaten the enemy, holding your sword behind you in warning.

Those who do not heed the warning shall be punished with a strike of pure malice.

Merchant's Guard

In this guard, you peddle your poisons to the enemy. You have something for everything.

Give them whatever they need.

Ilidar looked out towards the training area, the sun setting.

Purple. Such a gaudy color. But they were no merchant. They were only an assassin...

I will be a merchant. Yes, a merchant of death.

I will find you, assassin... I failed in my duty, but I will not fail to bring you to justice.

You will die forever.

That is my promise.

That is my seller's guarantee.

Luxyruss

Silver-white particles flew through the ether like a thousand shards of glass, a god shattered. They hurtled through the emptiness, propelled by some unknown force, homing in on The Red Moon.

The particles rained down through the atmosphere and slammed together, a sudden retraction.

The Divinity Converged on Faal. His eyes washed blue, the dust swept away.

He was on a high cliff with a smooth, flat top—red stone. Sitting before him, was Skotathis, facing The Faalan Shadowrise. He had stuck the tree's roots in a plastinated head—what looked like a woman's skull. The head sat in a pool of water from Judas, shimmering.

The Adversary had stuck a second pair of roots in his head, the black tendrils wriggling deep into his ears. He was meditating on something, experiencing a memory.

Whose memory it was, Luxyruss didn't know, but it must have been old...

Maybe he's looking for me? But who would remember me?

Well, whatever. Look no more, Skotathis, for I am here.

Luxyruss Called Purifire. The Fallstreak burst into flames because he willed it.

The Divinity didn't lunge forward. He approached slowly, cautious.

For anyone else, posting no guards would have been reckless, but this demon was another story entirely. Even blind and deaf, he could still see. Knowledge wouldn't leave him so defenseless, and his obsidian hide was as good as armor.

A twig snapped; The Divinity swiveled.

Lilith'in, Skotathis' lover, had climbed the steps carved into the cliff.

So they're still together, after all this time... I would say it's surprising that she stayed with him, but the woman's no innocent. She's just as bad as he is.

Her voice was sluttish and derisive.

"Luxyruss, what a surprise. I thought you'd be hiding at the edge of The Kol System somewhere—hiding like a coward. But here you are, about to stab your own brother in the back. Less cowardly than hiding, but not by much."

"I don't stab people in the back, Lilith'in. If anyone would know about backstabbing, it's you and your ilk."

To think that, in another world, she could have been my sister-in-law. But now a demon stands before me in place of a damsel, and Fang'rial is no longer my brother.

Lilith'in Called a whip from the ring on her finger, an acidic yellow.

So you have Theonium too. No matter.

"Skotathis was the one who was betrayed. Our kind is what you made us. All we've done—all that we've become—has been to fight injustice. You were not the eldest. It was not your destiny to take the **throne**."

"Destiny? Destiny is a sham, made up by **tyrants** and despots. My father denied Skotathis the Throne because he knew that he would be a bad King. He always played the loyal son, the dutiful son, but secretly, he hungered for money, power, and women, like he always has. You're merely his concubine, his plaything, yet you think you have some **greater purpose**, that you're spiritual and deep? What care you for destiny?"

Lilith'in cocked her head. A scowl flickered across her face, lips pressed together, but she composed herself again. Though she tried to look confident, she was stiff in her movements.

"Are you scared, little girl?" The Divinity asked, sarcastic. "Then you shouldn't have lived a life of evil."

"Maybe you're right—maybe you're wrong," the succubus remarked, indifferent. She stopped, planting her feet. "The question is: what are you going to do now, old man?"

"Whatever it takes," Luxyruss vowed.

"Ugh! You're so self-righteous! You're a fool to fight me, but you'll do so anyway, professing it's your duty. So be it. I'm not one to complain. Skotathis has been searching for you everywhere; now he'll wake up to your head on a platter."

Luxyruss scoffed, pointing his sword at her.

"I have nothing more to say to you. Either fight me, or get out of my way."

Lilith'in cracked her whip. The air shrieked. She walked forward slowly, hand to her side, and approached, cold menace.

Luxyruss remembered the scars that lined M'Cael's back.

M'Cael... I'll bring you justice.

Luxyruss made a cut for the Lilith'in's waist, but she sidestepped, swinging her whip. Dragontail wrapped around The Divinity's neck like a boa.

Leaping, the demoness got behind him and collapsed his knee, but his wings poured out like white fire. The old angel flapped backwards, wingtips boxing in her ears.

Lilith'in staggered. The Divinity pulled the whip off of his neck in one, fluid motion and tried to knock her over with a reverse sweep, but she did a back walkover over it. She swung her stock whip at him, whose smooth, pointed, black stinger he reflexively caught.

The spike buzzed with intensity, inches from his eye.

The Divinity twirled the banana-yellow cord around his arm, gaining leverage on Skotathis' mistress, but when he pulled her in for a punch, she took the initiative and punched him first.

Luxyruss flew backward, rolling against his wings. He coughed up blood and broken teeth. Lilith'in whipped him in the lower leg.

The Divinity cried out, doing a windmill up to standing position. Bleeding from his mouth and leg, he was already injured.

That's enough. I haven't even gotten to fight who I came to fight, yet.

Begone, small fry.

Lilith'in swung her whip again, looking to cripple him, but The Divinity blocked, Dragontail wrapping around Purifire's polished, white blade. With a flick of her wrist, she disarmed him, thinking herself masterful. Luxyruss raised his hand and Unified the air, the succubus frozen in steaming ice.

There's no aura around you. I should have realized earlier.

He really is arrogant.

Lilith'in looked at Luxyruss with wide, terrified eyes from within the ice. Without hesitation, The Divinity kicked her off the cliff.

The Adversary stirred.

He senses that her life force has changed, but he's not yet aware that she's dead.

Good. Let him lose someone he cares about for once.

Done with his conference, Skotathis pulled the wooden earplugs from his ears and shook his head, blinking.

"So gross," he complained, open-closing his mouth dryly. He started talking to Lilith'in, but she wasn't the one standing behind him.

"So, tell me, my dear, what would you like to do before I leave? I know I wasn't in the mood before, but maybe we could—"

Luxyruss pressed Purifire's smoldering point against Skotathis' neck, glassy, obsidian skin beginning to smoke.

"I'm afraid Lilith'in won't be doing much of anything anymore. She just took a dive off the cliffside. But you probably already suspected as much, so why pretend?"

Skotathis put his hands up, chuckling.

"Luxyruss—King of The Angels—here at last... You're just in time. My followers are waiting for me... They're awaiting the arrival of their god."

"You are no god. You are but a child who wants to sit a throne. You'd go to any length to gain power, but I'm not going to let you make landfall."

"Oh, man... You sound just like Mother, Luxyruss... You know, it's funny— she was just telling me about you. Well, as much as she could, anyway."

"What are you talking about?"

Hooked wings poured from Skotathis' back, the demon doing a tunnel flip to the right and twisting the Fallstreak out of Luxyruss' hands. Then, The Adversary did a spinning jump-kick, hitting The Divinity in the chest and pushing him backwards, creating distance.

"Let's not lose our heads yet, Y'shan, especially since Mother's watching. We wouldn't want to upset her, now, would we? She always hated when we fought."

"Mother? What—"

The skull.

It's a woman's skull. And that birthmark on her skin, the birthmark above her brow...

It can't be.

"What did you do to her?! I thought she— What did you do to our Mother?!"

"I don't know; I mean, see for yourself." The Adversary shrugged his shoulders casually. He rolled the sodden head over to Luxyruss. It came to a stop with a *plop*. Red dust turned to mud, a brown stain on igneous.

The wind picked up, howling.

Kneeling, Luxyruss picked up his mother's desiccated head with a shaky sort of hesitation. She tried to speak, but was unable to without a throat or lungs. Her mouth moved, like a fish out of water. He tried to listen, but she was just mouthing random words.

Luxyruss' heart nearly stopped.

Mom?!

Oh, Mother, what has he done?!

You vile man!

"Shadowrise sap... Skotathis—Shadowrise sap on your own mother... You're a monster."

"And you're weak, old man," The Adversary whispered.

"At least I am a man, creature!" The Divinity shouted, indignant. "Do you have any morals left?! Is there a crime you've yet to commit?!"

"Hmmm..." Skotathis mocked him, cocking his head and taking on a quizzical look. He put his hand to his chin performatively. "You know, technically speaking, fratricide... But I think I'll check that off my list in a minute," he smiled. It was the same smile Luxyruss remembered.

The Adversary towered over Luxyruss, though the siblings were but a year apart. The Divinity looked decrepit and old—unnaturally so. He had looked that way for a long time.

"Age has defeated you, Brother. It was foolish of you to come here in such a state."

Luxyruss' eyes were hard.

"Your mistress was just as arrogant as you, Skotathis, and now she's gone. M'Cael— Initiator rest his soul—even he couldn't beat me, and he used to be the best of us, so don't be so cocky."

"Lilith'in's not gone. I can sense her presence still, though it is weak... But so what? You may have defeated her, defeated that oaf of an Archangel, but you know you cannot defeat me."

The demon approached, swelling with power. The Shadowheart embedded in his chest glowed a bright, bubbling red, infusing him with souls.

Luxyruss didn't back down, sword-flame billowing quietly.

Skotathis' voice was resonantly low, his eyes like green fire.

"Luxyruss...my weak, old brother... I am Fang'rial, Father of The Archdemons, and I cannot be stopped. Your followers fear me as they do death, and they believe you to be omnipotent! They even have a name for me to match your own, little nickname... They call me The Adversary, or have you not heard?"

"Foul demon, all I hear are the cries of the innocent!"

Skotathis' tone was scathing.

"Demon... It's ironic that you call me that. It makes me wonder what your followers would call you. What would they call you if they knew the truth of what you've done? I wonder how they'd react, if they learned how many innocents you've killed... After all, you were the one who started all this— you and your man, Xersus. The dragons, the Goblins—everyone knows the monsters I've created... But your sins go unknown, and yours are the worst of all. Tell me, do you think they'd call you "demon" too, if they saw you forge his blade, that blade with the red edge?!"

The Divinity swept his sword across the rock, a veritable line in the sand.

"It is irrelevant! I did what I had to do! I don't need to justify myself to you! I wasn't about to let The Kol System die for someone to imitate you and your power-hungry gambit! I saw you destroy one world—no more! Even genocide is better than total annihilation."

Skotathis shook his head almost pityingly.

"You make it out like it was a necessary evil... But we both know that you did what you did, because you were scared, scared that there could be another Adversary—an equal who could rival you in power. Despite what you say, you want to be at the top. You think yourself noble and worthy, but you don't have what it takes to rule. You failed as both a King and a god, and now, centuries later, you fail as their messiah. You think you can stop this, but you're misguided... You think this isn't necessary?"

The Divinity's voice rose in incredulity, almost shrill.

"Necessary? You've been trying to conquer Avenshra for three hundred years! Do you see a planet needing your rule? The Nations are divided because of you; your followers are the very criminals and zealots responsible for what's happening! Demons race across the plains, raping and pillaging! You think that to rule is to crush... What I did was unjust, but there was no other way. It was my responsibility to avert the death of yet another sun. And don't make it seem like you didn't further the damage. I should have had a firmer grasp on Xersus, but you turned him completely mad. The first blood is mine to bear, but the second is all yours."

Skotathis scoffed.

"You lecture me about responsibility, but it was you who unleashed chaos on

Avenshra, you and that Xandromen butcher. You can't cry foul now that your attack dog was turned against you. As for today... You're right; I am behind this rebellion, but it would have happened with or without me. The blight you brought down as The High Empire has eaten away at the hearts of men for generations. I just offered them the knife—the knife they could use to cut it out. And lo, their hearts bleed for my cause, and you have no choice but to rekindle Elementality, the power you tried so hard to destroy! Do you think I would be a worse tyrant than The Red Meteor?! You're delusional if you think you're a positive influence on the world!"

The Divinity's face was shadowed.

"Maybe I am delusional. Maybe you're right about that," he admitted, sinking into Scarab Guard. "But I've come too far to quit now. I took out your mistress; I'll take you out too. Though I do not profess that I'm a god like you do, these people say that I am one. And these people—they pray for my help; they beg me to save them... It's time I answered their prayers."

"You're going to take me down? Me? Then give it your best shot, Brother."

Skotathis Called Lighteater. He twirled the crystalline machete, snickering, then Divided the air, a green fireball sent at Luxyruss.

The Divinity dodged.

Skotathis threw another fireball, but Luxyruss brought his hands together, Unifying a pillar of air that exploded against the viridescent plasma.

The old god Called Purifire again, getting into position to make a downward cut for Skotathis' left shoulder, but the demon got into a low Guard, so he switched sides, shifting his feet. The Adversary made some small feints, half-hearted and toying, but The Divinity deflected them all unperturbed, keeping as little space between himself and his opponent as he could. He had to avoid the green fire.

He's testing me...

That's fine, Skotathis; keep hiding behind The Power of Division like a shield. Keep playing your games. This duel can only end one way.

I'll only let it end one way.

Skotathis moved forward to cut the muscle of Luxyruss' thigh, but the angel did a corkscrew over the cut, revealing a limberness The Lord of Sulphur had not expected.

Luxyruss still didn't have the upper hand, as, when he tried to make an overhead cut to Skotathis' head, the demon pushed him back with a flap of his wings, a black gale.

The Divinity stumbled; The Adversary rushed to meet him. A quick, downward swing clipped Luxyruss' ear, but he Unified the dirt around Skotathis' left foot, throwing him off balance, and putting an abrupt halt to the exchange.

The brothers got their bearings again as The Adversary Divided the construct around his foot.

He's taking me seriously, now. I can't hold back.

Before he could swing Lighteater, Luxyruss cut for Skotathis' clavicle, but the demon let it glance off of Oil Guard, which he rested on his shoulder.

The Adversary immediately surged forward, bulldozing through Luxyruss' fruitless attempt at grappling and breaking the angel's nose with the blunt, back edge of his Devourer's Sword.

Luxyrusss felt pain, white-hot blood spouting from his nostrils.

The Divinity roared. He didn't know why it hurt so much, but his vision was blurred by primal anger, and he swung Purifire in all directions.

Skotathis shoved him and began bathing him in flames, plasma crackling as Division tore the air apart, corpuscle by corpuscle.

Luxyruss kipped up into a backflipping kick, blood streaming from his burnt nose. He hit Skotathis in the chin, but the demon kicked him back, dislocating his left elbow as he landed in a ready stance.

Bone splinters crunched against each other.

"Pfaaah!" Luxyruss bellowed. He pulled himself together, but he was shaking, wobbly. The pain was immense.

The ragged Divinity switched to a one-handed grip, shifting his feet again. *Karibdione, it hurts...*

Giving him no respite, The Adversary came at Luxyruss again with a thrust to the intestines, but the old god stabbed his sword into the ground and jerked the handle to the side, deflecting his opponent's machete with a haphazard blade-beat.

Lighteater went deep into The Divinity's left oblique.

"Hrmf! Ahaah!"

Luxyruss cut his blade out of the rock, oblique tearing as Purifire reignited in a spurt of blood.

The Divinity pulled Skotathis into the bind, growling. His Fallstreak's edge was so damaged that there were more than a dozen points glowing red, Theonium healing slowly. The angel gritted his teeth as strands of solid Lifeblood bridged the gap, living metal scabbing over.

Move!

Feeling that the demon was weak in the bind, Luxyruss stabbed for Skotathis' waist in an angled, downward thrust. However, The Adversary anticipated this, moving to the side in Scarab guard, and making a doubling swish to the angel's temple.

Luxyruss whipped his mangled arm upwards, using his off-hand to block the machete with Unification.

Lighteater bounced to the side as solid air broke. Luxyruss drew Purifire across Skotathis' armored abdomen, entering Archer's guard and waiting for counterattacks.

None came. The Adversary touched his side, strings of green goo stretching from the wound as he pulled his hand away.

"Fuck," Skotathis muttered.

Luxyruss wiped his nose with a certain satisfaction, blood smearing across his knuckles. Then he set his elbow back in place, grunting.

The two men found their footing again, circling each other. Drawn in by his aura, Lifeblood coalesced around Luxyruss, swirling.

The Divinity got into Scorpion Guard, holding his sword behind his back and placing his weight on his back leg—a stance brimming with power. Skotathis shifted his footwork to protect his injured side. He got into a ready stance for single-hand swords, his machete pointed upwards in line with his right knee, feet perpendicular to each other.

Aiming to blow right through, Luxyruss made the most powerful cut his brother had ever seen, Purifire screaming towards the demon's left shoulder. Barely evading, The Lord of Sulphur pivoted to the left as Luxyruss took a step forward, slashing through his rotator cuff.

Cutting off The Divinity's robed right arm, Skotathis made a devastating follow-up attack, drawing his sword upward to open up the angel's stomach, but Luxyruss leapt back, holding his shoulder in pain and shock. The haircloth at his stomach frayed. Lighteater had scraped it.

The god grit his teeth. Without his Callring, he couldn't use his Fallstreak, and that meant that Skotathis was virtually unstoppable. Still, he couldn't give up.

Skotathis made a bevy of savage, downward cuts, Luxyruss deflecting them with well-timed dodges and pillars of solid air, but as more and more pillars came together, Skotathis' movements became more and more volant, shimmering pillars breaking apart. As the demon got faster and he got weaker, Unification would soon be rendered useless.

My arm—my sword! Everything hurts so much! But I can't focus on the pain. I need to keep moving.

Another pillar was vaporized before it could even solidify, Lighteater's edge speeding towards him, but Luxyruss did a one-arm triple back handspring, creating ample distance between himself and his Adversary. He skidded to a halt, fine silt hanging in the air.

I've got to turn this around somehow! He's Dividing the molecules faster than I can Unify them!

But Unification is all I have.

Skotathis scorned his cowardice.

"Luxyruss...you bloody fool—you stupid, yellow-bellied fool! Do you really attempt to abscond from this fight? Will you retreat to some backwater planet to lick your wounds, or is this some other form of craven trickery?!"

Luxyruss blue eyes glistered, visible even in the dust. He prepared to try something he had never tried before.

The Adversary yelled, angry.

"Well, I'll tell you now, Luxyruss, you little bitch—your tricks won't work! You will face destiny, and you will die. Dust isn't yours to hide in. Dust is my cape, the herald of The Demonium!"

Lighteater's striped blade blurred to white as the dust around Luxyruss dispersed. The machete cut deep, finding flesh.

Or what should have been flesh.

Instead of blood, fragments of dry ice sprayed everywhere, frictionless pieces sliding off the cliff and tumbling into the valley below.

Lighteater had bitten into a buckler cast from air and Faalan dust, the homemade armament stronger than any gaseous construct Luxyruss had ever created. The shield's handle started to freeze the god's bony fingers, but he bore it, summoning all his willpower.

It was difficult. Cold, cold, eschar spread across The Divinity's palm like spilled ink, frostbite running across his innervated hand.

No, you're the one who's a fool, Skotathis. I would never run.

Even if I lose my every limb, even if you endeavor to kill me, to plastinate me, I will not run. This is my purpose. To oppose The Power of Division, what comes from its great power. History offers me no alternate recourse.

The Divinity broke his brother's ankle with a foot and punched him hard in the lip with his newly formed buckler, causing whiplash, but The Adversary headbutted him in the throat as if he didn't care, and then Divided the small rocks beneath his feet.

Luxyruss stumbled as pebbles disintegrated from underfoot and he lost purchase, clawing at his larynx. The Adversary swung for his exposed stomach, looking to deal the final blow.

The Divinity brought his wings together to take the cut instead. Wings cut in half, he managed to protect his vital organs, but it didn't change a thing.

Skotathis hit the ground, Dividing dusty rock.

And the ledge on which Luxyruss stood cracked from the peak, taking him down with it, a hundred-foot drop down unto death—unto defeat.

END OF VOLUME I

The Language of Dismaeol

The Power of Order
Protection—Reflectrica
Travel—Evanesire

(Aegis) Water
???

(Therius) Fire
???

(Solitus) Earth
Stone—???
Stone Spike—???

(Haskaleon) Lightning
Lightning Bolt—???

(Aeol) Wind
Flight—???

(Pagon) Ice
???

(Entoxis) Poison
Poison Spray—Venymlash

(Medalacus) Metal

???

(Radiol) ???

???

(Cryptus) Darkness

???

ACKNOWLEDGEMENTS

Although the past seven years have mostly consisted of me straining my eyes, destroying my back, and ruining my keyboard, the completion of *The Fallstreak Arsenal: A Sound of Steel* wasn't achieved through sheer force of will or superhuman writing skill. The fact is, there are many people who deserve my gratitude. And although this book may be too dark and too violent for most of them, I'd like to take the time to do that here.

Thank you to my family for all their love and support.

Ma, Da, thank you for all the sacrifices you've made for me. I know you don't like fantasy, but you allowed me to pull this off.

My younger brother, Adrian, is too young to read the unfiltered book right now, but he knows a good chunk of the plot, and he's been with me every step of the way. Without his input, writer's block would have stopped me long ago. Adrian—if you see this when you're older, thank you for being my best friend and the first real fan of *The Fallstreak Arsenal*.

Barb, Baba, thank you for your love and care, and thank you for helping to fund my college and my advertising campaign. Writing this book would have been impossible without a higher education, and it would have never succeeded without robust marketing.

Giagia, thank you for saying that my cover looked good, and thank you for always being my number one promoter. I hope to someday be as good as you think I am.

Giorgos, Zacharena—you guys are the best. One motivation for writing this book was to show you that, with enough time and effort, you can achieve your dreams, even if they look daunting. I look forward to seeing what you do in the future.

Aunt Mary, Uncle Billy, Aunt Dori, and Uncle Mark, thank you for standing by me during rough times and always doing nice things for me. Jimmy, Uncle Alan, and Mrs. Phillips, you're like family, and I'm grateful that you're a part of my life.

Thank you to all of my friends, especially Noah and Westley, who have stuck by me longer than anyone else, and Ethan, Ryan, Rocky, Leo, and Andreas, who have made my life in Bozeman a lot of fun. To my friends from the past, I wish you good health and good fortune.

Arguably, my biggest thanks go out to my friend Noah Hursh. He did an incredible amount of work as my alpha reader and editor, and he always helped me whenever I was stuck. Noah—you did a fantastic job. I am forever in your debt.

Special thanks to my friends Sarah, Chloe, and Kylie, who were there for me when things were difficult. You gave me the confidence to believe that my drawings in the lunchroom could become characters someday, and now, they are.

Special thanks to Mr. Russo, Dr. Vines, Joy, and Monica, for lending a listening ear when I was struggling. I can't overstate how much you helped me. Special thanks to Prof. Jeoffrey Gordon at Texas State University. Though we'll probably never meet, your article from 2009 saved my life. Thank you to Ben Lionel Scott on YouTube for always keeping me motivated. You kept me going when I wanted to quit.

Thank you to all of my friends at Lost Arts Historical Fencing (@lostartshf on Instagram), who threw away my preconceived notions of fighting and taught me how to really use a sword. Special thanks to Graham, Eric, Robert, and Calder, who were my mentors in sword-fighting and in leadership. I will always be grateful for the lessons you taught me. Equally special thanks to my friend and rival, Ethan, for all the amazing fights. You forced me to push past my limits.

Special thanks to William and Ethan for being the first people to say that they'd buy my book back in 2021. It might have seemed small to you then, but it meant a lot.

Thank you to Mrs. Frock and Ms. Cole for letting me attend The Alternative School for Math and Science. Going to ASMS helped steer my life in a positive direction.

Big thanks to the teachers who helped me improve my writing over the years: Prof. Corriel, Prof. Broome, Mrs. Leshke, Mrs. Possemato, Mr. McTigue, Mrs. Pierce, Mrs. Miller, Mrs. Kuehner, Mrs. Ijaika, and Mrs. Walker. You helped me find my confidence, and I was able to write this book because of you.

Mrs. Walker, Mrs. Ijaika—thank you for lending me your books. You made me passionate about reading. Mrs. Morse—thank you for making the library a welcoming place. Mrs. Pierce, Mr. McTigue, Prof. Broome-thank you for challenging me to live up to my full potential.

Equally big thanks to my art teachers over the years: Mrs. Fusco-Benoit, Mr. Ryan, Mrs. Wolf-King, Mrs. Halpert, Mrs. Ortiz, and Mr. Horton. I was able to illustrate this book because of you.

Mr. Horton, Mrs. Ortiz, Mrs. Wolf-King—thank you for uplifting my art. Mr. Ryan—thank you for giving me the opportunity to do an individual study. You gave me a space to express my feelings through art during a tumultuous period in my life. Mrs. Fusco—thank you for your kindness and continued support.

Thank you to Prof. Michele Corriel, Brendan Gibson, Leo Dilles, Calder Larsen, Ben Churchwell, Eric Welch, Natalia Alonzo, Sophia Irem, McCants Meinders, my dad, Ioannis Roudas, Alan Wysocki, Kalina Roussev, and all of the talented people at The Creative Writing Club at MSU (@creativewritingclub msu on Instagram). Speaking to fellow writers, both past and present, inspired and motivated me. Check out Prof. Corriel's books at www.michelecorriel.com, follow Brendan on his journey to publication at gibby.video.blog, and keep an eye out for the rest. To anyone who wants to write a book, remember—many people start, but not everyone finishes. All it takes to be an author is to keep going. If you have to scrap it, scrap it as many times as you need to, but don't give up. I believe in you.

Thank you to officers Ben, Hollin, Phoebe, and Genina for not just allowing, but helping me promote my work through The Creative Writing Club. It was a huge help, and pushed me to continue marketing when I was discouraged.

Big thanks to all of my ARC readers for taking a chance on my book. It made me both proud, and determined to improve.

ACKNOWLEDGEMENTS

Special thanks to Brendan for being my first and only subscriber on Word-Press for the longest time, and special thanks to Prof. Corriel for being the first person to offer me their help with editing. Though I didn't end up taking the offer, it was good to know that someone had faith in me. Thanks to my old neighbor Barbara for rekindling my interest in reading. Helping you sort books at the recycling center was a great experience.

Thank you to Arto Fama for helping me improve my fencing. Learning from you was an honor. Thank you to Jack Dagger for teaching me the basics of knife-throwing, and thank you to Luke Walker for teaching me how to use a bow. Your lessons helped make the fighting in this book a little more real.

Thank you to RollForFantasy.com for letting me use their map and solar system creator, and special thanks to Emily from fantasynamegenerators.com. Your website helped me come up with names for characters and locations. Also, thank you to the creators of Graphic Image Manipulation Program (GIMP) and G'MIC-Qt, which allowed me to make my maps and cover.

Lastly, and, most importantly, I want to thank you, the reader, for investing in this book. I wrote it for two reasons: to write the kind of book I want to read, and to write the kind of book you want to read. When I set out, I wanted to write a book that wasn't only epic in scope, but truly meaningful. This proved difficult, and I can't say that I've achieved that for sure. What I can do, is make a promise. I promise that *The Fallstreak Arsenal* will be a break from modern fantasy trends, and I won't rush or drag out the completion of the series. I'll stay true to my original narrative, and I won't change things to generate shock value or subvert expectations. I aim to write genuinely good books, and I hope you'll join me on that journey.

If you enjoyed this first *Volume*, or even if you didn't, please leave a review for me on Amazon. Feedback is how I grow as an author. If you want to keep up with my writing, please consider following me on social media. This is just *Volume I*. *Volumes II* and *III*, as well as the unified omnibus (an ebook), will be released soon. I anticipate that the second and third installments in the trilogy, *A Shadow of Blood* and *A Blaze of Light*, will be short enough to be released as individual books, but I can't provide a release date, or any further details just yet. In any case, I hope you're as excited for those as I am!

Till next time,

-Nick

About the Author

Nicholas Roudas spent his childhood in the Peloponnese, where he made swords out of sticks and was inspired by the heroes of Greek mythology. Growing up, he became a voracious reader, obsessed with swords, sorcery and mythical creatures, and since 2012, he has been building his characters and world through illustration. In 2018, he finally put pen to paper, and later, in 2019, he joined Lost Arts Historical Fencing at Montana State University, rising to the rank of president in 2020. Through LAHF, he learned more about the realities of historical combat, weaponry, and weapons mechanics, which he hopes to spotlight in his debut novel, *The Fallstreak Arsenal: A Sound of Steel*.